46

By
Lynn Ames

46

PRINT EDITION
ISBN: 978-1-936429-20-2

OTHER AVAILABLE FORMATS
eBOOK EDITION
ISBN: 978-1-936429-21-9

PUBLISHED BY
PHOENIX RISING PRESS
ASHEVILLE, NORTH CAROLINA
www.lynnames.com

This is a work of fiction. Names, characters, places, and incidents are the product of the author's imagination or are used fictitiously, and any resemblance to actual persons, living or dead, businesses, companies, events, or locales is entirely coincidental.

CREDITS
EXECUTIVE EDITOR: ANN ROBERTS
AUTHOR PHOTO: JUDY FRANCESCONI
COVER DESIGN: TREEHOUSE STUDIO

Dedication

To all those who believe that love is the strongest force in the universe. Keep shining light until the darkness recedes.

Acknowledgments

The idea for *46* was born of my meditations on how we as a country and part of a global community could heal from this extraordinary time of divisiveness, polarization, suspicion, and darkness. I knew what part I would play to be a difference-maker: it would be my job to shine light in the darkness, to give readers hope. *46* is my love letter to all of you. I hope that in Emma McMasters, I've given you the president your heart yearns for—the kind of leader who will unite us and restore our faith.

In order to write the most authentic, realistic, accurate tale for you, I relied on an incredible "Who's Who" of content experts. The depth and breadth of expertise is breathtaking. Any factual errors in this book belong solely to me.

My most sincere gratitude and thanks to the following extraordinary people. I'm blessed to have your input and your friendship. To Brigadier General Deborah Shea, whose bravery and experience is unparalleled and who breathed life into Palmer Estes' career and character. To Major General Tammy Smith, whose insights and careful attention to detail were invaluable to the accuracy of my portrayal of Palmer and military protocol. To Brigadier General Rose Loper, the first female test pilot in Boeing's history, for teaching me how to virtually fly a Black Hawk. To former Press Secretary to the President of the United States Ari Fleisher, for forty years of friendship and for ensuring the detailed accuracy of presidential/White House protocol. To State Department expert Dana Francis, one of my oldest and dearest friends, for help with issues of diplomacy and State Department protocol. To Doctor Christopher Stark, whose real account of emergency room trauma blew my mind and ensured heart-stopping accuracy. To retired criminal defense attorney Carsen Taite, who helped me dot my "i's" and cross my "t's." To Tracey Hepner, whose detailed first-person account of attending a State of the Union infused my story with realism. To my first readers, Doctor Jenni Levy and retired Lieutenant Commander Elaine Roberts for taking every ride with me. To the best cover designer in the history of cover designers, my little sister of choice, Ann McMan. To my crack editor, Ann Roberts, whose attention to detail gives my work a fine polish. To my final proofreaders, Laura Nastro and Anne Geary, whose keen eyes give me that last boost of confidence.

To my amazing wife, Cheryl Pletcher, who is the best sounding board, head cheerleader, and support system an author could ask for, and whose endless patience made this work possible. Darling, with you, everything is possible. Always together.

And finally, to you the readers, who continue to support my work. Thank you all for taking the journey with me.

Other Books by Lynn Ames

Stand-Alone Romances
Secrets Well Kept
Chain Reactions
Bright Lights of Summer
All That Lies Within
Eyes on the Stars
Heartsong
One ~ Love

Romantic Comedies
Great Bones

The Kate and Jay Series
The Price of Fame
The Cost of Commitment
The Value of Valor
Final Cut

The Mission: Classified Series
Beyond Instinct
Above Reproach

Anthology Collections
Outsiders

Specialty Books - Humor
Digging for Home

Lynn Ames books are available in multiple formats through www.lynnames.com, from your favorite local bookstore, or through other online venues.

CHAPTER ONE

She could hear them out there stamping their feet, clapping their hands, chanting her name, "Emma! Emma! Emma!" And her campaign slogan, "*United We Stand!*" She twisted the wedding band on her left ring finger. She didn't wear it for optics, but rather to honor her dead wife and their thirty-one years together. Heather had sacrificed everything, including her life, to support Emma's career.

"I wish you were here to see this."

"What was that, ma'am?"

Emma could see the makeup artist's eyebrows rise in question in her reflection in the mirror as she retouched the back of Emma's hair.

"Nothing."

Nichelle Johnson swept into the makeshift Green Room. She carried a folder in hand and wore a smile that was as wide as the Mississippi River valley from which she hailed. She had joined Emma's staff back in the days when Emma was a wet-behind-the-ears state senator from New York. "Well, Madam President-elect, are you ready to face your adoring public?"

"Don't you 'Madam President-elect,' me, Nichelle. It's bad enough everyone else is saying it."

"From where I'm standing, you've worked long and hard to earn that title. If I were you, I'd wear it with pride."

"Was that a pun from my always-serious campaign manager and soon-to-be chief of staff?"

"Was what a pun?" Nichelle's features scrunched up in confusion.

"Wear it with pride? Said to the first lesbian president-elect?" Nichelle blinked.

"Yeah. I didn't think so." Emma stood and addressed the makeup artist. "Thanks so much. I don't think I've ever looked this good before."

"Are you kidding me? I got to do makeup for the hottest president in history on one of the most important nights in our country's existence." The makeup artist swallowed hard as tears pricked her eyes and all pretense of lightheartedness melted away. "I'm sorry, ma'am. I don't mean to be impertinent, but I should be thanking you. As someone who puts the 'T' in LGBTQ, you make me proud to be an American again. You give me hope." Her voice faltered, and she wiped away a tear. "You *are* going to sage that place before you move in, right?"

Emma choked on a guffaw and cleared her throat. "I hope you'll always be proud to be an American. And if I do something that makes you feel less than that while I'm in office, I hope you'll call me out on it."

"Oh, you can count on that, ma'am."

"Madam President-elect. We really do need to get going. Secret Service estimates there are upwards of 300,000 people out there."

"I hope they're not ruining the grass."

"That's what you're worried about?"

"It's the Great Lawn in Central Park. It's iconic and it has survived concerts by some of the biggest names in rock 'n roll. I don't want to be known as the one who destroyed a New York landmark." Emma winked, turned on her heel, smoothed the lines of her suit, and followed Nichelle into the wings at the side of the stage. "Did David incorporate the changes I asked for in the speech?"

"He did."

"And the updated version is what's loaded into the teleprompter?"

"It is."

"Okay." Emma rolled her shoulders to release the tension.

"You're going to be great. They love you. Seventy million of them voted for you—the largest number of popular votes ever amassed by a candidate of any party."

"It's not the ones who supported me I need to address tonight. It's the rest of the country. I'm their president too." The night air was crisp, but the stars shone brightly and the temperature was warm enough that she'd eschewed a winter coat. Emma briefly closed her eyes and inhaled deeply.

Snippets from the campaign trail scrolled like a highlight reel through her mind: the endless speeches, interviews, debates, and fundraisers; the late-night strategy sessions, the sleepless road trips, the concerns for her safety as death threats rolled in...

But, first and foremost, she saw the faces of the people she'd met along the way. They were white, black, and brown; they were gay, lesbian, straight, queer, bi, pan, and transgender; each of them had a story they wanted to share with her, a need they hoped she would address.

She would carry them all with her. She would lift them up and show them they mattered. This was her duty, her solemn oath. This was why she had wanted to be president. This was her life's purpose—to make a difference.

"It's time." Nichelle touched her gently on the arm as she handed her the folder.

"Where's the vice president-elect?"

"He'll join you on stage as soon as your remarks conclude."

"Okay. I'm ready."

"Yes, you are." Nichelle signaled the speaker at the podium.

"Ladies and gentlemen, the next president of the United States, Emma McMasters!"

∽ふ❧

Palmer Estes, top advisor to the chairman of the Joint Chiefs of Staff and currently the nation's only female four-star general, shrugged out of her Army greens and threw on a pair of Army-issue sweats. The meeting with her boss had run late, but there was a lot of ground to cover with the upcoming transition of power to a new president.

She checked her watch, grabbed the leftover salad and dressing out of the refrigerator, and settled down on the couch in front of the television. Tonight was historic, and Palmer didn't want to miss seeing the winning candidate's acceptance speech. The idea that the

United States had elected the nation's first female president, who also happened to be a lesbian, seemed incomprehensible.

Palmer leaned forward on the couch, television remote in hand, and turned up the volume. She wanted to weep with joy as fifty-two-year-old President-elect Emma McMasters strode to the podium in Central Park. Here was her soon-to-be commander in chief, a woman four years her junior, who represented everything she admired.

Emma exhibited grace under fire from misogynists and bigots who attacked her ability to lead because she was a woman—and not simply a woman, but a lesbian. She handled every insult hurled at her with aplomb, conducted herself with dignity, and acted with integrity.

"And since you're not yet my commander in chief, I can admit to myself that you're stunning." Had that been her outside voice? Well, it was true. Emma's youthful features, penetrating green eyes, high cheekbones, and thick black hair with a hint of gray created a flawless face. Her form-fitting suit showed off her obviously workout-toned body to perfection. Yes, Emma McMasters was gorgeous.

"Oh, my God. You're as bad as the guys!" Palmer tossed the remote onto the couch in self-disgust. "This capable, intelligent person, with a vision for this country that you believe in, is about to be your boss. Shape up, soldier!"

"Hello!" Emma waved to the crowd. Her brilliant, white-toothed smile lit up the night. The massive audience went berserk, chanting her name. She allowed the adulation to continue for a moment, then tried, to no avail, to quiet the crowd. She stepped to the side of the podium, seemingly embarrassed by the attention, and paused before she endeavored once more to speak.

"Oh, my goodness. Thank you! Thank you all so much. Thank you for being here tonight to celebrate with me. United we stand!"

The crowd erupted again.

"Tonight we gather on hallowed ground. Not just because this Great Lawn has been the site of some of the most amazing concerts ever..." Emma nodded as the audience laughed. "You know I'm right. Barbara Streisand, Diana Ross, Bon Jovi, Elton John... I mean, come on!"

She's got them eating out of the palm of her hand. Palmer sat transfixed. *Me too.*

"But that's not the reason I chose this location to accept this most solemn, most monumental honor. No. Did you know that in 1931, during the height of the Great Depression, this very spot served as the home of displaced residents—folks who were down on their luck, cast out of their homes, many of them without a place to go, and most of them stripped of dignity and hope?

"For too long, too many of us have felt the same way. We've felt like outsiders in our own country, cast aside, hopeless, desperate for better days when we would once again feel safe, valued, whole, and a part of something larger than ourselves.

"Well, my friends and fellow Americans, that day is today; now is your time. Together, we will heal this *one* nation, under God, indivisible."

The audience went wild and Emma had to scream to be heard. "Mine is a big tent, where all are welcomed, treasured, and vital, regardless of race, immigration status, religion, ethnicity, sexual identity, sexual orientation, income level, or political affiliation. *You* are the fabric of this nation, and, as your president, I serve *all* of you."

The chants began again. "Emma! Emma! Emma!"

"E pluribus Unum," Emma shouted. "Out of many, one."

Someone in the crowd shouted, "E Pluribus, Emma!" The president-elect's eyes grew wide and she laughed. Palmer thought she'd never seen a more beautiful sight.

For the next half hour, she watched and listened as Emma expertly weaved a narrative that was equal parts history lesson, vision for the future, and rallying cry. The president-elect finished with a flourish and was joined onstage by the vice president-elect, along with his wife and children, all of them standing together, hands linked and raised to the sky in victory.

"I wish you had someone there for you, Madam President-elect," Palmer muttered aloud. On what undoubtedly was the most triumphant night of her career, Emma McMasters cut a solitary figure. Palmer felt sorry for her. Surely, this night was meant to be shared with loved ones.

Palmer mostly ignored stories about the personal lives of the candidates in the run-up to the election. She had no stomach for attack ads, smears, innuendo, or overly intrusive media profiles. Everyone was entitled to privacy, even the most public figures. She'd studied the candidates' positions on the issues, watched the debates to get a sense of each potential nominee, and chosen her candidate accordingly.

As a result, Palmer knew nothing about Emma, beyond the fact that she was a lesbian, she had lost both her parents to cancer, and that she was widowed. Now, sitting here watching her in this historic moment, Palmer wanted to know so much more.

She grabbed her iPad and tapped the Google app. She typed, "Emma McMasters," in the search parameters. Instantly, thousands of entries filled the screen. At the top was a sponsored ad with a link to Emma's official website. Directly below that were newspaper stories from *The Wall Street Journal*, *The Washington Post*, and *The New York Times* followed by a link to Emma's Wikipedia page. Palmer clicked to open the Wikipedia entry.

Emma Jean McMasters (born April 23, 1968) is an American politician and lawyer, serving as governor of New York since 2015. She was formerly the Senate minority leader in New York State, a state senator from New York's 27th Senate District, and before that, district attorney in Manhattan. She is a member of the Democratic Party.

Palmer scanned farther down the page.

McMasters is a graduate of the University of Connecticut and the University of Michigan Law School, where she was president of the prestigious Michigan Law Review. Although she was heavily recruited by many of New York City's most notable law firms, McMasters chose a life in public service, joining the Manhattan District Attorney's office as an assistant district attorney, where she successfully prosecuted cases involving high-profile white-collar crimes, political corruption, murder, and organized crime.

"So, you've got some mettle and you're not afraid of a fight. That's good." Palmer noted the crawl on the bottom of the television screen indicating that the Republicans had retained control of the U.S. Senate by a one-vote margin. "I have a feeling you're going to need those qualities, Madam Soon-to-Be-President."

The coverage shifted to the network studio, where the anchor intoned, "Who is Emma McMasters, really? Our own Judith

Abernathy sat down with Governor McMasters during the campaign for an in-depth interview."

Palmer shoved the iPad aside and gave the television her full attention.

"Governor McMasters, your opponent and his proxies have painted you as a security risk who can't be trusted with the keys to the front door of the White House. What do you have to say to that?"

If the reporter's question rattled or irked Emma, Palmer couldn't tell from her demeanor. Emma, seemingly relaxed and at ease, sat across from the interviewer wearing a sharply tailored dark business suit and a white shell underneath. She was the picture of calm dignity.

"I would say that the American people are smart enough to recognize a desperate smear campaign when they see it, which is exactly what this is. My opponent can't win on the issues, so he and his associates resort to personal attacks. The American people know that this is a weak attempt to deflect attention from the important work that needs to be done.

"Now is the moment to unite our country, to heal the deep wounds of partisanship that have dominated our government and our people for too long. The White House is the peoples' house, and all that represents. As president, I will be the custodian of a democracy of the people, by the people, and for the people. I will undertake this solemn responsibility with humility and integrity."

"I understand that, Madam Governor. But they've intimated that your sexuality and the fact that you're single—"

For the first time since the interview started, Emma's eyes flashed fire. She sat forward and planted both high-heeled shoes on the floor. The camera zoomed in for a close-up. "I'm a widow who lost her wife and partner of thirty-one years to a tragic car accident three years ago. There isn't a day that goes by that I don't bear that burden and that sorrow. Anyone who would suggest differently has never lost someone they loved."

"I want to show you something." The reporter pointed to a television monitor and hit the play button.

A gravelly, disembodied voice intoned, "This is the type of thing you can expect to see entering the presidential residence at the White House if Emma McMasters gets her hands on the presidency." The picture on screen showed a revolving door underneath the White House portico and several obviously masculine-looking women entering and exiting.

When the ad finished, the reporter turned to Emma. "What's your reaction to that?"

Sitting in her living room, Palmer fumed. "Would you ask a straight male candidate the same question?"

Emma was forceful in her response. "It seems to me that my opponent is intimating that LGBTQ and/or gender fluid individuals should not be welcome in their own house. United we stand. Mine is a big tent. I intend to include in my administration people of all faiths, all sexual identities and orientations, all ethnicities, and all political parties."

"Understood, Governor. But I believe the purpose of the ad was to suggest something more on a personal level…"

"From the beginning of my public life, I have been on the record and transparent about my personal relationships. At eighteen, I met and fell in love with my college roommate, who happened to be a woman. We were together for more than three decades until death parted us. Period. I have had one constant, faithful, loving relationship in my life." Emma stared unflinchingly into the camera. "How many other candidates for president can say that?"

"Impressive, Madam President-elect," Palmer said. Anyone with a pulse knew the answer to that question, and Emma had made her point without resorting to mudslinging.

Palmer's phone buzzed and she checked the screen. Immediately she muted the television and took the call. "Estes."

"Sorry to bother you, General. I know you just got home, but we've got a situation."

"I'll be there in ten." Palmer clicked off the call and the television and strode into her bedroom. Her various uniforms hung in neat rows in the walk-in closet. She shucked off her sweats and chose a fresh set of Army greens. Whatever was afoot, a summons at this hour portended high-level, classified briefings and a potential trip to the White House.

She didn't want to waste precious time standing on ceremony and calling her driver. Tonight she would take her private car.

At this hour, the drive from her home on the Fort Myer base to her office in the Pentagon took less than eight minutes.

At the entrance to the Pentagon grounds, she scanned her badge, parked in her assigned spot, and hustled inside. Her aide, Brigadier General Maxwell Jeffers, came crisply to attention as she entered the building. Palmer noticed, not for the first time lately, that his closely cropped afro was considerably grayer than it had been when they'd first served together all those years ago in Desert Storm.

"General, they're waiting downstairs." Downstairs meant below ground, in the most secure area of the building.

When they were alone in the elevator leading down to the basement, Palmer asked, "Who have we got?"

"CIA, NSA, OSD – J2."

Palmer sighed. If the Central Intelligence Agency, the National Security Agency, and the general in charge of the Office of the Secretary of Defense/Joint Forces were involved, this was serious, indeed. Fleetingly, she thought about Emma McMasters. Whatever Palmer was about to discover, she was grateful it no doubt would be a distant memory by the time the president-elect took office in January.

CHAPTER TWO

Not for the first time, Emma wished the occasion called for more practical footwear. She smiled ironically as she recalled Ann Richards' famous quote about Ginger Rogers doing everything Fred Astaire did, but backwards and in high heels. No doubt the deceased governor of Texas would've said the same of a female president.

Emma stamped her feet to restore feeling and shivered inside her winter coat. Why couldn't this Inauguration Day have emulated Ronald Reagan's first inauguration, when the temperature in Washington, D.C. had reached a balmy fifty-five degrees? She exhaled and watched as her frozen breath rose skyward. At least the sun was shining and the wind had died down a bit after last night's light dusting of snow.

She stood by herself in the private, enclosed Ross Garden, at the rear of the President's Guest House, Blair House, across the street from the White House. In another few hours, she would walk through those iconic doors as president of the United States of America.

We made it, Heather. God, she wished her wife were here to give the speech one last bit of polish. Heather was so good at that.

Emma bowed her head as the all-too-familiar stab of pain pierced her heart. They were supposed to be doing this together. Heather should have been holding the McMasters family Bible as the chief justice of the Supreme Court administered the oath of office. In Heather's stead, Emma had invited her mentor, her mother's best friend and the woman whom she'd grown up emulating, to do the honors.

Nichelle materialized next to her. "Madam President-elect, it's time to go to St. John's for the morning service."

"You have got to stop sneaking up on me."

"I thought it was part of my job description to be discreet."

"Is that in the Presidential Chief of Staff handbook?"

"It worked for Martin Sheen in *The American President*, not to mention John Spencer on *The West Wing*."

"You're shaping your role based on fictional characters you admire?"

Nichelle shrugged. "It works for me."

"Well, I'll tell you this much—I'm not Michael Douglas, you're not Martin Sheen, we're not playing billiards, and you're not going to get to tell me off in colorful language if you think I have my head up my wazoo."

"Aww. I was looking forward to that."

Emma linked arms with Nichelle as they strolled. "Promise me that you'll never let me take myself too seriously."

"I promise."

Emma pulled them up short. "And that you'll always tell me the truth, even if I don't want to hear it."

"You've got it."

"And that you'll keep the crazies away from me."

"Don't push it. Some of those crazies are your constituents."

"All of those crazies, at least the American ones, are my constituents, and some of them are elected officials."

"Too true." Nichelle urged them forward again. "Are you really going to stand in the freezing cold without a coat to deliver the inaugural address?"

"I am. It sends a strong signal."

"Yeah. It tells people their president doesn't have an ounce of common sense."

"It worked for Kennedy, Reagan, and Clinton."

"You know two of those three got shot and the other one got impeached, right?"

"Okay. Maybe those weren't the best examples." Emma said goodbye to Nichelle and nodded at the Secret Service special agent in charge of her detail, or SAIC, as he surveyed the area around the presidential limousine. She liked Scott. He was a burly ex-football player with a square jaw and biceps the size of her thighs. He was a family man with a wife and twin teenage girls whom he adored. His team obviously respected him, and more importantly, so did she.

Over the course of the last four months of the campaign, from the time when she'd first become eligible for Secret Service protection, they'd spent plenty of time together. Emma's status as the first lesbian major party presidential contender made her a target for every alt-right hate group and every individual who saw her existence as an abomination or a menace, and there were many of those.

Scott and his team had been by her side through all of it, interfacing with the Federal Bureau of Investigation to vet and investigate every credible threat. While Emma was certain she never would feel completely safe, especially in large, open spaces filled with seas of humanity, she knew that Scott and his team would do everything in their power to protect her, including take a bullet for her if it came to that.

"We're here, Madam President-elect." One of the Secret Service agents opened the door and Emma stepped out. She was greeted by the rector as she entered the Episcopal Church where almost every modern-day president-elect and vice president-elect attended service on inauguration morning.

Emma took her place in the traditional presidential pew, pew fifty-four, and settled in for the brief service. As much as she tried to take in the details, she couldn't keep her thoughts from straying to the precedent-breaking moment that would come next.

For only the fourth time in United States history, the incumbent president had chosen not to accompany the president-elect from the White House to the U.S. Capitol for the inauguration. As a student of history, this bothered Emma. Even Woodrow Wilson, who refused to attend his successor, Warren G. Harding's inauguration in 1921, rode with the next president to the Capitol before departing.

Beyond that, word of the snub was dominating headlines and news shows everywhere and the hashtag #poutingPOTUS was trending on Twitter. While that was a modest improvement over the far right's preferred hashtag, #lezziegohome, it still detracted from the dignity of the occasion and the traditional transition of power.

Emma received the letter yesterday, on White House stationery, signed by the president, informing her of his decision. She consoled herself by admitting inwardly that, on a practical level, it would be nice not to have to deal with the awkwardness of the moment. She imagined the photographers snapping away as she and the outgoing president, who at every turn during the course of the campaign had defamed and debased her, exchanged a handshake and an insincere smile as he and his wife boarded Marine One for the last time. No, she wouldn't be sorry to miss that photo-op.

Then, later in the day, the chairman of the Joint Congressional Committee on Inaugural Ceremonies informed her via telephone that the incumbent president had made it known that he and his wife would depart at exactly noon from the South Lawn of the White House, the very moment Emma would be standing on the west terrace of the U.S. Capitol taking the oath of office. Even for this president, the blatant show of disrespect for tradition, for her, and the office of the presidency, was astounding.

"We're so sorry, Madam President-elect. We never imagined..."

"Of course not. Please, don't worry about it. It wasn't your decision to make."

"Yes, but the plan calls for you to go from the service at St. John's directly to the White House, where you were to be met by the president at the North Portico and ride together to the Capitol for the oath and inauguration ceremony."

"I'm familiar with the tradition."

"Under the circumstances, you'll be going directly from St. John's to the Capitol. I'm concerned that you'll be waiting in the holding room for an additional half hour to forty-five minutes."

Emma hated the idea of cooling her heels in some Capitol ante-room simply because the current resident of the White House rebuffed her. She smiled as the perfect solution presented itself.

"I know precisely what I want to do with that extra time. If the logistics don't present too much of a nightmare, I'd like to make a stop along the route."

"A stop?"

"Yes. I think it would send the perfect message if I paused on the way to taking the oath of office to visit the original copies of the Constitution, the Bill of Rights, and the Declaration of Independence."

After a moment of silence, the chairman replied, "That's brilliant. The National Archives is directly on the route. I'm certain the Secret Service can secure the rotunda without too much trouble. We can allow the press to photograph you—"

"Hold it right there. I will allow the photo-op, but only from a distance looking into the rotunda. I don't want them in the rotunda itself. And I think I'd prefer if this was an unannounced stop."

"But—"

Emma felt her heart settle. "No. This is more than just a photo-op for me. The Constitution stands for something. Those documents stand for something, and so do I. I don't want the moment sullied by treating it cynically."

"Understood, Madam President-elect. We will make it happen."

"Please convey my apologies for the last-minute scramble to the committee and the security forces."

"This isn't your fault."

"Maybe not, but it's going to inconvenience people." Emma considered. "If possible, I'd prefer it if the archives themselves remained open during my visit and only the rotunda was unavailable to the public. I don't want to deprive visitors of the opportunity to spend time at one of the most important treasures in our capital."

"I'm not sure the Secret Service is going to like that, but we'll do our best."

"I know you will."

Emma snapped her focus back to the present as the reverend said, "I know you all join me in wishing our president-elect Godspeed as she undertakes her new role. May God watch over her and watch over all of us. Amen."

"Amen," Emma murmured. The service concluded and the vice president-elect joined Emma. They exited the row of pews together.

"Nice service."

Emma nodded as he helped her into her coat. She knew most of the press and half of the public believed she'd chosen Harrison Elder as her running mate because he was Black, had Washington experience as a U.S. senator, and polled well in some of the early primaries. But the truth was that she genuinely liked him. She found him to be intelligent and level-headed, his ego didn't require constant stroking, he offered a world view different from her own, and he was both progressive and pragmatic. Furthermore, he was willing to speak up when he disagreed with her, but was discreet enough to do so in private.

"Are you ready for this?" she asked.

"The real question is, are you?" he countered.

"I hope so."

"I know you are." They walked together to the back of the church, where Harrison's family waited for him.

Emma knelt in front of Harrison's youngest daughter. "It's an exciting day for you."

"Yes, ma'am."

"You should be very, very proud of your daddy. He's a great man."

"Yes, ma'am."

"Okay. I'll see you all in a little while."

"Yes, ma'am."

"I'm sorry about that. She's so shy." Harrison's wife, Beverly, straightened her daughter's sleeve.

"It's okay. I was that shy at her age too, and look what happened to me." Emma winked. "Take care of this guy." She jabbed a finger in Harrison's direction. "I need him."

"I will," Beverly assured her.

"I'm sorry you'll be stuck in a holding room at the Capitol for longer than we hoped," Emma said.

"No problem. We've arranged for lunch for the kids and promised them they could watch *Toy Story 4* again until it was time to go outside."

"Now I want to be one of your kids."

Beverly laughed. "No, you don't. Just ask them."

Emma caught a glimpse of the Secret Service agent standing rigidly inside the door. She addressed Harrison. "I'll see you all soon." She nodded at the agent, who opened the door for her and took up his assigned position as she closed the distance to the limo quickly and climbed inside.

In seconds, the motorcade was underway. "Here we go," she muttered to herself.

৯৩৯

Palmer, the members of the Joint Chiefs of Staff, and a handful of other high-ranking military officers stood on the risers above and to the left of the podium where the president-elect would take the oath of office. As they waited for the ceremony to get underway, she looked down on the sea of humanity below the west terrace of the Capitol and wondered idly if the crowd would top President Obama's 1.8 million-plus people. The waves of brightly colored outfits stretched all the way to the Lincoln Memorial at the other end of the National Mall.

Members of both houses of Congress, Supreme Court justices, past presidents and vice presidents, celebrities, and others Palmer didn't recognize milled around on the risers, chatting amiably.

Nearby, one of the late arrivers informed several people around her that she'd gotten a news alert on her phone on the way to the Capitol that the president-elect had apparently made an unscheduled stop at the National Archives. The news had blown up social media. Several news organizations had tweeted photos of the president-elect, solitary and looking pensive, viewing the glass-encased Constitution.

Palmer tried not to pay much attention to things like Twitter, but it had been hard to avoid the chatter about the presidential snub over the past two days' news cycles. She'd felt badly for Emma. Now, hearing about her visit to view the Constitution, Palmer felt a swell of pride. Without saying a word, Emma was making a point. *Good for you, Madam President-elect.*

The United States Marine Band played, a disembodied voice thundered the announced arrival of the president-elect, and Palmer and the other generals around her snapped to attention.

Emma looked regal and dignified in a perfectly tailored, power-red, dress-and-jacket ensemble with matching three-inch pumps. Palmer was surprised to note that she wore no overcoat or gloves. She was surrounded by an entourage—the chairman of the inaugural committee, the majority and minority leaders of both houses of Congress, and the sergeants-at-arms of both the House of Representatives and the Senate.

As she descended the stairs, the president-elect paused to greet well-wishers and friends along the way. Palmer watched, mesmerized, from her perch less than twenty feet away. *You're even more spectacular in person than you are on TV.*

Emma's smile was radiant, her manner warm, welcoming, and unassuming, and yet it was as if the air around her shifted and crackled with electricity. She commanded attention not because she

25

was trying to do so, nor even because of the occasion. She was the kind of person whose mere presence lit up any space. Palmer tried to put her finger on it. Charismatic. Self-possessed but not cocky. Beautiful but unpretentious and unselfconscious. All of these things were true, but there was something else…

For a brief instant, Emma's gaze turned in her direction. Had the president-elect really looked directly at her? Palmer swallowed hard. *Now you're imagining things.* Perhaps so, but she was happy to allow herself the moment.

⋘⋙

Emma couldn't remember ever being this cold. *Whose bright idea was it to go coatless? You'll be lucky if the entire world doesn't hear your teeth chattering together.* At exactly 11:55 a.m., she rose to take the oath of office.

Her left hand shook on the family Bible held by her mentor, Ruth Weinstein, as she recited after the chief justice of the Supreme Court, "I, Emma Jean McMasters, do solemnly swear to faithfully execute the Office of President of the United States, and will to the best of my ability, preserve, protect, and defend the Constitution of the United States, so help me God."

"Congratulations, Madam President." The chief justice shook her hand.

The crowd erupted in applause, and Emma blinked away unexpected tears as Ruth embraced her and whispered in her ear, "Your mom, dad, and Heather are so proud of you, and so am I. I hope you know I stand here representing all of them. You're going to be a great president."

Unable to speak, Emma simply nodded. Harrison appeared to her left and she accepted congratulations from him, Beverly, and the leaders of Congress. The United States Army Herald Trumpets played four ruffles and flourishes. Then, following a twenty-one-gun salute, the United States Marine Band broke into "Hail to the Chief."

The chairman of the inaugural committee intoned, "Mr. Vice President, members of Congress, distinguished guests, ladies and gentlemen, I introduce to you the president of the United States, Emma J. McMasters."

Emma had pored over dozens of presidential inaugural addresses for style, substance, and length. She'd taken suggestions from her speechwriters, respected U.S. historians, and two past presidents. In the end, she'd used their inspiration to find her own unique voice. She'd crafted every word of the address herself. At 2,347 words, and allowing for applause, she'd be finished talking in about nineteen minutes.

"This is your moment," one of her predecessors told her. "This tells the nation and the world who you are and what kind of leader you'll be. All eyes are on you. Make it memorable, and enjoy it. Not everyone gets to do what you're about to do, and you may only ever do it once in your lifetime."

Emma inhaled deeply and let go of the last of the nerves that had taken up residence in her stomach. She approached the podium and focused her eyes on the horizon before her.

"One nation, indivisible," she began. "One," she repeated, pausing for emphasis, "nation, indivisible. Three simple words that form the backbone of a thirty-one-word pledge most of us can recite in our sleep.

"E pluribus unum. That's Latin for 'out of many, one.'" Emma shifted her gaze to her left and picked up her place on the second of the two teleprompters placed diagonally in front of her. "Right about now, you're asking yourself, 'Where have I seen that expression before?' Might I humbly suggest that you pull the change out of your pocket? It's engraved on our currency. Depending on how good your eyesight is, you can also find it on the face of this lectern, above the wings of the bald eagle in the Seal of the President of the United States.

"Throughout this remarkable country's history, our greatest leaders have implored us to celebrate unity and to lift each other up. Why? Because they recognized what I know in my heart. Together, we're stronger. There is so much more that unites us than that which divides, so much common ground on which the foundation of this grand and powerful nation exists.

"What legacy will we leave for the next generation of Americans as citizens of this country and of the world? Will we look them in the eye and tell them we didn't get it done because it was too hard, or because we disagreed with someone else's vision and so we shut them down? Will we spend our days gazing inward in fear of those whose backgrounds, faiths, ethnicities, orientations, immigration status, or economic situation doesn't mirror our own?

"Or will we roll up our sleeves, step outside our own lanes, and open ourselves to the truth that we each add value, that we each have the ability to learn from and teach each other... That if we listen more than we talk, if we stop talking *at* each other and talk *to* each other, if we practice kindness instead of divisiveness, if we consciously lift each other up instead of tearing each other down..."

Emma no longer felt the cold. This was the moment. She would lay out her vision, set forth her hopes and dreams for the next four years, and if she did her job right, help to heal the deep schism that had torn the very fabric of the country she loved. She rested both hands on the sides of the lectern and leaned in.

CHAPTER THREE

The music was loud and the crowd was in high spirits at the Commander in Chief Ball inside the National Building Museum. Palmer stood off to the side, nursing a Diet Coke, as the anticipation built to a crescendo. Word was that President McMasters and Vice President Elder would arrive any minute.

This would be the seventh ball of the night for the president. Palmer imagined she must be exhausted. News alerts had been filled all day long with the president's nonstop schedule—the traditional luncheon with select members of Congress, the Inaugural Parade in which she walked most of the route, her late-afternoon arrival at the White House, the Senate confirmation of several of her Cabinet choices, and now a series of first dances and an endless stream of speeches to different crowds at the balls.

Palmer eyed the Joint Chiefs, all decked out as she was in their mess dress uniforms, the attire prescribed for formal occasions. They were an impressive group, dedicated to serving their country with excellence and honor. Her boss, Army General Charles Dutton, the chairman of the Joint Chiefs, was exacting but fair. She respected his office, but more than that, she respected the man, his experience and judgment, and his conduct.

General Dutton was due to rotate out of the chairmanship in October, a fact that had played heavily into Palmer's decision to retire after thirty-five years of service. At the moment, he was deep in discussion with newly-confirmed Secretary of Defense Lester Buchanan and Chief of Staff for the National Security Council Mark Nelson.

"I hope that's a friendly social gaggle over there," Max said.

"Me too," Palmer agreed.

"Ladies and gentlemen, the president of the United States," a disembodied voice announced.

Palmer and every military member in the room snapped to attention as the band struck up "Hail to the Chief" and all eyes turned to the stage.

Seconds later, Emma emerged and strode to the podium. She was resplendent in a floor-length, emerald green, off-the-shoulder gown. If she was tired, she hid it well.

This was Palmer's second in-person opportunity of the day to observe the new president in action. This president had presence—an undeniable magnetism that inspired confidence.

As she'd done at the inauguration earlier in the day, Palmer studied the faces and body language of audience members, many of whom had their phones out and were filming and live-streaming as they watched and listened to their new commander in chief. For the first time in longer than she wanted to admit, she saw on their faces something akin to hope. *Brava, Madam President.*

The president finished her remarks. "Well, what did you…" Palmer stopped talking when she realized Max was no longer standing next to her. She glanced around the ballroom. It was unlike him to venture far from her at what amounted to a working event.

After several moments, she spotted him standing not twenty feet from the president, talking to a very attractive woman in a stylish white gown. *Smooth, Maxwell. Very smooth.* Leave it to him to find the one civilian in a ballroom full of service members.

⤙⤚

Emma concluded the traditional dance with an enlisted service member. Her feet ached and her stomach reminded her she hadn't eaten dinner. After too many nights spent studying briefing books and working on her inaugural address, what she really wanted was to fall into bed and get a good night's sleep.

As the song ended, the lance corporal stepped back. "Thank you, ma'am."

"Thank you." Emma shook his hand. "You stay safe out there."

"Yes, ma'am."

This marked the conclusion of her formal responsibilities at the ball. She'd enlisted Lady Gaga to perform live, and she was sure to be a crowd-pleaser. Past presidents at this point waved and moved on to the next ball. But she wasn't past presidents, and she had something else in mind. She glanced to the wings where Nichelle was standing by, only to discover that Nichelle wasn't there. Instead, she was out front, deeply engaged in conversation with a dashing one-star general.

The sight warmed Emma's heart. She couldn't remember the last time Nichelle had allowed herself to have a life outside of work. That didn't mean that Emma wouldn't tease her about it later.

As if sensing that she was being observed, Nichelle's gaze jerked up to meet Emma's. Embarrassment stained her cheeks. She took a step forward, but Emma held up a hand and strode toward her, instead.

"Who's this?" she asked, as the officer snapped to attention. "At ease," she added.

"General Maxwell Jeffers, ma'am."

"A pleasure to meet you, General."

"The general was telling me about his job," Nichelle explained.

"Was he?" Emma smiled knowingly.

Nichelle glared at her. "I'll tell the Secret Service you're ready to go."

"Not so fast." Emma put a hand on Nichelle's arm to keep her in place. "I bet the general could help me with something."

Nichelle raised an eyebrow, and Max again came to attention. "Yes, ma'am."

"I don't want to cut and run just yet. I know the tradition is for the president to dance the first dance with the chosen enlisted person and then move on, but I want to shake it up a little. I'd like to be introduced to some of the brave service members who are defending this great nation. Could you help me with that? Who would you recommend I meet?"

The general's eyes lit up. "Yes, ma'am. I'd like to start, if I may, by introducing you to my direct superior, General Estes. She's the chairman of the Joint Chiefs of Staff's advisor to the White House. We served together in Desert Storm. Bravest soldier I ever saw. It's an honor to serve by her side."

"Lead on," Emma said. She winked at Nichelle, who studiously pretended to ignore her.

The general turned smartly and Emma fell into step alongside him. The Secret Service agents discreetly cleared a path for them. The general stopped in front of a lean, long-legged, fiery-redheaded four-star general.

"Madam President, may I introduce you to General Palmer Estes."

Emma signaled her "at ease" and extended her hand. "It's a pleasure to meet you, General Estes." She had to blink to avoid getting lost in the deep, shimmering blue of the general's eyes.

"The pleasure's mine, Madam President. I hope you're having a good time tonight."

Her voice was deeper than Emma had expected. "I am. So much so that I thought I'd linger a few minutes longer."

"That will make the troops very happy, ma'am. We're all aware that you have many events on your dance card tonight."

"Don't remind me," Emma said, smiling.

"Speaking of which…" Nichelle purposefully checked her watch.

"General Estes, meet my chief of staff, Nichelle Johnson. She's a stickler for keeping me on time," Emma complained.

"Nice to meet you, General. Madam President, you'll thank me later when the press doesn't complain that you were two hours late to the next ball."

Emma rolled her eyes and General Estes laughed. The sound was rich and full. "Please excuse us. General Estes, General Jeffers, it was a great honor to meet you both."

Emma allowed Nichelle to guide her toward the exit. She paused along the way to greet and take selfies with a line of enlisted military men and women that had queued up on her route. As she exited the museum, she took a moment to silently pray for the safety of each one.

❖❖

Palmer and Max left the ballroom together. "You certainly seemed like you were having a good time." Palmer jabbed Max playfully with an elbow.

"I'm sure I don't know what you're talking about."

"Nichelle Johnson, that's what I'm talking about. She's awfully attractive."

"She was a marvelous conversationalist."

"I could tell from the way you hung on her every word."

"You're imagining things."

"I don't think so." Palmer wasn't ready to give up her fun just yet. "I'll have to do a little research on Ms. Johnson."

Max shook his head. "Get off it."

"Is she single? Does she have references? This could take some time."

"For your information, she is single—"

"Aha! You've already inquired. That's an excellent start."

"It's not like that..."

"Like what?" Palmer feigned innocence.

"Come on. Cut me some slack."

"You're right." Palmer pulled them up short and held Max's gaze. "It's been too long since you had someone in your life, my friend. I just want to see you happy. Ms. Johnson is obviously a professional woman with an impressive resumé, she's single, she most likely is as devoted to her work as you are to yours, and she understands dedication to service and keeping odd work hours. I say, go for it."

"And I say you're reading too much into it. This was a casual conversation at a work event—"

"With an interesting, self-possessed, intelligent...did I mention *single* woman?"

Max groaned. "You might have mentioned it once or twice."

Emma wasn't sure what came after tired...weary to the bone, maybe? Whatever it was, she was there. She closed her eyes in the back of the presidential limo on the way back to the White House from the last ball.

The White House—where she now lived. The White House, which, in less than a day, had been transformed from the tastes, styles, personal items, furnishings, and even favorite foods of the previous president to her own. It was surreal.

33

"We're here, Madam President."

"So we are. Thank you." Once outside the car, Emma addressed her Secret Service contingent. "You've all had a long day. I hope you get some well-deserved rest tonight."

"Thank you. You too, Madam President."

Upstairs in the master bedroom—her bedroom—Emma kicked off her heels and stretched. Apart from using the restroom, this was the first time she'd been alone since early this morning. Momentarily, she closed her eyes and listened to the silence. Relief washed through her as the tension her body held washed away.

"What a day." She twirled around and took in the room. The muted beiges and pale lapis her designer had chosen for the room complimented each other well. The light colors kept the room from feeling too heavy or dark. The textures of the chairs, sofa, and the intricately carved wood and handblown glass breakfront added depth. The canopy over the queen-size bed was too fussy for her taste, but Emma was cognizant of the history of the house and its centuries of tradition, so she'd relented on that point, although she'd insisted on picking out her own mattress and box spring. She eyed the bed longingly on her way to the dressing room and the bathroom, as a new wave of exhaustion flowed through her bones.

She knew she shouldn't have been surprised that her clothes were hung or folded and organized exactly as she'd had them in the Executive Mansion in Albany, or that new versions of all her favorite toiletries were all present and logically stowed for easy retrieval and use.

Still, the idea of all the work the White House chief usher and his staff had accomplished in the time between when the outgoing occupant had vacated the residence at noon, and the time Emma had arrived at the White House to change clothes between the Inaugural Parade and the evening balls, was head-spinning.

Every detail had been attended to, all the way down to the heat and humidity levels, the artwork on the walls, and even her preferred brand of toilet paper.

Emma made a mental note to seek out the chief usher and thank him and his staff personally tomorrow. Right now, all she wanted was to get some much-needed sleep. Five a.m. would come soon enough.

∽ô↣

The pre-dawn mist hung over the Potomac River. Yesterday's frigid temperatures had moderated only slightly, which accounted for the dearth of runners on the trail. "Time to get the lead out, lads," Palmer called out to her executive officer, or XO, and the enlisted aide assigned to provide security for her. The XO ran lead, ten feet in front of her, and the enlisted aide, a new addition to the team, followed ten feet behind her. She lengthened her stride and picked up the pace.

"You're killing us, ma'am" Ted, the young aide running behind her, grumbled.

"This is the Army, Corporal. You're supposed to be in shape. You're going to let a middle-aged woman outrun you? Pitiful."

"With respect, ma'am, you're a middle-aged former track-and-field star who barely missed the Olympics. That's not the same," he huffed. His breath came in short puffs.

Palmer eyes widened in surprise. How did he know such a personal detail? Less than a handful of people knew about that part of her past. What else did he know? Was he aware of the circumstances that had shattered her teenage Olympic hopes and dreams? If she questioned him about it, she'd appear defensive and call attention to something she'd spent almost four decades burying. Still...

"General?"

Perhaps she should look into the corporal's background...

"General?" her XO called out, more urgently.

Palmer blinked as her surroundings came back into focus. "Yes?"

"Any special reason you're trying to outrun your detail, this morning, ma'am? Was it something we said?"

Was it something we said? The question reverberated in Palmer's mind and her pulse jumped. "No." Her denial was swift—maybe too swift. Also, she was shocked to realize that she was within two strides of overtaking her XO. "I—I'm sorry, XO. I've got a lot on my mind."

"No problem, ma'am. But if anything happens to you on our watch, General Jeffers will have us drawn and quartered."

Palmer laughed and moderated her pace. "Is this better?"

"Much. Thank you, ma'am."

Palmer finished clocking her six miles. As the XO peeled off, Palmer called, "Corporal? A moment, please."

"Yes, ma'am."

Palmer swallowed hard. *If you ask this question, there's no going back.* Maybe she could phrase it so that it seemed like she was casually curious. Who was she kidding? Was there ever any such thing as "casually curious" when a subordinate was asked a question by his commanding officer?

The young soldier stood rigidly before her, his eyes focused straight ahead.

"Relax. You look like you're ready to face a court martial." Palmer bent down to re-tie the shoelace that wasn't loose. "Out of curiosity, how did you know I ran track?"

"Oh, that's easy to tell by your form, ma'am. But the Olympic part? I was bragging about working for you to my aunt—my mother's sister. She asked your name, and when I told her, she said she knew you. She said that you'd trained under the same coach as teenagers."

Palmer's ears began to buzz. She put her hand on the ground to steady herself and untied and tied the other shoelace to buy time and avoid eye contact. "No kidding? What's your aunt's name?"

"Britney Reynolds, ma'am."

There it was. The buzzing grew into a full-fledged swarm of bees. Palmer's breathing became shallow as panic threatened to swamp her.

"Do you remember her, ma'am?"

Did she remember her? Dozens of images flashed through Palmer's mind. What should she say? *There's no use denying that you know her.* "I do. She was faster than lightning."

"She said you were the most talented hurdler she'd ever seen."

Palmer stood, relatively certain that her legs would hold her now and that she could look the corporal in the eye without giving anything away. "I haven't seen Brit since we were young, idealistic teenagers."

"Yes, ma'am. She said it was a shame your parents made you quit to focus on academics."

Relief flooded through Palmer. So, Britney hadn't told him. "Thank you, Corporal. I've got a meeting at 0630. I'd better get going."

Palmer cranked the heat up on the shower water and let it pour over her, as if it could wash away her bittersweet memories and the awful stain of that last, abbreviated afternoon together with Britney. She leaned her forehead against the still-cool tile and closed her eyes.

"I'll race you to the dorm." Everything was a competition to Britney. "If I win..." She let her gaze linger on Palmer's heaving chest and moistened her lips.

Palmer gulped in air as her nipples grew erect. They'd only managed to be alone together for brief moments over the past two weeks during the summer training camp for pre-Olympic hopefuls. Between the other kids and the coaches, there were too many people around—too much opportunity to get caught.

"What do I get if I win?" Palmer asked.

Britney's coal-black eyes bored into her. The intensity there should've made her look away, but Palmer's gaze was transfixed on the hunger in her expression.

"You get me, of course." Britney cocked an eyebrow. "Win-win." She crouched down. "Ready, set...GO!"

"No fair! You got a head start." But Palmer quickly made up the ground until they matched each other stride for stride.

In the end, Britney crossed the threshold first, Palmer right on her heels. They fell onto Palmer's bunk, laughing and gasping for air.

Britney reached up and caressed Palmer's face with her fingertips. "I love you, Palmer Estes. I don't know much, but I know that I want to spend the rest of my life loving you."

Palmer blinked. They were only sixteen. How could Britney be so certain?

"I-I love you too, Brit."

"Not good enough." Britney arched and claimed Palmer's lips, kissing her doubts away, until Palmer was panting and desperate for more. "Tell me you want me forever."

Palmer would've told her anything right then, as long as it meant she'd keep kissing her like that.

Britney slipped her fingers inside the edge of Palmer's running shorts.

"I want you forever," Palmer proclaimed.

"Surpr—"

Palmer's head whipped around. It couldn't be.

"Palmer Estes, what in world is going on here?" At the sound of her father's booming baritone, Palmer's blood turned to ice. For the barest of seconds, she saw the fear in Britney's eyes that matched her own. Britney's hand fell away and Palmer vaulted off the bed.

"N-nothing, sir."

"Nothing? Nothing?" He stepped further into the room and Palmer instinctively backed away. Britney pulled her knees up to her chest and cowered in the opposite corner.

Palmer ran out of real estate and her back hit the cold wall. "W-what are you doing here, Dad?"

"Your mother and I came to watch tomorrow's track meet and see for ourselves the great progress your coach has been raving about. We thought we'd surprise you and take you out to dinner tonight. It seems, however, that the surprise is on us."

For the first time, Palmer noticed her mother, standing in her father's shadow, her face pinched and pale, her eyes downcast.

Palmer's father glanced over his shoulder at Britney. "Who is this…this person?" He said it with such derision that Palmer saw Britney visibly cringe in fear.

Palmer's nostrils flared. He might try to intimidate her, or her mother, but Britney was off limits. "That's my friend, Britney. She's going to the next Olympic games. She runs the fastest one hundred meters in camp."

"She's Black. Of course she's fast. Those people are built for that." Her father unapologetically tossed the racist hand grenade out there without a thought. That was how he was, and Palmer had no doubt he truly believed it.

"Her race has nothing to do with—"

"Silence!" her father bellowed, and Palmer's jaw clicked shut. "I'm going to assume that that…person," he spat the word, "was attacking you."

Palmer couldn't stand it anymore. "No. Britney was not attacking me, Dad. We're in love." He flinched and then the anger within him escalated until he visibly shook with it.

"You don't know what you're talking about. She forced herself on you. She's an animal and—"

"She's beautiful, gentle, smart, and I love her."

"No daughter of mine is one of those…those…queers!"

"What's going on here?" Tony Valdez, Palmer and Britney's coach and trainer, burst into the room. "A dozen kids just came running into my office, telling me that they're afraid someone's being attacked in here. I hope that's not true."

Palmer's father rounded on him. "Is this the kind of program you run? You're supposed to be training these girls for the Olympics. Instead, I find out you're training them to be porn stars in some perverse—"

"What are you talking about?" The coach's gaze swiveled from him to Palmer, to Britney, and back again.

Palmer's father crossed his arms and glared. "You really don't know, do you?" He jabbed a finger into Palmer's chest. "Tell him. Go ahead. Tell him what you and that…person…were doing."

Palmer blinked as tears leaked from her eyes. Britney's lips quivered. They loved Coach Tony. He believed in them. She couldn't disappoint him…

"Argh! You disgust me. All of you. One last chance." Palmer's father loomed over her. "Tell me that…person…assaulted you and I'll have her thrown in jail and we can put this repugnant business behind us."

It was the last straw. Palmer pushed past her father, strode over to Britney, and gave her a hand up. She could feel Brit shaking. Palmer stood in front of her, as if to shield her from her father's bellicose bigotry.

"That's it then. We no longer have a daughter. We will never, ever speak your name again in our house. Do you understand me?"

Palmer's mother gasped and reached for his arm. "Paul…"

"Never!" He wheeled on the coach. "You're fired." He turned his attention back to Palmer, and she saw the malice in his eyes. "I don't care where you go from here, but you'll never step foot in our house or come near your mother or me again. Pervert." He turned on his heel, grabbed his wife's arm, and practically dragged her away.

Palmer choked on a sob and turned off the water. It was the last she'd seen either of her parents. She shook her head and blew out an explosive breath. *Clear your head, soldier.*

There was no point in dwelling on the past. After all, she had much for which to be grateful. The events of that fateful afternoon were the reason she was standing here now.

At the coach's suggestion and with his help, Britney transferred to a training center in Colorado. Palmer stayed in Oregon and got her high school diploma while living in Coach Tony's basement. They'd never again spoken of what transpired that day.

After graduation, she'd managed to secure an ROTC scholarship to pay her way through the University of Oregon. The Army became her family and her anchor.

She'd never heard Britney's name again...until today. How would she feel if they ever came face to face again? Palmer had no interest in rehashing the past. Too much life had happened since those days.

It's never going to come to that. Let it go. Besides, if she didn't hustle, she'd be late for her meeting.

CHAPTER FOUR

At 6:30 a.m., after a workout, shower, perusal of the morning papers, and a protein shake, Emma was ensconced at the historic Resolute desk used by so many presidents before her. For her first full day as president, she wore a navy A-line skirt suit with a white silk shell and navy pumps.

Later in the morning, she would attend the traditional day-after-Inauguration Day prayer service at the Washington National Cathedral. In the intervening hours, she would get to work on keeping her promises to the American people.

The intercom on her phone buzzed. "Madam President?"

"Yes, Jeannie?" Jeannie Tribden, a divorced single mother who had raised three great kids on her own, had been Emma's personal secretary for the past dozen years. Emma had attended the college graduations of all of Jeannie's offspring. When Heather died, it was Jeannie who took care of all the arrangements, including making sure that Emma ate at least one good meal per day. Other than Nichelle, Jeannie was Emma's most trusted team member.

"Vice President Elder, Chief of Staff Johnson, Press Secretary Dewey, and Senior Advisors Peters and Griggs are here to see you as requested."

"Thanks, Jeannie. Send them in."

"Madam President," the group said in unison.

"Thank you all for coming in so early." Emma came around the desk and took a seat in one of the upright chairs arranged around the sitting area. She motioned for everyone else to sit as well.

Olivia Dewey, Emma's press secretary, and Trent Peters and Miranda Griggs, her two closest senior advisors, chose one of the two couches. Vice President Elder chose the other upright chair. Nichelle remained standing.

Emma began, "When we started down this path to the presidency, I called this group together and informed you that when we won, our first order of business would be to restore integrity, dignity, and humanity to this office. I swore that within the first one hundred days, we'd alter the tenor of the conversation and the vibe in this country and enact real, measurable changes to lift up our citizens, save our planet, and repair our relationships abroad. Do you all remember that?"

Heads nodded.

"Now we're going to convert the talk into action." Emma turned to her vice president. "Harrison, we're going to need your congressional experience and good relationships across the aisle to build a bridge on our signature issues, starting with climate change and health care. I want you to put together two working groups and I want everyone at the table.

"For climate change, I want the leading scientists, environmentalists, fossil fuels representatives... I want them all. For health care, I want hospitals, doctors, patient advocates, cancer survivors, insurance companies, pharmaceutical companies, those for whom the system works, those for whom it doesn't, representatives of large companies with private health insurance plans, small businesses that can't afford to offer plans...and any other stakeholders you think I've missed.

"We're going to do this with full transparency, with each of these groups knowing what the other is trying to peddle. I want a clear understanding from all of them that this administration is going to tackle the big issues head-on. We're not going to be bought by those with deep pockets who can afford top-shelf lobbyists. Everyone gets equal time and access to make their case, and at the end of the day, we're going to do whatever it takes to address the needs of our citizens and improve their lives and the lives of the next generation and the next. Understood?"

"Yes, ma'am."

"I'm setting a March 1st deadline for recommendations on meaningful steps we can take in these areas, including how we're going to pay for it all. Then, once we've agreed on the way forward,

I want you to engage a bipartisan team to draft legislation with real teeth that we can get passed by both houses."

"Ask me for something small, why don't you?" Harrison said it with a smile.

"I hear you. But we have the will of the people on our side and a mandate on the heels of this election that we're going to leverage. The House shouldn't be hard to convince. They're already aligned with us. That one-vote-margin deficit in the Senate, though... Even though they're chastened by losing a few seats, their president, and majority leader, we're going to have to be very persuasive."

"I agree, I'm just not sure it's achievable," Harrison said.

"I have absolute faith in you, Mr. Vice President."

"No pressure here."

"On a related front, right after the election," Emma continued, "I asked our climate change and health care transition teams to put together exhaustive lists of every executive order passed under the previous administration that flies in the face of climate science and improvements to our healthcare systems. They are working on blueprints for actionable steps I can take right now, even without Congress's help, to set us on the right path in those areas. I'll have them interface with you."

"Perfect," the vice president said.

"Harrison? I'd rather have everything codified into laws, but I'm no wild-eyed idealist. I want you to give me a realistic assessment of what you think we can get done legislatively, and what we'll have to achieve via executive order."

"Yes, ma'am."

Next, Emma addressed Trent and Miranda. "Trent, your first priority is gun violence. I'm counting on you to bring together key federal agencies, state and local officials, grassroots advocates, gun manufacturers, concerned parents and kids, school districts, colleges and universities, faith groups... I want a coalition so broad that it's literally bulletproof. Again, real, measurable steps. I want town halls all over the country. I need folks to know I understand their fear and pain. I want to look them in the eye and tell them I've got their backs and that we're going to do something about this epidemic. And then we're going to do it with an army of citizens in our arsenal... Puns intended."

"Yes, ma'am."

"Miranda? I need you to shepherd our Cabinet and agency nominations through confirmation. We need the entire team onboard ASAP. No foot-dragging in the Senate on our choices. I want timely, expedient, fair hearings."

"I've got a list and I'm checking it twice."

"While you're at it, how's that interface with the American Bar Association coming? Did you get their list of every unqualified judicial nominee appointed in the past four years and those that are presently in the pipeline?"

Miranda smiled broadly. "They were exceedingly happy to supply all the details, along with several hundred names of truly qualified candidates."

"I bet they were. The transition judicial watch team has the full list of current vacancies on the federal benches. Now I need you to prioritize which openings and judicial nominees we push for first, and what, if anything, we can do about the incompetents shoved through by the last Senate majority leader, may he rest permanently retired." Emma shook her head in disgust. "Next to winning, him getting thumped in his home state was the highlight of election night."

"No kidding," Nichelle muttered.

"What about the ambassadorships? Do you want me to address those nominations too?" Miranda asked.

"Not right now. State is working on the ambassadorships with my admonition that we're not handing out any political favors or appointments. I want seasoned, deserving, knowledgeable career foreign service officers with integrity and grit. Period. Full stop."

Finally, Emma nodded at Olivia. "It's Day One, and we're going to send a very clear, unambiguous message to the public and the media."

Olivia sat with pen poised over her notepad.

"I want you to hold an official press briefing at 2 p.m., in the White House Press Briefing Room. In advance of that, I want you to work with the White House Correspondents Association to ensure full representation of all the recognized, mainstream news outlets. Everybody gets treated equally. We're going to restore faith in the media, and we're going to start today."

"Got it. Anything in particular you want me to spin?"

Emma tapped her chin thoughtfully. "I don't want you to spin. I want you to tell them the truth. Tell them we're already hard at work on our major priorities, that I'm fully engaged and focused, and that I'll be personally meeting with leaders of both parties in Congress for lunch to establish a strong working relationship and open communication for the good of the American people."

"Okay."

"Tell them that you'll be holding regular press briefings."

"Roger that."

"And then I'll stop in to emphasize that they won't need to be shouting questions at me on the South Lawn. If they want answers, they can be sure they'll get them directly. I welcome all unbiased, fair, high-quality reporting, whatever the outlet."

Emma stood, and the group rose with her. "Thank you, everyone. It's a brand-new day. Here's to getting off to a strong start."

Palmer pinched the bridge of her nose where a headache had taken up residence. She'd spent the bulk of her day with her colleagues from the Central Intelligence Agency and the National Security Agency briefing the new chairpersons and minority leaders of the Congressional Intelligence Committees, reading them in on situations around the world. Having spent much of her time on Capitol Hill, she now sat in her office, buried under a mountain of paperwork.

"Come," she called, in answer to a rap on her office door.

Max stuck his head in. "You look done in."

"I feel done in."

"So, now's a bad time to ask for your advice?"

"Depends on the topic."

"Best restaurant downtown to share a killer meal and a quiet conversation."

Palmer rolled her chair back and steepled her fingers as she studied him. "Ambiance matters?"

"Paramount."

"Price point?"

"Sky's the limit."

Now Palmer raised an eyebrow. "Those are three words I never thought I'd hear come out of your mouth. This must be serious."

Max shifted uncomfortably from foot to foot.

"Anybody I know?"

"No."

She nodded knowingly. "It's that presidential aide from last night, isn't it?"

"Chief of staff. She's the chief of staff to the president of the United States."

"Aha! So, I'm right."

Max narrowed his eyes. "I don't want to hear another word out of you."

"Hey, you're the one asking for the recommendation, not me." She held up her hands, palms forward. "Besides, I heartily approve. I told you, I think she's got great potential. I just can't believe my normally cautious, play-it-cool friend moved this fast."

"Who says I made the move?"

Palmer smirked. "If you weren't the one making the moves, you wouldn't be standing here looking for the perfect place to wow the woman. She would've picked the spot."

Max opened his mouth to say something, but apparently thought better of it. "Do you have a suggestion or not? Because I've got to get going."

Palmer's eyes widened. "You're taking her out tonight and you don't have a reservation?"

"I told her I'd pick her up at 2000, and to dress for a classy place," Max answered defensively.

"Did you translate that to eight o'clock for her?"

Max rolled his eyes. "I did."

"Good." Palmer was enjoying Max's discomfort. "Food preferences? Is she vegan or a pescatarian? Does she have any food allergies? Does she like spicy food? Savory? What?"

Max stared at her as if the idea of asking his date those questions never occurred to him.

"Ugh. Never mind. If you don't know her tastes, play it safe. That rules out Rasika, Jaleo, or Bobby Vans. You can't go wrong with the Old Ebbitt Grill. If she's new to D.C., the history of the establishment should appeal to her, the food is consistently good, and the mahogany and original artwork add class."

Max nodded. "That might work."

"Open Table is your friend, Max. Get a reservation, because standing around waiting for a table…not cool."

"Not my first date, boss," Max threw over his shoulder.

"No. But it's your first date in this decade," Palmer called after him.

"Which is more than you can say for yourself."

Palmer was grateful Max already had disappeared from sight and couldn't see how the truth of his rejoinder stung.

By the time Emma finally retired to the residence at nearly eleven o'clock, she was more than ready to fall into bed. That's when she remembered her promise to Olivia that before she called it a night on her first full day as president, she would compose and send a tweet.

Although Emma had no great love for Twitter or social media in general, she understood the symbolism of a positive, uplifting, unifying message on that particular platform, at this particular moment.

She picked up her phone, opened the app, and pondered what she could convey in two hundred eighty characters that would set the social media tone for her presidency. She considered several options and discarded them all. Eventually, she typed:

Thx to the American people for your trust. United we stand. Day 1 agenda: Address climate change solutions, affordable health care, gun violence, bipartisanship, restore confidence in media. ✓

Pleased with herself, she reread the tweet, sat back, and hit send. Within seconds, the reactions, re-tweets, and comments began to pour in. She knew she should close out the app and get some much-needed sleep. Instead, she scrolled through the first series of comments, curious to see how people had received her message.

The first few responses thanked her for her tone and for restoring civility and dignity to the office. The fifth tweeter spewed nonsense about her taking away his second amendment rights. The next tweet—crosshairs of a gunsight superimposed over a picture of her giving the inaugural address—sent a chill down her spine.

The Secret Service and F.B.I. no doubt already would have flagged the tweet. Still, the level of vitriol, especially the image of her in the crosshairs, provided a stark reminder that, as long as she lived, she'd be a flashpoint and a target for all manner of unbalanced individuals and fringe groups.

Emma started to put the phone down, when another response caught her attention.

Ur so-called wife's death is on ur hands. You should've died w/her. It should've been u 2. You both should've died for ur sins. Now u have 2 live w/letting her die alone 4 the rest of ur life. How does that feel, bitch? Don't worry. U'll burn in hell w/her when ur time comes.

The phone fell from Emma's shaking fingers. The sound of the protective case hitting the wood of the coffee table echoed loudly in the quiet of the night. She wrapped her arms tightly around herself. *Ignore the troll. He's only trying to get under your skin.*

Intellectually, Emma understood the intent. This was exactly like all the other horrible, anonymous broadsides aimed in her direction.

Yet, somehow, this time it felt different. Emma jumped up and strode out of the living room, down the Center Hall, into the Yellow Oval Room, and out onto the Truman Balcony.

A blast of frigid winter air hit her in the face, cooling her overheated skin. She stared out at the Washington Monument, brightly lit and standing sentinel over the Mall.

Heather! She wanted to scream her beloved's name out loud. Instead, she stared at the dimly lit reflection of light glinting off the diamonds in her wedding band and heard the echo of their vow to love each other until death do they part.

Emma closed her eyes as a tear leaked out. For the thousandth time, she replayed their last conversation.

"What's wrong?" Heather asked.

Emma's hair stood at odd angles from where she'd run her fingers through it in frustration. "What's wrong is that I haven't yet figured out a way to clone myself."

"Thank God for the rest of the world." Heather came up behind her and hugged her around the waist.

"Very funny." Emma turned into the embrace.

"Bad timing?"

"Colossally bad timing."

"What's the issue?"

"The budget negotiations are at a critical point and require my personal attention. The deadline is midnight tomorrow night, and I'm this close," she held her thumb and forefinger a millimeter apart, "to getting the Assembly and the Senate to agree on final numbers."

"Well, that sounds promising."

"It is. But I'm scheduled to be in the North Country tomorrow for the opening of that state-of-the-art wellness and comprehensive health care facility I pushed so hard for."

"Surely, they can understand that the budget is a statewide priority."

Emma shook her head. "Improving rural healthcare was one of my signature issues in the campaign. I have to be there."

"Can't they put it off and wait for you?"

"They've had the date set up for months and it's been all over the media."

"Okay. I'll do it."

"What?"

"I'll be you."

"What are you talking about?"

"I'll go and christen the facility, or whatever you do at those things. I'll be your surrogate."

Emma started to object, and Heather silenced her with a kiss.

"You said yourself, you can't be in two places at once. Let me do this one thing for you. You're so stressed. I can't do the budget for you, but this I can do."

"It's not the same—"

"You're right. You look better in a skirt than I do." Heather lifted Emma's chin with two fingers. "Look at me." Emma did as she was told. "I've got this. I want to do it."

"Nobody wants to go to the North Country to cut a ribbon, turn around, and drive back to Albany."

"Okay, you've got me there. But I want to be there for you. Besides, my driver is the one who'll be dealing with the tedious part. I'll just be a backseat passenger."

Emma grumbled.

49

"It's settled," Heather said. "I can get some uninterrupted work done on the way there and back."

"That's hardly an argument in favor of your going," Emma replied. "You said it yourself. You have your own work to do. You shouldn't have to be doing my job."

Heather moved an errant strand of hair off Emma's face. "Remember when we made the decision for you to run? I told you I was all in and that I'd do my best to be the perfect first lady of New York state. This is what first lady's do. It's in the handbook."

"Show me where."

"It's one of those fine-print thingies you never read even though your lawyer tells you to."

"Uh-huh."

They'd made love after that, and Emma had felt lighter than she had in weeks.

At 2:14 the next afternoon, as she was deeply ensconced in final negotiations with the Assembly speaker and Senate majority leader, the superintendent of the New York State Police appeared personally to inform her that the official state car carrying Heather and a New York State trooper who was a member of the first lady's security detail had been in a collision with a tractor trailer on the Northway as they returned home from the event. The truck driver had walked away, but Heather, her driver, and the state trooper had been killed instantly.

Emma turned from the balcony and headed back inside the White House as a new spasm of guilt tore through her.

I'm so sorry, Heather. It should've been me that day. Her therapist had called it survivor's guilt.

Whatever it was, Emma knew if she were going to survive the internet trolls and focus on her presidency, she was going to have to find a way to come to terms with the circumstances of Heather's death and move on with her life. It would be what Heather would've wanted too.

CHAPTER FIVE

Taking fire! Captain! Three o'clock! Three o'clock! Multiple sources. We're taking too much heat... Captain Estes, do you read me?"

Palmer blinked the sweat from her eyes, pushed the cyclic forward to increase speed, pushed down on the collective to reduce altitude, adjusted the tail rudder, and maneuvered the helicopter sharply to the left. "Negative. We're not going anywhere. Those troops need cover. Without us, they're sitting ducks.

"Sergeant Jeffers. I need you to take out that missile launch site at four o'clock. I'm going to get you as close as I can. You ready?"

"Ready, Captain!"

"Here we go." A searing pain ripped through her.

"You're hit!" her co-pilot yelled into the radio.

"I know."

"Abort."

"No. We're going to finish this. Jeffers, you've got one crack at this."

"I'll get that son-of-a-bitch for you, ma'am."

She pushed the helo into a steep dive and angled to the right...

Palmer jolted bolt upright. Her chest was slicked with sweat and pain shot through her left leg in the muscle just above the knee. She looked around wildly, trying to get her bearings.

She flicked on the light, focused on the bright splashes of color in the Jonas Gerard painting on the wall, and willed her heartbeat to settle into its normal rhythm. *Home.*

She was home, safely in her own bed. "This is not Desert Storm. I am not in Kuwait. It is not 1991. It's Tuesday, January 26, 2021. I'm at home in Arlington, Virginia, and Emma McMasters is president of the United States." She repeated this aloud three times in order to ground herself in the present day.

When she was sure her legs would hold her, she threw off the covers, wandered into the kitchen, and grabbed a frozen bottle of water from the freezer. She lowered herself to the floor in the living room, straightened her left leg, and spent fifteen minutes rolling the icy plastic against the scar that bisected her quadriceps muscle to loosen some of the scar tissue.

She tossed the water bottle back in the freezer, poured herself a glass of water, and went back to bed. Dawn soon would break on the horizon, and she had a flight to catch. Today, she'd be addressing the cadets at West Point. Hooah.

◈◈

Emma laid her reading glasses on the desk and rubbed her tired eyes.

"Why don't you go back to your sleeping quarters and get some shuteye?" Nichelle sat across from her in the Air Force One Oval Office.

"Because the president's work is never done?"

"The president's non-critical work can wait until we get home. You've just wrapped up an enormously successful first trip abroad. The Brits loved you, the press lionized you, and the American media covered it favorably. You deserve a break."

"Staying up works better for me. Less chance of jet lag." Emma stretched.

"Okay, then. Can I at least convince you to stop working for a minute?"

"It depends. What's my alternative?"

"You can give me dating advice."

"Let me get this right. You want dating advice...from me? The woman who hasn't been in the dating pool in the last thirty-five years?"

"Well, when you say it that way..."

Emma leaned forward, happy for the distraction from more weighty matters of state. "Are we still talking about tall, dark, and handsome? The general from the inaugural ball?"

Nichelle's eyes took on a faraway, dreamy quality. "Mm-hmm."

"I see. So, what is it I can help you with?"

"We've been on a couple of dates—"

"That was quick."

"Are you going to interrupt me through the whole story?"

Emma mimed zipping her lips.

"Anyway, I really like this guy. He's straight up and earnest. He's polite, well-read, and a real gentleman."

"Where's the problem?" Nichelle glared at her, and Emma held up her hands defensively. "Right. Shutting up now."

"Both times we've been together, he's spent at least a third of the date talking about his boss. I think he's got a massive crush on her. Maybe he's even in love with her and he doesn't know it."

Emma searched her memory bank. "Isn't his boss the general he introduced me to that night? The redhead?"

"That's the one."

Emma waved dismissively and leaned back in her chair. "Then, you've got nothing to worry about."

"How can you be so sanguine about that? You haven't been there and listened to him yammer on and on about her."

"She's not his type."

"What? How do you know what his type is?"

Emma bit her lip. Although this was an informal conversation between friends and had nothing to do with her or Nichelle's official capacities, she was still the commander in chief; the two generals in question worked for her. What would propriety dictate in this situation? It wasn't like she really knew anything. But she had a definite opinion. How could she make her point without actually making her point?

"You're obviously his type, or he wouldn't have asked you out in the first place. And he certainly wouldn't have asked you out a second time if he wasn't interested."

"But he wouldn't talk about her incessantly if he didn't have a crush on her. It's 'Palmer this,' and 'General Estes that.' I don't even think he realizes he's doing it."

Emma chuckled.

"What in the world is so funny? I could really learn to like this guy, and you're over there making fun of me. Forget I asked." She jumped out of her chair.

"Nich—sit," Emma said softly.

She did but continued to frown.

"What I'm trying to say, apparently ineffectively, is that if *you're* his type, she definitely isn't." Emma waited for that to sink in.

Nichelle scrunched up her features. "You're saying he's into women of color, therefore he can't have a crush on a white woman? Of all the things I've ever heard you say—"

"Nich! Stop talking and *listen* to me." Emma leaned forward earnestly. Clearly, she was going to have to spell it out in less oblique terms. "I'm going to say it again, a little differently this time, and I want you to really think about it, okay?"

"Okay." Nichelle drew out the "O."

"Your man is not *her* type."

"You don't even know her..." Nichelle's voice trailed off and her eyes grew wide as Emma's meaning became clear.

"You think she's..."

Emma nodded. "Eureka! Let's just say I'd bet a week's salary you're more her type than he is."

Nichelle narrowed her eyes. "How do you know that?"

Emma shrugged. "I suppose I could be wrong, but I'm not usually in such instances."

Nichelle popped up and began to pace. She glanced over her shoulder back at Emma. "You really think so?"

Emma nodded imperceptibly.

"Well, that changes everything."

"I should hope so." Emma winked at her.

The shrill ringing of the telephone in the dead of night jolted Emma bolt upright. She shook the cobwebs from her head and snapped up the receiver. "Yes?"

"It's Nichelle, Madam President. Sorry to disturb your sleep, but there's been an incident."

Emma was instantly fully awake and alert. "What kind of incident?"

"A VIP flight carrying a bipartisan delegation of U.S. senators was forced down over northern Syria in the border region between Syria and Turkey about an hour ago—that would be 9:00 a.m. local time. We have confirmed that the flight crew and the senators all survived the crash. The three crew members were killed by hostiles on the ground. The senators were taken away at gunpoint by what appeared to be ISIS fighters before backup could arrive."

"How do you know that?"

"The pilot's helmet cam was recording. Our forces secured the helicopter, the bodies of the crew members, and the footage."

"Which senators?"

"Tannebaum, Lawson, Friese, and Wicks."

Emma groaned. Republican Senator Friese of Tennessee was one of her fiercest critics. Texas Senator Wicks, also a Republican, was one of her predecessor's closest allies. While her response to such a crisis would be closely watched anyway, the fact that the hostages included two of her most vocal detractors would invite a new level of scrutiny. Tannebaum and Lawson were Democrats. All four men served on the Senate Foreign Relations Committee.

"I assume all pertinent agency heads and personnel are up to speed and hard at work on the situation?"

"Yes, ma'am. Already gathering intel, filling in the blanks, and mapping strategies."

"Good. I'll meet with Defense, State, the NSA, the CIA, and the chairman of the Joint Chiefs in the Roosevelt Room in thirty minutes, at which time I'll expect a full update and actionable intelligence."

"Yes, ma'am."

Emma hung up and headed for the shower. She hoped the heat of the spray would clear her head for what would be the greatest challenge yet of her week-old presidency.

Palmer, who was running point for the Department of Defense, wearied of the cross-chatter around the table. "How confident are we of the intel, folks? Is this solid? Because the president has requested actionable intelligence and options to be presented to her in the next..." Palmer checked her watch. "...twenty minutes."

She sat on the near side of the conference table in the Situation Room. The Director of National Intelligence sat across from her, flanked by top staff members from the Central Intelligence Agency on one side and the deputy chief of staff for the National Security Council on the other. The undersecretary for political affairs, the special presidential envoy for hostage affairs, and the director of the FBI's Hostage Recovery Fusion Cell rounded out the group.

"Our sources and information are solid." The answer came from the CIA station chief in Ankara via a closed-circuit secure satellite feed. "They're holding the senators in a remote area in Kurdistan in a small shack. Aerial surveillance has verified heat signatures we believe to be six hostiles and the four senators. The flight manifest shows four passengers and three flight crew. The number of listed passengers matches the helmet cam footage recovered."

"The helicopter and the bodies of the flight crew are secure?" Palmer asked.

"The crew has been removed and transported back to base where they'll be prepared for the final flight back to Andrews. The helicopter and accompanying technology have been destroyed per protocol."

On another one of the six flat screen television monitors, the deputy commander for U.S. Central Command, or CENTCOM, based in Tampa, Florida, chimed in. "We have multiple teams in range. We don't want to risk the hostages' lives going in without cover of darkness. With a green light to retrieve the senators, the 160th can drop a team from the 75th Rangers and SEAL Team Six within twenty klicks at 1800. They'll go the rest of the way on foot, putting them on site between 2100 and 2200. The Rangers will take care of securing the perimeter. Six will execute the rescue, and the 160th will circle back and pick up the packages."

"We want equal time to present a diplomatic solution," the special presidential envoy chimed in. "We believe we have diplomatic assets in Russia and Turkey we can work with on this."

The head of the FBI-led team stood up. "Put your best intel and solutions in report form. The presidential briefing is upstairs in the Roosevelt Room, fifteen minutes from now. We'll meet again after that."

Palmer rose. She needed to bring Chairman Dutton and Secretary of Defense Buchanan up to speed so that they could brief the president. They were waiting for her upstairs in the Cabinet Room.

Ensconced upstairs in the Oval Office, Emma pored over the dossiers of the missing senators. Folders with the bios and pictures of the deceased flight crew lay open on the desk. A half-empty cup of coffee sat forgotten nearby.

The intercom on her phone buzzed. “Madam President?”

“Yes, Jeannie?”

“Vice President Elder, Nichelle, Olivia, Trent, and Miranda are here to see you as requested.”

“Thanks, Jeannie. Send them in.”

“Madam President,” the group said in unison.

“I’m sorry to have called you all here in the middle of the night, but we’ve got a lot of work to do. You’ve all been read in, so I won’t waste any time rehashing what little we’ve already established.” Emma came around the desk and motioned for everyone to sit.

As had become their custom, Olivia, Trent and Miranda chose the couch on the near side. Vice President Elder chose the upright chair opposite Emma’s seat. Nichelle remained standing.

“We’re about to go into a strategy session where I hope to God I’m going to hear some very specific details and action plans. When we come out of there, I need to make a firm decision about how, when, and what to tell the Senate and House leadership, and then the American people and the world.”

“Do you want me in the strategy session?” Olivia asked. “Plausible deniability. Easier for me to stand in front of the press and tell them I don’t know if I really wasn’t present.”

“Good call,” Emma agreed. “I want to be as transparent as I can be without endangering lives and/or compromising security. I’d prefer it if you stayed behind and monitored activity to see if anyone in the media is aware of the situation.”

“Yes, ma’am. I checked just before I came in here. So far, all is quiet. Everyone’s still focused on your recent overseas trip and speculation about the fate of your first hundred days agenda.”

“I sincerely hope it stays that way,” Emma said. “It works in our favor that it’s the middle of the night here in the States, and that the senators’ trip was under wraps. But I don’t doubt for a minute that this terrorist group didn’t go to all this trouble to keep quiet about taking such high-profile Americans.”

"Assuming they knew who they shot down," Nichelle said. "On the outside, that Black Hawk looks just like any other."

"If they didn't know, they sure got lucky," Vice President Elder chimed in.

"If they didn't know initially and they know now…" Miranda let the sentence hang in the air.

"Let's focus on the tasks at hand. We'll deal with the rest after the update," Emma said.

"I drafted the statement you asked me to put together." Olivia removed a sheet of paper from a manila folder and handed it to Emma.

Emma read the copy once, and then again as she crossed out and replaced some of the verbiage.

> *Today,* ~~*just days after*~~ little more than a week after *America celebrated its most sacred rite of passage—the peaceful, democratic transition of power from one freely elected leader to another—* ~~ISIS~~ a ruthless terrorist cell *committed a heinous act of violence against the United States.*
>
> *Four U.S. senators on a* bipartisan *fact-finding mission on the Syria-Turkey border were forcibly taken* as they fulfilled their Constitutional oversight duties. ~~Sadly~~ *Tragically, three of our bravest soldiers from the Army's A-Company, 5th Battalion, 158th Aviation were killed by these terrorists.*
>
> ~~President McMasters~~ The United States *strongly condemns this outrageous act.* President McMasters *has scheduled* ~~a morning~~ *an address* for later this morning *to update the nation and the world as the situation develops.*

Emma handed the document back. "Make the changes and hold this for now. The only scenario in which I want to release that statement is if it appears the news is about to break ahead of us. If that happens, alert me before you do anything else. I want to keep this quiet as long as we can to give us the best opportunity to get our people back without added complications."

Emma rose. "Thank you all."

CHAPTER SIX

G ood morning." Emma claimed a chair near the middle of the conference table in the Roosevelt Room and slapped a series of manila file folders down in front of her. "Please, take your seats."

The members of the Joint Chiefs, Vice President Elder, Secretary of Defense Buchanan, Secretary of State Dalton Neville, National Security Advisor Christian Edwards, CIA Director Lisa Fishel, and Director of National Intelligence Robert Tarbor took their places around the large conference table. Their support staff and Emma's top advisors settled into seats against the wall.

It was four o'clock in the morning, and Emma knew that all of the people in this room had been awake as long as she had or longer, each of them determined to do the job required of them under the most difficult circumstances. Those assembled around the main conference table represented either her hand-picked choices or those she had chosen to retain to advise her on foreign policy, intelligence, and military matters.

Each of these individuals had years of experience and expertise in their fields, but ultimately, only Emma would decide what course of action would be taken. The people of the United States had put that onus squarely on her.

Trust and advise, Emma. Trust your experts, value their advice, make the best decisions you can based on the information presented, and advise them what course to take. She gathered herself and squared her shoulders.

"Ladies and gentlemen, I know that every second is precious here and we've got a lot of ground to cover. Let's get right to it. In this meeting, we're going to talk about the hostages and their situation, actionable plans, family notification status, and what, when, and how we release any information about this incident. First, I want the most current sit rep. Do we have eyes on the hostages?"

"Madam President," NSA Edwards spoke up, "we've utilized drone technology to ascertain what we believe is their current location."

"How confident are we that we're right?"

"Ninety-five percent, ma'am."

Emma raised an eyebrow. "Impressive, although I'd prefer one-hundred percent reliability."

"Madam President," CIA Director Fishel added, "within the past ten minutes we've heard chatter indicating that, at a minimum, the hostiles are aware that they have high-value American targets."

"At a minimum?"

"Yes, ma'am. It's not yet clear whether they know exactly who the senators are or the nature of their positions."

"Thank you. Are we certain that ISIS is who we're dealing with?"

Director of National Intelligence Tarbor replied, "We are, based on the language, the dress, and the weapons picked up by the helmet cam footage."

"To the best of your knowledge, have they made any announcements or demands?"

"Not yet, ma'am, but it's only a matter of time before they either make demands or make an example of the hostages."

"Which do we think is more likely?"

Secretary Buchanan, Director Fishel, Secretary Neville, Director Tarbor, and Chairman Dutton all spoke at once.

"Stop! I understand that you all come from different vantage points. I want to hear the best argument for each case." As a lawyer, Emma was used to weighing the evidence and having to choose between strategies. *Same approach, different arena. Listen carefully, ask questions, make informed judgments.*

Secretary Neville spoke up first. "Madam President, because we've essentially shut down ISIS to the point of dysfunction, I can envision a scenario in which this cell sees an opportunity to use the hostages as bargaining chips to make a show of power, thereby elevating their standing in terrorist circles, gaining them recruits, and putting them back in business."

"And killing the hostages wouldn't give them more street cred?"

"If they kill them, they've got nothing to bargain with."

Emma opened the first folder to reveal the pictures of the three deceased members of the flight crew. They were so young, so proud, and had so much of their lives in front of them. *Until those terrorists took that away from them. Whatever choices you make this day, remember, these were real people, with real lives and loved ones.* She tapped each picture. "These service members gave their lives in service of our country."

She flipped open the next folder and spilled the pictures of the four senators onto the table. "These four senators' lives hang in the balance because they were executing their Constitutional responsibilities." Deliberately, she laid the seven photos side by side facing outward toward the assembled group.

"The people who murdered these soldiers and took our lawmakers hostage are terrorists. The United States of America doesn't negotiate with terrorists. As long as I am president, our people will never be used as bargaining chips. End of story."

The room went silent.

Emma took a deep breath and let it out slowly. "Okay. We've covered the possibility that the hostage-takers keep our senators alive to use them for some unachievable perceived advantage. Who wants to argue the other side?"

As if by silent agreement, all eyes turned to Secretary Buchanan. "With all due respect to Secretary Neville, Madam President, these men are fanatics. They're not the least bit interested in negotiating anything. They'll kill our men with all the viciousness they can muster, and record it or livestream it for all the world to see."

Emma steepled her fingers underneath her chin. "If you're right, why haven't they done so already? And why not take the flight crew alive as well? Create a macabre public show out of killing our finest brave service members?"

"Taking trained military assets alive is risky, ma'am. And murdering them in cold blood is designed to instill fear and ensure the compliance of the senators in following their orders."

Emma envisioned the scene and the horror of watching those trained soldiers die. Yes, that would inspire terror in the hearts of almost anyone.

Director Fishel chimed in, "As for why they haven't killed the hostages yet, the answer is threefold. One, they would want to torture the senators to see if they can get any useful information out of them and/or if they can get them to beg for their lives and renounce America on camera.

"Two, if, as we suspect, the capture of such high-value targets was an inadvertent bonus, there is likely great disagreement among the group as to what to do now. Simply shooting down an American Black Hawk is a victory. Capturing part of our government is quite a coup."

"And the third reason?" Emma asked. She respected Lisa Fishel. She was a career CIA officer with extensive experience in infiltration and covert operations. She was sharp, with a keen, analytical mind and she had firsthand experience in surviving more than one harrowing situation involving ISIS fighters.

"Three, if these terrorists are small fry and they shot down the helo with the idea of making themselves more prominent players within the ISIS hierarchy, then they're likely reaching out to the powers that be and bolstering their standing even as we speak. In that case, they would offer the senators to those higher up the food chain. It's likely it would take some time for those big guns or their surrogates to arrive on site."

Compelling possibilities. "If you're correct, Director Fishel and Secretary Buchanan, and for now I'll emphasize the if, how much time do you think we have before the terrorists…?" She left the rest of the sentence hanging.

"It's hard to say, ma'am," Buchanan answered into the silence.

"If I might, ma'am," Chairman Dutton waded in, "The challenge for any rescue mission is the conditions on the ground."

"Meaning?" Emma asked.

"Optimum conditions for our special operations teams to create a successful outcome are after dusk or at dawn."

Emma consulted her watch. Her eyes opened wide as she calculated the seven-hour time difference. *It's barely eleven o'clock in the morning in Syria.*

"You're telling me that we need to wait out any attempt at retrieving the senators for another..." She consulted her watch again. "...seven to nine hours, until after sundown there?"

"In order to achieve opti—"

"I know," Emma held up a hand to forestall the rest of the answer. "In order to give our team the best chance for success."

"Yes, ma'am. But that seven to nine hours only gets us until we can drop the team in the zone. We estimate it will take another three to four hours to reach the hostages."

The idea of leaving the hostages in such a vulnerable, volatile, unpredictable situation for the balance of the day was nearly intolerable. On the other hand, it made sense that for the mission to succeed, the rescue team required the cover of darkness, or dusk at the very least, to give them sufficient cover.

You can't leave the hostages as sitting ducks without trying to do something to give them a fighting chance. "Secretary Neville, Director Fishel? I need you to buy us, and most importantly, the senators, some time. What can you suggest to me as a ten- or eleven-hour distraction?"

Director Fishel weighed in. "We could insert an agent posing as a Russian. He could pretend to be negotiating on our behalf."

"Wouldn't that alert the terrorists that their location is known?"

"We wouldn't do it in person. That's too risky. We'd have to make contact via the same chatter channels they use to communicate with other cells and interested parties."

"And the terrorists would believe that we'd turn to Russia for help?" Emma asked.

All of this seemed so...tenuous. Emma surveyed the array of experts around the room. As she glanced at Chairman Dutton across the way, she noticed General Palmer Estes sitting against the wall behind him. *Wonder what her take is on all this?*

"Does anyone have another idea or any thoughts about the suggested distraction?"

No one spoke.

"Folks, we're going to have one shot at this. We're not talking about something theoretical. We're talking about real people, with lives and families. Whatever we do, we must succeed. If any of you can think of a better way, or if you think what the director is suggesting is an unworkable tactic, now is the time to speak up."

Emma purposefully made eye contact with everyone in the room. "Look, I understand that there's a necessary chain of command and natural hierarchy in this room. But you might have noticed that I tend to ignore tradition when I believe it is counterintuitive to what serves the highest good in any given situation. In this particular instance, there is no corner on the market for great ideas and plans. Each of you is here because you are experts in your fields."

Emma pointedly indicated those seated at the main table. "I know I speak for all of your direct supervisors here when I say, now is not a time to stand on ceremony or worry about proper protocol in meetings like this. I know that all of you around the perimeter of this room have poked, prodded, brainstormed with each other, and hashed through scenarios and given your supervisors your best recommendations.

"I also recognize that this situation is fluid. For instance, as Director Fishel told us not two minutes ago, we now know two new facts. One, the terrorists are not radio-silent—they're chattering to some external entities. And two, they know they have high-value targets. While we might've assumed they'd figure out the latter, confirming these facts, nevertheless, changes the dynamics."

Again, no one spoke out. Emma sighed in exasperation. *Try a different tactic.* "I accept that it best serves the mission to wait until after dusk to mount a rescue—and we're going to get to what that looks like in a minute.

"Can anyone in this room please give me a workable solution as to what our options are if we do as Director Fishel suggests and contact the terrorists through back channels and either our cover is blown or they don't bite? Or, if for any other reason our working theory about the terrorists goes out the window and they suddenly choose to execute the senators ahead of our desired rescue timetable?"

Emma watched a whispered exchange between Chairman Dutton and General Estes. It was Palmer who spoke up. "Madam President, as you know, we have Unmanned Aerial Vehicle—UAV—technology that is giving us eyes on the location. Unfortunately, without being physically inside the premises and achieving absolute visual confirmation of target identity, using a remote, weaponized instrument to achieve a daytime rescue carries the very real risk of mistaken identity or potential imprecision.

"But I may have a way we can modify Director Fishel's proposed use of one of her assets in order to get us valuable information and one-hundred-percent reliable data as to the status of the hostages, their precise location in the premises, the layout of the place, and more."

"Go on, General Estes," Emma encouraged. She smiled at Palmer's obvious surprise at being addressed by name.

"If we could place an agent posing as a villager or some other local close enough to launch it—within four kilometers—we can send in a drone as small as a bee that will give us eyes inside. The agent can operate the drone remotely from anywhere within that four-kilometer radius with adequate signal and can feed live, secure images back to the Situation Room and anywhere else we designate.

"The drone only has the capacity to be in the air for a maximum of thirty minutes, but it can provide clear images and the software can run facial recognition so that we can ascertain the exact position of the hostages, the layout of the rooms, take pictures of the terrorists, etc. If it's clear to us that the hostages are in imminent threat of execution, we will have a plan and a team in place to implement an immediate, daylight strike upon your command."

"A daylight operation jeopardizes the potential success of the mission, correct?"

Chairman Dutton chimed in, "It's very true, Madam President, that we should only order such a strike if it is clear waiting any longer will result in the imminent death of the hostages. But our team will carry out whatever order you give."

"Director Fishel? What do you think about getting one of your agents within range to use this drone?" Emma asked.

The director nodded. "It could work. We have assets in proximity that we should be able to get close enough to insert as vendors at a nearby open-air market, if there is one, or something similar. It will take some time, but it's achievable."

"How much time?"

"Maybe a couple of hours. Their cover won't be perfect, and the setup is not without risk, but we should be able to fudge enough to get through the day."

"Does anyone have a better idea or a reason why the plan on the table isn't a good one? Speak up now." Once again, Emma surveyed the room. "Okay. Let's get that part of the operation underway."

"Yes, ma'am." Director Fishel motioned to her deputy director, who immediately took his leave.

"Now brief me on the proposed specifics of the rescue, please," Emma said.

Chairman Dutton took the lead. He slid a briefing book across the table to Emma. "With a green light to retrieve the senators, the 160th SOAR—Special Operations Aviation Regiment—can drop a team from the 75th Rangers and SEAL Team Six within twenty klicks—roughly twelve-and-a-half miles—at 1800—6:00 p.m. They'll go the rest of the way on foot, putting them on site between 2100 and 2200—9:00 and 10:00 p.m. The Rangers will take care of securing the perimeter. Six will execute the rescue, and the 160th will circle back and pick up the senators."

Emma digested this information as she leafed through the book, which contained background on each of the teams involved, along with detailed topography maps and markings for the teams' insertion, route, and target. "I assume this is the course of action all of you have agreed on? Does anyone have any objection? Now is the time."

"Madam President, CENTCOM believes this is the most effective way to go, and Secretary Buchanan and I concur," Chairman Dutton said.

Emma trusted her military advisors. She trusted Buchanan. Still, lives most likely would end this day because of an order she gave. She glanced over briefly to where General Estes sat. She seemed resolute and for some reason, that settled Emma's nerves. "So ordered." She held up a hand. "Unless we get information in the intervening hours that requires us to act sooner."

Secretary of Defense Buchanan signaled to his deputy, who grabbed his briefcase and exited through the main door leading to the hallway.

"Now that we've got an action plan that we're all confident provides the best chance of success, where are we with the families of the deceased and the families of the senators? Have they been notified? Who's been interfacing with them?"

"Madam President," a tall, bespectacled young man sitting at the farthest point on the perimeter stood. "I am FBI Special Agent Hiram Esocur. I'm in charge of the FBI Hostage Recovery Fusion Cell. We're a multi-agency team whose job is to recover hostages abroad and interface with their loved ones. Our Family Engagement Team has been alerted and is standing by."

"The families of the senators haven't been notified yet?"

"No, ma'am. We recognize this is a highly sensitive situation. I've held off on the order to contact the families until we had direction from you as to how, what, and when, you wanted us to share."

"Thank you, Special Agent Esocur." Emma knew exactly how it felt to be on the receiving end of the gut-punch of horrible news. *You can't leave this to someone else to do.* "I'd like to inform the families myself and hand them over to you."

"Yes, ma'am."

"Obviously, the element of surprise and secrecy about this rescue operation is of paramount importance. Based on your experience, how long do you believe I can delay before making the calls? In the end, I must balance the needs of the families with the integrity of the mission."

"Honestly, ma'am? It depends on the personalities involved. Some loved ones ask dozens of detailed questions, such as what time did this happen? Others are more outcome focused."

"And of those families that fixate on the details, I imagine if we tell them their loved ones were taken hours ago, they want to know why they haven't been informed before now?"

"Yes, ma'am."

"Thank you for your candor, Special Agent Esocur."

Emma turned to the secretary of the Army. "Secretary Carsen? Have the next of kin for the deceased been notified?"

"Not yet, ma'am. As you know, we send a notification officer and a chaplain to deliver the news in person. Notification takes place within four hours of the death and between 0600 and 2200. As it is not yet 0600 here, the notification has been scheduled for roughly 0800. Also worth noting: it is Army policy not to release the names of the deceased for twenty-four hours after notification of next of kin."

"Okay." Emma rubbed the back of her neck, where tension had assumed squatter's rights. "I think we have to assume that sooner or later, and most likely sooner than later, the terrorists are going to do or say something to call attention to themselves and their cause. We cannot have loved ones find out about this on television or by the media ringing their doorbells and camping outside their homes."

Emma sucked in a sharp breath at the unbidden memory of that fateful visit telling her Heather was gone. She'd been driven nearly mad by the intrusive clamor of the media for a reaction from her even as she grappled with her grief. *This is a part of the process you understand. These loved ones are going to need your empathy and any protection you can give them. Empathy is a strength, remember that.*

"When we leave here, I'll personally notify the senators' loved ones. That will be followed immediately by contact from your people, Special Agent Esocur. I will emphasize, and your people should as well, that the lives of the senators depend upon our ability to carry out the mission covertly. That means we need their cooperation, and to the extent possible, a media blackout. Also, I want teams in place ready to set up perimeters around the senators' homes and the homes of their loved ones to protect their privacy should that become necessary."

Emma gathered up the contents of the folders and tidied them. "Finally, we come to the issue of informing the senators' staffs and the public. I'll be discussing this with my senior advisors and my communications team."

Although she would never say so in this room, the fact that two of the hostages were openly hostile to her complicated this state of affairs. She worried that their staffs would foolishly publicly criticize her handling of the crisis while it was in process, thereby further escalating an already-dangerous situation. *You need to tread delicately here.*

"Special Agent Esocur? Does your team also deal with the workplace in the instance of a high-profile kidnapping?"

"Yes, ma'am. We'll work in conjunction with the special presidential envoy for hostage affairs to secure the cooperation of the senators' staffs."

"Please make it abundantly clear to them that any statements they make, privately or publicly, put their bosses' lives further in jeopardy."

"Yes, ma'am."

"At whatever point I deem it necessary to make any public pronouncements regarding this situation, I will have my office inform you all in advance. I don't want any surprises on my end or on yours. Are we clear?"

"Yes, ma'am," everyone said in unison.

"I want hourly updates. More frequent if the situation warrants." Emma stood. "I have tremendous faith in all of you, as well as in your people. The senators' lives are in the best possible hands. Thank you all for your dedication and professionalism. That's all for now. I've got some difficult phone calls to make."

She turned on her way out. "Special Agent Esocur? You're with me."

CHAPTER SEVEN

Emma slugged down a bottle of water. If she could hydrate enough, perhaps the incessant pounding in her head would subside. Of course, navigating her way through four challenging conversations with senatorial spouses, two of whom were preconditioned to despise her, hadn't helped.

"Are you okay?" Nichelle asked gently.

"Define okay." Emma massaged her temples. "The first existential crisis of my presidency centers around two allies in the Senate, and two self-avowed 'Never Emma' Republicans whose wives apparently believe every ridiculously untrue thing their husbands have told them about me."

Nichelle perched on the edge of one of the visitor chairs. "For what it's worth, I thought you handled the calls perfectly. You were kind, compassionate, and empathetic. You gave them as much information as was safe to share without compromising any details of an active, classified operation. Honestly, I don't know what more you could've done under the circumstances."

"I could bring their husbands home safely."

"And you will."

"I certainly hope so."

"Do you have confidence in your team?"

"Of course I do!"

"With good reason. Trust in your choices, and trust in the team to get the job done."

"Speaking of which, I need you to do a couple of things for me. First, I need Olivia and her deputies, David, Trent, Miranda, and the vice president in here ASAP. I have to decide what, if anything, to say publicly, when to say it, and what form that takes. I want to have a robust discussion of the pros and cons before I make up my mind, and then I'm going to need David to draft my remarks."

"Okay."

"Next, I need you to interface with whoever has that helmet cam footage from the pilot."

Nichelle recoiled. "Please tell me you don't want to see that."

"What?" Emma's brow furrowed. "Why on Earth would I want to do that? No, I don't want to see it. That serves no purpose. However, if I decide to make a public statement, I need to know what, if anything, the footage shows of the senators."

"Because…?"

"Because it makes a huge difference whether or not there's any definitive indication they identified themselves to their captors."

"Director Fishel said—"

"Fishel said chatter made clear the captors knew they had high-value targets. That doesn't tell me whether they know their identities or that they're senators. For all we know, high-value targets to these terrorists could be American businessmen," Emma snapped. *Don't be a jerk. Nichelle doesn't deserve that.*

Emma intentionally moderated her tone. "I'm sorry. There's no reason why you should see where I'm going with this."

"It's all right. We're all stressed out and running on lack of sleep."

Emma acknowledged the truth of that. "This is where I'm coming from: If I decide to make a public statement, I sure as heck don't want to give the terrorists any information they don't already have. If I identify the hostages and those captors didn't already know who they were, that's a game-changer. On the other hand, if the footage shows that Friese, Tannebaum, Lawson, and Wicks revealed their status and identities when they were taken—"

"Why would they do that?"

Emma swiveled in her chair, stared through the French doors out into the Rose Garden no longer shrouded in the dark of night, and imagined the scene halfway around the world. "If they thought confessing their status would keep them alive longer, I suspect they'd do it. With the trauma of having watched those soldiers be executed, don't you think they'd say just about anything they believed would help them avoid the same fate?"

"I guess I hadn't thought about it that way." Nichelle rose and headed for the door. "I'll figure out who has the footage and have them scrub it for anything that gives us additional information."

"Thank you."

"Just doing my job, Madam President."

◈◈

Palmer's jaw tightened as she and her team reviewed the footage for the third time. With each viewing, her heart ached a little more, but this was her job. She owed it to these brave men to complete the mission. "Stop it right there."

The colonel manning the laptop paused the video.

"Now run it slowly."

"Yes, ma'am."

Palmer leaned closer to the screen. "See that? You see Senator Friese say something to the guy on the left? The one who appears to be in charge?"

"Yes, ma'am."

"I want a lip reader in here ASAP. I want to know for sure what Friese said."

"Yes, ma'am." The colonel took his leave.

Palmer clicked on the new secure message in her inbox. *Operation Bee Sting underway. Asset in place. Awaiting results.* "Best news of the day so far." She turned at the sound of a knock on the half-open door. "Come!"

Max stepped into the office. "The lip reader you requested will be here in five, ma'am."

"Roger that." Palmer closed out of the message. "Good news. The CIA asset is in place. Now we wait to see if he/she can get eyes inside."

"That is good news. Any idea how long it might take?"

Palmer shook her head. "You know what I know."

"Crappy way for the president to start her term."

"Understatement of the year there." Palmer thought about the way the president had handled the meeting earlier. She was calm, in command, efficient, and decisive. Now it was up to Palmer and everyone else involved in the op to ensure a successful outcome.

She would start by providing accurate and detailed information about the exchange between the senators and the captors.

"You've got that face thing going on."

"What are you talking about?" She'd almost forgotten Max was still standing there.

"You know, that thing you do with your jaw muscles right before you kick someone's ass and take no prisoners."

"Is that right? First, I didn't know that was a thing, and second, part of me wishes I could do more to get President McMasters a win here, you know? She's in an incredibly tough spot, and there are a lot of moving parts."

"I know you. You want to be the one flying that bird, making the drop and pickup."

Although Palmer scoffed at the comment, it was truer than she wanted to admit. She always gave her very best to a mission, but for reasons she hadn't yet put her finger on, she especially wanted to bring this one home for this president.

"Get out of my office and send in the lip reader, will you?"

❦❧

"If the information leaks out and we're not ahead of it, then we lose the ability to control the narrative. We'll be playing defense and having to explain our silence forevermore. The president ran on a platform of integrity and transparency. We simply cannot let anyone else break this story before we do," Olivia argued.

"I agree," Emma responded. "The American people have to hear this from me. The question is how much we share, knowing that our primary responsibility is to those four senators. Our priority is to keep them alive and get them home safely. To give them the best chance, I have to manage the information in such a way that it protects the mission at all costs."

"I say we issue a press release. That way, there are no questions, just a static statement," Olivia's deputy press secretary said.

"I disagree," Miranda said. "This is a huge story with big repercussions. Hiding behind a press release is an invitation for the media to go scrambling to other sources for video and reactions, and then everyone else's part of the story sucks up more airtime than ours."

"Okay!" Emma felt the heat climbing up her neck. "I've heard enough. First, this isn't about scoring public relations points. There are real lives at stake here and whatever I do or say could be the difference between life and death. Let's keep that foremost in mind, please."

"Yes, ma'am," the group replied in unison.

"Second, I'm going to address the nation at 8:55 a.m. It's still early enough to break into the morning news shows, even here on the east coast."

She picked up her pen, jotted some notes on a legal pad, and handed it to her head speechwriter. "David, this is the direction I want you to take. Get me a draft script in the next twenty minutes and we'll go over it."

"How long do you want to speak?"

Emma pursed her lips in thought. "No more than ten minutes, less if we can make it more succinct than that." She motioned to Olivia. "Better tell the networks what we'll need so they can put it in motion on their end."

"Where do you want to make the address, Madam President? What backdrop would you like?"

Emma took in her surroundings. "Here, I think. Behind the desk in the Oval Office. It speaks to the gravity of the situation."

The intercom buzzed, and Emma dismissed the staff before picking up the phone. "Yes, Jeannie?"

"Madam President, I have Secretary Buchanan on the line for you."

"Put him through, Jeannie. How are we doing on getting the Gang of Eight in here?"

"The Senate majority and minority leaders, the Speaker of the House, the House minority leader, and the Intelligence Committee heads from the Senate and the House are waiting for you in the Roosevelt Room, ma'am."

"Thank you, Jeannie." She waited for the click on the line. "Hello, Lester. What've you got?"

"Helmet cam confirmation that Friese identified who he was and that he was a U.S. senator to his captors. The others followed suit."

"You're positive?"

"Yes, ma'am. Verified by a lip reader and re-checked and verified by a second just to be certain."

One question answered. "Anything else of note? How did they appear physically? Were they injured from the crash?"

"They were a little banged up, but all appeared to be able to walk under their own power. I can't tell you much of anything else that will be useful."

"Okay. Thank you."

"You're welcome, ma'am. I'll keep you posted."

She filled him in on the upcoming address to the nation, hung up the phone, and then headed across the hall to the Roosevelt Room to brief the Congressional leaders on the situation.

The clock on the wall indicated it was 7:27 a.m. Emma did the math in her head; it was 2:27 p.m. in northern Syria.

Hang in there, gentlemen. We're coming for you.

⊷⊶

The first thing Palmer noticed about the president as she swept into the Situation Room was the crease in the middle of her forehead. Palmer recognized the look, as she'd observed it too many times on presidents faced with the burden of making life and death decisions.

Palmer had made similar calls in the heat of battle and understood only too well what the weight felt like. *My heart goes out to you, Madam President.*

The Joint Chiefs, Secretary Buchanan, NSA Edwards, and Director Fishel, all stood as she did until the president took a seat.

"I'm scheduled to address the nation thirty minutes from now. What Chief of Staff Johnson is handing you all is the preliminary draft of my remarks. While I haven't yet had time to put my own stamp on them, the tone and basic facts give you the gist of what I intend to say."

Palmer accepted the proffered sheets of paper and read through the speech. It was brief, informative without being overly specific, and to the point.

"I need to know now if anything that's in here will affect the ability of the team to successfully carry out its mission."

"No, ma'am," Secretary Buchanan answered. "But shortly before we came over here, we received some footage you're going to want to see before you take to the airwaves."

"Please tell me this is good news."

"It's a mixed bag, trending to the positive," Director Fishel answered. "It took some doing, but our asset was able to maneuver the drone into position and capture several minutes' worth of intelligence, including some images of the senators and a general sense of the layout of the premises."

"That's great, right?" the president asked.

"It's fortunate, yes."

"The images aren't pretty, Madam President," Secretary Buchanan said. "Prepare yourself."

"Secretary Buchanan, I'll remind you that I was the district attorney in the largest borough in New York. I'm no stranger to seeing difficult material."

"I apologize, Madam President. I didn't mean to suggest—"

"Apology accepted. We're all under a lot of pressure here. Please continue."

The secretary motioned to Palmer, who stood.

"Madam President, we were able to take the frames and construct a sort of time-lapsed sequence from them."

"Let's see it."

Palmer, with all her wartime experience in the field, still found the images jarring. *Madam President, I know you're tough, but I'd spare you and anyone else from seeing these if I could.* She opened the lid of her secure laptop which she'd already connected to a Situation Room projector, clicked on the file titled, "Operation Bee Sting," and the drone footage filled one of the six secure video screens in the room.

"The drone entered the building through the back door when one of the captors stepped outside to relieve himself," Palmer narrated. "The CIA asset was able to set the drone down on a table and gradually move it into position to ascertain the whereabouts of the senators."

Several people in the room gasped at the sight of the four men, bloodied and beaten, their heads lolling onto their chests. They were tied to straight-back chairs in the center of a filthy, otherwise empty room.

"Are they alive?" the president asked, barely concealing her anguish.

"The drone was in place long enough to capture movement, ma'am." Palmer said softly.

"How long ago was this footage taken?"

"Less than two hours ago, ma'am."

The images on the screen shifted to reveal several young men standing just outside the room. They carried large, automatic weapons slung across their shoulders. One had a cigarette dangling from his lips. The others appeared to be laughing.

When the footage froze on the last image, Palmer closed the file and the laptop lid and sat down. "That's what we've got, ma'am."

The president's clenched fists turned her knuckles white. She addressed the room. "I need your best professional judgment. Clearly our people have been tortured. They're barely alive, if at all. If we wait until after sundown, it might well be too late. Should we go in right now?"

Chairman Dutton spoke up first. "Madam President, those images are as hard to see for us as they are for you, but the good news is that we have definitive proof that the senators are all together, and they are alive."

"If we go in now, we put not only the senators but also our team at great risk," Secretary Buchanan added.

"And if we don't, the senators could be dead," the president shot back.

"Ma'am," Director Fishel said, "if those terrorists were going to kill them, they would've done so already. The fact that they are alive means that there's a bigger plan."

"What's your suggestion, Director?"

"Let this play out. Stick with the original plan. It takes guts, and I understand that it's damned hard to sit on your hands for several more hours, but it's your best option."

"Would anyone else care to weigh in? Anyone feel differently?" The president made eye contact with everyone in the room.

When her eyes locked on Palmer, the raw pain Palmer saw there made her breath catch in her throat.

"Okay, then. Please continue to keep me posted. Thank you for the excellent work and thank your people for me as well. I've got to get ready to address the nation."

Palmer checked the time. It was 0845. The president had ten minutes to polish her remarks and pull herself together. *If anyone can do it, she can. Stop worrying about her.*

Emma studiously ignored the hubbub all around her. Technicians fiddled with the lighting, the cables, the podium set up in front of the Resolute desk where she now stood, the teleprompter, the microphones, the drapes, and even the framed personal photographs on the credenza behind her. A makeup artist applied a last coat of lipstick to her lips and fussed with the sheen on her forehead created by the heat of the lights beating down on her.

"Five minutes," the television producer announced.

Emma closed her eyes and willed herself to channel into steely resolve the horrific images of four human beings, beaten nearly to death, strapped to chairs half a world away. *I promise you, I will do everything in my power and the power of this office to bring you safely home to your loved ones.*

"Madam President? Are you all right?" Nichelle touched her on the sleeve.

"I'm fine." Emma gathered the sheaf of pages before her and organized them into a neat pile. She always insisted on having a backup paper copy of her remarks in case technology and the teleprompter failed.

"It's a good speech."

"David did a nice job under difficult circumstances. Did I remember to thank him?"

"You did. And the changes and additions you made were spot on and necessary."

"You followed up personally and you're sure the families of the flight crew have been properly notified?"

"I did and I'm positive that everyone who needed to be notified has been so informed."

"Two minutes!"

Emma drew in a deep breath, blew it out, and rotated her shoulders to relieve the built-up tension.

"You're going to be great," Nichelle said as she stepped away.

"What I need to be is the right leader to get the job done for those men and the American people."

"Thirty seconds!"

"And you are," Nichelle said.

Emma cleared her throat.

"And five, four, three, two, one…"

CHAPTER EIGHT

One floor down, in the White House Situation Room, Palmer and the rest of the group from the earlier meeting sat riveted to the six flat-screen televisions. Each screen carried one of the four major networks, CNN, and MSNBC. The sound was from the CNN feed.

The CNN anchor intoned, "Again, we haven't been given any advance notice what it is President McMasters is planning to say. We were told only that this is a matter of urgency and import to the American people."

Suddenly, the president's image filled every screen. Palmer's heart thumped hard. *No, Madam President, I needn't have worried about you at all.* Whereas in the Situation Room ten minutes earlier the president seemed shaken, pained, and haunted by the drone footage, now she appeared strong, fully in command, and in control.

In hushed tones, the anchor said, "Looks like President McMasters is ready to address the nation."

"Good morning," the president began. "Several hours ago, a U.S. Army helicopter piloted by a skilled crew and carrying four of our United States senators was targeted and brought down by a ruthless band of terrorists in northern Syria.

"The four senators, Senator Daniel Tannebaum of New York, Senator Robert Friese of Tennessee, Senator Ted Lawson of Minnesota, and Senator Nathaniel Wicks of Texas, were on an unpublicized trip in the region to review conditions on the ground. The senators all sit on the Senate Foreign Relations Committee and were fulfilling their Constitutional and Congressional oversight duties. All seven individuals onboard the helicopter survived the crash landing. The three brave military members of the flight crew were murdered in cold blood. The four senators were taken captive."

The president leaned in toward the camera, and Palmer unconsciously leaned in too. "Let me make this perfectly clear: The United States of America will not be held hostage by terrorists or entities hostile to our country. We will defend and protect our people, and our nation's ideals, wherever, whenever the forces of evil would seek to challenge or intimidate us.

"To terrorists anywhere, I say this: On 9-11, and in the intervening years since, any number of terrorist organizations and cells have tested our resolve. In each instance, we have defeated and decimated these entities and captured or killed their leaders. Terrorists, and those who would aid them, are no match for the strength, determination, and resilience of this country and our people.

"This day is no different, and this president's resolve is unwavering and absolute."

The president took a deep breath. The expression in her eyes softened and her posture relaxed slightly. "To the American people: I ask that you keep the senators, their families, the slain service members, and their loved ones in your prayers and thoughts. In times of our greatest challenges, we rise together and prevail. E Pluribus Unum. Out of many, one.

"Thank you. May God bless you. And may God bless the United States of America."

The CNN anchor returned. "There you have it. The president of the United States, speaking to the nation from the Oval Office, informing America that four U.S. senators have been taken hostage by terrorists. I'm going to bring in our panel of experts, beginning with CNN White House correspondent…"

At the signal from Secretary Buchanan, the watch officer in the Situation Room killed the sound. "She did good," he said.

"She did better than good," Chairman Dutton answered. "She was steady, strong, and in control."

"She was," Secretary of the Army Carsen agreed. "And I appreciate that she didn't play politics with it and give the senators any more weight than the soldiers."

"She was genuine," Director Fishel said. "If the terrorists saw it, they know she means business."

NSA Edwards' phone buzzed and he stared at the screen. "Oh, my God."

"What is it?"

"They saw it, all right." To the watch commander he said, "I'm sending you a link. Can you bring it up on screen? And reach out to the president's chief of staff. President McMasters needs to see this."

Seconds later, a YouTube livestream appeared on the television. In front of a curtained background, four masked gunmen stood over the chairs of four slumped, bound figures—the captive senators.

Palmer closed her eyes briefly and said a prayer for the men. As she finished, President McMasters hustled into the room.

"What's going on?" Her eyes drifted to the screen and she froze.

One of the terrorists yelled something to the prisoners.

"Get a translator in here," NSA Edwards ordered the watch commander.

The terrorist yelled the same phrase again, and this time poked the gun under the chin of the nearest hostage. Senator Daniel Tannebaum raised his head. Both of his eyes were nearly swollen shut. Blood dripped from his nose, the side of his mouth, and his left temple. His cheekbone sported a lump the size of a golf ball.

The president murmured, "Oh, Dan. What have they done to you?"

Palmer understood the reaction only too well. She'd had to witness too many fellow service members and friends return from a battle bloodied or worse. The shock of it always left her feeling sick inside.

The gunman poked the senator again, this time screaming at him while holding the muzzle of the weapon against the side of his head. "Tell them," the terrorist said in heavily accented, broken English.

When Tannebaum balked, one of the other terrorists stepped forward and pointed his weapon at the center of the forehead of the hostage next to him. The first terrorist hissed, "Tell them or he dies."

"Don't do it, Dan," the second hostage said.

A tear streaked down Tannebaum's cheek. "Bob, I have to. It'll be all right."

"Enough!" The first terrorist motioned to the second. He said something Palmer didn't understand.

"He's telling him he's going to count to three and then give the order to shoot to kill."

Palmer hadn't noticed the translator's arrival.

The second gunman pushed his weapon more forcefully into Senator Friese's forehead.

The president stepped closer to the screen, as if by doing so she could somehow intervene. The movement placed her right next to Palmer. Waves of anger and indignation radiated outward from her. Even in the darkened room, Palmer could see the anguish and pain visible in her profile.

The first terrorist spoke. The sound of his voice, even in another language, oozed menace.

"One, two..." the translator relayed.

"Wait!" Tannebaum shouted. "Don't shoot."

Again, the first terrorist spoke to the second.

"Back away, but keep that thing pointed at the bastard," the translator shared.

The first terrorist put his mouth next to Tannebaum's ear and hissed, "Tell them."

Tannebaum wet his cracked lips and looked directly into the camera. "I am U.S. Senator Daniel Tannebaum," he said softly.

The gunman poked him in the ribs with his weapon. "Tell them."

"Senators Friese, Wicks, Lawson, and I apologize for the injustices perpetrated on the Islamic State..." Tannebaum paused, which earned him another prodding with the gun and another harangue by the lead terrorist.

"He's telling him to say it the way it was rehearsed, or his friend will die where he sits," the translator explained.

Tannebaum ran his tongue across his lips again. "...*unfairly* perpetrated on the Islamic State by the cowardly United States government. In exchange for our safe return, ISIS demands the release of the wrongly imprisoned heroes on this list by midnight tonight. If these terms are not met, our lives will be forfeited."

Suddenly, the screen filled with a rumpled, handwritten list of names. The list filled the screen for thirty seconds and then was replaced with a close-up of each of the faces of the four captives. Finally, the lead terrorist's filthy visage filled the screen. "You have until midnight or these pig infidels die." The transmission went blank.

The lights came up, and everyone, including Palmer, turned to the president. Her face was ashen and her hands were balled into fists by her sides. "Do we know if that broadcast was from the same location where we last knew they were being held?"

NSA Edwards barked into his phone, "Did we get a fix on the location?" He listened for a moment. "Keep trying. You got a still image of that list? Send it over, ASAP." He hung up the phone. "We're working on it, ma'am."

"Please work quickly. Also, I want a vetting of that list. I want to know who they're demanding, where we're holding them, and everything we have on them."

Secretary Buchanan stepped forward. "Madam President—"

"Hold that thought, Lester," the president said. "I have no intention of giving in to these demands; I simply want to know who they covet and why."

She planted both palms on the table, her eyes laser sharp. "Correct me if I'm wrong, but my calculation is this: These bastards believe they're negotiating with us and that they have the upper hand. True?"

"Yes," Director Fishel responded. "First, they're testing American resolve. But, even more than that, they believe they have the upper hand because the president of the United States is a woman, and they are an organization that doesn't value women and believes they are weak."

The president smirked. "In this case, that hues to our advantage. The truth is, they just gave us a tremendous gift—the gift of time— and a firm window of opportunity. If their deadline is midnight, that indicates they'll keep the hostages alive at least until they know whether or not we've acceded to their demands. The timing of the rescue mission puts our team on site no later than ten o'clock."

She singled out Secretary Buchanan, Chairman Dutton, NSA Edwards, and CIA Director Fishel. "You all told me earlier this morning that the timing of this operation was optimal and it is your expert opinions that it will succeed. Is that still the case?"

"Yes, ma'am," the group answered.

"Have you seen or learned anything here to give you pause with regard to that plan?"

"No, ma'am."

"Is there anything wrong with my calculus that we'll have our men back safely and this ordeal will be over long before that midnight deadline?"

"No, ma'am."

The president rapped her knuckles on the table. "All right then, let's get this thing done. I'm certain there are four very anxious families out there who'd like to see their loved ones come home.

"If the gunmen offer no resistance or threat, take them into custody to be tried under our terrorism statutes. If they pose an imminent danger to our team or our senators, I authorize the team, at its discretion, to take them out."

&⸎&

The words on the legal pad blurred together. Emma laid down the pen and rubbed her temples. She swiveled around and glanced out at the serenity of the perfectly manicured lawn and grounds and contrasted that with the scene she'd witnessed a few hours earlier. "Hang in there, guys. The cavalry's on the way. We're going to bring you home and send a chilling message of our own to bad actors everywhere."

"Don't mess with the United States or her badass commander in chief."

"Exactly." Emma whirled back around to see Nichelle leaning against the doorjamb that opened into the private corridor. The chief of staff's office was at the far end of that corridor, beyond the president's private dining room, study, the offices of the president's two senior advisors, and a reception area.

"How's that State of the Union speech coming?" Nichelle closed the door and helped herself to the near-side visitor's chair.

"Slowly. I seem to be having some difficulty focusing today."

"I can't imagine why."

"Any backlash from the families, the senators' staffs, the Hill?"

"The FBI's Hostage Recovery Fusion Cell checked in with the families shortly after that horrible spectacle. They were really rattled, but hanging in there. They've been assured that we're doing everything we can, but they're frightened and despondent about the senators' physical appearance."

"They're not alone." Emma closed her eyes tightly. "I can't imagine what these guys have been through. How do you come back from that?"

"With a lot of help, love, support, and time, I imagine."

"Have we been able to keep the press away from the families?"

"For now. They're all hunkered down, and Capitol Police and local law enforcement are providing protection."

"And the senators' staffs? Are they behaving?"

"As promised, the majority and minority leaders have taken charge and are sitting on them. They understand that this is a matter of life and death, and they need to stay on the sidelines and trust that things are happening behind the scenes that will resolve this mess."

Emma glanced at the clock for what seemed like the hundredth time in the past two hours. "The teams are safely on the ground and on the move. They should be getting close to the location by now."

"Watching them drop into the zone in real time was impressive," Nichelle said.

"It was, and reassuring. I know these teams train specifically for situations like this, and they're the best in the world."

"But?"

Emma shook her head. "There is no *but*, except that this operation is on me. What happens out there today falls on my shoulders. I'm the one who ordered them in."

"Are you having second thoughts?"

"No. This is the right call."

"But something's bothering you." Nichelle said it as a statement, not a question.

"At the end of this day, it's highly likely that lives will have been lost because I ordered a capture or kill strike. Brave service members will commit acts they'll carry with them for the rest of their lives. Marks on their souls. Four senators will suffer unimaginable, additional trauma with bullets and bodies flying before their very eyes. These are not facts I take lightly."

"Of course not," Nichelle said softly. "But let's also consider that today, you're saving the lives of four U.S. senators who are in grave danger. You're bringing them home to their families. You're sending a message to terrorist groups throughout the world and their allies that the United States is strong and will not flinch when it comes to protecting her people and values. You're making it clear that you won't hesitate to take action."

Emma knew all of that. Still, the tug of war between her head and her heart persisted. *That's okay. Putting lives at risk should never be easy. If it is, you're doing something wrong.*

"Madam President, you know as well as I do the mountains we had to climb to smash that glass ceiling—to overcome the obvious and sometimes subconscious sexism and misogyny. Decisive action now shuts down the argument that a woman isn't up to the job and won't make the hard decisions. And I'm not even going to mention the optics of you saving the lives of two of your biggest critics in the Senate. That's a beautiful bit of poetic justice."

Emma's nostrils flared. "Stop right there. I want to be really clear about something, even in private." Her voice shook and her face reddened. "I don't care about the politics of this mission. I don't give a rat's rear end about making the Republicans in the Senate and the misogynists in the world eat crow for underestimating me and every other woman. Optics are the last thing on my mind. I am the commander in chief of our military forces and the leader of the entire United States of America, not just the people who voted for me. There are four U.S. senators out there—legislators who did nothing more than set out to fulfill their Constitutional responsibilities—clinging to life, clinging to hope, and praying for a miracle. It's my deep honor to answer their prayers, regardless of who they are, what party they represent, or how they feel about me personally. Do you understand?"

"I do, Madam President. I apologize. I meant no disrespect to those men or what they're going through."

"Madam President?" Jeannie's voice over the intercom cut through the tension of the moment.

"Yes, Jeannie?"

"They're ready for you in the Situation Room."

"Thank you. Please tell them I'll be right down."

⟡⟡

Emma slipped quietly into the Situation Room. For once, she didn't want to stand on ceremony; she didn't want to be a distraction. She simply wanted to observe undetected for a moment.

The air in the room crackled with energy. A dozen people, including the vice president, the director of national intelligence, the national security advisor and his first deputy, the director for counterterrorism, the chairman of the Joint Chiefs, Secretary Buchanan, Secretary Neville, Director Fishel, Nichelle, General Estes, and a brigadier general Emma didn't recognize, crowded around the conference table, pouring over laptops.

Other than Lisa Fishel, Nichelle, and her, Palmer Estes was the only other woman in the room. At the moment, she was engrossed in something on her laptop, her brows furrowed in concentration. *You're a four-star general—only the second female in the Army's history to reach that rank—how did you get there? What's your story?* Suddenly, Emma was really curious. Cracking the glass ceiling in the military had to be nearly as hard as winning the presidency. She made a mental note to review Palmer's file.

Emma planted herself against the wall just inside the doorway and continued her survey of the room. The television screens were alive with activity. On the first screen, the combatant commander in charge of the mission barked orders from CENTCOM in Tampa, Florida to the Special Ops team on the ground in Syria. A second screen featured live helmet-cam views transmitted by that rescue team. A third screen featured a live aerial view high above the strike location transmitted from a drone hovering undetected above.

Chairman Dutton spotted Emma first. "Madam President."

All activity ceased and everyone came to attention.

"At ease."

Dutton indicated the one person in the room Emma didn't recognize. "Madam President, this is Brigadier General Adam Fulton, Assistant Commanding General of the Joint Special Operations Command—JSOC. He'll be our eyes and ears, keeping us connected to CENTCOM and to the action on the ground. He's in charge of what you see on these screens."

Emma nodded to the general at the end of the table. In front of him was a laptop. "Glad you're here, General." Emma took a seat in the middle of the table.

"Thank you, ma'am. We're about ten minutes away from 'Go time.' At the moment, we're assessing whether or not we can send another bee UAV to get a final look inside."

Dutton continued, "While the team is getting in position and working on logistics, I thought we'd have General Estes take us through the set up and what we can expect."

"Good afternoon, Madam President." Palmer entered several keystrokes on her laptop. She pointed to the fourth television screen, which had come to life. "I've pulled up some satellite images of the region, overlaying the route our team took to arrive at the strike site. As you can imagine, this path was intentionally circuitous, which allowed the team to move more freely with only limited exposure."

"Did we encounter any opposition along the way?" Emma asked.

"No, ma'am." Palmer projected another image on the screen. "These are a series of snapshots taken by the RQ-170 drone less than twenty minutes ago. The red outline is the structure where the senators are being held. As you can see in the next slide, we are able to make out four figures milling around outside the building—two in the front, and two in the back."

"Are we still thinking there are six gunmen?"

"Thermal imaging indicates six heat signatures inside, which would seem to confirm that there are two hostiles present along with the four senators. All of them are clustered in one of the six rooms in the house. To ascertain anything more specific, we'd need to get inside."

Emma addressed General Fulton. "Any decision on whether to send in the bee?"

"The team believes it would be too risky, ma'am. We absolutely don't want to tip off the hostiles at this point."

A radio squawked. "This is Bravo One. In position. Perimeter is secure. Awaiting your signal, Alpha One."

"Check. Alpha One requesting permission to complete the mission."

"Bravo One is the platoon commander of the Rangers affirming they have the area around the strike site blanketed and have cleared the way for the rescue," Palmer supplied. "Alpha One is the commander of the SEAL team that will be going in to neutralize the enemy and secure the hostages. Once they have the senators secure and triaged, we have Black Hawks in range to retrieve the entire force and head back to base."

Emma appreciated Palmer's commentary. It was concise, informative, and yet didn't condescend simply because Emma was a woman and a civilian with no military experience.

"Thank you, General."

"Madam President?" The combatant commander at CENTCOM asked. "Requesting permission to complete the mission, ma'am."

"Permission granted. Godspeed."

"Alpha One, Bravo One, permission granted. You are a go!"

"Check."

Instantaneously, the grainy, night-vision footage from the helmet cam shifted as the SEAL team moved in on the target. With gestures, Alpha One directed traffic, as men splintered off in opposite directions.

Emma's breath came in short spurts as the action unfolded before her. The scene hurtled from left to right as first one, and then the second gunman raised their weapons to fire. The sound of gunfire pierced the air. Both terrorists' heads jerked and each fell backward, their arms flailing in the air, their bodies crumpled on the ground.

Seconds later, a SEAL came into view. He fired two more shots, one at each terrorist's chest, and kicked their weapons out of the way.

"Alpha One to Alpha Two, we're clear back here."

"Check. Clear in front."

"Check. Breaching the back."

"Check. Breaching the front."

Another member of the team placed a charge on the door, jumped to the side, shielded himself, and the door blew open. Three members of the team moved forward into the building. The first whispered, "Left room, clear."

The second followed, "Right room, clear."

Alpha One said, "Should be the next room on the left."

The first SEAL stopped just short of the room. The second ducked past him and took up a position on the other side of the door. At a nod from Alpha One, the first SEAL turned the knob and opened the door a crack.

Alpha One burst through the open door. Emma's heart beat triple time as the four senators, each bound and with black hoods covering their heads, came into view. Their heads snapped up at the sounds of the chaos around them.

The gunman standing behind them screamed something in Arabic and raised his weapon. Before he could shoot, a blast from Alpha One's rifle hit him above the left eye, snapping his head backward. His weapon fired and several shots splintered the wall. He landed on the floor with a thud. Alpha One put an insurance bullet in the center of the terrorist's chest.

One of the senators cried out, "Who's there?"

"United States Navy SEALS, sirs. We've got you. Alpha One to Alpha Two, we've got the packages. Clear."

"Check. We're clearing the rest of the house. Took out one charging toward us."

"Check. That makes six. Clear the premises to be sure." Alpha One addressed the two SEALS with him. "Sweep the place."

Alpha One removed the hostages' hoods one by one. Tears streaked down Nate Wicks' cheeks leaving tracks through the grime and blood on his face.

"Can you identify yourselves, please?"

"T-Ted Lawson. And boy, am I glad to see you guys."

"We're glad to see you, Senator. The president sends her regards to all of you. She's looking forward to seeing you all back in Washington."

Emma smiled at the unscripted, unprompted mention. Indeed, she couldn't wait to check on the senators in person, under much different circumstances.

"Bob Friese."

"Dan Tannebaum."

"Nate Wicks."

Emma blew out an explosive breath, closed her eyes tightly, and offered up a quick prayer. "Thank you, God, for keeping them alive until we could get there." She opened her eyes again. Palmer Estes smiled at her and nodded.

Emma nodded in return and mouthed, "Thank you," before she returned her attention to the television screen.

On screen, Alpha One used a knife to cut through each of the senators' restraints. "Can you all stand?"

One of the SEALS returned to view. "We're all clear out here."

"Okay. Let's get those birds back here and take these gentlemen home."

"Check. I'll make the call. Beta One, we're clear in here."

"This is Beta One. All quiet out here. Ready for a ride?"

"Check."

"ETA ten minutes."

"Check."

"CENTCOM, this is Alpha One."

"Go ahead, Alpha One."

"All packages are safe. We're going to triage here and move out."

"Job well done, Alpha One, Beta One."

For the next fifteen minutes, the only sounds in the room were the scratchy radio transmissions of the teams in the field as the helicopters arrived and the senators, SEALS, and Rangers were loaded and safely on their way to the U.S. base.

When it was clear the helicopters were out of danger of attack, the combatant commander at CENTCOM headquarters looked directly into the camera. "Madam President?"

"I'm here, General."

"Mission accomplished, ma'am."

"I can see that." She cleared her throat as emotion threatened to overwhelm her. "Congratulations everyone, on a job well done. Today, democracy and freedom won. To everyone in this room, your staffs, to all of you at CENTCOM and our Special Ops units in the field, you have my heartfelt gratitude. You've made all of us proud. Thank you. Now let's bring our men home."

CHAPTER NINE

P almer hung up the phone and gazed out her office window at Arlington National Cemetery. Days from now, three fresh graves would be dug and three more heroes who died in service to their country would be buried.

Your deaths were not in vain. We got the bastards. It would be cold comfort to the families of the flight crew, Palmer knew, but it would take at least a little of the sting out of it.

"You did a great job today, General." Chairman Dutton stood in the open doorway.

Palmer straightened in her chair and swiveled to face him. "Thank you, sir. So did you. Everyone did. Objective achieved." She closed a folder on her desk. "You told the president the senators have been stabilized and are en route to Landstuhl Regional Medical Center?"

"I did. She was much relieved to know that. She personally informed the families and arranged for them to fly over to be with their loved ones."

"What time is her address to the nation tonight?"

"1800 hours." The chairman consulted his watch. "Which is to say, about two minutes from now."

"Care to watch it with me?"

"You go ahead. I'm recording it to watch as soon as I get home. My wife is complaining that it's been so long since she's seen me, she's forgotten what I look like."

"Have a good night, sir."

"You as well. Don't stay too late tonight; it's been a long day."

When he'd gone, Palmer tuned in to the CNN livestream on her computer.

"This is President McMasters' second address to the nation today in what is proving to be an extraordinary first week on the job," the CNN anchor intoned. "We were not given any advance information about what the president will say, although we can certainly speculate that this has to do with the fate of the four senators who are being held captive... The president is at the podium. Let's hear what she has to say."

"Good evening. Tonight, I can report that a few hours ago, I authorized an operation that resulted in the rescue of the four United States senators who were captured and tortured earlier this morning by a ruthless band of terrorists in northern Syria. Senators Tannebaum, Friese, Wicks, and Lawson are safely in U.S. hands and en route to our military hospital in Germany for further treatment and to be reunited with their families.

"The rescue operation was carried out professionally, smoothly, efficiently, courageously, and without injury to any American. During the course of a firefight, all of the terrorists involved were killed.

"My deepest gratitude to our Special Operations Forces on the ground, our commanders in the field, and our intelligence, national security, defense, and military chiefs and their staffs, all of whom combined to ensure the success of this mission."

The president paused for a beat. Palmer had observed her under difficult conditions enough today to recognize that she wasn't simply pausing for effect. *You feel things so deeply. It's personal for you. That empathy is part of what will make you a great president. But mind your heart, Madam President. I fear what four or eight years in office will do to you.*

"Today, we lost three brave service members—the crew of the downed Black Hawk helicopter so brutally murdered in cold blood as the senators were being taken captive. These were patriotic Americans who will never come home to their families, never see their children grow up, never live to grow old. They died in service to their country, doing a job they loved. They died because there are extremists in this world who are so poisoned and consumed by hatred for the ideals we Americans hold dear—

freedom, democracy, peace, and diversity—that they would seek to destroy us.

"To those of you who would follow in their wake, know this. Each time you have sought to bring harm to our nation, our people, our allies, and/or our way of life, you have been defeated. It will ever be thus, for the principles we live by, the beliefs we adhere to, and all that we hold sacred, are grounded in love. Love for our country and all she stands for, love for our fellow human beings, and love for liberty and justice. Your hatred and hate-filled rhetoric and actions can never overcome our indomitable spirit and humanity. Our resolve is unshakeable, our cause is just, and our American heartbeat is strong.

"To the American people, I stand with you and keep always close to my heart those we lost on 9-11 in a senseless, cowardly attack on our shores. We will always remember that on that day, we came together as one nation, under God, indivisible, with liberty and justice for all. And so it is today, as it was then.

"Thank you. May God bless you, and may God bless the United States of America."

Excellent work today, Madam President. I hope someone tells you that. Briefly, Palmer recalled the scene on election night, with the president standing all alone on the stage absent any family. The thought saddened her.

The network cut away back to the anchor. "President Emma McMasters, announcing the successful rescue of four United States senators and sending a forceful message to terrorists that she will not hesitate to take action when challenged. Let me turn to our panel of experts…"

Palmer paused the newsfeed, exited her browser, and logged off for the night. She rose and stretched her back and shoulders in an effort to relieve the tightness. Her stomach growled, a stark reminder that she'd missed lunch amidst the organized chaos of the day.

She could do with a quick run on base, a nice dinner, and an early curfew, especially since her day had started in the middle of the night. Briefly, she wondered what was left on the president's agenda for the remainder of the evening. *I hope you get some well-earned rest tonight, Madam President. And may days like today be few and far between for you.*

Palmer snapped off the light and closed the door. *Here's to an easier tomorrow.*

&ঙ৯

Emma kicked off her shoes and stretched out on the sofa in her personal quarters aboard Air Force One. The adrenaline rush of the day was wearing off and exhaustion had set in. Although Nichelle, Miranda, and Trent had argued against it, she was determined to make this trip to Germany. She needed to see the senators for herself.

Olivia had pleaded with her to allow television cameras to accompany her into the hospital—the public relations opportunity would be invaluable. Emma had shut her down. This trip wasn't about scoring PR points or making a spectacle. These men had been through hell. She wanted them to know that she understood and empathized.

The media would be allowed no closer than the hospital parking lot, where Emma would update them on the condition of the senators once she'd seen them.

She'd also arranged for the bodies of the three flight crew members to be shipped back to the States with her on Air Force One tomorrow. She wanted to be present to greet the families at Joint Base Andrews when the caskets were unloaded.

She roused herself with great effort and headed for the sleeping quarters. Right now, what she really needed was some rest; they'd be landing in a few hours.

&ঙ৯

"Madam President!" As Emma entered the hospital room, Claire Friese jumped up from where she'd been sitting vigil by her husband's bedside. "We didn't expect... We didn't know you were coming." Tears pricked the woman's eyes.

Emma hugged her. "Sit, sit." She swallowed the lump in her throat. Bob Friese lay motionless in the bed. His face resembled raw meat and his left arm sported a cast. "How is he?" she semi-whispered.

"He's heavily sedated, thank God," Mrs. Friese answered. "Last time he woke up, he screamed bloody murder. He kept flailing around and cowering like someone was going to hurt him. No one could convince him he was safe. They had to s-sedate him to keep him from doing himself harm." Her composure slipped and Emma took her hand.

"It's going to take time, but hopefully the memories of what he's been through will fade along with the physical injuries. If there's anything I can do to help—"

"Anything you can do to help? You saved my husband's life! I still can't believe it. I-I know that Bob hasn't always been your biggest fan. He's said a lot of nasty things about you. I think about all that now, and I'm ashamed. I know he is too."

"She's right." Senator Friese's hoarse affirmation surprised both women.

"You're awake," his wife said.

"Barely." He cracked open one swollen eye. "I owe you a big apology, Madam President...about a lot of things. It took balls to make the call you did. And that you did it for an ass like me who's done nothing but run you down... Well, that takes a special kind of person."

"You're welcome, Senator. And you really should be resting."

"Thanks to you, I'm getting the best care in the world."

"I'm looking forward to seeing you back in Washington."

The senator fumbled for the bed controls and raised the head of the bed to a semi-reclined position. He glanced around the room. "You're alone?"

"The Secret Service is waiting outside."

He shook his head and sucked in a sharp breath. "Ouch. Remind me not to do that." He took a sip of water from the straw his wife held for him. "I didn't mean that. I meant, there's no press? No official photographer?"

Emma furrowed her brow. "Why would I invade your privacy like that? I came because I wanted to see for myself how you were doing."

Senator Friese began to shake his head again, and caught himself. "I don't understand you. This is probably the best PR you could get, and you take a pass. Remarkable. You do have a photographer with you, don't you?"

Emma chuckled. "It's a hazard of being president. They tend to insist everything I do is documented for posterity."

"Well, where is he?"

"She," Emma emphasized the pronoun, "is probably getting a cup of coffee in the cafeteria."

"Well, Madam President, could you get her in here?"

"What?"

"I thought I was the one whose ears got boxed. Get her in here. I want her to take a picture of you visiting and shaking hands with me."

Emma blinked. *What in the world?*

"Stop looking at me like I've lost my senses. I've been in politics a long time now. A picture is worth one thousand words. I'm going to make sure that picture is splashed everywhere, along with my words of gratitude for what you did."

"Why would you do that?"

"Good God. I'm giving you a gift. Take it. I was wrong about you, Madam President, and when I'm wrong, I say so. Not many presidents would've staked their standing in the first week on the job on a risky op that so easily could've gone sideways. But you did. Because you did, I'm here. Respectfully, that doesn't mean I'm not going to continue to kick your ass when it's deserved, but there's no one else I'd rather be in a foxhole with, and that's saying a lot coming from a grizzled old Vietnam veteran like me."

"Don't think you're going to hog all the limelight."

Emma wheeled around to see the other three senators parade into the room, all of them in wheelchairs pushed by their wives.

"Yeah, what Dan said," Senator Nate Wicks echoed. "We heard there was quite a commotion going on in here. We had to come see for ourselves."

"Now we can see that it's Friese once again trying to steal all the attention." Senator Ted Lawson's smile revealed a newly cracked tooth, no doubt courtesy of his captors.

Emma knew she was grinning like a fool, but she couldn't help it. Here they were, all four men, alive and playfully carping at each other.

"President McMasters," Senator Tannebaum paused to collect himself. "On behalf of all of us, and our wives and kids too, we can't thank you enough. Now the rest of the country and the world know what I've been saying about you for more than a year on the campaign trail—you're more than tough enough for this job, and you've got a heart to match that grit."

"Did I hear Bob ask to take a picture with you? Heck, there must be a contingent of press around here somewhere, right?" Senator Wicks asked.

"In the parking lot, whining that I wouldn't let them any closer," Emma said.

"Let's get them in here," Senator Lawson said.

Emma couldn't believe her ears. "You've all been through an ordeal—"

"That's true," Senator Tannebaum agreed. "But, because of you and the troops you sent, we're here to tell the story. America needs to understand the magnitude of that."

"Besides," Senator Friese joked, "Dan has never looked this good."

Fifteen minutes later, an impromptu press conference was set up in the hospital conference room. In addition to detailing their ordeal, each of the four senators praised Emma for ordering the strike that saved their lives.

Bob Friese especially went out of his way to emphasize that Emma hadn't brought any press inside with her, and in fact, even had barred her official photographer from taking pictures.

"The only reason you all are standing here grabbing footage and photos and quotes for your stories, is because we four insisted on it. So, you can thank us for overcoming the reluctance of a too-modest president." Friese tried to wink at Emma. "Well, I have to have something negative to say about you. Otherwise the press will think I got hit on the head once too hard."

Everyone in the room laughed.

An hour later, Emma took her leave. As she was getting ready to board Air Force One, she noticed three flag-draped coffins being loaded into the rear of the plane. She reversed course and headed for the honor guard and the transfer cases.

The head of the honor guard ordered his troops to halt. "Attention!"

"I'd like to pay my respects." Emma touched each transfer case as it was loaded into the cargo hold. *Rest well, and thank you for your service.*

She proceeded back to the steps and boarded the plane. She would wait until she was alone to process the grief she felt. Presidents, after all, grieved in private.

CHAPTER TEN

Palmer stuck her head into Max's office on her way to the bank of elevators. "Burning the midnight oil? I thought Nichelle was back from Germany and you two had a date tonight? Don't tell me the bloom's already off the rose."

"Very funny. No, I'm wrapping up the paperwork my boss so nicely dropped on my desk a while ago. Then, I'm making Nich a nice dinner at home."

"You're cooking?"

"Something wrong with that?"

"No. What're you making?"

"I'm making chicken cacciatore on a bed of wild rice, salad, homemade dinner rolls, and for dessert, my mama's recipe for blackberry pie."

"What time is dinner? I'm thinking that sounds a whole lot better than the leftover rotisserie chicken and spinach salad I've got planned."

"No can do. This is a dinner for two."

"Okay, love bird." Palmer smiled. "I hope she's impressed." Palmer had one foot out the door before she turned around. "I'm seriously thrilled for you if you've found your person, Max. She's a lucky girl."

"I'm a lucky guy. I wish you'd find your person. Nobody deserves love more than you."

Palmer sighed wistfully. "Yeah, well, I'm married to the job, so…"

"That's an excuse and you know it," Max countered.

"Goodnight, Max."

At the elevator bank, Palmer pressed the down button and waited. A pang of loneliness stabbed at her heart. She rotated her shoulders and shrugged, as if the motion would help her slough off the emotions. Still, an unshakeable sadness settled over her. Perhaps a good, long run would do the trick.

The elevator door opened, and absently, Palmer stepped inside.

"General Estes. Just the person I was hoping to find."

"Hmm?" Palmer glanced up. She hadn't seen Ted since the running incident. Quietly, she'd filled that running detail slot the next day with another of her staff members. She'd felt less exposed that way. Vaguely, she recalled that he'd put in for a promotion. The upgrade meant that he'd be rotated to the Middle East.

"Ma'am, my family is in town to see me off. They were desperate for a tour of this place before I shipped out, and I wanted them to meet my commanding officer."

The elevator doors closed.

"Are you going down, General? We'll go down with you. Also, I remembered that you were old friends with my aunt and—"

"Hello, Palmer. It's great to see you."

Belatedly, Palmer noticed the other two occupants in the elevator. Her eyes widened and her heart rate spiked. Even all these years later, she'd know that voice and that face anywhere. "H-hi, Britney. It's good to see you too."

"Hello, General Estes. I'm Ted's mother, Yolanda. Ted's told us so much about you, I feel as if I know you already."

"It's a pleasure to meet you, ma'am. You should be very proud of your son. He's a fine soldier, and an even better young man. I'm sorry to be losing him, but happy to send him on his way to bigger and better things." Palmer felt Britney's eyes on her; she barely controlled the impulse not to squirm.

"That's very kind of you to say. We sure think he's pretty special."

"Mom."

"Don't you 'Mom' her," Britney chided. "You're too old to be embarrassed by such things."

"On the contrary," Palmer offered, "I've found you're never too old for a good, old-fashioned blush." As soon as the words left her lips, Palmer wished she could reel them back in.

"Case in point," Britney said, as Palmer felt the heat suffuse her neck and cheeks. "I see some things never change. It always was easy to get a rise out of you."

Palmer felt a sudden urge to bolt. Had Britney meant the double-entendre? Thank God they'd reached the ground floor. She addressed Ted's mother, "Well, it was a pleasure to meet you. Good to see you again, Britney—"

"That's it?" Yolanda glanced from her sister to Palmer and back again. "I remember you guys used to be tight. Why don't you take a few hours to catch up? Brit, Ted can finish showing me around and we'll meet you back at the hotel."

"Um…" Britney's brow furrowed, which Palmer interpreted as discomfort with the idea.

"Really," Yolanda continued. "This may be your only chance for who-knows-how-long."

"Palmer might have other plans…"

Palmer wanted to hide under a rock. Britney gave her an apologetic shrug.

Palmer couldn't see any graceful way out of the situation. "N-no. Catching up would be great. My driver is out front. If you're hungry, we could grab a bite and I'll drop you off afterward."

"It's a plan." Yolanda gave Britney a shove. "Go on, you two."

"Do you—"

"How about—"

They both spoke at once. "You go first," Palmer said.

"This is your town. Anyplace you pick will be fine with me. And I'm sorry for my sister."

"No need to apologize. It's crazy not to catch up." Palmer considered and discarded several options. First and foremost, she wanted to go home and change into civvies. But that would mean inviting Britney into her home, which seemed way more intimate than she wanted this meeting to be. No, she would have her driver drop them off so that she could pick up her personal car and they would go directly to the restaurant without having to go inside.

"I hope this is all right," Palmer said. The restaurant was quiet, and because she knew the maître d', she'd been able to secure a booth toward the back, away from the noise of the crowd and the kitchen.

"It's great. Palmer, I'm sorry for throwing you a curveball. When Ted said he wanted us to meet his boss, I should've made an excuse and begged off. I'm sure I'm about the last person in the world you wanted to see." Britney looked miserable.

Palmer felt like a jerk. "Listen, Brit. I won't deny that seeing you makes me uncomfortable as heck—"

"I can go—"

Palmer put a hand on her arm and just as quickly removed it. "I wasn't finished yet. But now that we're here, I realize this is our chance to heal what happened. I've been carrying around this hole in my heart for far too many years. Maybe bumping into each other is a blessing in disguise."

Britney looked up at her from under long lashes. "Maybe so," she said softly.

The server appeared. "Would you like to order?"

"We haven't had a chance to look at the menu."

"I can come back."

"No. I'll have the salmon and a Diet Coke, please," Palmer said, cognizant that she still was in uniform.

"I'll take the sea bass, and a glass of chardonnay," Britney said as she handed him the menu.

When he was gone, Britney said, "As scared as I was for myself that day, my heart broke for you. Your father was awful. I've replayed that scene a billion times in my mind over the years, wishing that I'd had the guts to stand up to him like you did. You were fierce. If I'd stood up for you…"

"If you'd stood up for me, you'd have gotten hurt. I don't know what he would've done, Brit. I wasn't frightened for me. I'd seen his rages many times. But you…" Palmer blinked to hold back tears that seemed suddenly too close to the surface.

"I felt like I abandoned you," Britney said. "We didn't even get to say goodbye. I left you there without a home to go to, without my love and support. You lost your life that day, not to mention your dreams…"

"It wasn't your fault. We were kids without any power over our own lives. I was glad you were going to get a fresh start in Colorado. You were so talented, I only wanted you to reach for the stars and set the world on fire."

Britney fidgeted with the edge of the cloth napkin. "Honestly, for a long time, I was a mess. I blamed myself for what happened. I ruined your life."

"Look at me, Brit." Palmer waited until Britney reluctantly raised her head to make eye contact. "You did no such thing. The only bad actor in that scenario was my father, and trust me, losing him probably did me more good than either of us can fathom." *But losing my mom—that was a different story.*

Palmer rubbed the sore spot over her heart as a familiar stabbing pain in her chest left her temporarily breathless. She didn't want to talk about the hurt and anguish caused by being ripped away from her mother. There was no point to it. To Palmer's knowledge, her mother never had defied her father or tried to reach out to her.

The server set down their drinks and once more disappeared.

"Are you okay?" Britney asked.

"What?" Palmer dropped her hand to the table. "Oh, yes. I'm fine." The glare of the spotlight made her squirm. *Time to shift the conversation.* "Tell me about you. Why didn't I ever see you at any of the college track meets? Or in the Olympics?"

"Freshman year at Oklahoma I blew out my Achilles."

"Ouch."

"It took me a full year to get past that, and then the first meet back, I tore my ACL. So, I missed the '84 Olympics to rehab. By the time the '88 Olympics in Seoul rolled around, I'd lost too much off my acceleration to make the team."

"I'm sorry to hear that."

"Yeah, I spent the latter part of the '80s being totally pissed at the world," Britney said. "How about you? Why didn't I see you at the Olympics? I kept turning on my TV, expecting to catch a glimpse of you on the starting block."

"Thanks to Coach Tony, I got my credits transferred from home and finished high school while living in his basement. He helped me get into the University of Oregon, even though I wasn't on their radar for track."

"How could you not have been on their radar?" Britney asked.

Palmer smiled at her indignation over the slight. "They had a killer team and a limited number of scholarship slots. I walked on and made the team, but we had three top-five elite women on the squad besides me. No scholarship funds left over for me."

"That's just not right," Britney said.

"I appreciate your confidence in me, but I wasn't in the same class as those girls."

"The heck you weren't." Britney crossed her arms.

Warmth suffused Palmer's heart. *You always were my biggest fan. I guess some things don't change with time and distance.* "Anyway, the only path for me to be able to afford college was to go the Reserve Officers' Training Corps—ROTC—route."

Britney nodded and her posture relaxed slightly. "That's how you ended up in uniform."

"Right. I quickly realized that the most important thing I could do to survive in this world was to focus on a career."

Britney indicated the four stars on Palmer's shoulders. "Looks like you made the right choice."

"What about you? What've you been up to for the past..." Palmer calculated in her head. "...forty years?"

"Those who can't...teach. I became a teacher and girls' track coach."

"You followed in Coach Tony's footsteps."

"I did."

"Seems like he was a major figure in both of our lives."

"All the great educators are."

"I'm sure your students would say the same."

Britney ducked her head. "I don't know about that."

"Don't be modest. You've got the perfect temperament for coaching and I don't know anybody who had better technique and form."

Their meals arrived, and they spent several minutes eating in awkward silence. Palmer studied her plate. *You know it's coming.* So far, they'd managed to cover every subject except for their personal lives.

"Anybody special in your life?" Britney asked.

There it was. Palmer sucked in a deep breath. "No. The Army's my family."

"Sounds like an excuse, if you ask me." Britney smiled gently. It was a line she'd thrown at Palmer many times when they were young. "What's the real story?"

Britney always had been able to see through her. Palmer shrugged. Maybe it would be cathartic to say it out loud. Finally, she said, "I mourned you for a long time, Brit. It was so sudden—like a death, or a part of my soul being shredded."

"I mourned you too." Britney briefly laid a hand on top of Palmer's before withdrawing it.

Palmer continued, "When I finally stopped spiraling after that day, I was too scared to get involved with anyone. Coach Tony opened his home to me. I couldn't disappoint him."

"I get that."

"Then, when I joined the ROTC, I had to go so deep in the closet I couldn't have found my way out with both hands."

"And now? Surely that's not the case now?" Britney's eyes searched hers. They were filled with empathy and kindness.

Palmer stopped playing with the food on her plate and set down her fork. "No. But I spent so many years focusing on my career that it became easier to stay alone. I picked up and moved...a lot. War zones, political appointments, promotions... I convinced myself that I didn't have time or room in my life for a relationship."

"Sounds incredibly lonely."

You have no idea. "Sometimes."

"Why don't you do something about it?"

"I'm too old now."

"Pfft," Britney scoffed. "Fifty-six is not too old to find love. Heck, the best part of your life is still ahead of you."

"Enough about me. How about you?"

"Well, after that whole fiasco, I tried my hardest to convince myself that I didn't really like girls like *that*—it was just you I felt that way about."

"How'd that work out for you?"

Britney laughed. "Okay, for a while. Until a girl named Vanessa turned my head in chemistry class at Oklahoma. We had a thing for a while, but she wanted different things from life, so we split after graduation."

"I'm sorry."

"Don't be. I wasn't in love with her the way I was in love with you, Palmer. Even at sixteen, I meant what I said. If your father hadn't intervened, I think we would've spent our lives happily together."

Palmer swallowed the lump in her throat. "So, what happened after Vanessa?"

"Ah, something unexpected." Britney bit her lip and unconsciously twirled the ring on her finger. "I met Jason and figured out that I was bisexual."

"You got married."

Britney nodded slowly. "Yeah, we got married. We've got two grown kids."

Palmer smiled broadly. "Good for you, Brit."

"You're not disappointed?"

"Disappointed? Why would I be disappointed?"

"Because I married a guy."

"Are you kidding me? I'm thrilled that you found someone you wanted to spend your life with. Does he know that you're...?"

"Bi? Yeah. I was completely open and upfront with him right when we met. He was so chill about it. That's part of how I knew he was the right one."

"I'd love to meet him sometime."

"Seriously?"

"And the kids too."

"Okay, then. It can be arranged."

"Would you like coffee or dessert?" the served asked.

Palmer looked to Britney. "Nothing for me, thanks."

"Just a check, please," Palmer said.

"I'm glad we did this," Britney said, as they walked to Palmer's car.

"Me too," Palmer answered. She really meant it. It would take her some time to process her feelings, but she felt lighter, as if an unsettled question had been answered.

"By the way, I never said a word to Teddy about any of this," Britney said as Palmer drove. "It's your story to tell to those you choose to share it with, or not."

"I really appreciate that, Brit. In my position, I have to—"

"Be a role model?"

"Be discreet."

"Palmer Estes. Stop making excuses to distance. Just...stop. Do you have any idea how many LGBTQ+ military service members would benefit from knowing that the highest-ranking woman in the Army is one of them?"

Palmer stared at a spot over Britney's head. "I've announced that I'm retiring in October when my boss cycles out of the chairmanship of the Joint Chiefs. That's eight months from now."

"You're going to fritter away another three-quarters-of-a-year so you can remain hermetically sealed in the closet?"

"It's not like that." Palmer's cheeks flushed bright red.

"Really?"

"Really. It's not as if no one knows…"

"Who knows?"

They arrived at Britney's hotel and Palmer got out of the car and came around to say goodbye. *Why are you pressing me?* "My closest aide knows. He's been with me forever. Served with me in Desert Storm." Her tone sounded defensive, even to her own ears.

"Well, that's something." Britney finally relented and her tone softened. "Hey. I only want you to be happy. I know you say the Army's your family, and you're clearly doing well professionally. But there's so much more to life, and the Palmer I fell in love with was a risk-taker."

"You saw where that got me."

"Ouch. Okay, I'll give you that." They were quiet for a moment. "What are you going to do after you retire?"

"I don't know yet. My core fields are aviation and intelligence."

"And leadership, obviously."

Palmer nodded. "I do a lot of public speaking these days, and strategic planning."

"In other words, you can write your own ticket."

"I suppose."

"Palmer, promise me you'll open your life and your heart. Everyone needs love. You can't marry a career, especially one that's winding down. Your soul is too beautiful and you've got too much to offer to rot away by yourself somewhere when it's over. It's time for you to enjoy life. Unclench your fists and let go of that iron control. Life happens while you're busy trying to control it."

"When did you get to be so wise?"

"About half an hour ago," Britney replied, "when I realized my dear friend Palmer needed my sage advice."

"Uh-huh."

Britney's eyes bore into hers. "Don't waste your one wild, precious life, to paraphrase the poet Mary Oliver."

"Now you're quoting lesbian poets?"

"I'm a woman of many mysteries." Britney winked. "Come visit us when you retire."

"I'll do that."

"I hope so." Britney reached up and kissed Palmer on the cheek. "I'm so glad we had this time."

"Me too. It does my heart good to know that you're happy and living your best life, Brit."

"Now we have to make that true for you."

"You couldn't resist, could you?"

"You know I always had to have the last word."

Britney's laughter echoed in Palmer's ears as she waved goodbye.

For reasons she couldn't fathom, a line from *The Sound of Music* popped into Palmer's head. It was a line from the scene when the Reverend Mother kicks Maria out of the abbey to become the governess for the Von Trapp family.

When the Lord closes a door, somewhere He opens a window...

Obviously, her emotions were on overload. *If you start singing "Climb Every Mountain," I swear...* Palmer shook her head to clear it. It was time to go back to her life and leave the swirl of emotions behind her. Her head could fool herself into believing it was that simple, and surely her heart would follow and fall back into line.

CHAPTER ELEVEN

Emma wiped the sweat from her face with a fresh towel and headed for the shower. As had become her habit, she detoured through the Yellow Oval Room to take in the pre-dawn view of the South Lawn and the Washington Monument from the Truman Balcony. The majestic beauty of the nation's capital before the city awoke settled her spirit.

As her body cooled down, a chill winter breeze raised goose flesh on her bare arms and she shivered. *Probably not the brightest move to stand outside in your workout gear in early February.*

Thirty minutes later she was dressed and ready when her national security team showed up in the Old Family Dining Room for the daily morning briefing. She'd decided to offer them all a working breakfast as a nice change of pace.

When the group filed out a little less than an hour later, Nichelle lingered behind.

"Did I forget something?" Emma sat back and crossed one leg over the other.

"No." Nichelle kicked her toe at the carpet, a gesture Emma recognized from years of shared experiences.

"You're uncharacteristically nervous. What's going on?"

Nichelle folded her arms and bit her lip.

"Come on. Out with it, whatever *it* is."

"I'm deciding whether bringing something to your attention constitutes a conflict of interest."

Emma raised an eyebrow. "I see. Well, that's hard for me to judge without knowing what it is. Do we need to play twenty questions to figure it out without you giving anything away?"

"What?"

"For instance, does this thing have to do with a person?"

"Yes."

"Does it involve a personal favor?"

Nichelle squinted in thought. "Yes, and no."

"Aha. Does this thing have anything to do with tall, dark, and looks good in a uniform?"

That startled a laugh out of Nichelle. "Maybe…tangentially."

"I see." Emma considered. "Does this thing personally benefit you or Max in any way?"

"No. Unless you count righting an egregious wrong for someone he truly cares about as personally benefiting him, and thus, indirectly, me."

"Hmm. Four questions in, I'm feeling pretty good about this. I think we're safe to discuss and if I change my mind when I hear what it is, I'll shut you down. Fair enough?"

"Fair enough," Nichelle agreed. She lowered herself to the chair opposite Emma. "Max made me dinner last night—"

"Oh. Sounds like things are getting serious," Emma teased.

"Are you going to let me talk?"

"Okay, okay. By the way, I approve. I really like this guy."

"Please. You don't even know this guy."

"I'm a great judge of character. Everyone says so."

"Who's everyone?"

"Not you, apparently." Emma laughed. "Continue."

"After a while, the conversation turned to Palmer…General Estes."

"I know who she is. I already told you, she's not your competition, and not simply because she's his commanding officer."

"Are you going to let me finish? That's not at all where this conversation is headed."

Emma made a motion as if to zip her lips.

"After watching Palmer in action during the hostage crisis, I understood why Max admires her so much. And I got curious about her. You know, who is she really? How did she get to be the highest-ranking woman in the Army?"

Emma caught herself before admitting out loud that she'd been wondering the very same things.

"It took a whole lot of poking and prodding… Lord, that man knows how to keep a confidence." Nichelle shook her head. "I finally got him to tell me the story of how they met."

"How did they meet?" Emma's curiosity got the best of her.

"Palmer was a captain and Max's platoon leader in Desert Storm. They were both assigned to the 101st Airborne. Max says she was the best pilot he ever flew with."

Palmer was a flyer? Emma filed that away for further examination.

"On a mission in Kuwait, they were in a Black Hawk offering aerial cover for some ground troops who had come under enemy fire. They were out there alone and came under heavy fire from some surface-to-air missiles and artillery. Palmer was the pilot. Max was the gunner. Everyone on the flight crew wanted to turn back, but Palmer wouldn't do it. She wouldn't leave those troops uncovered."

"Apparently, she took a bullet in the leg through the fuselage and still refused to give up. She maneuvered the helicopter into position so that Max could take out a missile launching site. Then, she stuck around to make sure the threat truly was neutralized before she finally pointed them back to base."

"Wow. That's heroic." Emma meant it.

"You bet it is. She earned the Purple Heart for being wounded in combat, of course, but Max insists that her actions that day qualified her for the Silver Star. The company commander said so himself. He filled out the paperwork and sent it on up the chain of command. But nothing ever happened. Max thinks the paperwork must've gotten lost someplace between Kuwait and Fort Bragg in the chaos of the war."

"Let me guess. Is this where I come in?" Emma asked.

Nichelle regarded her sheepishly. "By everything Max said, Palmer really deserved that award, Madam President. The Silver Star—"

"Is the third-highest award exclusively for combat valor," Emma finished for her.

"Yeah. How did you know that?"

Emma tapped her head. "I've been doing my homework, and you might recall, my powers of retention are quite good."

"So they are. Anyway, only six women have ever been awarded the Silver Star, and four of those were nurses in World War II."

"You want me to award the Silver Star to General Estes? That's the favor?" Emma asked.

"N-no. I only wanted to ask if you would review her files and then, and only if you think she's worthy, you could award her the Silver Star. I just want her to get the consideration she deserves."

Emma nodded. What Nichelle was asking was fair. It was a file review. She'd done plenty of those. If she didn't believe that Palmer's actions rose to the level of the Silver Star, she could simply let the issue go.

"Okay. I'll order the Pentagon to send me her file and all supporting materials."

"Oh, thank you. Thank you, Madam President." Nichelle jumped up from her chair and hugged Emma.

"Don't thank me yet. I haven't done anything."

Palmer hated days like this—the anguished cries of loved ones, the mournful sound of taps as played by the Army bugler, and the three-volley salute to the fallen heroes. It was her solemn duty to honor the dead and their families and something she took very seriously. But no matter how many times she bore witness, it never got any easier. In this instance, the deceased were the airmen that had been killed in the terrorist attack while on escort duty for the senators.

She took her seat in the Memorial Chapel next to Chairman Dutton and Secretary of the Army Mack Carsen. She leaned forward and caught a glimpse of the four formerly captive U.S. senators seated across the aisle in the second row. They still looked pretty banged up, and Senator Friese's left arm remained immobilized in a cast and a sling.

Palmer had seen the news footage last night of the four deplaning at Joint Base Andrews, where they were met personally by President McMasters. The coverage had included video from the Landstuhl press conference. The senators seemed in far better shape today than they had in the three-day-old footage.

Suddenly, the mourners were on their feet and those in uniforms came to a crisp position of attention. Palmer followed suit. She assumed the families of the three airmen were entering the chapel, and so she was taken aback when President McMasters strode down the aisle and took a seat in the front row. She wondered if her superiors were as surprised as she was at the appearance. Judging from the expressions on their faces, they hadn't been informed either.

A contingent of media took up positions in the back of the chapel, including still photographers, television cameras, and reporters. The Secret Service members stationed themselves discreetly against the walls at various points around the chapel.

Every eye in the place was on the president. Palmer glanced surreptitiously at the president's profile. If she was aware that everyone was watching her, she seemed unfazed by it. Palmer tried to imagine what it would be like to live in a fishbowl where her every movement and expression were so scrutinized. *No wonder every president that comes into office with a full head of youthful hair leaves gray-headed.*

Palmer fantasized about what Emma McMasters would look like when her gorgeous inky black mane turned gray. At the moment, there were but a few stray silver locks that glinted in the right light. *You'd be even more attractive, more distinguished looking.*

As if sensing Palmer's gaze, the president shifted and made direct eye contact with her. Heat bubbled up from the pit of Palmer's stomach and she willed herself not to fidget. Then, Emma smiled at her and nodded. Or had she imagined it?

Palmer tore her attention away from the president as the families of the deceased filed in and took their places.

The president hugged each of the parents and wives. Then she knelt so that she was eye-level with two small children who clung to the hands of their mother. She said something to each of them, hugged them tightly, and kissed them on the cheek.

Palmer had never been prouder of any commander in chief than she was right now. When the president stood, Palmer could see that she had tears in her eyes. It tugged at her heart.

That whole thing with Britney has you on emotional overload. That's all it is.

The president delivered the eulogy, a stirring tribute to the lost soldiers, in soaring rhetoric that was at once personal and universal to all who serve and sacrifice.

As she descended from the altar, Chairman Dutton leaned over and whispered in Palmer's ear. "She's something else, isn't she?"

"Yes, sir, she really is. I'm always proud to serve, but a little more so today, I think."

"Me too, General. Me too."

❧❧

Emma ensconced herself at the Treaty Table, the magnificent Victorian desk first used as a cabinet table by Ulysses S. Grant in 1869. These days, Emma tended to use the Treaty Room as her study late at night, when sleep eluded her. The quiet of the space allowed her to focus on the work items she hadn't gotten off her plate earlier.

She clicked on the desk lamp and opened the thick file jacket she'd brought to the residence from the Oval Office. The name, neatly typed on the tab, read: Estes, Palmer L. – General. In addition to Palmer's Officer Evaluation Reports, Emma had requested that the Pentagon send over her military record, her personal biography, mission reports, and all materials relevant to any awards and/or commendations she'd received.

Emma knew she'd cast a wide net—perhaps unnecessarily so— but she was considering Palmer for an extraordinary honor. She wanted to be sure she had all the facts. *That's a rationalization, and you know it. The truth is, you're intrigued and you want to know more.* There. That wasn't so hard to admit, was it?

Emma skimmed the Officer Evaluation Reports. In every instance, at every level, Palmer Estes achieved outstanding marks from her superiors. Raters gave her their highest marks for character, presence, intellect, ability to lead and get results, and develop herself and those around her.

A natural-born leader; embodies the Army Values in all that she does. Palmer leads by example and lifts others around her, builds trust, and extends influence outside the chain of command. Excellent communicator. Confidence and resilience in expected duties and unexpected situations. Excellent problem-solving and decision-making skills. Excels at critical thinking, engaging others, presenting information and recommendations, and persuasion. Uses all influence techniques to empower others; proactive in gaining trust in negotiations.

"Seems you are universally beloved and respected, Palmer Estes." Emma flipped through until she found Palmer's bio.

Military Schools Attended: Officer Advanced Course, Intelligence Advanced School, United States Command and General Staff College (Master of Science in Aviation Intelligence), United States Army Command and General Staff College, United States Army War College (Strategic Planning). Other Educational Degrees: University of Oregon (Bachelor of Science in Engineering), Princeton University's Woodrow Wilson School of Public and International Affairs (Ph.D. in International Relations).

Emma raised an eyebrow. *Wow. Next to you, I feel practically underqualified.* She scanned farther down the page to view the section on promotions and major duty assignments.

1986: 2nd Lieutenant assigned to the 101st Airborne; 1987: 1st Lieutenant Pilot & Platoon Leader..." Emma continued to scan down the long list. *"Air Assault Commander in Desert Shield/Desert Storm; Aviation Intel Officer... Executive Assistant for Aviation and Intelligence Warfare to the Chairman of the Joint Chiefs; Chief of Staff, Fort Bragg; Corps Executive Officer (Brigadier General) in Kuwait; Deputy Commander, CENTCOM; Deputy Commander (Major General) Baghdad; Office of the Secretary of Defense/Joint Forces (Intelligence for all Services); Multi-National Security Transition (Lieutenant General) in command of all military in Iraq... Director of Intelligence (General) for all services; Commanding General, Forces Command (Director of All Services for the Middle East); and current assignment, Chairman of the Joint Chiefs of Staff Advisor to the White House.*

Emma whistled. "That's quite a career, General Estes." Her eyes alit on the last section of the bio: US Decorations and Badges. *Combat Action Badge, Senior Army Aviator Badge, Air Assault Badge, Basic Parachutist Badge, Army Staff Identification Badge, 101st Airborne Division Combat Service Identification Badge, 101st Aviation Regiment Distinctive Unit Insignia, Six Overseas Service Bars, Defense Superior Service Medal with one bronze oak leaf cluster, Legion of Merit with three oak leaf clusters, Bronze Star Service Medal, Joint Service Commendation Medal, Air Medal with bronze award numeral seven, Army Achievement Medal with two oak leaf clusters, Meritorious Unit Commendation with two oak leaf clusters, Superior Unit Award with oak leaf cluster, National Defense Service Medal, Afghanistan Campaign Medal with service star, Global War on Terrorism Expeditionary Medal, Global War on Terrorism Service Medal, Humanitarian Service Medal, Army Service Ribbon, Army Overseas Service Ribbon with award numeral three, and Purple Heart (2).*

"Purple Heart times two?" Had Nichelle said something about a second instance where Palmer was wounded in battle and she'd missed it? Emma rifled through the documents.

Dread crept in and settled in the pit of her stomach. She didn't want to examine the emotion too closely. *It's a natural reaction to finding out that someone was harmed in action. The fact that it's someone you've met merely heightens that reaction.*

Finally, she found the report she sought.

On September 11, 2001, Colonel Palmer Estes was serving as the top assistant to the Chairman of the Joint Chiefs of Staff for aviation and intelligence. Her office was located on the fifth floor of the Pentagon Building. Emma's heart skipped a beat. Palmer was in the Pentagon when the plane hit?

At the time the plane struck the Pentagon between the Army and Navy wings of the building, Colonel Estes was traversing a passageway located in proximity to the point of impact. She was thrown into a wall and suffered a dislocated shoulder and a severe blow to the head. Despite bleeding from a head wound and her displaced shoulder, Colonel Estes made her way up to the fifth floor, where she helped to evacuate the civilian leadership and removed them to a secure room in the basement of the Pentagon.

Once she had ensured the safety of the civilian leaders, Colonel Estes waded back through the smoke, water, and debris to ensure that all of her staff had safely evacuated. Only then did she continue outside, where she took charge and ordered the creation of a berm for defense purposes.

For her heroic deeds and for being wounded as a result of an enemy action, Colonel Estes was awarded the Purple Heart Medal.

Emma sat back heavily. She'd once dislocated her shoulder too, and it had been the most painful injury she'd ever sustained. She envisioned Palmer fighting her way through impossible conditions with a concussion and a dislocated shoulder to save others even as she must've been in agony. She easily could see Palmer shrugging off any sort of attention or adulation for her heroism. She didn't seem like the kind of person who would want attention called to herself.

How would you feel about receiving the Silver Star, General Estes?

As Emma returned the materials to the folder, she noticed a jump drive tucked into a pocket of the jacket sleeve. She pulled her laptop close and plugged in the drive. The icon for the drive populated on her home screen: Action Footage – Captain Palmer Estes, Desert Shield.

Emma opened the drive and clicked on the video file. The footage from the Black Hawk was grainy and crude, but clear enough. The chatter over comms between crew members inside the helicopter was distinct, as was the sight of incoming fire from enemy forces.

Emma unconsciously dodged and weaved along with the helicopter as it evaded the onslaught and fired back. She could see the troops on the ground also under attack.

"Taking fire! Captain! Three o'clock! Three o'clock! Multiple sources. We're taking too much heat. We need to get out of here. Captain Estes, do you read me? If we don't get out of here now, they're going to shoot us down. We don't have any backup."

Emma held her breath as the helicopter nosed downward and veered sharply to the left. Her heart hammered harder when she recognized Palmer's steady, determined voice.

"Negative. We're not going anywhere. Those troops need cover. Without us, they're sitting ducks. Sergeant Jeffers—Gunny—I need you to take out that missile launch site at four o'clock. I'm going to get you as close as I can. You ready?"

"Ready, Captain!"

He sounded younger, and scared, but Emma had no trouble picking out Max's deep tones.

"Here we go."

Emma clutched at her chest as Palmer swung the Black Hawk around and headed almost directly toward the location of the gunfire. Seconds later, Emma heard a loud, whistling sound, followed by a low growl. Another voice came over the comms.

"You're hit."

"I know." It was Palmer, her voice sounding somewhat muffled.

Emma lowered her head. Had she really just borne witness to Palmer being shot? She reached for the mouse to stop the video, not wanting to know what came next. But she had to know. She pulled her hand back.

"Abort," the unknown voice said.

"No," Palmer answered. "We're going to finish this." Her voice sounded sure, but weaker. "Jeffers? You've got one crack at this."

"I'll get that son-of-a-bitch for you, ma'am."

Emma's eyes opened wider as the Black Hawk dove steeply and to the right. A fusillade of bullets hailed down at the now-clearly-visible rocket-launcher's nest.

"Direct hit! Direct hit!"

A massive cloud of desert sand billowed up from below. Emma pumped a fist in triumph.

"I'll take one more pass to confirm that our guys are safe," Palmer said. The helicopter circled the area once more.

"Clear. All clear," the unidentified voice said.

"Let's take this bird home," Palmer answered.

"I've got it from here, ma'am." Emma realized that the unidentified voice must belong to the co-pilot. "You saved them. That was some damn fancy flying. Let's get you home, soldier."

The video ended and Emma unclenched her fists. She was breathing hard, as though she'd been on board with the crew. *Oh, Palmer. I'm so glad you survived that.*

Nichelle had said that the wound was to Palmer's leg. Did she have a limp? If so, Emma hadn't noticed. As for the Silver Star… Oh, yes. Emma would see to it that she'd receive the award she so richly deserved, and soon.

CHAPTER TWELVE

Palmer couldn't remember the last time she'd been this nervous. The president of the United States was about to present her with the Silver Star. *Surreal.* Fleetingly, she considered making a run for it, even as she knew she couldn't do that. Instead, she paced back and forth in the Green Room, where she'd been directed to wait by one of the president's aides. She could hear the murmurs of attendees traversing the Cross Hall as they headed toward the East Room.

"General Estes?"

Palmer whirled around at the sound of her name. "Yes?"

"President McMasters would like a moment with you before the ceremony. Would you please come with me?"

"Of course."

The aide led her through a doorway into the Blue Room. The president cut a solitary figure, standing in profile, outlined by the sun as it shone in through the massive window. She wore a stylishly flattering red dress that hugged every curve. Palmer glanced around the room, surprised to find that they were alone. Her pulse jumped and she swallowed hard. Where had the aide gone?

Pull yourself together, soldier. "Madam President." Palmer came to attention as the president turned to face her. Her smile was radiant, and the sunlight shone like a halo over her head.

"General Estes. At ease. If it's all right with you, since it's just the two of us here, I'd love to set aside the formalities."

"Of course, ma'am."

The president motioned for Palmer to join her at the window. "Sometimes, I wish I could run out there and bury my bare feet in the grass—although not in the middle of winter."

Her laugh was rich and deep and she smelled like sunshine on a spring day.

"You're the president of the United States. I'm pretty sure it says in the handbook you can do that. After all, it's your lawn."

The president turned fully to face her and Palmer's heart stuttered. At this distance, the green of her eyes was even more vivid and her smile more dazzling.

"Correction. It's the people's lawn. I'm just the caretaker who doesn't have to mow it."

"Valid point."

"Since we only have a few minutes, I'll be brief. We haven't spent much time together, General, but I get the strong sense you're not the kind of person who enjoys being the object of fanfare."

"That's an understatement."

"Right. So, first, thank you for allowing me to put together this well-earned, long-overdue moment of recognition."

"When the president calls, I answer. That's in the military handbook."

"Touché." There was that smile again. "In any event, if it helps you to feel more comfortable, please try to view this award as a victory for all female military personnel. Honestly, that you were overlooked thirty years ago is a travesty."

"With all due respect, ma'am, I simply was doing my job, and I know how things are in wartime. It's entirely possible that the paperwork really was lost in transition."

"Perhaps so; all the same, I'm happy to be in a position to correct an egregious wrong."

The aide knocked and leaned her head in. "Madam President? Everyone's seated."

"Thank you. We'll be right there." When the aide closed the door, the president said, "One more thing before we go in there. I would appreciate it very much if you would be one of my guests for the State of the Union address on Tuesday."

Palmer wasn't sure she'd heard her correctly.

"I promise not to make too much of a spectacle of you." The president's eyes twinkled with mischief. "Please?"

"Of c-course, Madam President. It would be an honor. I didn't mean to suggest otherwise—"

"You're fine, General. Although you did have a bit of that deer-in-the-headlights look." The president hesitated, then added, "Of course, you are welcome to bring a guest—a spouse or partner, your mother or dad—to the pre-State of the Union reception. They are welcome to stay and watch the event in the White House theater along with other guests' loved ones..."

Palmer glanced away. The invitation hung in the air between them. How much did the president know about her personal situation? The president was someone who chose her words carefully. She hadn't said *husband or boyfriend*. No, she'd said *spouse or partner*. Palmer tucked that away for later examination. "Thank you. That's very generous of you, Madam President, but I'll be attending alone."

The president paused as if processing that piece of information. Finally, she glanced at the door and sighed. "We'd better go. The natives are probably getting restless in there."

They reached the entrance to the East Room and the president put a hand on Palmer's arm. "Not yet. We need to wait for the rest of our party."

A moment later, they were joined by Chairman Dutton, Secretary of the Army Carsen, and former Chairman of the Joint Chiefs during Desert Storm and former Secretary of State Colin Powell. All three men greeted Palmer warmly.

A White House aide instructed in hushed tones, "General Estes, you'll enter first, followed by Secretary Powell, Secretary Carsen, Secretary Dutton, and finally President McMasters."

All nodded their understanding.

Secretary Powell leaned over and whispered to Palmer, "I'm sorry this took so long. I wish I'd known about it at the time."

"I'm honored that you're here, sir."

"When President McMasters called and made me aware of the oversight, I was grateful for the opportunity to be present and participate."

"Good afternoon ladies and gentlemen," the master of ceremonies began. "On behalf of President Emma McMasters, Chairman of the Joint Chiefs of Staff Charles Dutton, Secretary of the Army Mack Carsen, and former Chairman of the Joint Chiefs of

Staff and former Secretary of State Colin Powell, it's my pleasure to welcome you to this special Silver Star Award Ceremony. Today, we gather to honor the heroic deeds of then-Captain Palmer Estes. Her courageous actions on February 24, 1991, saved many lives.

"The president would like to extend a very special welcome to former Battalion Commander Lucius Wright, former Warrant Officer Anselm Oakes, and then-Sergeant Maxwell Jeffers. Ladies and gentlemen, I ask that you please rise for the arrival of the official party."

"That's our cue," the president said.

✎✎

Secretary Powell recited the events of the action for which Palmer was being recognized. As he did so, Emma focused on the faces of Palmer's fellow service members. It warmed her heart to see the admiration and affection for Palmer in their expressions. These were the men who crewed that fateful flight with her—who faced enemy fire with her—and their genuine excitement for her on this day spoke to the kind of soldier and person Palmer Estes was.

Out of the corner of her eye, Emma snuck a peek at Palmer. She stood stiffly and without expression to Emma's left. Emma could feel Palmer's body vibrating next to her, signaling either her nervousness or her discomfort at the glare of the spotlight. Her humility only reaffirmed for Emma the importance of personally bestowing the honor upon her.

Secretary Powell said, "By her bold initiative, undaunted courage, and complete dedication to duty, then-Captain Palmer Estes reflected great credit upon herself and upheld the highest traditions of the United States Army. President McMasters, would you please do the honors?"

Emma turned to Palmer and smiled. Under her breath so that only Palmer could hear her she murmured, "Please act as though I'm not torturing you here." Out loud she said, "As Commander in Chief, I am exceedingly proud to know that our military has someone like you on our side. Congratulations, General. Well deserved."

"Thank you, Madam President. It's been an honor, and it's a privilege to serve under your command."

Carefully, Emma pinned the medal to Palmer's left chest. Then she shook Palmer's hand, gave her the certificate that accompanied the award, and posed for pictures with her.

The master of ceremonies invited Max to the podium to say a few words. He nodded to Palmer and winked before stepping to the microphone.

"I'm not a man of many superlatives, as anyone who knows me can tell you. And I want to start by saying that the fact that General Estes is my boss has nothing to do with what I'm going to say next." He said it teasingly and the audience laughed in response.

"I have never been so proud to serve alongside someone in all my years in the military. It was true on that fateful day, and it remains true today." Max's voice cracked and he paused to gather his composure.

"What General Estes did that day—the way she performed with such valor and courage—I don't honestly know anyone else who could've done what she did. She had nerves of steel, and she's the best darn pilot I've ever flown with. Even after she got hit, and with us continuing to draw fire, she managed to bring that bird around and get me into position to take out that nest. Anybody else would've turned back, but she wouldn't do it. She refused to leave those ground troops unprotected. I've never seen anything like it before or since. If you ask me, and no one did, this award is long overdue, and I'm so happy for her that this day of recognition is finally here." He turned to face Palmer. "Congratulations, ma'am. Well done. I'm honored to serve with you." He snapped off a smart salute, and Palmer drew him into a warm hug.

Emma could see that both of them had tears in their eyes.

Warrant Officer Oakes, Palmer's co-pilot that day and her battalion chief spoke next, each extolling Palmer's virtues. Then, it was Emma's turn.

"Being president of the United States involves making difficult choices all the time. The decision to award General Estes the Silver Star for her courageous and exemplary actions on the battlefield thirty years ago was a no-brainer. As I listen to her fellow service members speak about her with such admiration and affection, I am reminded that great leaders, even in their nascency, lead by example. General Palmer Estes—then Captain Palmer Estes—has been leading by example throughout her storied and historic military career. It is an honor and a privilege to present her this long-overdue honor today. General Estes, would you please say a few words?"

As they passed, Palmer smiled at her shyly, a blush creeping up her neck to stain her cheeks red. She adjusted the microphone higher. "Thank you, Madam President, Secretary Powell, Max, Oak, and Commander Wright. I'm not sure I'm worthy of such beautiful words, but I'll try to live up to them every day, in all that I do. Chairman Dutton, Secretary Carsen, I'm honored by your presence.

"From the time I was a young girl, I was fascinated by flying. When I wasn't busy running track, I was up in the air, soaking in the flying lessons I started taking in college. Choosing aviation in the Army was akin to choosing breath. I couldn't imagine anything I wanted to do more than serve my country and fly at the same time.

"To fly with the team I had onboard that day..." Palmer gripped the podium tighter and dropped her chin to her chest to collect herself. When she raised her eyes to the audience again, moisture glistened her eyelashes. "I had the best with me; your valor under tremendous pressure is something I carry with me every day. I'd fly with you any day of the week. It was an honor to serve with you and to successfully fulfill our mission. Hooah."

"Hooah!" came the resounding reply.

Palmer checked herself in the full-length mirror on the back of the closet door. She ran her fingers through her hair and fussed with the sleeves of her Army Service Uniform. She told herself this wasn't about vanity. After all, she'd already met the president multiple times. No, tonight, before a nationally televised audience, she would be representing the United States Army. If she happened to make a good impression on President McMasters in the process, well, that was a bonus.

Palmer checked the time. Her driver would be here soon to pick her up for the short drive to the White House for the pre-State of the Union reception and dinner with the president.

Dinner with the president. That invitation, which had arrived two days ago along with the official, autographed picture of her with the president at the Silver Star ceremony, had come as a complete surprise. Palmer had read the handwritten note from the president so many times she had it memorized.

Dear General Estes,

I'm not sure if you're aware, but the normal presidential tradition prior to delivering the State of the Union is for the president to share a quiet dinner with family before heading to the Capitol.

It seems awkward and somewhat depressing to dine alone on such an auspicious occasion as the delivery of my first State of the Union address, and I was wondering if I might impose on you, since you'll be coming to the reception and the address anyway, to join me in the residence for the traditional (now non-traditional) pre-State of the Union meal?

If you are available, please call the number on the enclosed business card and the White House Social Secretary will take care of all the details.

Congratulations again on your well-deserved award. I hope you enjoy the enclosed memento of the occasion.

All the best,

Emma McMasters

Palmer shook her head in amazement. The president hadn't used her title, nor commanded that she appear—she'd extended an invitation without pretention. *...if I might impose on you...* "As if," Palmer mumbled out loud. She grabbed her overcoat and headed for the door.

Emma rubbed her eyes.

"If you hadn't stayed up until two o'clock in the morning working on the speech, you wouldn't be exhausted now," Nichelle admonished.

"If I hadn't stayed up until two o'clock in the morning making adjustments to the text, I'd be one unhappy president right now," Emma countered.

David burst into the Roosevelt Room where Emma had been rehearsing the State of the Union. He was out of breath and his hair stuck straight out at odd angles. "I've got the changes you asked for.

I think you're particularly going to enjoy the turn of phrase when you pivot to talking about the need for bipartisan cooperation."

"I'm sure I will." Emma accepted the fresh version of the speech from him and scrolled through until she located the section she'd revamped in the middle of the night. "It's good. Very good. Thank you, David."

"So, that's it, right? The final version?" He resembled a little boy handing in a homework assignment on which he hoped to score a top grade.

She couldn't resist playing with him just a little. "Until I decide to change it again," she said. The look on his face was priceless; she thought he might collapse on the spot, and so she took pity on him. "Yes, that's it. I can't promise that I won't ad lib a line or two, though. After all, I've got to do something to keep you on your toes."

He groaned audibly.

"Great work to you and your team, David. I really appreciate it."

"Madam President," Nichelle said. "The reception has been underway for a while. They're expecting you to greet the guests."

"Right. On my way." On the walk, Emma reviewed the list of special guests and their plus ones. Each guest represented a priority in Emma's speech, or an achievement she wished to highlight.

Normally, the pre-State of the Union reception was hosted by the first lady. In this unprecedented moment, Emma had settled on having the event hosted by the vice president and his wife, with a special surprise appearance by the president.

When she arrived, the event was in full swing. Vice President Elder and his wife chatted amiably with Caleb Rick, the CEO of EcoGlobal, a forward-thinking company that was converting single-use plastics like shopping bags and diverted landfill material into reusable, recyclable, multi-purpose heavy-duty mats with multiple applications called Ekomats.

Elsewhere, guests were engaging one another in conversations, trading stories, and enjoying the food.

"We should announce your arrival," her social secretary suggested as Emma stood on the threshold.

"No. I'd rather keep it low-key and make my way around the room."

"You don't have long. The group is scheduled to leave for the Capitol via caravan at 7:30 p.m."

"I'm only planning to stay fifteen minutes or so."

"Don't forget, you have dinner with General Estes at 7:15 p.m."

"I haven't forgotten." Emma spied Palmer standing near the fireplace in deep discussion with Dalilah Muhammad, Team USA track star and 2016 Olympic gold medalist in the 400-meter hurdles. Although she wanted to start there, Emma detoured in the opposite direction. She'd have her opportunity to get to know Palmer better soon enough. For now, she should focus on the rest of her guests.

CHAPTER THIRTEEN

P almer scrutinized a picture of a jubilant young girl in a Speedo. She held aloft a trophy. *Look at you, Emma McMasters, swimming champion.* A second framed photo featured Emma giving the valedictory address at her law school graduation. She looked so earnest. *What was your message to the class, Madam President? What words of wisdom did you share? And what would you tell them now?*

"Oh, my God. Don't look at those. I call those the awkward years. Of course, they've pretty much all been awkward years."

Palmer faced the president and out of habit, came to attention.

"At ease. Please, this is an informal, private social occasion. I hope you won't feel the need to stand on ceremony, if only for the hour we have. Let's throw caution to the wind and toss protocol out the window. Just a couple of friends sharing a meal. Unless you feel uncomfortable with that..."

"Not at all."

"Excellent." The president held out her hand. "Hi, I'm Emma. Nice to meet you in a not-official-capacity." There was that smile again, this time more relaxed.

Palmer took the proffered hand and shook it warmly. "Hi. I'm Palmer. It's a pleasure to make your acquaintance."

"I'd give you the full tour, but unfortunately, my staff tells me I'm on a schedule tonight. Something about an address to Congress, I think."

"Huh. I believe I heard something about that."

Emma led the way down the Center Hall and into the Old Family Dining Room. "I hope the meal will be to your liking."

"I'm sure it will be far better than the leftover spinach salad in my refrigerator."

Emma raised an eyebrow. "I don't know. That's a pretty high bar you set."

If the president was the least bit nervous about her upcoming speech, it didn't show. Palmer wanted to tell her so but was loathe to break the easy casualness of the banter.

The wait staff served the first course, a cold cucumber soup, and disappeared.

"Thank you for accepting my invitation, Palmer. I'm not someone who has a lot of close friends... Okay, I don't really have any."

Palmer liked the way her first name sounded coming from Emma's lips. "I'm honored that you asked."

"I hate that it's tricky business, and I want to acknowledge the elephant in the room up front. I'm your commander in chief. I can't change that. But in you I sense a kindred spirit and someone I think would make an excellent friend. I sure could use one of those."

Warmth suffused Palmer's insides. "I'd like that." *I'd like that very much, in fact.*

"If you feel the least bit uncomfortable or if you feel it's inappropriate, I understand perfectly. If you'd prefer if others were present, I'll make that happen."

"That's completely unnecessary, Emma. I trust you with my life, and I know you to be a person of great integrity. I'm a lot like you— a loner who's built impenetrable walls, even as I occasionally long to let someone in. Also like you, my position often makes it difficult not to blur lines. My aide, Max, whom you've met, is the closest thing I have to family. And yet, he's in my direct chain of command. We always manage to maintain those dualities, but it isn't easy."

Emma gazed thoughtfully over Palmer's head. "That's exactly right."

They finished the soup and the wait staff appeared again to replace the first course with a small beet salad with goat cheese and fresh, hot cornbread.

"Oh, my God. This is fabulous." Palmer closed her eyes and savored a bite of the cornbread.

"I know, right? Horrible for my waistline, but it tastes so good."

"You don't need to worry about your figure…" The words were out before Palmer could take them back. The blush began at her chest and ran all the way up her neck to her ears and cheeks.

Emma threw her head back and laughed heartily. "I wish you could see your face."

"And this is why I can't go out in public," Palmer mumbled unhappily.

"I'm not making fun of you. I think it's endearing that a highly decorated military officer, who would rush into enemy fire without hesitation, gets tangled up over words."

"Trust me, facing enemy fire is easier than a one-on-one conversation or having attention called to myself."

"Nonsense," Emma said, as she tucked into the salad. "You just need more practice."

"Can we change the subject now?"

"Of course."

"I see you were a swimmer. Nice trophy, by the way."

"I was and am a swimmer, although these days it seems all I can manage is a quick pre-dawn workout in the gym upstairs."

"Did you swim collegiately?"

"I did. 200-meter fly was my specialty." She took another bite of the salad. "You must've been a runner with those long legs."

"I was. University of Oregon track team. I fell just short of qualifying for the Olympics in the 400-meter hurdles. Then I graduated college under the ROTC plan, and the rest, as they say, is history."

A shadow passed across Emma's face. "The Desert Storm incident. You were shot in the leg. Did that… Could you…"

Palmer read the concern in her eyes. "I still run every day. I'm not going to break any land speed records, and the hurdles are out, but a good, albeit painful, run soothes my nerves and gets my day off to a great start."

"It's an endorphin thing," Emma said.

"Agreed. It's also a great way to conduct meetings and get in a workout at the same time."

"Ah. The advantage of being in a military environment where everyone keeps in shape. If I did that with my people, they'd all pass out in the first fifty yards."

The wait staff delivered the main course—sea bass with a roasted red pepper and broccoli purée.

"You'd better be careful. Keep feeding me like this and I'll be back nightly at dinnertime." The sea bass was amazing, as each course had been. "My compliments to the chef."

"I'll be sure to pass that along." Emma swallowed a few bites and pushed the plate away. "I don't want to overeat and be sorry about ninety minutes from now."

"Tell the truth, you're just saving room for dessert," Palmer countered.

"That too."

"So, what's for dessert?"

Emma shook her head. "It'll be a surprise to both of us." Emma fiddled with her fork. "Speaking of surprises, you do know that your Max is dating my Nichelle."

"I do." Palmer leaned forward. "What do you think of it?"

"I love it. Max seems like a true gentleman and a real catch. In all the years I've known her, I've never seen Nichelle this hung up on a guy."

"I can say the same for Max. He's got it bad. And I'd be happy to vouch for his character. He's a class act all the way. One of the nicest, most thoughtful men you'd ever want to meet."

"Well, he's getting quite a catch, himself. Nich is as honest as they come, with a heart of gold. She's a workaholic, and this job isn't helping to cure her of that…"

"They're made for each other. Max has an incredible work ethic. He'll get promoted one of these days soon, maybe before I retire."

"You're retiring?" Emma's voice rose almost to a squeak.

"That shocks you?"

"I don't know. You're so young."

Palmer laughed. "It's the red hair and freckles. Fools them every time. I'm fifty-six. I've been at this for thirty-five years."

Emma still looked shell-shocked.

"Chairman Dutton cycles off in October. That seemed like a natural point to call it a career."

"What will you do next? You're way too young and talented and I can't imagine you sitting around on your rear end eating bonbons."

"Tempting. I don't know," Palmer answered, and she meant it. "I haven't gotten that far yet, nor have I made an official announcement of any kind. It's been an ongoing internal monologue."

"Maybe you'll change your mind by then."

"I don't think so. It's funny. I've never known anything else in my adult life. But I'm not afraid. I've been frugal and saved well. I can afford it financially, even if I never wanted to take another paying job. I'll have to move, of course."

"Move? Why?" Emma's fork slipped and clattered to the plate.

"I can't stay in base housing once I retire."

"Ah. Of course not. But you'll stay in D.C., right?"

Palmer cocked her head to the side. "Does it matter?"

They were silent for a moment as dessert was served.

"Oh, my God. Chocolate mousse pie? You obviously don't eat like this every night or you couldn't look the way you do…" Again, Palmer blushed crimson.

"No. If it's a normal night, I might have time for a quick salad or four ounces of protein and a vegetable. I think the chef secretly wishes she'd taken another gig. I'm no fun at all to cook for."

"Are there any? Normal nights, I mean?"

"A few. Not as many as I'd like, to be sure." Emma pushed the pie around the plate. "If you didn't stay in D.C., where would you go? Where's home? Do you have aging parents somewhere you have to take care of?"

"What? No." Palmer said it too quickly and looked away. She jerked when a warm hand touched hers and then withdrew.

"I'm sorry. Obviously, I touched a nerve. I shouldn't have asked something so personal."

You're an idiot, Palmer. Now she feels badly. What had Britney said? It was time to take down some of the walls around her heart. If she really wanted to get to know Emma better and be friends, she'd have to start by cracking open the door and letting her in.

Palmer bit her lip. Surely, she could trust Emma to hold her confidence. "The truth is, my parents disowned me when I was a teenager."

"They did what?" Emma growled.

"They sent me away for the summer to train with a world-renowned track coach. He was working with some of the most gifted young athletes in the United States. A few weeks later, they surprised me with a visit. I was just figuring out my sexuality, and Britney and I... Let's say if I'd known my folks were going to show up at that moment, I would've made sure I was alone."

"Oh, Palmer. I'm so sorry."

Palmer let out the breath she held as relief flooded through her. Where she'd anticipated judgment, she found compassion. "Yeah, well... I never saw them again. That was forty years ago."

"Are you telling me that in all that time, they've never reached out to you?"

"Yes."

"How old were you?"

"Sixteen. My coach was a great guy. He and his wife took me in and let me live in their basement. He made sure I finished high school. Then, right around the time all my friends were college shopping, I saw an Army recruitment ad. I figured that was the only way I was going to punch my ticket to college." Palmer shrugged. "The Army became my family and I've never looked back."

"For the life of me, I will never understand how a parent can turn his or her back on a child. It's so..."

"Cold?" Palmer supplied.

"For lack of a better word, that will have to suffice." Emma neatly folded her linen napkin and placed it on the table. She brushed her fingertips over Palmer's sleeve. Immediately, Emma realized that the gesture might be construed as being too intimate. She dropped her hand into her lap.

"For what it's worth, the loss was entirely theirs. I agree with your men. There's no one I'd rather be in a foxhole with. You're an amazing woman, Palmer Estes, and for so many reasons. I'm so glad our paths have crossed. I'm looking forward to forging that friendship, if that's something you think you'd enjoy too."

"I absolutely would."

"Excellent. The next dinner's on you."

"What?"

Emma stood and winked. "I hate to dine and dash, but I've got to change and get put together. Showtime in an hour."

Palmer stood as well and glanced down at her watch, surprised to see how quickly the time had passed. "I'm sorry to have kept you—"

"You didn't. I wish I had longer. Next time." Emma escorted Palmer to the door leading back to the Center Hall. Two Secret Service agents stood ramrod straight outside in the hallway. "Nick will make sure you get back to the entrance. Your driver is taking you to the Capitol? Did I hear that correctly?"

"Yes." He's waiting for me."

"You know where you're going to meet up with the group of invited guests?"

"Yes, I've been thoroughly briefed."

"Perfect. I'll see you soon."

"Thank you, Madam President."

Emma nodded in acknowledgment of the slip back into their official roles. "Thank you, Nick. Take good care of General Estes. She's one of our finest."

"Of course, ma'am." He turned to Palmer. "If you'll come with me, please, ma'am."

As much as Palmer wanted to catch one last personal glimpse of Emma, she resisted the urge. After all, Emma had promised a return engagement, hadn't she?

❧❧

Emma was two-thirds into her speech. Predictably, she'd gotten raucous cheers from the Democrats and mixed responses from the Republicans. She'd been heartened to see a host of moderate Senate Republicans stand and cheer for her climate change initiatives and her commitment to reducing the national debt. When she welcomed back Senators Friese, Tannebaum, Wicks, and Lawson, the entire House chamber erupted in a prolonged standing ovation.

She waved to each of them and applauded as well.

Senator Wicks mouthed, "Thank you, Madam President."

Emma nodded her acknowledgment. She shouted to be heard over the noise. "These four men are here to share this night with all of us thanks to the heroic efforts of our intelligence community and our brave military men and women." She waited for the applause to ratchet down.

"The United States has the finest fighting force anywhere on the planet. While diplomacy is our weapon of choice, we will not hesitate to defend our nation, our people, our ideals, and the principles of freedom, humanity, and democracy the world over." Again, Emma waited for the applause to die down.

"Our military members and their families unselfishly endure long separations, often over multiple deployments, and, tragically, they sometimes pay the ultimate price. Tonight we are joined by the wives and young children of three members of the Army's A Company, 5th Battalion, 158th Aviation who were killed in action as they escorted the senators on a fact-finding mission."

Emma gestured to the balcony and motioned for the families to stand. "Our nation owes you a huge debt of gratitude. Please know that our hearts are with you." She leaned forward and addressed the children. "I want you all to grow up knowing that your dads were real-life heroes who made a difference. They were very brave, just like you and your moms."

One of the little boys snapped to attention and saluted, and the audience gave him a standing ovation. It was such an unexpected moment. Emma's hand flew to her heart. She fought back tears and gave him an equally sharp salute in return. If she could've transported herself up to the balcony, she would've hugged him.

Instead, she took a deep breath, gathered her composure, and continued with her remarks. "The War on Terror has claimed too many lives, over too many years. Generations of heroes have been forged in the heat of battle... Heroes like Silver Star and double-Purple Heart recipient, General Palmer Estes, who is here with us tonight." Emma pointed to Palmer, who sat two rows behind Vice President Elders' wife, Beverly.

"General Estes is only the second female four-star general in the U.S. Army's history and currently the highest-ranking. In 1991, she was a twenty-five-year-old captain flying Black Hawk helicopters in Kuwait during Desert Storm. She was shot and wounded while flying oversight to protect ground troops pinned down by enemy fire. Even as her helicopter endured a barrage of surface-to-air missile and ground fire attacks, she refused to turn for home until she knew those soldiers below were safe and out of harm's way.

"Her crew mates have said that her heroism and skill as a pilot saved the lives of an entire platoon." Emma schooled her expression. Even from this distance, she didn't want to telegraph the surprise as she made eye contact with Palmer.

Emma leaned casually against the podium. "General Estes, did you ever know the names of the men whose lives you saved that day?"

Palmer raised both eyebrows, obviously caught off-guard by the direct question. She shook her head. "No, I did not, Madam President," she answered. Her voice carried clearly in the chamber.

"General Estes, please turn to your left and meet Doctor Seth Radin. Today, Doctor Radin is one of the leading experts in curing spinal cord injuries. His work has improved the outcomes of thousands of patients, including many military veterans.

"In 1991, Doctor Radin was Captain Radin, leader of that platoon you and your crew saved. For years he wondered who that pilot was—the one that saved his life and enabled him to pay it forward. We did a little digging and determined the position of that platoon relative to the position of your Black Hawk and found a definitive match. Tonight, he wanted to travel here from his home outside New York City to thank you in person."

The surprise on Palmer's face was priceless. Doctor Radin stood, saluted Palmer, and then lifted her into an emotional hug. The audience roared its approval.

Emma's heart nearly burst. *Sometimes, it's good to be the president, especially when you can do cool things like this.* "As I said, we have the finest fighting force in the world. After decades of conflict, we have brought the major terrorist organizations to their knees. Now it is time to pivot and develop new and effective strategies to counteract terrorism throughout the world.

"Where hatred rears its ugly head, we will meet and defeat it. Where extremism seeks to take root, we will plant love and democracy instead. Alongside our allies, we will win the fight for the hearts and minds of the next generation before the poison of 'other-ism' sets in, combatting fear, misinformation, and ignorance with knowledge and truth. Together, we can and will win this fight, and we will do it by adhering to this absolute: as citizens of the world, we share far more in common than we have differences.

"The same is true for citizens of this country. We are, all of us, created equal. Where suspicion, ignorance, and fear breed domestic terrorism, bigotry, and persecution, we will instill the American values of unity, compassion, and tolerance. Education is the key.

"My Department of Education, under the leadership of Secretary Ahern, will work with school districts across the country—all stakeholders—to create and enhance curricula that reflect the full truth of our history. Where there has been erasure, we will restore the experiences of every racial, ethnic, and cultural cohort. Our children are our greatest resource and our greatest hope to create a more perfect union, one in which hatred—which is born of ignorance and fear—is replaced by knowledge and understanding.

"We fear that which we do not understand. Knowledge, born through comprehensive teaching and learning, holds the key to ending prejudice and division in this country and, indeed, throughout the world.

"Ladies and gentlemen, we are the stewards of our present. Our children are the custodians of the future. I look forward to working with Congress and the American people to ensure that we create the kind of world in which our children, and our children's children, and generations to come will thrive. This is our solemn duty, and we are up to the task. I believe in us. The state of our union is strong. E Pluribus Unum—out of many, one.

"Thank you. May God bless you, and may God bless the United States of America."

        ✎✎

Palmer stood in line with the president's other special guests, who all were excitedly talking about the State of the Union speech and how fabulous it had been. They gathered in the coat room where they would retrieve their personal items and be herded into the vans that would return them to the White House.

"Leave your coats and follow me," an aide said.

Now the group buzzed about where they might be going. Someone jokingly said, "Maybe we're going to see the president again."

Someone else poo-pooed the idea. "Surely, the president has press and other obligations right now."

"Okay, let's go," the aide announced. "You're going to see the president."

Palmer smiled affectionately. Leave it to Emma to put it all out there in the speech and still find the energy to personally greet her invited guests afterward.

They reached the end of a hallway. The aide lined them up against the wall and provided each of them with a small card. On the card was the presidential seal on top and their name. Palmer waited in line with everyone else.

When it was her turn, the aide escorted her to the door, took her card, and announced her name. Palmer walked into the room. One aide stood at the entrance door, and another at the door through which she would exit at the opposite end of the room. Other than the president, the only other person present was a photographer.

Emma smiled broadly as Palmer approached and came to attention.

"At ease, General." She took Palmer's hand in a gesture that seemed somehow more personal than a handshake. Or had Palmer imagined that?

"You gave a magnificent speech, Madam President."

"Did you really think so? Or are you just blowing smoke?"

Palmer guffawed. "I really thought so. You'll find I never blow smoke. The surgeon general says it's bad for your health."

"Ha, ha."

Palmer's brow wrinkled in concern. "You look tired."

"You try giving a forty-five-minute speech to that raucous bunch."

"Thanks, but no thanks." Palmer turned serious. "I can't believe you found Doctor Radin. That was…remarkable…and so thoughtful."

"You're very welcome. For the record, I didn't do that for show or theater. What you did was heroic, and I wanted you and the country to see the ripple effect of your actions."

"Well, point made, Madam President." Palmer glanced around. "I'm sure you have to keep this thing moving. You really should get some sleep tonight. You earned it."

"Thank you. Will you take a picture with me?"

"Of course."

The photographer had been standing a discreet distance away. Emma motioned her over now. She put her left arm around Palmer's waist and shook her right hand, posing for the camera.

"Remember, the next dinner's on you. Smile as though you like me."

Palmer had no trouble following the president's order.

CHAPTER FOURTEEN

Palmer finished the last five reps of her chest presses, placed the weight bar on the stand, and sat up. At this hour, she had the fitness center to herself. It had been a good workout, and her muscles were satisfyingly spent.

Her head jerked up as she heard a familiar voice emanating from the large, flat-screen television suspended in the corner of the room.

60 Minutes teased the episode with a clip of Emma talking about her recent trip to Europe, where, among other things, she triumphantly re-entered the U.S. into the Paris Climate Accord Agreement.

"We'll also talk to the president about her first one hundred days in office—her successes and failures—and what we can expect in the next one hundred days. It's May 2nd, 2021. All this and more next, on *60 Minutes*."

If she hurried, Palmer could be home in time to watch the episode in the comfort of her living room. Guilt gnawed at her gut as she raced back to her place. More times than she cared to count, she'd stared at the crisp business card with the fancy presidential seal and Emma's private cell phone number in her neat script scrawled on the back.

Palmer almost had missed the card, which fell out of the large, manila envelope that had arrived in the mail two weeks after the State of the Union address. Inside the envelope was a glossy, eight-by-ten signed photograph of Palmer and Emma, posing together for the camera after the speech.

Palmer let herself into the house and made a beeline for the living room and the remote control. She switched to CBS just as the show was coming back from commercial. The first twenty-minute segment focused on the European trip. Palmer thought Emma looked transcendent at a ball in her honor thrown by the French president and his wife. At the ceremonial signing of the re-entry into the Paris Climate Accords, she radiated calm leadership, surrounded by American allies.

On the commercial break, Palmer walked over to the mantel where she'd placed the now-framed picture. Emma's eyes sparkled up at her. Palmer's stomach clenched. This was why she'd resisted making the call. *She's just a friend. Remember that. All she wants is to be your friend.* Palmer could do that.

As the broadcast finished after two segments on Emma's first one hundred days in office, Palmer reached for her cell phone. She scrolled through her contacts until she found the entry for *EJM*. She'd copied the contact information into her phone in case she ever misplaced the card. She'd decided to use only Emma's initials in case her phone ever got compromised. Now she selected the number marked *private cell* and hesitated only a moment before placing the call.

"I was beginning to wonder if I'd ever hear from you."

Emma's voice washed over Palmer like a warm summer breeze. "Am I catching you at a bad time?"

"Not at all. Just reading some scintillating budget updates."

"I saw *60 Minutes*."

"I should've gone with the other navy suit."

Palmer laughed. "I don't know, I thought the one you wore was a good choice." She gripped the phone tighter. "It was a great show."

"Did you really think so?"

These small moments of insecurity always baffled Palmer. "Of course. Didn't you?"

"Never ask a perfectionist if she could've done better."

"You're too hard on yourself. What you accomplished in the first hundred days is mind-boggling. That you did it with a Republican majority in the Senate is even more impressive."

"I'm glad you think so."

"I do. How was the weather in Paris?"

"Springtime in Paris. What could be better than that? Except that I never got outside."

"I'm sure."

"I'll be glad to be home for a while, that's for certain."

"Speaking of that…" Palmer bit her lip. "I believe I owe you a dinner."

"So you do. After all this time, I figured you were trying to weasel out of it."

"You've been out of the country."

"For three months?" Emma asked, incredulously.

"Okay. You've got me there. Still, you have to admit, it's intimidating having the president over for dinner."

Emma's laugh was lighthearted. "Stop making excuses. Having your friend over for dinner shouldn't be rocket science. You can always order a pizza."

"Are you kidding me? My friend would never go for those kinds of carbs."

"Is that right?"

"It is."

"There's always the leftover spinach salad in your refrigerator."

"How do you know—"

"Please. You're the kind of woman who always has a leftover salad in her refrigerator."

"Typecasting now, are we?"

"Am I wrong?"

"That wasn't the point."

"I'm pretty sure it was."

"Okay, Madam President. How about dinner at my place Saturday night at say, 1900 hours."

"Seven o'clock it is. What can I bring?"

"You mean other than a team of Secret Service agents?"

"Yes."

"Just yourself. And Emma?"

"Yes."

"Jeans and a hoodie would be formal for this."

"Got it. I'll have my people call your people. See you Saturday, Palmer."

"See you then, Emma." Palmer disconnected the call and held the phone against her chin. She couldn't wipe the grin off her face. Emma was coming to her place for dinner six days from now. *Oh, my God. What the heck am I going to serve her?*

❧❧

Emma brushed her hair one more time and checked her teeth in the mirror. She should floss again. *Why are you so nervous? It's just dinner with a friend.* She smoothed her jeans and settled the hood on her sweatshirt.

Her security detail had informed the provost at Fort Myer several days ago of her impending visit. For once, she wished she could eschew the formalities, the security screenings, and the logistical machinations, and enjoy something as simple as a lovely dinner with a friend, where she drove herself there and back without dozens of eyes watching.

It wasn't that she resented the Secret Service—quite the opposite. She was incredibly grateful for their professionalism, their dedication to duty, and for the fact that they kept her safe. But at moments like this, when she only wanted to be a private citizen doing something millions of people did on a regular basis, she longed for the freedom privacy afforded.

She sighed and threw open the bedroom door. "I'm ready to go, Jemelle."

"Yes, ma'am." The Secret Service agent, who had been waiting outside the door, murmured into her comms, "Pioneer is on the move."

As was tradition, Emma had selected the security code name from a list curated by the White House Communications Agency. It had been the name they'd hoped she'd embrace for the historical significance of her candidacy and now her presidency.

The ride was short and cut through Arlington National Cemetery to the back gate of Fort Myer. On base, the motorcade came to a stop in front of a quaint, turn-of-the-Twentieth Century, red-brick, two-story house. Emma recalled that the military base was built on property the famous confederate General Robert E. Lee owned. The historic nature of the place was evident everywhere.

She noted members of her Secret Service detail fanned out over the grounds of the property. Others already would've swept the house and taken up positions inside.

Jemelle opened Emma's car door. Surrounded by the remainder of her protection detail, she bounded up the walk and mounted the steps. She reached the front door just as it opened.

Emma did her best not to stare. In a pair of worn jeans and an Army sweatshirt, Palmer looked years younger, carefree, and…

"Hi."

Emma blinked. "Hi, yourself. I hope I'm not late." She turned to the agent to her left and retrieved the basket from him. "I wasn't sure what to bring, and I didn't want to show up empty handed." She thrust the basket at Palmer. "The roses are a couple of weeks away, but the tulips looked so beautiful in the Rose Garden, I thought—"

"They're beautiful. Thank you." Palmer accepted the basket of blooms and motioned for Emma to come inside. The accompanying agents would take up positions at the front door. "I'll get these flowers in some water. Give me a second."

Emma took in the details of the house as she waited in the center hall. The spotless floors and woodworking appeared to be worn but well-cared-for oak. The walls were painted in muted colors, and the artwork consisted of various depictions of Civil War battles and Lincoln delivering the Gettysburg Address. The staircase leading to the second floor sported a richly red oriental-patterned carpet up the center, with exposed wood on the edges and an ornately-carved wide, wooden banister.

"Sorry that took a minute. I had to find a vase. Come on in." Palmer beckoned for Emma to follow her into the living room. "Dinner will be served shortly. Can I get you something to drink?" Waves of nervousness radiated off Palmer.

Of course, she's nervous. It isn't every day the president and a host of Secret Service agents invade your home. That would be nerve wracking—even for a four-star general. "If you have any sparkling water, that would be great."

Palmer returned a moment later with a tray. On it were two glasses of sparkling water, a plateful of bruschetta, and other tasty hors d'oeuvres.

"I thought you'd come up with a low-carb dinner. How did you know I love bruschetta?"

Palmer shrugged. "Lucky guess?"

"Uh-huh." Emma eyed her suspiciously. Then, she took a bite and moaned with pleasure. "Oh, my God. This is incredible."

"Glad you approve." Palmer smiled, selected an hors d'oeuvres, and sat opposite her on the couch. "Thanks for the picture, by the way."

"I see it's got a place of honor." Emma gestured to the framed photograph on top of the marble fireplace mantel.

"How do you know I didn't move it there just for this occasion?"

Emma snickered. "That would be cynical. Did you?"

"No." Palmer shook her head. "You don't strike me as the kind of person who has patience for being fawned over."

"I don't, eh?"

"No, you do not."

Emma cocked her head, intrigued. "So, what kind of person am I, then?" She tried not to squirm as Palmer took her time measuring her. Instead, she sampled another tasty treat.

"You're earnest, not jaded. You don't suffer fools lightly, yet you're patient and prefer to dole out positive reinforcement rather than harsh criticism." Palmer pursed her lips. "Let's see... You measure your words carefully so that you say what you mean and mean what you say. You have the ability to synthesize situations and information quickly and act decisively, but refuse to do so until you feel confident you have all the facts."

"I don't know who this person is you're describing, but she sounds pretty nice."

Palmer steepled her fingers under her chin. "I've been lucky enough to see her in multiple situations now, and I think she's got...potential. She's principled, generous, and kind—not attributes normally associated with a politician. That automatically sets her apart."

"I suspect you set a low bar."

"Quite the contrary."

A petite, serious-looking woman in a chef's blouse ducked into the living room from the adjacent dining room. "Dinner is ready, ma'am."

"Thank you, Master Sergeant Miles."

When she'd gone, Emma raised an eyebrow. "And here I thought you were going to cook for me."

"And here I thought you'd like something more satisfying than a spinach salad."

"Touché. Although I was certain you'd see this opportunity as a challenge to be mastered."

Palmer motioned for Emma to precede her into the dining room. "There are many ways to master a challenge. A wise tactician chooses the most efficacious path to success."

"Spoken like a true general." Palmer held the chair for Emma, a gesture she found both gallant and surprising. It was the kind of thing one did on a date, and this wasn't that. Right?

The dining room was a formal affair. A large, mahogany table and mahogany chairs with fussy hand-carved feet and flourishes dominated the space. A matching sideboard and glass-front hutch filled out the room.

The table was covered with a perfectly ironed white linen tablecloth. The place settings featured linen napkins, fancy good china plates and bowls, and sterling silver silverware. Pewter candlesticks with white tapers burned on either side of the centerpiece, which was a gorgeous cut-glass vase filled with Emma's fresh tulips.

Emma wondered what had been there before she'd upended the tableau, although she appreciated the effort. She'd asked for a pair of snippers and personally selected and cut the flowers herself.

Once Palmer was settled in her chair, the chef brought in the first course. "I hope you like ceviche."

Emma raised an eyebrow. "Another personal favorite. I'm beginning to smell a rat."

"I don't know what you're talking about." Palmer feigned innocence.

"Uh-huh." Emma took her first bite of the Peruvian specialty and savored the tangy explosion of lemon/lime citrus-infused raw seafood on her tongue. "My compliments to the chef."

"You'll get to tell her so when we're done."

They finished the appetizer in companionable silence. When the plates were removed, Emma asked, "Have you thought any more about what you want to do next?"

"Not really. The military is all I've ever known."

"Are you sure you want to be done?"

Palmer nodded. "It's time."

They paused the conversation as the chef brought in the main course, a delicious-looking paella that Emma couldn't wait to try. "Now I know I smell a rat."

"I don't know what you're talking about, Madam President."

"Don't Madam President me. You can't possibly go three-for-three in favorite dishes without having gotten some insider information. Spill."

Palmer appeared unmoved.

"Spill, or I'll order your chef in here and pry the truth out of her."

Palmer laughed. It was a rich, full sound that Emma enjoyed more than she should've.

"Okay, okay. I can't have you browbeating my favorite cook. It's possible that I might've suggested she contact your chef and get a few clues as to dishes you might like that you don't get to experience often enough."

"Aha! I knew it!"

"You don't mind, do you?"

"Mind?" Emma scoffed. "Not in the least. I'm flattered that you and your chef went to the trouble." She meant it. Palmer didn't have to go to these lengths for a simple Saturday dinner between friends, but she had. It showed thoughtfulness and consideration, and Emma was touched by the effort.

Palmer swallowed and said, "I'm open to suggestions, by the way."

"Suggestions?" Emma queried. What had they been talking about? She'd found herself caught up in observing the delight on Palmer's face as she sampled the meal.

"Yes. You know, my post-military future?"

"Ah. That." Emma tapped the fork against her chin. "Of course, I'm sure the private intelligence sector would love to have you. With your expertise and experience, you could write your own ticket."

Palmer made a face. "I'm loathe to be a gun-for-hire. It just feels...wrong."

"I can understand that. Honestly, I'm a little relieved that's not something you'd want." She took another appreciative bite. The lobster obviously was fresh, as were all the other ingredients. "You could take a teaching position. Perhaps a professorship in international studies at a major university like Harvard, or Yale, or even your doctorate alma mater, Princeton."

Palmer's eyes lit up at the prospect. "I hadn't really thought about it, but I suppose that could prove interesting."

A knot formed in Emma's stomach. *Yes, except I don't want you to move away.* "You're already used to lecturing and mentoring. You certainly know the subject matter intimately. You'd be a natural."

"I'll put that in the to-be-given-serious-consideration pile."

The two of them finished their last bites and sat back.

"That was amazing." Emma patted her stomach.

"We're not done yet."

"Oh, my God. I don't think I can eat another bite."

"Don't say that yet. You haven't seen what's for dessert."

Emma groaned. "What is it?"

"A surprise." Palmer pushed back her chair and rose. "But I'll tell you what. Let's give our dinners a little while to settle before dessert and coffee."

"An excellent suggestion." Emma rose as well, and followed Palmer into a dark-paneled library at the opposite end of the house.

Without asking permission, Emma gravitated to the books on the fully stocked shelves. She recognized first-edition classics by Mark Twain, Emily Dickinson, Oscar Wilde, F. Scott Fitzgerald, Ernest Hemingway, Charles Dickens, and Edith Wharton.

Another section held contemporary literary fiction from Alice Walker, Toni Morrison, and Dorothy Allison, among others. Still another set of shelves was dedicated to presidential biographies and memoirs, along with books on the theory of war.

"Feel free to borrow anything." Palmer came up alongside her and warmth spread through Emma's body.

"Thanks. This is quite a collection."

"I'm not a Neanderthal."

"Palmer Estes," Emma turned and they were in each other's space. "I would never suggest such a thing." Emma needed to lighten the mood. She was feeling things she hadn't felt in too long. Her body was reacting in ways that were at once pleasant and unwelcome. "Of course, it's entirely possible that the collection resides here and wasn't personally curated by you."

Palmer, perhaps sensing a change in the atmosphere as well, took a step back and covered her heart as if she'd been mortally wounded. "I can't believe you'd accuse me of such a thing."

"I note that you haven't answered."

"Once a lawyer, always a lawyer, I see. The collection is wholly mine, I assure you."

"In that case, I'm impressed."

At that moment, the chef appeared with a tray. On it were two cups of black coffee and two slices of lemon meringue pie.

Emma's mouth watered. "Oh, my." The chef set the tray down.

Palmer put a hand on the chef's shoulder. "Madam President, I formally present to you Master Sergeant Elizabeth Miles, chef extraordinaire."

"I'm honored to meet you. This was a fabulous meal. If you ever get tired—"

"Hey!" Palmer interrupted. "You can't steal her."

Emma laughed. "On the contrary. I could, but I won't."

"Thank you, Madam President. I can't tell you what an honor it is to cook for you."

"And I can't tell you what an honor it is to eat what you prepared."

"Master Sergeant Miles has aspirations to open her own five-star restaurant in Paris someday."

Emma smiled at her. "When that happens, please let me know where you land. I'd love to be your first customer."

"Yes, ma'am."

"If you've got everything under control, you can go, Master Sergeant."

"I do, ma'am."

"Thanks for everything. You outdid yourself tonight."

"Thank you, ma'am."

Palmer and Emma finished the pie and the last of the coffee. Emma glanced at her watch. It was 9:45. Where had the time gone?

"You have to go." Palmer said it quietly. The soft glow of the lamp made her look even more youthful and beautiful. They were standing less than two feet apart.

Emma swallowed hard. "Alas, I do."

"I'm glad you came."

"I'm glad you invited me. I was beginning to lose hope."

"Don't ever do that." Palmer appeared as though she were going to reach out with her fingertips and stroke Emma's face. Instead, her hand fell to her side.

"I won't, as long as you promise not to be a stranger."

"I promise. Although, the ball's in your court now."

"I'm going to have to up my game."

"Your game is just fine the way it is."

Emma nodded, unable to find the words she sought, unable to articulate how she felt—how Palmer made her feel.

"Thank you for a beautiful night, Palmer. I can't remember the last time I enjoyed someone else's company so much."

"Happy to be a place of respite, Emma. Keep in touch."

"I will. You too."

"I will."

Emma smiled up at her one last time. When they exited the library, a Secret Service agent was standing watch outside the door, staring straight ahead. "I'm ready to go, Robert."

"Yes, ma'am." He spoke into his comms. "Pioneer is on the move."

Yes, she was.

CHAPTER FIFTEEN

Palmer completed her third running circuit around the base. Eighteen solitary miles, and she still hadn't been able to outrun her jumbled emotions. She bent over and put her hands on her knees. Sweat dripped from her chin, leaving a pattern of droplets on the pavement. A slight summer breeze ruffled her hair. She shook out her arms and legs and executed a series of stretches to help her cool down. But no amount of physical exertion tamed her renegade heart.

In the intervening two months since that magical evening with Emma, Palmer had immersed herself in her work. She convinced herself that she owed it to whomever would follow her to get her professional house in order before her retirement, but the truth was, she needed the distraction.

It seemed as though every waking hour of personal time—and most nights during her dreams—Palmer's mind, heart, and body were filled to bursting with Emma. Emma, gazing up at her under long lashes in the library. Emma's laughter floating on the air between them on the living room sofa. Emma's penetrating gaze memorizing her face, her words, her mannerisms. Emma's voice, soothing the jagged places in Palmer's soul.

Dozens of times a day, Palmer picked up her personal cell, opened an encrypted text message, and stared at the blinking cursor. Sometimes, she would compose an entire message in her head without committing any of it to the screen. Other times, she would begin to type out a message, only to delete the incomplete sentiment seconds later. She was always careful not to select a recipient—she didn't want to accidentally send something she couldn't retract, or that could be misinterpreted.

Misinterpreted? Who was she kidding? Her thoughts couldn't be misinterpreted, unless one was completely oblivious. And even Palmer wasn't that clueless. She knew what it meant—understood the import and the truth. She simply didn't want to admit it. Not to herself and certainly not to Emma. It was inappropriate; it was impossible; it was madness.

Instead, Palmer literally ran herself into the ground. She willed herself to ignore the ache in her belly, the longing in her loins, and the way her heart rate accelerated every time she glimpsed Emma's face on the news programs, which was, of course, nightly.

Not that she was one to confide in others—she wasn't—but even if she had been, there wouldn't have been a soul in whom Palmer could've confided. Not about this. So, she continued to battle with her burgeoning feelings in isolation.

She didn't dare reach out to Emma in this state. Besides, it wasn't as though Emma had tried to contact her either. Palmer wasn't sure what to make of that. Did Emma feel as she did? Or had Palmer imagined the spark between them?

Emma's life was complicated. Of course, it was. She was president of the United States. Beyond that, she was a widow who'd tragically lost the only partner she'd ever known three years ago. Was she still grieving for Heather? Could anyone take Heather's place in Emma's heart? Was there room for someone else there?

Argh. Enough! Why do you torture yourself? This isn't getting you anywhere. Palmer trudged up the steps, through the front door, and into the bathroom, where she stripped and headed for the shower. Maybe that would help. Heaven knew, nothing else had worked.

Emma picked up her personal cell phone for the third time, only to toss it back on the bed again when it was clear she'd had no messages. *Palmer's not going to reach out. The ball's in your court. She told you so before you left that night.*

Emma turned, punched the pillows propped against the headboard to fluff them, and scooted up higher. She snapped up the book from the nightstand and flipped to the bookmarked page. She was re-reading Lillian Faderman's 2003 memoir, *Naked in the Promised Land*, reissued last year. The prose was classic Lillian—elegant and filled with unvarnished, if difficult, truths.

After re-reading the same paragraph for the sixth time, Emma re-inserted the book mark and laid the book back on the nightstand. She ditched two of the pillows, laid the other one flat, snapped off the light, and tried to settle in for the night.

Myriad images filled her head. Palmer as Emma pinned her with the Silver Star. Palmer blushing over an unintentional double entendre. Palmer smiling that toothy grin at her over dinner. Palmer, Palmer, Palmer... *Ugh!* Emma pulled the pillow over her head. Why couldn't she will herself to stop thinking about her?

When Heather died, part of Emma died with her. Never in her wildest dreams did Emma believe that she'd ever be capable of falling in love with another woman.

Was that it? Was she falling for Palmer? Emma tossed off the pillow and bolted upright. The sheet and blanket pooled around her waist.

How was that possible? They'd had exactly two social interactions, both of them perfectly chaste and friendly. Apart from that, they'd crossed paths professionally less than a handful of times over the course of her seven months in office. No. This was a classic case of it being lonely at the top and Emma suffering from a dearth of personal social contact, and especially contact with other lesbians.

Even as she tried to convince herself of this, Emma knew it was a lie. It might've been nearly thirty-five years since she'd experienced that rush of first attraction when two people clicked, but she hadn't forgotten what that felt like. She and Palmer had chemistry aplenty.

That wasn't all either. Too often, Emma found herself daydreaming about what Palmer would think of this or that, or what it would be like to have Palmer accompany her to this reception or that dinner. Most of all, though, she yearned to get to know Palmer—really get to know her. Emma longed to see what lay in Palmer's heart, behind the walls she'd erected to keep everyone at a distance.

Given what Palmer had shared with her about her teenage years—the lack of parental love and support, and her early relationship experiences—it hardly was surprising that she'd learned to turn inward. Add to that the exigencies of rising in the Army under the aegis of *Don't Ask, Don't Tell*...

Emma wished she could heal all of that for Palmer. *I want you to know what it feels like to be truly loved and cherished as you deserve. I want to give you that gift.* Emma's heart constricted with loneliness and longing.

She snatched up the phone once more. This time, she opened her encrypted text app, selected Palmer from her list of contacts, and typed: *Is it October yet?* She bit her lip and stared at the message and the blinking cursor. Would Palmer understand her meaning? Would she recognize the cryptic reference and the importance of circumspection? Would she read between the lines and know how Emma felt?

Before she could reconsider, she hit send. Her heart raced and she dropped the phone to the bed, afraid to know what would happen next.

Palmer's personal phone buzzed and she dredged herself up from a restless sleep. Who would be texting her at this hour? She cracked open an eye and fumbled for the phone. She caught it as it tumbled off the nightstand and stared at the screen. Her eyes opened wide and her heart hammered double-time. *Emma.*

She shot up and clicked on the bedside lamp, even though she could see the backlit screen perfectly in the dark. She used her thumbprint to unlock the phone and opened the message. Four words. That was it? Where was the rest of it? Palmer blinked and read the text several times.

"Is it October yet?" Palmer read aloud. She frowned. *What are you trying to say? Am I supposed to know what that means? After months of silence, you send me a text out of the blue, and this is it? No preamble, no, "Hi. Sorry I've been so quiet, I've been busy being president?"*

Palmer shook her head and tossed the phone on the bed. Obviously, Emma worried that her texts would someday be public or could be hacked. Even so, this message either was too cryptic, or Palmer was too obtuse.

She threw the covers off and paced around the bedroom. *Think it through. What's the significance of October? Columbus Day, Halloween, fall foliage... Is fall your favorite season?*

Palmer reached the window and spun around. *October.* Perhaps she was thinking about this wrong? Maybe this wasn't about Emma as much as it was about her?

She stopped short as realization dawned. *Oh, my God. Are you saying what I think you're saying?* Her hands shook as she dove on the bed for the phone. "Is it October yet?" she muttered out loud again. *Are you counting down to my retirement?* Palmer's heart stuttered. *Breathe. Just breathe. You need to be certain that's what she means before you make an ass of yourself.*

Palmer sat up and threw her legs over the edge of the bed. She rocked unconsciously and chewed the inside of her cheek as her mind raced. Finally, she typed: *Looking forward to it...* The blinking cursor stared back at her. *That's not enough. C'mon. Think.*

Her fingers trembled over the tiny letters. *Perhaps a celebratory meal afterward?* Palmer debated. Was that too presumptuous? Too forward? Too much? Her pulse pounded in her ears. Yes. Anyone could read between the lines there. She deleted the sentence and instead typed: *Does that explain the silence?* After another moment of paralysis, she exhaled and sent the text.

Seconds later, she received her reply: *Yes. Necessary, at least for me...*

Palmer measured Emma's words. "Are you telling me you want more than friendship, and that's why you need to keep your distance until I retire?" Was Emma staying away to avoid any impropriety, knowing nothing could happen between them until Palmer was no longer under her chain of command? Could it be true? Or was that wishful supposition on Palmer's part?

Emma was a lawyer and no doubt razor-precise with language, even with punctuation. Palmer re-examined the text. The comma was a pause. What if the ellipses represented Emma asking if Palmer felt the same way? "What if you're completely misreading this whole thing?" she mumbled. Yes, it would be incredibly embarrassing if she misconstrued Emma's meaning. On the other hand...

Yet again, Britney's admonition played in Palmer's head. *Unclench the fist around your heart. Unless you do, you'll never find the love you deserve.* Palmer sighed. If she refused to take a risk here, she could lose the best opportunity she'd ever get with Emma.

Whatever the risk for you, triple that for Emma. Surely, Emma had even more at stake than she did.

Palmer's fingers flew over the keys. *Me too. So, October 9th, then?* Her retirement ceremony was scheduled for Friday, October 8th. She hit send before she could re-think it.

She didn't have long to wait.

I'll have my people call your people.

Palmer knew she was grinning like an idiot. She didn't care.

Emma sucked in a deep breath and prayed for patience. After the fourth time listening to the Senate majority leader suggest language that would once again water down protections against unlimited corporate and union spending on political campaigns, she slammed her palms down on the table and stood. Papers skittered across the conference table in the Roosevelt Room and her chair nearly tipped over backward.

Vaguely, she registered the shocked expressions on the faces of the majority leader, the speaker of the House, the legislative staffs and her own people. She was beyond caring.

"Enough! We've been at this for three hours, and we've gotten exactly nowhere. I want legislation on my desk before the October recess—that's one week from today—that fixes the morass caused by Citizen's United and also sets out robust, iron-clad protections for the integrity of our elections.

"Free-flowing corporate contributions and money from Super PACs rate as the most corrupting factors in our elections today, followed close behind by foreign interference. We all know it. And for the record," Emma pointed directly at the Senate majority leader, "we've got the votes in your chamber to ram a full-strength version of the bill through. Those six Republican senators from vulnerable districts are being outspent five to one, thanks to union donations and Super-PACs working to defeat them. You want to hold onto your majority in the midterms next year? This legislation, with the full weight of its protections, is in your best interest. Get on board or get out of the way."

Emma kept to herself that Senators Friese and Wicks already had called her with their support as a thank you for their rescue. She gathered up her papers and stormed out of the meeting.

Her staff scrambled behind her. When she reached the Oval Office, she slammed the door closed behind her, tossed the folder onto her desk, and strode over to the doors that led outside. She threw open the doors and headed toward the Rose Garden path.

The fresh, crisp fall air cooled her overheated skin. She breathed in deeply and exhaled slowly several times until she felt more under control.

"Want to talk about it?" Nichelle came up alongside.

"What?"

"Madam President, I've known you a very long time, and never, in all our years together, have I ever seen you blow your top in a meeting like that."

"Was it undeserved?"

"No." Nichelle drew out the word.

"Was I wrong?"

"No."

"So, what's the problem?"

They walked for a moment in silence. "As I see it, the problem, whatever it is, has little or nothing to do with campaign finance and election reform."

Emma closed her eyes briefly. *Here it comes.* "I have no idea what you're talking about. And be careful here, Nich. You're treading on thin ice. I wouldn't want you to fall in."

To Emma's great surprise, Nichelle threaded her arm through Emma's and gave her a squeeze. "Do you remember what you said to me on Inauguration morning?"

"I said a lot of things."

"Uh-huh. Let me refresh your memory and I'll paraphrase here. 'Nich, promise me you'll always tell me the truth, and that you'll never let me take myself too seriously.'"

Emma nodded. "I hate when you throw my words back at me."

"It's in the job description."

"Damn fine print."

"Now stop prevaricating."

Emma arched an eyebrow. "Was I evading?"

"You know you were. What's going on with you? Something's wrong; I just don't know what it is."

I do. It's the beginning of October and Palmer retires in a little over a week. I need to decide my future. If we go forward and explore a relationship, everything about my life will change. Am I ready for that? Is it the right thing for me? Is it the right thing for Palmer? Is it the right thing for the country?

"Madam President?"

"Yes?"

"Care to share?"

"I'm just tired, that's all. I've been pushing too hard and not getting enough sleep." *All true statements.*

"How about a retreat to Camp David? You haven't taken a vacation since before the Inauguration. No one could fault you for taking a long weekend."

Emma pondered the suggestion. What Nichelle said was true. But taking a break this weekend would negate her strategy for the following weekend. If she didn't get cold feet, she'd ask Palmer to join her in New York for dinner and a Broadway show, followed by the rest of the long Columbus-Day weekend at her cabin in the Adirondack Mountains. The fall colors were predicted to be near their peak in the North Country.

"Madam President?"

"Hmm?"

"A Camp David retreat? What do you think?"

Emma half-smiled at Nichelle. "I appreciate the good intention. I think I'd rather plan something for the following weekend."

Now it was Nichelle's turn to raise an eyebrow. "Really? What do you have in mind? I'll let the appropriate staff know so they can start preparing."

"It can wait." Emma turned them back toward the Oval Office. "Do you think I need to smooth any ruffled feathers?"

Nichelle seemed to accept the change in topic. "Nah. He had it coming to him. I think the staff was impressed. They've never seen you lose your temper. It's not a bad thing for them to know that you'll go balls to the wall when it's called for."

"Is that what I did? Go balls to the wall?"

Nichelle laughed. "Yep. You were a real badass."

Emma stood up a little straighter. "Go, me."

"Please, don't do it again anytime soon."

"You spoil all my fun."

"That's in my job description too."

Palmer capped her fountain pen and sat back in her chair. This would be her office for only three more days. She took stock. The only personal items on her desk were a picture of her hurdling victory in the 1985 NCAA Championships and the signed picture of Emma pinning the Silver Star on her. She'd left the picture of them together after the State of the Union on her fireplace mantel at home.

Emma. Merely thinking her name sent a jolt straight to Palmer's gut. True to her text, Emma hadn't reached out to her in any way, and Palmer had respected that, following suit. That hadn't stopped her imagination from running wild.

Would Emma show up at her retirement ceremony? Wouldn't that be something? The president's presence would be highly irregular in such an instance. Secretary of Defense Buchanan, Chairman Dutton, and Secretary Carsen were all scheduled to attend, along with a host of senators and members of Congress with whom Palmer had worked, fellow generals and service members from her past and present, diplomats, and members of the intelligence community.

No, Emma wouldn't surprise her with an appearance. The risk would be too great that someone, after the fact, would wrongly add two plus two and get five if word of any future relationship leaked out.

"A penny for your thoughts?" Max stood in the doorway.

"I'm not sure my thoughts are worth that much. C'mon in, Max."

He selected the nearest visitor's chair. "Have you figured it out yet?"

"What?" Palmer's eyebrows shot up. Had she telegraphed anything?

"You know, what's next for you."

Palmer let out a relieved breath. "Not yet. I've gotten a bunch of offers."

"I know that. And yet, you haven't done anything about any of them. I've been asking myself, why is that?"

"What do you mean?"

"I mean, the Palmer Estes I've known for thirty-plus years is always five steps ahead. She's got everything planned out far in advance."

"Is that so?"

"You know it is. And yet, here you sit with your whole life stretched in front of you, and you haven't lifted a finger to plot your next course. So, why?"

Palmer's heart pounded. She shrugged. "Maybe I'm done being structured."

"Pfft. Yeah, that's never going to happen." Max waved a hand dismissively. "Where are you going to live?"

Palmer swallowed. "I haven't decided yet. I've got at least thirty days before I have to move out of base housing." *And I'm not yet sure whether I'll be in a relationship that requires me to stay here in D.C. or go far away to heal my heart. How can I entertain job opportunities and locales when any decisions I make are dependent on a certain someone else's choices?*

"Uh-huh."

"What's with the inquisition?"

"Nothing. I'm just worried about my friend."

"You don't need to worry about me, Max. I'll be fine." She needed to change the topic. "I put in a good word on that promotion for you. I'm hopeful it will come through before the end of the week."

"Nice deflection."

"It's the thought that counts. You know if it were up to me, I'd promote you in a heartbeat. Speaking of hearts… Don't you have a date with Nichelle tonight?"

"I do." He rose. "I can take a hint, but we're not done talking about this."

"I'm still your boss, you know."

"You're my friend," Max said softly. "And what happens next for you matters to me, okay?"

"Understood. Don't worry about me. I'll be fine. I promise."

After Max left, Palmer allowed herself to ruminate. Would she be fine? What if Emma was having second thoughts? What would Palmer do if she'd changed her mind?

Palmer shook her head to dispel the doubts. *That's not going to happen. Emma's just exercising an abundance of caution, that's all.* Palmer snapped off the light. More than anything, she wished she could reach out to Emma and ask. Instead, she'd satisfy herself by packing yet more boxes and daydreaming about the future she hoped would be coming to fruition soon.

CHAPTER SIXTEEN

E mma stared blankly through the inky early-morning darkness at the Washington Monument in the distance. Today was the day. She couldn't put it off any longer. If she were going to spend the weekend in New York with Palmer, she would have to make the call now.

The Deputy White House Chief of Staff would have to scramble the Secret Service and the motorcade and procure the hotel and the theater tickets. Scott, her Secret Service Agent in Charge, would have to interface with New York City police, JFK International Airport officials, the Wall Street landing zone, the New York State Police, and vet whatever restaurant Emma chose for dinner. The cabin would have to be opened, secured, and stocked. And then there was the issue of the White House press corps.

The trip would appear on the official presidential schedule with the time of departure and the simple notation: The President departs the White House en route Joint Base Andrews; South Lawn; Open Press (Final Gather – 5:05 p.m. – North Doors of the Palm Room). Then, a second entry would indicate the time (roughly fifteen minutes after the takeoff from the South Lawn) and the notation: The President departs Joint Base Andrews en route to New York City, New York; Joint Base Andrews; Travel Pool Coverage.

No, Emma wouldn't have to disclose her traveling companions, if she had any, nor her exact itinerary on the schedule. She wouldn't have a public schedule for the trip either. But the press pool was ubiquitous. It wasn't as though she could sneak away without them tagging along.

For Emma, this was the sticking point. Up until now, she'd never taken unofficial guests with her, well…anywhere. As a result, there'd never been anything of interest to the press with regard to her personal life. In truth, she had none. Emma could just imagine the headlines if Palmer traveled with her now.

And what about Palmer? For her entire military career, Palmer had avoided any personal entanglements—anything that might call negative attention to herself. She'd never come out, even when it was safe to do so. The idea that she'd welcome—or even tolerate—the harsh glare of the spotlight that would shine on her as a result of being seen with Emma… Emma couldn't fathom it.

"That's not your decision to make," Emma muttered into the empty space. She shook her head and crossed her arms. *Come on, McMasters. Stop dreaming up obstacles and be truthful, at least with yourself. This isn't about Palmer. It's about you.*

Well, that was honest. Her hesitation had far more to do with her own issues than it did with Palmer. Emma was frightened out of her mind—scared to open her heart again, scared to take a risk, scared that entering into a romantic relationship would damage the Democratic party at the midterms and hurt her own reelection chances, scared of the scandalous headlines and the Republicans' inevitable taunts, "I told you she would besmirch the White House with her lesbianism," scared that every good thing she'd done as president up until this point would be subsumed by her personal life. Scared. Scared. Scared.

The phone rang and Emma practically jumped out of her skin. She snapped up the receiver. "Yes?"

"Good morning, Madam President."

"Good morning, Nichelle."

"Did you still want me to join you for breakfast in the residence?"

Emma closed her eyes. As her panic had increased in the middle of the night, she'd sent an email to the one person in whom she could confide and asked if the two of them could have breakfast together before the start of the day.

She needed a sounding board. She simply wasn't thinking clearly. Nichelle had been with her when Heather was alive. Nichelle would understand why this was so hard—why it felt like a betrayal of her relationship with Heather. Nichelle knew her better than almost anyone. Emma trusted her to tell her the truth and to be discreet.

"Yes, please."

"I'm on my way."

Five minutes later, there was a knock at the door. "When you said you were on the way…"

"I was in my office catching up."

"Ah. Come in."

They walked to the dining room without saying a word. The silence stretched until breakfast had been served and they were alone. Nichelle put her hands in her lap and stared at Emma.

"What?"

"You tell me, Madam President."

"What do you mean?"

"Let's see… You've been distracted all week. You're jumpy and far more brooding than usual. You sent me an email from your private account to my private account in the middle of the night when you should've been sleeping. You're out of sorts. Hence, the reason I'm here at oh-dark-thirty before the workday starts. You're obviously struggling with something personal. I'm just waiting to be enlightened."

"Don't look at me with that smug expression."

"What smug expression?"

"The one that says, 'I know I'm right, so why don't you admit it and spill already?'"

Nichelle arched an eyebrow. "You read all that from one look?"

"Yep."

"Huh. Remind me not to play poker with you. Am I right?"

"Of course you're right."

"Okay, then. I'm all ears. What's got you so wound up?"

Emma bit her lip. Once she said it out loud, she could never un-say it.

"Come on. It can't be that bad," Nichelle prompted.

"Whatever I tell you remains in the strictest of confidence."

"That goes without saying. You know that."

Emma nodded, more to herself than anything else. Where should she begin? "I-I'm…" She blew out an explosive breath. This was hard.

Nichelle leaned forward and touched Emma's hand until she made eye contact. "I'm on your side, remember? Whatever it is, I'm with you."

"I know." Emma sucked in a deep breath and started again. "I'm interested in someone," she blurted.

Nichelle's face lit up. "You are? That's fantastic! Oh, I'm so happy for you."

Emma pulled back her hand and scrunched up her forehead. "You are?"

"Of course I am. You've been alone for more than three years. You're lonely and this job is so damn isolating. You need and deserve someone to share your life with. Heather would tell you as much, and you know it."

"But you don't even know who it is yet."

Nichelle smiled broadly. "I've got my suspicions."

Now Emma was intrigued. "Do tell."

"Nu-uh. This is your story."

"Well, you seem so sure of yourself. I'm curious who you think it is."

Nichelle laughed. "How very high school of you. I'll tell you what. I'll write the name down on a piece of paper. You tell me who it is, and then check me to see if I was right."

"That's juvenile."

Nichelle shrugged as if to say she didn't care.

Emma relented. She retrieved a pad of paper and a pen from the side-table drawer and slid them over to Nichelle. Nichelle scribbled something, tore the page from the pad, folded it in fourths, and put it underneath her palm.

"You're not going to give it to me?"

"Not until you 'fess up."

Emma groaned. Could this be any more awkward? "It's Palmer Estes."

Nichelle tried to keep a straight face but failed miserably. She slid the piece of paper over to Emma. "Open it."

Emma stared at the name. *General Palmer Estes.* "How did you know?"

"For one thing, according to Max, she's been acting every bit as squirrelly as you."

"She has?"

"Uh-huh. Max says she's been staring off into space a lot, she hasn't made any firm commitments for what she's going to do next, or where she's going to live. Very unlike her, he says."

Emma took in this information. So, she wasn't the only one struggling. "Has she said anything to him?"

"Not a word."

"But you two clearly have been talking."

"We care about you. Both of you have been alone for a long time. You're fabulous people who deserve every happiness. So, yes. Maybe Max and I have been engaging out loud in a little wishful thinking."

Emma couldn't sit still any longer. She jumped up to pace. "It's fraught with political implications, Nich."

"Let's talk about it. Have either of you done anything that could raise red flags? Have you engaged in any behavior that would be construed as inappropriate?"

"Absolutely not."

Nichelle nodded. "Is there anything for anyone to find, if they were digging?"

"Absolutely not. We didn't have feelings for each other when you asked me to review her actions for the Silver Star. Other than that, we had an innocent, friendly dinner here the night of the State of the Union. As you know, she legitimately deserved to be one of my special guests at that address, and she got no special treatment at the event or afterward above or beyond what any other of my guests received."

Emma turned and paced in the opposite direction. "Some time later, she invited me to her place for dinner, as friends. I went. We had a friendly dinner. Nothing happened of a more personal nature, but that was the night when I began to realize I had feelings for her. So I left and came home. Period."

Emma thought about their text conversation. She told Nichelle about that for good measure. "That's the last back-and-forth we exchanged, and that was months ago. I knew I was falling for her, so I cut off all communications. She understood why and said she was looking forward to hearing from me on October 9th, the day after her retirement ceremony."

Nichelle nodded sagely.

"Well, say something." Emma stopped pacing.

"Sit down, you're making me dizzy."

"Very funny." But Emma did as she was told.

"Look. You've done everything with complete integrity and honesty. No one can argue otherwise."

Emma scoffed. "You know as well as I do that perceptions can be altered with the twist of a comment or a misinterpreted photo op."

Nichelle held up a hand. "Let's unpack this one aspect at a time. First, let's forget about the optics and politics. Let's talk about how you feel and what you want. You're human, Emma, and allowed to have a life outside of the office."

The fact that Nichelle had used her first name wasn't lost on Emma. That was rare these days. She understood that Nichelle was trying to humanize the situation. This wasn't about politics; it was personal.

"It's complicated," Emma finally said.

"You bet it is."

Emma twisted her wedding band. She only became aware that she was doing it when Nichelle stilled her hands. "I've been thinking about taking it off," she said hoarsely.

"Are you ready for that?"

"If I'm ready to start dating, then I need to be ready to say goodbye, don't I?"

"I didn't ask you that. I asked—"

"If I was ready to let go of the last tangible sign of my marriage—of us."

Nichelle nodded. "Yes, that's the first and most important question."

"Because if I can't let go of Heather, I can't let Palmer in. Not really, anyway. And that would be monumentally unfair to Palmer."

"Exactly."

Emma resisted the urge to jump up and pace again. "I-I think I could really fall hard for Palmer. She's nothing like Heather, so it's not a case of projection or replacement."

"That's for sure."

"Palmer has a quiet strength and noble beauty about her." Emma wanted to be careful not to betray Palmer's confidence about her young adult experiences, so she phrased the next bit carefully. "She's got a bruised and battered heart—one that will require special care and tending. But she has such a capacity to love; it's palpable."

"I don't know her the way you do, but anyone can see she's something very, very special."

Emma smiled and allowed herself to moon for a minute. "Yes, she sure is. She's smart, analytical, mostly unflappable unless you embarrass her, big-hearted, compassionate... You wouldn't know it, but she's got a very sly, subtle sense of humor, and a shyness that's both surprising and quaint. She's humble and stoic, and..."

"You're already in love with her," Nichelle said quietly.

Emma glanced up with a shock. "Yes... I suppose I am."

Tears pricked Nichelle's eyes. "Good."

"Good? I already told you, this is fraught with danger on so many levels—"

"Maybe so. But where there's real, deep love, there's the armor to withstand any attacks that may come your way."

"You, better than anybody, should know what's coming. All those Republican fearmongers who tried to whip up the bigots before the election with scenarios of wild, debaucherous sex in the White House will have a field day with this. It could do serious damage to the party before the midterms right when we've got a real shot to win the Senate.

"It will distract from our agenda and overshadow every initiative and every other newsworthy topic."

"Correction," Nichelle held up her forefinger. "Coverage of your personal life might eclipse other topics, but your relationship with Palmer will not be a distraction to the agenda itself."

"That's semantical and you know it. We can't win that argument. It's unsustainable."

"Do you want us to poll or conduct a focus group to gauge reaction to you undertaking a relationship?"

"What? Put together a focus group to test whether or not voters believe I'm entitled to have a life?" Emma asked.

"Indignation. Excellent. That's exactly the appropriate reaction to such an absurd idea. Also, it reinforces my point. Yes, you will undoubtedly catch flack and the far right and social media trolls will be brutal about it. Yes, something this salacious will dominate the headlines for a while once it comes to light—"

"And it will."

"But," Nichelle continued as if Emma hadn't interrupted her, "I've never known you to be cowed by push back. The Emma McMasters I know withstood withering, vicious attacks on her character, her sexuality, her morals and scruples, through every campaign for every office starting with the district attorney's office. Not only did she withstand them, she turned them to her favor."

Emma wanted to interrupt again, but Nichelle was on a roll.

"She stood tall and faced the criticism and the lies head on by being honest, transparent, and unflappable. She took the high ground, ceded nothing, and won everything. That's the Emma McMasters I know, and the one I'm proud to call my friend and my boss."

"Are you finished yet?"

"No," Nichelle said. "One more thing. Is Palmer worth fighting for?"

"What?"

"Is Palmer worth fighting for?" Nichelle asked slowly.

"Yes."

"Right. Then I'll be proud to fight alongside you for your right to live and love the woman of your choosing and I'll happily marshal an army that will stand with us."

Emma smiled wanly at her friend. "Thank you, Nich. You're one in a million."

"Lucky for you." Nichelle folded her napkin and placed it on the table. "Now let's talk logistics and strategy."

Emma's heart swelled with gratitude for her friend and fiercest ally. "Okay, let's do."

≼⊱

Palmer stood ramrod straight as the master of ceremonies for her retirement ceremony, Chairman Dutton, extolled her virtues. A virtual "Who's Who" of dignitaries and former bosses and team members strode to the podium to have their say as well.

She hadn't thought she'd be so emotional, but it was all Palmer could do to hold it together. Thirty-five years was a long time—a lifetime. As she gazed out into the audience, her mind clicked through the tours of duty and all of the postings and situations she'd endured, both harrowing and good. She'd met and worked beside so many wonderful, special people. They'd filled the void left by her parents' absence. More than that, because that really didn't give them enough credit, they'd become her surrogate family.

Palmer also reflected on the faces that weren't there—those who had been lost in action along the way. She swallowed hard. *Now's not the time, soldier. Later...* Later she could engage in a proper retrospective and mourn those she'd lost under her command, those who had served so bravely and made the ultimate sacrifice. She remembered every single one of their names and the circumstances under which they'd been killed. Some of their families were in the audience today.

Palmer blinked as she realized Secretary of Defense Buchanan had turned to address her.

"I wanted to read you this personal note directly from President McMasters. She asked me to convey this to you on the occasion of your retirement."

Palmer's eyes nearly bulged out of her head. Emma had sent an emissary with a personal message to be read in front of hundreds of people? Her palms started to sweat.

"On this, the occasion of your retirement from active military duty, I wish to congratulate you, General Estes. For more than three decades, you have served with courage, honor, and valor. No one could have represented the uniform better. I know I speak for all above and below you in your chain of command when I say, 'Well done.' On behalf of a grateful nation, I wish you well in your next endeavors. Your country thanks you for your service."

Secretary Buchanan stepped back and handed her a proclamation bearing the text he had just read. There, on the bottom with a flourish, was Emma's distinctive signature.

"Thank you, sir. And please, thank the president for me."

"I certainly will. Congratulations, General Estes."

The remainder of the ceremony was a blur. Afterward, Palmer felt like she'd shaken hands with, or hugged, everyone in the room. As the line to greet her thinned, she noticed Nichelle standing off to the side with Max.

As Palmer approached, Max peeled off. Palmer frowned in confusion. "Where's he going? Something I said?"

"No," Nichelle laughed. "I told him to get lost."

Palmer raised both eyebrows.

"I needed a moment with you—alone."

"Okay." Palmer drew the word out.

"I have something for you." Nichelle slipped a blank note-card-size envelope into Palmer's jacket pocket. "You're going to want to read that when you're alone. I've included my personal cell number. Call when you're ready."

Palmer knew she must've looked bewildered.

"All will become clear to you when you read what's in the envelope. Congratulations, General Estes." Nichelle winked and disappeared into the crowd.

CHAPTER SEVENTEEN

Palmer turned over the note in her hands for the umpteenth time. She didn't need to read it again—she'd already memorized the contents.

My dearest Palmer,

I hope you don't mind that I sent a trusted personal courier to put this safely into your hands. I trust Nichelle with my life and you can too.

I deeply regret that I was unable to be there in person to deliver this note and my official remarks. I do intend to make it up to you by congratulating you in private, if that is still something you'd like to explore.

On the off chance you're thinking of saying yes, you should know up front, nothing about this will be easy. Every detail of my life is scrutinized, and, according to some, open for public debate. That includes my private life.

Where normally one might take things slow and private, i.e. go out for coffee two or three times, followed by a dinner or three, and maybe a concert or a show as the parties get to know each other better and determine whether/how to proceed, I do not have that luxury. The simple act of going out for coffee involves a contingent of Secret Service agents and a coterie of reporters.

You are so fiercely protective of your privacy, Palmer. I wish, more than anything, I could assure you that I can protect you in this. Please know that I will try, but I cannot promise you with any certainty that I will succeed.

All of this is by way of saying, I certainly will understand if you decide pursuing the possibility of a relationship with me isn't worth the risk of exposure and/or the attention being seen with me will garner. Please, think carefully about this. Everything about your life will change the moment you say yes.

Your sexuality will be exposed, and everything you've ever done personally or professionally (and many things you haven't) will become fair game for pundits and prognosticators. That's a lot to withstand without any guarantee that you'll want to pursue an ongoing relationship once you get to know me.

Now that I've given you every reason to say no, please rest assured that I have been counting down the days and I have no reservations or doubts.

I've put together a plan for a quiet weekend getaway. If you decide that you want to throw caution to the wind, please call Nichelle's private number and she will fill you in on the details and logistics.

Whatever you decide, please know how proud I am of you, Palmer. You've had an exemplary career and deserve every accolade and the most perfect post-retirement life. I wish for you every wonderful thing life can offer.

Affectionately,
Emma

Palmer wandered into her home office and gazed at the pictures on the wall. The first photo featured her in fatigues, flanked by her flight crew in Kuwait during Desert Storm. They had their arms around each other as they mugged for the camera. "We were so young and cocky back then."

The next photo showed Palmer's promotional ceremony when she received her fourth star. To her own eyes, she appeared wistful and a little sad, and she had been both. In addition to her friends and co-workers, the ceremony should've been attended by her close family. Her father should've been the one to pin the stars on her shoulder. Instead, the chairman of the Joint Chiefs had done the honor.

The final photo showed her delivering the commencement address at the Army War College last year. The theme of her address had been, *Proud to Serve*. Palmer smiled wanly. She'd always been proud to be Army strong, proud to wear the uniform, proud of her country and her fellow service members.

She'd dedicated her entire adult life to serving and representing her country. The Army had given her a purpose, an education, a home, and a family, all invaluable commodities to Palmer. In return, she'd given the Army her full attention and effort for thirty-five years.

And now it was over. For the first time since she'd signed the papers committing her to service, she was a free woman. Her choices and decisions were hers alone, and the consequences of those choices also fell only to her.

What was it Britney had asked? It was part of a Mary Oliver poem, wasn't it? "What will you do with your one wild, precious life?" Palmer recalled out loud.

Indeed, what would she do? Emma's note had laid bare Palmer's choices. If she went forward with the weekend Emma had planned for them, she should assume the media would suss out the reason for her presence and jump all over it.

Emma was right, nothing would be sacred—not her career, her family, her accomplishments and awards, her friendships—everything would be subject to intense scrutiny. The knot in Palmer's stomach tightened. All this time, she'd avoided even a whisper of scandal or personal entanglement. As far as she knew, with the exception of Max, no one had any reason to suspect she was a lesbian.

Emma was the most out, visible lesbian in the universe. Even if nothing happened between them beyond an innocent dinner, Palmer would be presumed to be gay by association. Every corner of her life would be examined and exposed. All that careful work to maintain her privacy would be forfeited in the blink of an eye. Emma had said as much, and she was right.

The weight of her choices settled on Palmer's shoulders like a shroud. She sat down heavily in her office chair. Panic welled in her chest, constricting her airway.

"How can you be perfectly calm and clear-headed in the middle of a battle, with bullets flying all around you, and yet be completely freaked out at the thought of committing to a personal relationship?"

Palmer's eyes flew open wide. That was it. This wasn't just about people finding out she was a lesbian or digging into her life. She was kidding herself. Yes, of course she had to consider the potential damage to her reputation and honor should her tie to Emma become public knowledge. But the crux of the matter had far more to do with her fear of intimacy and commitment than it did with the rest of it.

Britney had been right. Palmer was terrified of letting anyone into her heart. Her parents, Britney... The lesson from that formative situation was that people you loved abandoned you. Secondary to that had been the shame and judgment heaped upon her. Everyone at the track camp heard some version of what had happened. She heard them whispering behind her back. Their judgmental gazes burned holes in the back of her head as she packed her bags and left camp.

The abandonment issues hadn't gotten any better as she lost fellow service members in various actions through the years. Those experiences simply reinforced the notion that people you cared about left you, so it was best not to get too attached, and not to let them get too attached in return.

She frowned as she remembered Ellen Arnold. They'd been captains together in Desert Storm. Like Palmer, Ellen had been wounded in action. They'd gone through rehab simultaneously, pushing each other to heal. The shared experience bonded them together.

One day, they'd been alone in the rehab room, working on range of motion and strength conditioning. Ellen had been spotting Palmer as she settled on the weight bench to do chest lifts. If she closed her eyes, Palmer still could see Ellen clearly, the dimple in her cheek prominent when she smiled, as she was doing then.

Palmer's heart rate had soared when Ellen bent over and kissed her. Her lips had been so soft, the taste of them so sweet.

"I've been released," Ellen whispered. *"I ship back out tomorrow."*

"You do?" Palmer swallowed hard.

"Yeah. I got my orders. What do you say we get out of here and enjoy my last night?"

At a loss for words, Palmer merely nodded. Ellen knew a place where they could have privacy. Despite Palmer's trepidation, she'd acquiesced. It had been so long...

Ellen shipped out the next day. A week later, Palmer got word that she'd been killed in action. It was the first and last time in the Army that Palmer had let down her guard. Never again would someone get underneath her armor.

Palmer ran her fingers through her hair. *That was then, this is now.* Emma was not Ellen, or Britney, or her parents, or any of the dozens of good soldiers she'd lost along the way.

"You either can spend the rest of your life avoiding human connections in order to keep yourself safe, or you can have a little faith, trust your heart to show you the way, and open yourself to the possibilities." When Palmer said it out loud, the choice seemed so obvious.

She glanced again at the wall. Although the pictures marked personal milestones, there was very little personal about them. For so long, she'd been existing instead of living.

Emma, so full of life, so vibrant and real... Emma was reaching out her hand. She had every bit as much to lose as Palmer—probably more. And yet, she was willing to take the risk.

Palmer picked up the business card from the center of her empty blotter and punched in a phone number. "Hello? Nichelle?"

Emma ignored the shouted questions from the gaggle of reporters gathered on the South Lawn. Resolutely, she made her way to Marine One for the short helicopter ride to Andrews. So far, the coverage had been positive. The press seemed to respect that the president was about to take her first breather since getting into office. They'd even run a favorable story this morning highlighting the amount of "personal" time taken by her predecessor versus her first official long weekend off.

Emma was painfully aware that all that stored good will could, and likely would, evaporate in less than a nanosecond if they learned that she wouldn't be alone on this trip.

Palmer. When Nichelle called last night to say everything was a go, Emma's heart skipped a beat. Right now, Palmer would be on a commercial flight to New York with Nichelle. Together, they'd meet Air Force One at JFK so Palmer and Emma could take the last leg of the journey together.

Emma knew it would've been more discreet simply to have Palmer proceed to the hotel, where Nichelle had booked Palmer her own room. But, knowing Palmer's affinity for flying helicopters, Emma thought she might appreciate the short hop to the Wall Street landing zone aboard Marine One—a Sikorsky Sea King VH-3D, piloted by HMX-1, the special Marine unit tasked with flying the presidential fleet.

Emma laughed at herself. *Tell the truth—you just wanted to impress the girl.* Again, Emma's stomach did that funny, flip thing it did every time she thought about this weekend and Palmer. She'd said yes. In spite of everything Emma had laid out in her note, Palmer had said yes.

Palmer wiped the palms of her hands against her trousers. *It's just a weekend away getting to know one another.*

"Nervous?" Nichelle asked gently as their plane skidded to a halt on the runway at JFK.

"Me?" Palmer squeaked. "What gave me away?"

Nichelle squeezed her arm. "If it helps, she's skittish as a colt too."

Palmer digested that information. "She is?"

"Oh, yeah. You should've seen her trying to pick out outfits. My God, she had an easier time figuring out what to wear to meet the Queen of England."

That made Palmer laugh. "I'm sure she'd look great in a burlap sack."

"Aren't you just the sweetest thing."

"No one's ever accused me of that before."

"First time for everything."

The plane taxied toward the jetway, and Palmer's pulse quickened. "Are you sure we shouldn't just go right to the hotel? I mean, there's press on Air Force One with her, right?"

"Yes, there's press. And no, we're not going to change the plan now. If I don't deliver you to Marine One as expected, the boss will have my head." Nichelle shifted in her seat so that she faced Palmer. Her expression turned serious. "Unless you're having second thoughts…"

"No. No," Palmer repeated firmly. "I'm trying to be considerate here. I already thought through all of the potential consequences for myself before I made the decision to call you. But Emma… The stakes are off the charts for her."

"Trust me, she knows that. Emma is smart and probably the shrewdest, most astute politician I've ever met. She's studied this from every angle and played out the possibilities so that she's ten steps ahead."

"I didn't mean to suggest—"

"You didn't. Don't worry." Nichelle hesitated. "Palmer, I'm going to get personal here for a second. Emma would kill me if she knew I shared this with you, but I think it's important for you to understand."

Palmer nodded.

"I've been with Emma for a very long time—ever since she first ran for the New York State Senate. I've been by her side for every major decision and through professional ups and downs, personal triumphs and tragedies.

"What Emma did—what she's doing now—in opening her heart to you? This is a huge leap for her. You're the first person who's turned her head since her wife died. Truthfully, I think you might be the only person who *could've* done that."

Palmer understood that Nichelle was measuring her words carefully. Nichelle's devotion to Emma was so obvious. As if she hadn't already loved Nichelle for making Max so happy, Palmer's respect and appreciation for her soared now. There was much

Palmer wanted to ask, but time was short, and she didn't want to interrupt.

"When Heather died," Nichelle said, "a big part of Emma died with her. Emma convinced herself that what happened that day was her fault—it should've been her in the car, not Heather; it would've been Emma, except that she got caught up in a meeting. She's carried that guilt ever since. I think that unconsciously, Emma doesn't believe she deserves love and happiness in this lifetime after what happened."

Palmer's heart ached for Emma. "I can't imagine anyone who deserves those things more."

"I agree. She and Heather had a ten-year plan. They'd already decided that Emma should run for president. Honestly, I wasn't sure she'd follow through. I wasn't sure she could. But seeing that dream through to fruition became almost an obsession with Emma. It was the one thing she could do for Heather and by golly, she wasn't going to fail her again.

"I don't know what would've happened if Emma had lost." Nichelle bit her lip as her expression took on a faraway look. "Or maybe I do. She would've been lost, herself. The race, the presidency, Emma's honest, fervent belief that she can improve people's lives, that she can heal the country... These are the things that get her out of bed in the morning."

The plane rolled to a halt and passengers undid their seatbelts all around them.

"Palmer, Emma is ready, finally, to move past the grief, past the guilt, past the past. I don't know you well, but Max does. He talks about you with such reverence and love, I think I've come to fall a little in love with you myself." Nichelle smiled and winked. "If I didn't think you'd make Emma deliriously happy, I would've advised her against pursuing this. God knows, there are many practical reasons for her to avoid any sort of personal relationships.

"The truth is, I think you can save her. No pressure there for you. It takes two, though, and I hope Emma will make you every bit as happy as I'm confident you'll make her. If, after spending time together, you decide this won't work for you, so be it. Selfishly, I'm rooting for you two to fall madly, deeply in love and live happily ever after."

This time it was Palmer's turn to squeeze Nichelle's hand. "I understand what you're telling me. Trust me, if I wasn't already falling in love with Emma, I wouldn't be here. I'll take excellent care of her heart. You have my word."

"I'm counting on it." Nichelle rose. "Are you ready?"

"Yes, I am." And Palmer meant it.

CHAPTER EIGHTEEN

To Palmer, it all resembled a well-choreographed ballet, executed with military precision, as she would've expected. Secret Service agents met Nichelle and Palmer at the gate and hustled them out a side exit to a waiting limousine. The limo ferried them out onto the tarmac where Air Force One had just come to rest. A series of four identical Marine helicopters sat pre-deployed and at the ready, each manned by a pilot, co-pilot, and a crew chief. Black Secret Service SUVs ringed the area, along with New York City police cruisers, Secret Service agents on foot, and uniformed police officers.

Emma descended the steps. Palmer could've sworn she paused to look around for her, but she might've imagined it.

When Emma was halfway down the steps, Nichelle said, "That's our cue."

A Secret Service agent opened the limo door and Nichelle and Palmer exited. Another agent guided them toward the same helicopter Emma had boarded. Emma indicated that Palmer should sit next to her. Nichelle settled in a seat behind them. They buckled in and donned headsets as several more Secret Service agents joined them.

As they took off, Palmer looked back at the ground. Members of the president's staff, credentialed media, and Secret Service agents were piling into the remaining helicopters. When she returned her focus to her surroundings, she found Emma smiling a toothy grin at her.

Into her headset mic, Emma said, "I thought you'd appreciate the sweet ride." She indicated the Sea King.

Palmer laughed. "It's a neat upgrade. More bells and whistles than I'm used to, and a lot less dust and sand."

"I hope you're going to love the scenery," Emma said. "Those other helicopters take the direct route to the Wall Street landing zone. We'll take a circuitous route. The president never waits; that's the rule. So, we get a fabulous tour of the city—the Statue of Liberty, Wall Street, the Hudson River, the stadiums—every iconic landmark."

"Lucky me," Palmer said.

Emma arched an eyebrow, and, no doubt cognizant that everyone on the helicopter wore a headset and could hear every word, silently mouthed, "No. Lucky *me*."

Palmer thought she might melt on the spot. Instead, she settled for a broad grin of her own and a smile that she hoped reached her eyes.

As they descended onto the landing pad, Palmer noted the State Police divers and boats in the water, preventing anyone from getting close. A motorcade was set up and waiting; she watched the last of the other helicopters empty out and the presidential party and reporters scramble into the waiting limousines and SUVs.

Within seconds of touch down, Emma, Palmer, and Nichelle were off-loaded, hustled into one of the cars, and on their way to the hotel. As if by silent agreement, none of them said a word.

When they reached their destination, the Lotte New York Palace Hotel on Madison Avenue in midtown Manhattan, Emma surreptitiously brushed her fingers against Palmer's hand. "I'll be getting out first and heading directly to my suite. Once I'm safely inside, you and Nichelle will head into the lobby. Nichelle will get you checked in and see you to your room. Get settled in, and then she'll bring you up to the suite so we can sit and chat for a bit and have a nice dinner before we head out to the show."

"Check."

"I'll see you soon." Just before she exited, Emma turned back to her. "I'm really glad you're here."

"Me too," Palmer answered softly. "Me too."

❧❧

Emma stared out the window at the breathtaking view of the Empire State Building and *her* city. The sky was crystal clear and bluer than she remembered. So far, everything had gone off like clockwork.

Nichelle texted to let her know that Palmer was freshening up and would arrive shortly. When Emma asked how their trip from D.C. had gone, Nichelle answered with one word, *Splendid.* Naturally, Emma wanted to know more. What had they talked about? How was Palmer's mood? Was she as nervous as Emma? She asked nothing more. Nichelle wouldn't have told her anyway.

Emma heard a soft knock on the door of the suite and the murmur of voices as one of the Secret Service agents admitted Palmer.

Emma spun around in time to see Palmer step tentatively into the living room. She wore a slate blue suit with a white shell underneath and a pair of fashionable navy flats. The only jewelry showing was a pair of sapphire stud earrings. *Stunning.*

Belatedly, Emma realized she hadn't said anything out loud. "Hi. Come in. You look...amazing."

Palmer stopped just short of Emma's personal space. "That's because you've only ever seen me in uniform."

Slowly, Emma shook her head. "No. You look marvelous in a uniform too. But this," she indicated the tailored cut of the trousers and structured jacket, "this really suits you."

From this close, Palmer's eyes appeared cerulean. *I could so get lost in those baby blues.* For the first time since Emma had known her, Palmer wore her hair down, rather than in a tight bun at the back of her head. Waves of luxurious red flowed around her face and spilled onto her shoulders.

Palmer shifted uncomfortably under the scrutiny, and Emma blinked. "I'm sorry. I'm being rude. Come, sit down. Can I get you something to drink? I believe you prefer sparkling water with a twist of lime, right?"

Palmer's eyebrows shot up into her hairline. "You've got quite a memory."

"Hazard of the job, I'm afraid. I have to be observant."

"In answer to your question, yes, please."

Emma strode over to the sideboard, where sparkling water chilled in a bucket of ice. On an adjacent sterling-silver tray were a bowl of neatly sliced lemons and limes, an additional bucket full of ice, and two cut crystal glasses. She filled the two glasses and brought them over to the couch.

"Thank you." Palmer smiled at her shyly.

Emma couldn't help herself; she had to know why. "Explain to me how a four-star general can be so bashful?"

Palmer glanced away.

"See? That's exactly what I mean."

The blush began at Palmer's chest and spread upward.

"I'm sorry. I know I shouldn't—"

"Large groups, commands, and crises are easy. Those aren't about me. One-on-one personal situations have never been my forte. Truthfully, I haven't had much experience with those."

Emma nodded. "Understood." *Change the topic to something that puts her more at ease.* "I'm sorry I couldn't be there for your retirement ceremony."

"Don't give it a second thought. Your appearance would've been highly unusual. Under the circumstances, it made perfect sense for you to stay away."

"I know. I just want to be sure you're clear that I wished I could've been there." How was it possible they'd interacted with so much ease when they'd dined at Palmer's place, and now the conversation seemed so...stilted?

Palmer silently sipped her drink.

"Palmer?" Emma leaned forward and searched Palmer's gaze. "I-I know I conveyed to you in my note some of the challenges of dating the president—"

"Emma." Palmer slid her palm underneath Emma's and intertwined their fingers.

It was such a simple act, but it sent shockwaves of pleasure and warmth through every inch of Emma's body. She couldn't take her eyes off their joined hands.

"I get that you're concerned for my privacy. That's remarkably chivalrous, truly." Palmer increased the pressure of the contact. "I'm here because no one in my fifty-six years has moved me the way you do. I'm here because you fascinate me, not as the president, but as a woman. I'm here because—"

Emma couldn't help it. She closed the distance between them, cupped Palmer's face with her free hand, and brought their lips together. The kiss was gentle, soft, and tentative. As she drew back, she stroked the side of Palmer's face. "I probably shouldn't have done—"

Palmer pulled her close again and kissed her more thoroughly. The exploration was sweet…almost reverential. They broke the kiss and rested their foreheads together.

"Sometimes," Palmer said hoarsely, "words are overrated."

"Mm-hmm," Emma agreed. After a moment, and with great reluctance, she added, "We probably should have the appetizers. The chef went to a lot of trouble—"

"Right. Of course. Right," Palmer said again. She moved away.

Immediately, Emma felt bereft. She wanted to savor these first private moments alone together, before the world intruded.

As if reading her mind, Palmer said, "You need to know, I'm not done with you yet."

Emma trailed her fingertips along Palmer's jaw line. "I sincerely hope not." *You know you should have this discussion up front. Putting it off doesn't change the facts.* The appetizers would hold a little longer. "Palmer…"

"When you say my name like that, it sounds ominous."

It was Emma's turn to look away. "Not ominous, but important."

"I'm listening." Palmer re-joined their hands, and Emma focused her attention there.

"During my campaign, I promised the American people that I would be transparent in all I did. When the Republicans ran attack ads suggesting that, if elected, I would turn the White House into a den of lesbian iniquity—"

"I remember that ad," Palmer said. "It pissed me off on your behalf."

Emma chuckled and squeezed Palmer's fingers. "Yeah. Me too. But the press thought it made for good copy, so I had no choice but to address the issue, even though it was absurd on its face."

"I saw your answer in the interview they aired on election night. You were pitch-perfect. I even gave you a standing ovation in my living room."

That surprised a guffaw out of Emma. "Good to know." She turned their hands over. Palmer's hands were bigger than hers, with slender but strong fingers. *Out with it. Stalling isn't going to make this part any easier or change the facts.* "The thing is, if I use ruses to throw the press off track in order to give us more room to explore a relationship—"

"It will look like you're hiding something and trying to pull one over on the American people," Palmer finished for her.

"It certainly could be construed that way. The optics would be horrible. As it is, once they figure out that we're dating, I have no doubt that some media outlets will immediately assume that we were an item before I awarded you the Silver Star and invited you to the State of the Union. In fact, they'll intimate that our relationship was the very reason why you received those honors."

"I'm sure they'd like that to be the truth," Palmer said. Emma noticed that her posture had stiffened.

"It sells papers and it's too juicy a prospect to pass up."

"What do you want to do, Emma?"

For long seconds, Emma said nothing. Finally, she began, "Whatever I do or say affects us both, Palmer. I won't do or say anything unless you're on board with it."

"I appreciate that." Palmer raised their joined hands and examined them. Her eyes grew large. "You took off your wedding ring," she said, wonder evident in her tone.

"Yes," Emma acknowledged quietly. "I loved Heather with all my heart, but it's time to let *us* go. I wouldn't have sent you that text if I wasn't ready to make room in my life for someone new— for you."

"You know some eagle-eyed reporter will notice…"

"I do," Emma agreed. "But it would be disingenuous to continue to wear it when I'm falling in love with someone else." She raised her eyes to meet Palmer's. She needed for Palmer to see what was in her heart. "I won't hide behind that ring in order to maintain cover."

Palmer's incandescent smile said it all. She pulled Emma toward her and kissed her deeply. Emma's heart soared as she lost herself in the moment. How could she have wondered if this was right for her?

"I love you too, Emma," Palmer said against her lips. "I'm ready. I wouldn't have answered your text as I did if I wasn't, and I certainly wouldn't have placed that call to Nichelle. You gave me fair warning. I understand this could get messy. As long as we go through it together, I'll be fine."

Emma's heart hammered. She cupped the back of Palmer's neck and pulled her in for another kiss. "I promise, we'll take every step together."

"I'm sure you've thought this through. How do you think we should handle it?"

Emma sat up straight. She couldn't think clearly with Palmer this close. "Olivia—my press secretary—has arranged for the press pool photographer to take pictures of me arriving for the show. That's the only official photo op of the trip.

"We have two choices. You can arrive on your own, ahead of me, and be seated before I get there. Under that scenario, the pictures will indicate that I attended the show solo, or with aides."

"Why do I sense that's not what you have in mind?"

Emma smiled. She appreciated that Palmer had a keen mind for strategy. "Probably because, most importantly, it's not honest." She broke eye contact. "Palmer, I need to ask you a question, and I need you to be really frank."

"Okay." Concern creased Palmer's brow.

Emma jumped up, walked to the window, and gazed outward. She couldn't bear to see Palmer's face when she responded to the next question. "It's ridiculous to hope that you already know the answer to this, but the stakes are too high—for both of us."

She heard Palmer shift on the couch. *Here goes nothing.* "I know what you said before, but…" Emma searched for the right words. "On a scale of one to ten…" She shook her head. "No. Scratch that." "How likely is it…" Emma crossed her arms. "No, scratch that too." *Just spit it out already.* If she said it in a rush, it would be easier.

"Palmer, I know how I feel. Even in the ridiculously little time we've spent together, I know what's in my heart. I don't need five dates with you, or even two, to know that I want a relationship with you. But if you have any doubts at all, there's no reason to expose you—"

Suddenly, Palmer was behind Emma, wrapping her in her arms. "Stop, Emma."

Palmer spun her around and held her tight. "I'm positive what I want. I don't need time or to take us out for a test drive."

"You don't?" Even as she asked it, Emma could see the truth in Palmer's eyes.

"I think I knew it the very first time I saw you in person, standing outside in front of millions of people, coatless and shivering, delivering the best damn Inaugural Address I'd ever heard. And I certainly knew it when I watched you handle that hostage situation. I admired your leadership, resolve, and compassion, yes. But it was more than that. I simply chose to ignore what I felt because you were unattainable. Any scenario that I might've dreamed was impossible."

"Until it wasn't," Emma said.

"Yes. Until it wasn't," Palmer agreed. Her breath tickled Emma's ear, making it difficult for her to focus.

"If you're absolutely sure... Because there's no putting the genie back in the bottle once it's out."

"I know." Palmer's lips caressed the outline of Emma's ear.

Emma closed her eyes as liquid heat flowed directly to her center. Reluctantly, she pushed Palmer back. "I can't think when you do that."

"That sounds promising."

"Mm-hmm. But right now, we've got to work through this."

Palmer stuffed her hands in her pockets and moved out of Emma's personal space.

"Okay," Emma said. "I've given this a lot of thought."

"I'm listening."

"The theater seats seven-hundred-forty patrons. The chances that none of them notice me and snap a photo or video, or livestream on Facebook or YouTube, is—"

"Zero."

"Yep. And if they get shots of me, they'll get shots of you too. Someone is going to enlarge that picture to try to figure out who was sitting with me. It'll take less than two seconds to ID you and start tongues wagging."

"So, if our cover is going to be blown anyway..."

"The best defense is a good offense," Emma finished.

"True."

"We have several options." Emma began ticking them off on her fingers. "One, we simply let the photographer take our picture together as if it's the most natural thing in the world and let the story unfold organically."

"That doesn't sound like going on offense to me," Palmer said. "That leaves tons of room for supposition."

"Correct. The only advantage to that approach is that it makes clear that we have nothing to hide and downplays the significance."

"You really believe a picture of you on your first date as president would ever be considered insignificant?"

"Fair point. Two," Emma held up a second finger, "we release a statement identifying you, make clear that this is our first date, and indicate that we're in the 'getting to know each other' stage."

Palmer made a face. "Accurate, but maybe a little defensive."

Emma cocked her head to the side. That was a nuance she hadn't anticipated Palmer understanding. *Impressive.*

"Three, I can select a reporter of my choosing and offer an exclusive interview to get the story out in my own words."

Palmer arched an eyebrow. "Why do I think you're leaning toward option number three?"

Emma patted her on the cheek. "Probably because I am." She led them back to the couch.

"I assume you already have a candidate in mind?"

"I do."

"Would we be doing this interview together, or would you be solo?"

"For now, I think solo works best. To do an interview together before the first date would seem somewhat...reality TV-ish, don't you agree?"

"I do.

"I plan to tell the truth. Our paths crossed several times in your professional capacity. I found you to be of excellent character, exemplary at your job, intelligent, and impressive. You were one of those responsible for the successful rescue of the four senators.

"A short time after that incident, I was asked to consider your file for receipt of the Silver Star. In reviewing your actions in Desert Storm, I agreed with your commander at the time that you were deserving of that honor, and that the honor had been delayed for so many years only through a clerical oversight.

"In speaking with you upon the occasion of the Silver Star ceremony, I learned that you were retiring in October. I determined that the circumstances of your heroism dovetailed with my State of the Union address, and, accordingly, invited you to attend as one of twelve honored guests.

"Upon your retirement, once it became appropriate for me to do so, and only then, I reached out to you on a personal level and asked if you'd like to accompany me to the theater. I am both delighted and nervous to be going on my first date since my wife was tragically killed in a car accident three-and-a-half years ago. If the reporter has any tips for my first date in nearly thirty-five years, I'd be happy to hear them. For our first date, we'll be taking in a Broadway show."

When she'd finished, Emma waited expectantly.

"I think it's a good approach. It's open and forthcoming, addresses up-front the obvious question of how many times we've been in the same room, and for what purpose. It makes clear that you didn't initiate the Silver Star investigation and explains my presence at the State of the Union."

"I recognize that I'm omitting the text messages."

"There was nothing untoward in those messages, and besides, you have no obligation to report every detail."

"Are you comfortable with me doing the interview?" Emma asked.

Myriad emotions crossed Palmer's face before she said, "Yes. I've seen you do many interviews. I know you'll handle this one just fine." Palmer's brow creased. "I do have one question, though."

"What is it?"

"When are you going to give the interview?"

"The reporter already has been alerted that I may want to sit for an interview. With your approval, I'll have Olivia round up her and her crew and do the interview here in the suite right after dinner."

"And where do you plan to stash me?" Palmer asked.

"That's easy. After we eat, you're going to head back to your room until the Secret Service comes to get you. Are you okay with that?"

"Sure."

"By the way, the caveat in exchange for the exclusive is that it must air at eight o'clock, the same time the curtain goes up on the show."

"I love a well-executed plan."

"That's the military tactician in you talking."

"I'll remind you that my fortes were flying and intelligence."

"So they were." Emma reached up and kissed Palmer gently on the lips. "Speaking of good execution, we'd better get this party started. Want a tour while we munch on hors d'oeuvres?"

"I admit to being curious, so yes. This suite is bigger than a house."

"Five thousand square feet, to be exact."

They stole glances at each other over hors d'oeuvres, as Emma showed Palmer around the palatial Champagne Suite.

"I understand the dining room, the two indoor living rooms, the balcony sitting area... I even get the conference room," Palmer said. "But the spiral staircase, now that I didn't see coming."

"I know. I feel as though I should make a *Sunset Boulevard*-type entrance."

"You are many things, Emma McMasters, but a diva is not one of them."

"Are you sure?"

"Positive," Palmer crooned in her ear.

The sultry sound of her voice sent a shiver down Emma's spine. "Right. You know, I'm guessing dinner might be ready." She glided away from Palmer before things heated up between them again. After all, they had a show to catch and she had an interview to do.

CHAPTER NINETEEN

Palmer lay awake staring at the ceiling, thinking about Emma, hopefully asleep several floors above her. The evening—in fact the whole day—had been magical and beyond anything Palmer could've envisioned. The Broadway show, a new revival of the musical, *1776*, brought down the house. It was the first time Palmer had seen a Broadway show from the presidential box, and she knew it was an experience she'd never forget.

The press-pool photographer snapped several pictures of them as they exited the limousine and entered the theater. Although Emma forewarned Palmer, the sudden explosion of flash against the dark night was jarring; it reminded her too much of enemy fire piercing the sky during some of her night combat missions.

Emma must've felt Palmer's reflexive flinch. As she waved to the crowd, she asked just loud enough for Palmer to hear her, "Are you okay?"

"I'm fine. Old baggage. Too much like Kuwait."

"I'm sorry. I imagine it's like re-living a bad nightmare on a continuous loop. This may not make any difference for you to hear, but you're safe here. The Secret Service has our backs, I promise you."

"I know."

Once they'd gotten inside, the atmosphere turned electric. Emma's entrance was timed so that they arrived at their seats and settled in seconds before the house lights dimmed.

"The president never waits," Palmer had murmured, more to herself than out loud, repeating what Emma had told her on Marine

One. Palmer understood that this practice wasn't because Emma was a diva—nor was it unique to her. The timing was a matter of security protocol. Less time waiting meant less time for the president to be a target.

Still, even with less than a minute between the time they were seated and the time the orchestra began playing the overture, the audience managed to recognize Emma. The buzz reached a crescendo as the first beats of the snare drums sounded and abated only when the actors began their dialogue.

When the play ended, the audience gave the cast a standing ovation. After the first curtain call, in an extraordinary gesture, the cast pointed to Emma. Benjamin Franklin stepped forward and shushed the crowd.

"On behalf of the cast of *1776*, we want to extend a warm welcome and our deepest gratitude and admiration to the forty-sixth president of the United States, Emma McMasters. President McMasters, it is a deep honor to perform for you. We applaud you, Madam President."

The cast broke into a hearty round of applause, and the audience members once again rose to their feet, this time for Emma. The ovation lasted a full five minutes. Emma seemed genuinely surprised by the gesture, and not a little bit embarrassed. She pointed back to the cast and applauded.

As the curtain came down, a disembodied voice asked all audience members to remain in their seats while the president departed. The Secret Service stepped in, and within seconds, Emma and Palmer were clear of the front of the house.

Emma spoke to one of the agents and flashed a mischievous grin at Palmer.

"What are you up to, Madam President?"

"Wooing the girl, of course. What else would I be up to?"

In short order, they were backstage, where they met the entire cast. Palmer wasn't sure who was more thrilled by the exchange, the actors or Emma. She introduced Palmer, joking that she owed the cast big time for ensuring her a successful first date.

The actors responded that it was a good thing they hadn't known the stakes ahead of time, it might've made them nervous enough to blow their lines.

Emma acquiesced to requests from the actors for selfies, although she was careful to ensure that Palmer wasn't visible in any of the pictures. They'd created enough of a publicity conflagration for one evening.

Palmer's cell phone buzzed on the bedside table, jolting her back to the present. She snapped it up. The text message on the screen read: *I hope you're sleeping soundly, dreaming of me. I wanted to thank you for a perfect first date. How about an encore?*

A frisson of excitement coursed through Palmer. *I'll see if I can fit you into my busy schedule. How about breakfast?*

Seconds later, Palmer received her answer. *Nine a.m., after my security briefing. Don't be late.*

I'm sure your detail will make sure I'm on time.

Another bonus of being president. Sweet dreams, sweet Palmer.

Sweet dreams, lovely Emma. See you soon. Palmer cradled the phone next to her happily tripping heart before setting it back on the table. She closed her eyes and was asleep in seconds.

"I'm not going to respond to that." Emma folded her arms.

Nichelle and Olivia exchanged glances. It was Olivia who spoke first, "Madam President, we simply can't let an accusation like that stand. If we don't answer—"

"Answer?" Emma exploded. She uncrossed her arms and balled her hands into fists. "Let me make this perfectly clear." Her voice was controlled fury, and she worked to moderate her tone. "I will not, today or any other day, address disgustingly inappropriate and salacious falsehoods or rumors about my personal life. Am I making myself understood?"

Nichelle stepped into the breach. "Madam President, I agree that we don't want to give any air time to such garbage, and that addressing baseless crap with direct statements only serves to lend credence to the initial story—"

"Good. Then there's nothing left to talk about."

"Madam President, please, let me finish," Nichelle pleaded.

Emma didn't want to hear another word. She'd known that her date with Palmer would result in an instantaneous firestorm of bullshit from her detractors and sexist and homophobic jerks everywhere. But this wholly made up interchange between her and Palmer at the Silver Star ceremony, replete with doctored video purporting to show Emma propositioning Palmer as she pinned her with the medal, went beyond the pale. Worse still, it was blowing up social media, trending on Twitter, showing up in memes on conservative websites, and driving the conversation on every conservative channel and talk show.

Palmer will see this piece of fiction. Who knows? Maybe she's already seen it. Emma's mood sunk lower. Noble, courageous, humble Palmer, who never had sought the recognition in the first place...

Nichelle said, "You don't need to say a word, but maybe we could put some surrogates out there—"

"Like who? Max? How long do you think it would take for them to figure out that you and Max are an item? That will only make it worse."

"No, ma'am. I was thinking of Generals Powell, Dutton, and Carsen. They were there, on stage with you. They can attest to what you really said. Not only that, but we have audio and video of the entire thing, from multiple angles. We simply need to have our own experts produce the real footage."

Emma closed her eyes and pinched the bridge of her nose. *What a cluster.* She should've seen it coming. Yes, they had anticipated push back, but this? She hadn't imagined anyone would outright fabricate something so audacious.

"Madam President?" Jemelle stuck her head into the suite's conference room.

"Yes, Jemelle?"

"General Estes is here."

Emma sighed heavily. "Send her in, please." Emma's heart raced.

"Madam President," Olivia started. Emma held up a hand to stop her.

"Hi." Palmer stepped into the room. Her head swiveled from Emma to Nichelle and Olivia and back again. "Bad timing?"

She wore a pressed pair of black slacks, a black turtleneck, and a baby blue sweater. Emma wanted to tell her she looked incredible. She wanted to take her in her arms and kiss her senseless. What was happening was so unfair. Instead, she said, "Never for you."

Palmer stuffed her hands in her pockets. "Let me guess, you've seen the creative interpretation of the award ceremony."

"Obviously, you've seen it too." Emma bowed her head. She should've known Palmer already would've seen it. She should've called her as soon as she heard about it. "I'm so sorry."

"Madam President?" Emma felt rather than saw Palmer approach. "Emma?" She stopped just short of Emma's personal space. Her voice was gentle and suffused with love. She tipped Emma's chin up to meet her eyes. "I knew what was possible—what could happen. I'm a big girl."

"You don't deserve this."

"Neither do you." Palmer stepped back. "So, I've taken care of it."

"You what?" Emma, Nichelle, and Olivia spoke in unison.

"You do remember that I spent my career in intelligence, right?"

Emma nodded slowly. Where was this going?

"I have friends in every corner of the intelligence community, with every skill set. I simply asked a friend to determine the originator of the manipulated video, right down to the IP address."

Emma's eyebrows rose into her hairline.

"And?" Nichelle asked. She slid into the nearest chair. "I think I'm going to want to sit down for this."

Olivia joined her.

"Does the name Rodney Winkler ring a bell?" Palmer asked.

Emma sucked in a sharp breath.

"Holy shi... I mean, seriously?" Nichelle asked.

"Mm-hmm."

"Rodney Winkler, as in the chief of staff for the majority leader of the U.S. Senate?" Olivia asked.

"The same," Palmer said. "Right about now, an investigative journalist for *The New York Times* is breaking the story, with quotes from two unnamed intelligence sources, irrefutable digital forensic evidence of the manipulated footage and the originating source, and, no doubt, a request for comment from the majority leader as to whether he authorized the fabrication."

Emma wrapped her mind around it all. Finally, she asked, "Are you one of the unnamed intelligence sources?"

"No." Palmer's gaze bore into her. "Emma, you have to know, I'm not going to sit idly by and let anyone besmirch your character. That's never going to happen on my watch."

Emma shook her head. "I think I grossly underestimated you, Palmer Estes."

"Common mistake," Palmer said. "I hope I didn't overstep?"

The insecurity of the question cut Emma to the core. "I don't know how to answer that. I have to admit, it never occurred to me that you might intervene. Nor did I ever consider that this was a problem we needed to address together."

"So, you assumed it was yours to handle; it was your job to protect me."

"Yes," Emma admitted.

"I'm not some fragile flower that wilts at the slightest foul wind."

"I know that."

"Do you?" Palmer addressed Nichelle and Olivia. "Could we have the room for a minute, please?"

The two looked to Emma, who motioned with her head for them to leave.

"Emma," Palmer swept Emma into her arms. "I love you. I need you to know that. But if we stand a chance of making it as a couple, it will be because we're equal partners in this relationship. That means we handle situations that affect both of us as a unit, not as a president and a mere mortal, nor as a presidential public relations problem to be solved. When it directly concerns us, you have to include me in the deliberations and discussions. Otherwise, we can't have a healthy, balanced relationship."

Palmer paused, and then continued, "I probably shouldn't have acted unilaterally in this situation—it was hypocritical of me—but I knew I could do something to put a quick end to this that you couldn't do. I did it without using a single government resource or paying some shady operative to get to the bottom of it. I apologize for not consulting you in advance. In this instance, it was better for you not to know."

Emma's head spun, both as a result of Palmer's nearness and because she was having trouble digesting what was happening. While she'd been brooding and allowing her anger and indignation to cloud her mind, Palmer had been out there solving the situation in the most perfect, ingenious way.

"Emma? Say something. Please."

Emma reached up and pulled Palmer down for a searing kiss. "I love you." Then, she backed away. She simply couldn't think clearly when Palmer held her like that. "You're right. We are, and have to be, equal partners. I spent the early morning hours worrying that you would see the video—that it would hurt you—and trying to determine how I could protect you. Meanwhile, you were busy rescuing my reputation with a surgically perfect strike."

"Yeah, well, we're just finding our sea legs. Don't beat yourself up too badly. Now how about you make it up to me with that breakfast you promised?"

Their troubles were far from over; more attacks would come. Emma knew that. But at the moment, all she wanted to do was concentrate on Palmer and stay present in the moment. They would tackle the rest—together. That knowledge made all the rest bearable.

Emma waggled her eyebrows. "I'll see if we can rustle something up." She traced Palmer's lips with her fingertips, then exchanged her fingertips with her lips. "Where were we going again?" she asked eventually.

"Breakfast," Palmer answered. Her voice was hoarse with desire and her eyes were unfocused.

"Right." Emma took Palmer by the hand, only relinquishing it when they reached the door. She opened it just as Nichelle raised a hand to knock.

"I'm sorry, Madam President."

Emma already knew by Nichelle's expression that all her carefully laid plans for the remainder of the long weekend were about to go by the wayside. "What is it?"

Nichelle's eyes cut to Palmer and back again. "I'm afraid we're going to have to head back."

Emma nodded. Although Palmer had top security clearance when she was active-duty military, that clearance no longer applied. Emma turned to her now. "Give me a second? I'll be right out, I promise."

"Of course." Palmer stepped outside the conference room to make way for Nichelle to join Emma inside.

When they were alone, Emma asked Nichelle, "What is it?"

"An attack on the U.S. Embassy in Afghanistan. Intelligence reports from the NSA and the CIA indicate a splinter group—"

"Casualties?"

"Two Americans and four of the attackers."

"Current situation?"

"The attack was repelled and the embassy is locked down."

"The Ambassador?"

"Safe."

"Who were the casualties?"

"Two members of the Marine security force. They were patrolling the perimeter and were able to signal the alarm, which saved a lot of lives and the integrity of the compound."

"Thank God for them." Emma considered her next move. "Right. Alert the team and have Olivia inform the press pool that if they want to make the flight, they'd better hustle. The motorcade is leaving in the next fifteen minutes. I want to be wheels-up on Air Force One on the way to D.C. in less than an hour."

"Roger."

"I want NSA Edwards in here in five minutes to read me in on everything we know so far. Tell Olivia she's with us in the limo. I want a statement out within the half hour condemning the attack in the strongest possible terms. We'll draft it together in the car on the way to Marine One. And I'll need to reach out to the Gang of Eight simultaneous to releasing that statement."

"Got it."

"Okay." Emma blew out an explosive breath.

"Madam President?"

"Yes?"

Nichelle smiled sadly. "I'm sorry about your weekend plans."

Emma nodded and squeezed Nichelle's arm. "Me too. More than you know." She exited the conference room and went in search of Palmer. She found her in the living room gazing out at the Empire State Building.

"Palmer—"

"Emma, you're president of the United States of America. Country above self. Always."

Emma brushed her fingers gently along Palmer's cheek. "That doesn't mean I can't be filled with regret for our lost weekend."

"Me too. But we'll always have last night." Palmer winked.

"Now you're quoting old movies?"

"Damn. Thought I'd get away with that one."

"Not a chance. You should play Trivial Pursuit with me one of these days."

"I'll look forward to it."

"Palmer—"

"Don't worry about me. Optics matter. I'll find my own way home."

The fact that Palmer was right didn't make Emma feel better. "I can have my assistant book a flight for you and take care of the rest of the transportation details."

"No. I've got this. You've got a country to run."

"I-I don't know when I'll be able to be in touch."

"I'm not going anywhere, Emma. You do what you need to do. We'll work it out."

"How did I get so lucky?" Emma allowed herself to get lost in Palmer's light, in her strength.

"I'm the lucky one." Palmer kissed her quickly. "Be safe, Emma McMasters. I'll see you back home."

"That's a promise and I always keep my promises."

"I know you do." Palmer nodded toward the exit. "I'll let myself out."

"I love you, Palmer Estes. Remember that."

"I love you, Emma. You remember that."

With great reluctance, Emma watched her go. Then, she returned to the conference room. The National Security Advisor should be here soon.

CHAPTER TWENTY

Palmer blew a stray lock of hair off her face as she rummaged through yet another box marked, *Home Office.* Somewhere in this morass was the binder that contained her research on the myriad job offers that had flowed in over the course of the past weeks.

"Ugh! Come on. I know you're here somewhere."

Her phone buzzed, and absently, she answered it. "Estes."

"That doesn't sound like someone who's happy to hear from me."

Palmer smiled at the sound of Emma's voice. She removed yet another box from the couch to make room and sat down. "Well, hi there. Sorry. I've got my head in a box at the moment. I didn't know it was you." Her brow knit together. "Why is it you? Aren't you still in Geneva?"

"Nope. At the moment, I'm on Air Force One, about twenty minutes out from Andrews."

"You are?"

"I am."

"How'd the meetings go?"

"Let's just say, incremental progress was made. How about if I tell you all about it, or, better yet, if we talk about other things, tonight over dinner?"

Palmer's stomach flipped. In the month since that aborted weekend in New York, they'd only been able to see each other once in person, and that was for a quick dinner. Nightly phone and text chats had been a poor substitute for in-person conversations.

"You shouldn't tease a girl."

"Oh, I hope to do that too."

Palmer delighted in Emma's rich, deep laugh. "You're on. Your place?"

"As much as I'd love to take you out for a night on the town, if we want privacy, that's the best option."

"Oh, we definitely want privacy."

"Seven o'clock?"

"I'll be there with bells on."

"Will you be wearing anything else?"

"You'll have to wait and see, now won't you?"

"We're about to land. I'll see you soon."

"I can't wait." Palmer disconnected the call. She knew she was grinning like a fool, but she didn't care. Tonight, she had a date with Emma.

∽⸱∾

Soft candlelight flickered, creating interesting shadows on Palmer's face. Emma knew she was staring. She didn't care.

"I've missed you." Palmer reached for her hand.

"I've missed you too." Emma reveled in the feel of Palmer's fingers wrapped around hers. "Have I mentioned how beautiful you look tonight?"

"You might've said something like that once or twice."

"Good, because you do."

"You must be exhausted, but it sure doesn't show."

"Wild horses couldn't have kept me from having dinner with you tonight."

"I'm glad. Also, that was the best food I've had in a month. Eating out of take-out containers while trying to unpack the kitchen doesn't cut it."

"No doubt. I'm so sorry I couldn't help you move in."

"Yeah, I'm sure the Secret Service would've been thrilled with having to protect you from flying boxes and television sets."

"Very funny. Sometimes being president is a pain-in-the-butt."

Palmer held up their joined hands and kissed Emma's knuckles. "Did you always want to be president?"

The question surprised her. "No. It's funny. If Heather hadn't given me a shove in that direction, I might not have pursued anything more than the district attorney's office."

"Really?" Palmer sat up a little straighter.

"True. Heather was the one who was always indignant about injustices and wrongheaded policies. She'd say, 'Emma, you need to run for senator, you need to run for governor, you need to run for president. You could fix this. You'd do a better job.'" Emma could hear Heather's voice in her head. But for the first time in a long time, thinking and talking about her didn't hurt.

"Why didn't she run herself? She was an attorney too, right?"

"She was. But she didn't have the patience for elective office. She wasn't much for compromise. She always said I was more diplomatic than she could ever be. She would've beaten folks over the head instead."

"Sounds like my kind of girl," Palmer said. She stumbled over the last part and Emma squeezed her hand. "It's okay. You would've loved Heather, and she would've loved you. That makes me happy."

"I'm glad."

"Anyway, at the time she passed away, we'd already put together the team, the game plan, the mechanisms, and I felt like I owed it to her to see her dream through." Emma smiled wistfully. "I hope she'd be proud of our win and the job I'm doing."

"I know she'd be so proud. You're a fabulous president, Emma—a born leader."

"I'll double what I'm paying you."

"I'm serious. This country needed so much healing. The divisions between left and right, gay and straight, women and men, conservatives and progressives... I couldn't imagine how we ever could restore civility and comity."

"I've still got a lot to do yet to knit the fabric of our society back together."

"You're bringing back humanity, empathy, and decency that were sorely lacking. You're re-establishing presidential norms and respect for the office, rebuilding global alliances and treaties, prioritizing people over profits, taking necessary steps to save the planet from climate change—"

"No, Palmer. I can only take credit for my own ethos, my personal behavior. The rest takes a village and certainly doesn't happen in a vacuum."

"It wouldn't be happening at all if it weren't for you."

"Yeah, well… There are moments when I wish I could shed my presidential skin for a little while and move about and behave like an everyday person." It was an admission Emma hadn't thought she'd make, but it was the truth.

"What would you do with your one wild, precious life, Emma McMasters?" Palmer gazed intently at her.

"I'd walk down the street holding my girlfriend's hand, buy her flowers, go for a hike together, picnic by a babbling brook in the middle of nowhere, and see a waterfall. Afterward, we'd stop for ice cream. And when we got home, I'd take her in my arms and make sweet love to her without a care in the world to weigh us down."

"That sounds like the perfect day," Palmer said softly. "Count me in."

"Oh, you're definitely in. You're the main attraction." Emma kissed the back of Palmer's hand.

"Do you not want to run for reelection? Your approval ratings are impressive, your polling numbers are high among every group except arch-conservatives, you've largely succeeded so far with your legislative agenda despite the Senate being in Republican hands, and mainstream media generally loves you."

"I don't know."

"Emma, you've almost single-handedly restored the American people's faith in the presidency, in our democracy. Imagine how much more you could accomplish before you're done. You'd barely be in your sixties when you left office, with your whole life in front of you."

"Now you sound like Nichelle, Trent, and Miranda."

"Maybe they're on to something, darling." Palmer pushed back her chair and lifted Emma to her feet. She drew Emma to her and cupped her face with both hands. "Emma McMasters, I want you to do whatever makes you happiest. Run again or don't. Become a recluse or don't. Work or don't. I will love you to the end of time, regardless of the choices you make."

"You will?" Palmer's nearness was intoxicating.

"I will. That's a solemn promise." She enfolded Emma in her arms.

"A normal person could ask you to stay the night without having to worry about what the press would write about it and whether or not the Senate Democrats would lose their shot at the majority in the midterms simply because their president fell in love."

"And you?" Palmer asked against Emma's lips.

"Stay, Palmer. Stay the night with me."

"Are you sure?"

"I'm sure that in this moment, I don't care what anyone else thinks. I know only that I ache for your touch and I'll combust without it."

Palmer's mouth formed an *O*. "Which way is the bedroom?" Her voice was husky and sent shivers down Emma's spine.

Wordlessly, Emma led her to the master suite. Once inside, she crushed her mouth against Palmer's and pushed her back against the door. The pressure of their combined weight clicked the door shut.

Palmer's hands were in her hair, her body firmly pressed against Emma's center. Palmer rocked against her, sending sparks from the top of Emma's head down to her toes.

Emma fumbled for the buttons on Palmer's shirt. "Too many clothes."

"Mm." Without missing a beat, Palmer helped Emma undress her. Emma stroked Palmer's bare shoulders, her collarbones, her chest. She outlined Palmer's bra with her fingertips, then kissed her way from Palmer's neck down to the tops of her breasts where they peeked out from her bra.

She reached around and unclasped the bra, teased it off her, and dropped it to the floor, luxuriating in the feel of Palmer's erect nipples against her palms. Vaguely, she heard Palmer groan as she pressed forward, increasing the pressure.

She wasn't sure how Palmer managed to get the advantage, but Emma felt herself lifted and hoisted gently onto the bed. Then, she was naked and Palmer was leaning over her, her thigh pressing rhythmically into Emma until she could barely stand the delicious contact.

"Please." It was the one word she could find in her fogged brain.

Palmer took her. Her ministrations were at once gentle, reverential, and thorough. Emma levitated off the bed, her body absorbing all that Palmer offered her and more.

"I love you, Emma."

"I love you, Palmer." When she could catch her breath, Emma rolled Palmer over. She explored every inch of her. She ran her hands up Palmer's long legs. Her fingertips stuttered over a raised area on her left leg. With a start, she remembered Palmer's bullet wound.

Palmer tried to pull away, but Emma held her fast. "No. Please, don't." Emma lowered herself to kiss and caress the angry scar, as if in so doing she could heal the wounds Palmer carried on her body and in her soul. Although Palmer flinched, she allowed the contact.

Emma continued her exploration, taking her time with Palmer, uncovering sensitive points and exploiting them until Palmer begged her. "Emma."

"Yes, love." With her heart exploding with joy, Emma finished what she'd started, holding tight to Palmer as aftershocks rocked her body.

When their bodies began to cool, Emma pulled them up in the bed and slipped the covers over them. She snuggled into Palmer's shoulder.

"Are you all right?" she asked Palmer.

"Oh, yes." She nuzzled the top of Emma's head with her lips. "I'm quite a bit more than all right. You?"

"Mm-hmm." Sleep crept in and Emma let it flow over her. "Goodnight, sweet Palmer."

"Sweet dreams, Emma."

⤙⤚

Palmer drifted up from sleep. Emma was curled against her side, nestled in her arms. She kissed the top of her head and brushed the hair back from her face.

"Why are you awake?" Emma murmured against her breast.

"Just cherishing the moment."

"That was…amazing."

"Mm-hmm." Palmer slid her hands along Emma's torso. She felt her respond and it sent another jolt directly to her core.

"Palmer."

Emma's breathless plea was all she needed. This time, Palmer explored at a more leisurely pace, her fingers and mouth memorizing every inch of Emma. She was so lovely, Palmer wanted to weep with joy.

As Emma crested, she took Palmer with her, their hearts racing in synchrony. They kissed and caressed for long moments more, reveling in each other and the newness of this most intimate expression of love.

Palmer couldn't remember ever being this happy.

"What are you thinking about?" Emma asked.

"Nothing. I-I just wanted to take a picture of this moment in my mind. I'm not sure I could ever be as happy and content as I am right now."

"I love you, Palmer. I hope to give you many more moments just like this one."

"Yes, please." Palmer caught sight of the bedside clock just as Emma started to drift off again. "Emma? Darling?"

"Mm?"

"As much as I hate to say this, it's 3:30 a.m. I'd better get out of here before it becomes too obvious that I spent the night."

"No," Emma mumbled and held her tighter.

"You know I'm right. There's no sense borrowing trouble."

Emma growled. "It's Saturday. I have no public schedule today."

"You still have a security briefing in four hours."

"I hate that you know that."

"I know." Palmer slid out of the bed and hunted around the room for her clothes. She dressed silently as Emma sulked.

"I protest."

"You'll thank me for the lack of tawdry headlines."

"I'm not a fan of your practical side."

"Noted."

"Spend the day with me?"

"What?" Palmer paused as she buttoned her pants.

"Spend the day with me. It's Saturday. I've got nothing so pressing that it can't wait. The weekend schedule is intentionally light so I can adjust to the time change. Please?"

Palmer knew that she couldn't say no. Emma looked adorably rumpled and gorgeous with the covers pooled around her waist. She returned to the bed and kissed Emma thoroughly. "I'll be back for brunch."

"Ten o'clock. Don't be late."

"Am I ever?"

"There's always a first time."

"There won't be." She kissed Emma one last time, imprinting the feel and taste of her lips. "How do I...?"

"I'll have a Secret Service agent escort you out and make sure you get back to your car."

"You know how weird that feels? To be sneaking out of the president's bedroom with the help of the Secret Service?"

"We can trust their discretion."

"I know. That doesn't make it feel any less...awkward."

"Get used to it, lover. I suspect this will be the first time of many. At least a girl can hope."

Oh, yes, Palmer thought. A girl could definitely hope.

⇜⇝

"A bowling alley? The White House has its own bowling alley in the basement?"

Emma tied her bowling shoes and handed Palmer a pair of size eight-and-one-halves, as requested. "It's not as if I can go out to Joe's Bowl-a-Rama and throw a few frames."

"True. So, whose brilliant idea was this?"

"The original bowling alley was installed in 1947 as a birthday present for Harry Truman. He didn't care for the sport, but he offered it for staff. You've actually been in that bowling alley."

Palmer's brow scrunched in confusion. "I have?"

"Yep." Emma stepped up to the single lane and squinted at the ten pins. "You'd recognize it as the Situation Room."

"The Situation Room was a bowling alley?"

"It was in 1947. The alley was dismantled and moved to the Old Executive Office Building in 1955. But it turns out that President Nixon and Pat were huge bowlers. So, he had this present-day, one-lane alley built under the North Portico in 1969. Welcome to the presidential bowling alley." She hurled the ball down the center of the lane, sending the pins flying.

"Not bad, Madam President."

"You know you're not allowed to beat the president, right?"

"That's a rule? Since when?"

"Since I have a feeling you're going to wipe the floor with me."

Palmer laughed as she stepped up and launched the ball directly down the center for a neat strike.

"When did you have time in the military to bowl?"

"Who says we did?"

Emma indicated the strike on the scorecard.

"Beginners luck?" Palmer shrugged.

"I smell a ringer." Emma laughed.

"You're the one who picked the activity. I'm the one who suggested a movie in the White House theater."

"That's this afternoon's activity. *Wonder Woman/Captain Marvel* double-feature, with real theater popcorn."

"That's what I'm talking about."

Emma regarded Palmer's relaxed profile, pleased with herself for finding a way to give them a day that came as close as she could arrange to a normal date.

As predicted, Palmer crushed her three games in a row.

"Uncle. I give." Emma tossed a white towel onto the polished wood floor. "I surrender. You are queen of the bowling alley."

"Don't worry. We'll find something you can beat me at." Palmer threw an arm around her and kissed her on the temple.

"Yeah, well I can tell you right now I won't challenge you to a shooting contest at the Camp David range."

"Camp David has a shooting range?"

"Yep. Behind the mansion. It also has a one-hole golf course. I haven't mastered either skill. But, when it's warm enough, I'll eat your lunch in the swimming pool."

"No fair. That was your sport. It would be like me challenging you to a foot race."

"That's not going to happen."

"Exactly my point."

They walked on for a bit in companionable silence. "It's a nice day, can I interest you in some fresh air?"

"Perfect. Honestly, anything sounds good, as long as I get to do it with you."

"Palmer Estes, you sweet talker." Emma led them out through the West Colonnade and into the Rose Garden. "How about a walking tour of the grounds?"

"I'm game."

Emma threaded her arm through Palmer's as they strolled. "Can I ask about your childhood? Or is that too painful?" Although she'd read everything the Pentagon had sent over when considering Palmer for the Silver Star, Emma yearned to know more.

"You can ask me anything. I'll tell you everything you want to know."

"Okay. Where did you grow up?"

"Pendleton, Oregon. My father owned a bar there, and my mother was the school librarian."

"Pendleton is in Umatilla County, right?"

"Uh-huh."

"As in, conservative Eastern Oregon?"

"That's the one."

"Oh, boy. Not a great place for a budding lesbian to grow up."

"Nope. As you might imagine, we didn't hear much about lesbians in Umatilla County. I knew I didn't like boys. I knew there was something different or wrong about me. But, until I met Britney at that track camp, I had no idea about my sexuality."

"That must've come as quite a shock."

"Not to me. That was the moment when all the pieces of my life finally fit together and I understood who I was and where I belonged."

"Which probably felt like such a relief."

"Right up until the moment when my father discovered me and Britney together."

"I'm sorry for all that, Palmer. You were so young. I can't imagine my parents turning their backs on me like that. It's horrible."

"As I said, I was probably better off in the long run. I have to say, the most hurtful part of all of it wasn't my father's reaction. It was that my mother never said a word. I remember staring at her, wordlessly imploring her to say something—to protect or defend me. Instead, she stood there like a statue or a deer in the headlights, unwilling to fight for me."

Emma envisioned the scene... A young Palmer bravely protecting the girl she loved and facing down a mountain of a man as her mother did nothing to help or to mitigate the situation. It made Emma's heart hurt. She told Palmer as much. "What kind of person was your mom?"

"My mom was this educated, soft-spoken, well-read moderate who instilled in me a love of learning and books."

"That explains your library collection."

"Yes. I was reading the classics while others were memorizing their A, B, Cs."

They passed the tennis court and the quarter-mile track Bill Clinton had installed.

"My father was a high-school-educated ruffian with a nasty temper, who drank too much and believed that women should be kept barefoot and in the kitchen. He was a thug."

"Doesn't sound like an ideal match."

"Far from it. I never could figure out how my parents' marriage worked. My dad's bar was the preferred hangout for every conservative and far-right nut-job east of the Cascade Mountains. Those were his people. My mother despised them. Once, when I was about ten and my father had taken his belt to me for some perceived wrongdoing, I asked my mother what she saw in him."

"How'd that go?"

Palmer shook her head. "She slapped me across the face and told me I should be grateful he put a roof over our heads and kept us fed and clothed."

Emma recoiled at the image. "But she had some independence. She had her own job."

"Yes. A nice, respectable position for 'the little woman.'"

Emma breathed deeply to tamp down her rising anger. "Did you have siblings?"

"No. I don't think my parents intended to have me, never mind a bigger family. My father hated kids. He didn't take an interest in me until I started showing promise as a runner. Then, I was useful to him—a point of pride for him to brag to his cronies about and a potential source of business for his bar. If only I'd not turned out to be a queer and made it to the Olympics, people would've come from far and wide to meet his prized pony," Palmer said bitterly.

Emma squeezed her arm tightly. "I'm so, so sorry. How in the world you grew up to become the wise, compassionate, grounded, educated, worldly, well-adjusted woman you are is beyond me."

"I got lucky. I had great role models along the way... My coach, my high school guidance counselor, my ROTC advisor, my platoon leader, my military mentors who saw potential in me and nurtured me along..."

"But you always kept yourself apart, didn't you?" It was as much a statement as a question.

"Yes. From a very young age, I learned that I was the only person who was going to take care of me. I always felt safest when I was by myself. I viewed opening myself to others as a vulnerability I couldn't afford. If I kept to myself, no one could hurt me."

Emma felt the pain of that young woman and she wanted to reach back in time and hold her. She pulled them up short and took Palmer's hands. "I love you, Palmer. I promise you with all that I am that I will never intentionally hurt you. I'm not going anywhere."

"I know that."

"You understand that on an intellectual level. I need for you to accept that truth in here." Emma laid her hand on Palmer's heart and kissed her softly on the mouth.

"I'm a work in progress, Emma." Palmer covered Emma's hand with her own. "I know you love me. I can feel that as surely as I feel my own heartbeat. But waiting for the other shoe to drop is engrained in my DNA. It's going to take time and consistency to overcome that."

"Fair enough. I need you to know, I'm planning to spend a lifetime proving myself to you."

"I like the sound of that." This time Palmer initiated the kiss, and Emma let go of everything except this moment.

CHAPTER TWENTY-ONE

Absentmindedly, Palmer massaged Emma's stockinged feet as they rested on her lap. The two women sat on opposite ends of the couch in the private residence's family sitting room. Palmer was grading essays from the students in the doctoral class in International Security she was teaching as a faculty member at Georgetown University's School of International Relations. Emma was working on a speech she was due to deliver at the United Nations.

Over the months, they'd fallen into this easy routine. Palmer would spend two or three nights a week with Emma when she was in residence at the White House, slipping out in the middle of the night to return to her apartment.

They hadn't ventured out together publicly since that first Broadway date. Initially, Emma had resisted this low-key, ultra-low-profile approach. "I'm not going to hide our relationship under a rock. That's why I gave that interview up front, so that we could live our lives openly."

"You saw the fallout. Yes, we were able to diffuse that situation with the bogus video and turn it to our advantage, but every week there's some other ridiculous story about us your team has to refute. Your numbers take a hit every time a pollster asks the question about whether or not the voters approve of the president dating another woman."

"Our relationship is not up for public debate. They don't get to have a say in my love life."

"True. But we can make it easier on ourselves if we limit our exposure. We're not denying the relationship—we're just keeping it private as we give ourselves the space to be together."

In the end, Emma had relented, especially as the polling numbers also indicated the Democrats' chances of flipping the Senate were being negatively impacted by the distraction of the president's personal life.

"How's it going over there, Professor Estes?" Emma asked. "By the way, I'm curious. You've got a PhD, you're a retired general, and also a professor. Do your students call you Doctor General Professor? Doctor General? Professor General? Doctor? Or just, Professor? It's a lot to take in."

Palmer laughed and swatted Emma's foot. "Very funny. Professor seems to be their preferred title for me, although I have no idea what they call me behind my back. In answer to your first question, you'd think by graduate school these kids could learn to properly conjugate a verb."

"Unfortunately, grammar seems to be a dying art."

"You're the president. Can't you raise the standards or something?"

"Not in time to impact your class, I'm afraid."

"That's a shame." Palmer stroked Emma's calf. "How's the speech coming?"

"Slowly."

"Why's that?"

"I seem to be distracted."

"Is that right? What might be distracting you, Madam President?"

"She's about 5'8" tall, red-haired, and sexy as all get out."

Palmer looked over her shoulder. "Huh. I don't see anybody else here."

Emma waggled her eyebrows suggestively. "Any chance I can entice the professor to come to bed?"

"I guess that depends."

"On?"

"What you're offering once we get there."

Emma stood up and offered Palmer a hand. "Guess you'll have to come with me to find out."

❦

Emma ran her fingers through Palmer's hair. Tonight's lovemaking had been exceptional. Who was she kidding? Every time they made love was exceptional. Palmer understood the rhythms of Emma's body better than Emma did herself.

Still, each time they were together like this was bittersweet. In another few minutes, Palmer would wake up and insist on going back to her place so as to avoid any scandalous pictures or headlines.

Emma sighed in frustration. Next week would be the one-year anniversary of that first date in New York—the date they'd never gotten to finish. Since then, although they'd seen plenty of each other, they hadn't stepped foot outside the safety of the White House grounds as a couple. On several occasions, they'd invited Max and Nichelle to join them for dinner in the residence, but these instances hardly substituted for anything approaching a normal relationship progression.

Palmer seemed content enough with this arrangement, but Emma recognized that Palmer's interest was in minimizing Emma's exposure to criticism. In the process of dating the president, Palmer had sacrificed any sense of normalcy. Emma hated that for her.

"Why are you still awake?" Palmer mumbled against Emma's breast.

Emma shifted so that she faced Palmer. "Do you know what next week is?"

"Columbus Day?"

"True. What else?"

"The anniversary of our first official date."

"Excellent. You get points for remembering." Emma sat up fully and switched on the light. "Palmer, I want us to celebrate."

"Of course we'll celebrate, darling."

"What I mean is, I want to take you out for a night on the town."

"Why would you want to do that when you have the best chef in town right here in residence?"

"Nice try. You're not going to win this time, Palmer Estes. It's a milestone event, and I'm determined to make a splash."

Palmer sat up as well. "Emma, we're less than a month away from the midterm elections. One wrong step now could hurt your chances—"

"It's not a wrong step to want to take my girlfriend out for a nice dinner to celebrate an anniversary." Emma knew her irritation was showing, but she was beyond caring. This shouldn't be so hard.

Palmer took her hand. "The date means a lot to me too. But going out and being the object of attention comes at a high price."

"It's a price I'm willing to pay."

"Is it a price the party's willing to pay?"

"Damn it, Palmer! For once, I want to do something every other couple in America can do on their anniversary. This is not some PR problem. This is my life."

"Okay." Palmer took Emma's face in her hands and kissed her forehead. "Okay. Let's go paint the town red."

Emma's heart rate slowed. "That's better."

"But I'm buying."

"What?"

"Those are my terms. You pick the restaurant. I get to buy."

Emma narrowed her eyes. "What if I don't agree?"

"First, you're the president; you're not allowed to have your own credit card or cash. Second, and more to the point, you'd have a hard time celebrating by yourself, now wouldn't you?"

"You wouldn't dare…"

"Do you want to test me?"

Emma looked Palmer up and down suggestively. "Yes, but not about that."

Palmer laughed and pulled Emma back down onto the bed. "You're beautiful when you're determined."

"And you're beautiful when you're insufferable."

"That works out well, then." Palmer reached over Emma's head, clicked off the light, and took her again before slipping away into the night.

Emma rolled over into the spot Palmer had vacated. The sheets still smelled like her. She wished more than anything that she could hold Palmer all night long and wake up with her in the morning. They'd have to work on a solution to that situation too. But not tonight.

≪੭ ੧≫

Palmer understood now why Emma occasionally yearned to be able to move about freely and unnoticed. Even the simple act of going just around the block to Bobby Van's Steakhouse on 15th Street required advance planning and coordination. Before they ever got in the limo, the Secret Service had descended on the restaurant to determine the best place to seat the president. They wanded every person in the restaurant and those who would come in the door while Emma and Palmer dined.

As a result, all eyes were on them as they walked in the front door. In a town where big-name politicians regularly dined out in peace, eating in the same restaurant as the president excited even the jaded.

Palmer did her best to ignore all the raised cell phones recording or livestreaming the moment, the flash of cameras, the requests for Emma's autograph and selfies, all of which she obliged, and the gazes that stared openmouthed at them.

Emma resolutely reached for Palmer's hand. She leaned toward her and whispered, "I love you, Palmer Estes. I know this is hard for you. Thank you for giving us this night."

The words sliced Palmer's heart. She smiled at Emma. "I'd give you the world if I could, darling. The least I can do is grant your wish to celebrate our anniversary like normal people." Palmer winked and rolled her eyes indicating the crowd, the electric buzz in the air, and the dozens of cell phone flashes creating a strobe-light effect all around them. At least she no longer flinched from the flashes. *Progress.*

Emma laughed; the sound reached deep inside and nourished Palmer's soul.

"You're a good sport." Emma held Palmer's hand all the way through the restaurant to the private room they'd reserved. While Emma had wanted to go out, neither one of them had relished the idea of dozens of denizens watching them eat.

The door to the private dining area closed behind them and the Secret Service agents discreetly took up their positions.

"Alone at last," Emma said, as they seated themselves. Her smile was radiant and infectious.

"Are you happy?" Palmer asked.

"Ecstatic. You?"

"Seeing that light on your face fills me with joy." Palmer took Emma's hands. "I love you, Emma McMasters. Saying yes to you one year ago today was the best thing I ever did."

"Asking you out one year ago today was the smartest thing I've done in a long time."

Palmer raised an eyebrow. "Smarter than winning the presidency?"

"Yes. Because walking through life with you by my side is forever. The presidency comes with an expiration date."

"We all come with an expiration date, Emma. But I'd like to believe that we'll have eternity together, however that works."

"I like that outlook. I hope so." Emma lowered her gaze to their joined hands. "Speaking of spending eternity together…"

Palmer's heart hammered. Was Emma going to…

"When I lost Heather, I thought I'd never find anyone else for me. And then I met you. Palmer Estes, I love you more than anything in the world. Finding you this late in my life… Well, it adds a sense of urgency to our time together, at least for me. I don't want to waste a minute."

Emma reached into her clutch and withdrew a small velvet box. She slid it halfway across the table and rested her hand on top of it.

Palmer covered Emma's hand with her own, holding it in place. She saw the panic in Emma's eyes a fraction of a second too late and the breath caught in her throat. *Oh, Emma. You have nothing to fear, my love.*

Palmer rushed the words out in order to correct Emma's apparent misconception and reassure her. "Darling, if I don't miss my mark, great minds think alike." She fumbled in the pocket of her tailored, women's tux and wrapped her fingers around her own little velvet box. She produced it and slid it halfway across the table next to Emma's box.

Tears pricked Emma's eyes even as a brilliant smile spread across her features.

"Emma McMasters, I was certain I was destined to spend my life alone and lonely…until I met you. You fueled my imagination and captivated my heart from the very first time I saw you. I knew even before that first date in New York that I wanted to live out the rest of my days holding you in my arms."

Palmer nodded at Emma. It seemed only right that they should ask the question together.

"Emma…"

"Palmer…"

"Will you please marry me?"

"Yes, darling, I'll marry you," Palmer responded. She struggled to see Emma's face through the blur of tears.

"Yes, my dearest Palmer, I'll marry you. All I want is to spend the rest of my life with you."

Palmer nodded and swallowed around the lump in her throat. "I'm not crying. You're crying."

Emma laughed easily. "I'm pretty sure we're both crying, love."

Emma pushed her box the rest of the way across the table. Palmer did the same.

"On the count of three?" Palmer waggled her eyebrows.

"Sure." Emma shook her head. "If this doesn't go down as the craziest marriage proposal of all time."

"Agreed. One."

"Two," Emma said.

"Three," they said in unison.

Palmer couldn't help it, although she opened the box, her focus was on Emma.

"Oh." Emma gasped. She raised her gaze to Palmer. Her eyes were a deep green, and in them Palmer saw her future. "This is…" Emma put her other hand over her heart.

Palmer reached across and gently lifted the diamond and emerald encrusted platinum ring set from its nesting place. "May I?" she asked.

Emma nodded.

Palmer pushed on the inner emerald-laden band with her index finger and pulled the two entwined rings apart. The remaining outer ring was comprised of two diamond-studded bands held together by a two-carat diamond solitaire in the center. "This part is the engagement ring." She held up the other part of the set—the platinum band embedded with emeralds she'd just removed—and slid it back inside the two outer diamond bands. "The emerald band is the wedding band." She held up the combined solid whole, with the emerald band surrounded on both sides by the diamonds.

"It's breathtaking," Emma whispered hoarsely.

"Just like you." Palmer held her breath, took Emma's hand, and slipped the ring on her finger. It fit perfectly. Palmer exhaled her relief.

"I'll give you the option to wear only the engagement ring portion, or to keep the entire ring intact with the emerald band in the middle."

Emma blinked. "I'm not sure I'm capable of making a decision with such far-reaching ramifications."

"You're right," Palmer agreed. "That decision is so much bigger than popping the question." She winked.

"Smart ass." Emma gestured to the box that lay open in front of Palmer.

For the first time, Palmer focused on what lay before her. Her heart cracked open wide. Emma knew her so well. She withdrew the classic, sleek platinum band ringed with princess-cut diamonds three-quarters of the way around.

"You're so hard on your hands. I couldn't envision you wearing anything that you'd have to worry about losing or damaging."

"It's perfect, darling. Very me."

"I know it's a wedding band more than an engagement ring…"

"It'll function as both."

"May I?" Emma asked. She liberated the ring from Palmer's grip and slid it on Palmer's ring finger.

"How did you know my ring size?"

"Lucky guess."

"Mm-hmm." Palmer rose and came around the table. She lifted Emma to her feet and spent long moments staring into her eyes. "I love you, Emma. I can't wait to be married to you."

"I love you, Palmer. I can't wait to be your wife." She wrapped her arms around Palmer's neck and pulled her down for a lingering kiss.

When they broke apart, Palmer returned to her seat. "By the way, where did everybody go?"

Emma chuckled. "I asked to clear the room for fifteen minutes."

"Perk of being the president."

"There have to be some."

As they tucked into their meals, Palmer said, "You know that people are going to notice, right?" She indicated the ring on Emma's finger that now twinkled in the candlelight.

"I do. I have a press release announcing our engagement ready to go as soon as you approve it."

Palmer shook her head in wonder. "You thought of everything, Madam President." She savored the last bite of her dinner. "Does the release name a date?"

"For the wedding?" Emma laid down her fork and wiped her mouth.

"That's the next logical step, right?"

"No. There's no date. Did you want to set one now?"

"Sometime in the next year or two?"

"That's specific."

"The midterms are a few weeks away. Let's at least wait until after that to pick a date," Palmer said.

"You know that after the midterms I'm going to have to start focusing in earnest on my reelection campaign."

"I do."

"There's always going to be something, Palmer," Emma said quietly.

Palmer covered Emma's hand with her own. "Yes, but your reelection campaign will go a lot more smoothly if we have a good result in the midterms. You have to prove you have coattails."

"Since when did you become such an expert on politics?"

"Since I hooked up with the president," Palmer joked.

"I'm tired of longing for you every morning when I wake alone in our bed, wishing you'd stay the whole night."

"And I'm tired of tearing myself away from you in the middle of the night, darling. But until we're married, I don't think the middle of the country is ready to accept the president's live-in girlfriend."

"Fiancée," Emma corrected.

"That either," Palmer said.

"I hate that you're so much more practical than me."

"And right. Don't forget that I'm right."

"You wouldn't let me."

"True." Palmer smiled into her coffee.

"All the more reason for us to get married quickly," Emma argued.

"In due time. All good things come to those who wait."

"Patience never was my strong suit," Emma muttered.

"Really? I hadn't noticed." Palmer sipped her coffee. "I promise to make the wait worth your while."

"Oh, I'll hold you to that, professor."

"I'm counting on it." Palmer couldn't contain herself. She and Emma were getting married. Her heart overflowed with love.

CHAPTER TWENTY-TWO

Social media, the newspapers, and the airwaves were filled with pictures and video of Emma and Palmer arriving at Bobby Van's. Emma and Palmer's quotes, via the press release the communications office put out shortly after the two of them returned from dinner, managed to make the online and early print editions of most of the major dailies and the morning network and cable news shows.

Enterprising amateur photographers at the restaurant somehow captured images of the rings, of Emma holding Palmer's hand, and of the loving looks that passed between them.

Well-wishes poured in from around the country and around the world. Mixed in with those were horrible, venom-filled diatribes railing against Emma, Palmer, homosexuality in general, and a host of other unrelated grievances.

"Stop looking at Twitter," Nichelle cautioned.

"It's like a train wreck. I can't stop," Palmer said.

"Nothing good will come of it," Emma warned.

The three of them sat around the breakfast table in the residence, eating Sunday brunch. In a few hours, Emma would depart for a two-day campaign junket through targeted areas where incumbent Republican senators were vulnerable and pegged by the Democratic National Committee for possible upsets.

"I wish you were coming with me," Emma said.

"I'm sure that wouldn't create any new fodder for the hatemongers."

"We can't run scared."

"Palmer is being practical and level-headed. You ought to listen to her more."

Emma pointed her fork at Nichelle. "Whose side are you on?"

"The side that wins us a majority in the Senate so that we can push through the rest of our agenda and get you reelected in a landslide."

"Listen to Nichelle. She knows things," Palmer said.

"Speaking of knowing things," Emma said, "when are you and Max going to tie the knot?"

"What?" Nichelle asked. "Where did that come from?"

"You two have been dating longer than we have, you're perfect for each other…"

Palmer picked up the thread from Emma. "You practically live together. Emma's right. When's the wedding? Inquiring minds want to know."

"Just because you two crazy kids decided to take it to the next level, don't be projecting all that settling down stuff outward."

Palmer laughed. "You've got cold feet."

"Do not."

"I know you, Nich," Emma chimed in. "You so do."

"Two against one is no fair."

"I know Max," Palmer said. "I've known him for most of my adult life. I've never seen him as head-over-heels as he is for you. He tells me he's asked you more than once, but you keep changing the subject. Don't tell me he's not good enough for you, because I'll fight you on that one."

"No. Max is perfect for me."

"Then what's the problem?" Emma asked.

"Who says there's a problem?"

"There's a problem," Palmer said to Emma.

"Sure sounds like that to me," Emma agreed.

Nichelle sat there looking from one of them to the other. "There is no problem. I'm very busy. I've got a dragon for a boss and no time off, and—"

"You set the date and I'll bet I can get your boss to give you some time off to plan the wedding," Palmer said. "I have sway."

Nichelle pointedly looked at her watch. "Madam President, you have a plane to catch. I think I'll give you two lovebirds a few minutes of alone time." She got up. "Ten minutes and not a second more."

"She's such a kill-joy," Palmer said.

"Yes, but she's my kill-joy," Emma quipped.

"What are you going to do for Columbus Day, Palmer? Surely, you're not teaching tomorrow?" Nichelle asked.

"Office hours. No rest for the wicked."

"Tell me about it," Nichelle agreed, with a pointed look at Emma.

"Stop your whining. At least I didn't make you come with me, Nich."

"Well, there is that." Nichelle headed for the door.

"I'll be on time. I promise." Emma waved as Nichelle let herself out.

When they were alone, Emma swept Palmer into her arms. "I don't want to go."

"I don't want you to, so we're even." Palmer claimed Emma's lips in a long, lingering kiss.

"You should've stayed for round three last night. I've made an honest woman out of you now."

"Engaged is not married. Just ask all those 'they' people who answer the polling questions."

"You have got to stop watching the polls. I told you, public sentiment is not going to dictate how or whom I love."

"I heard you, darling." Palmer kissed her on the forehead. *I just worry for you.* Maybe if she tried a different approach... "Have you read some of this crap on Twitter? These trolls would never say such things face to face. They hide behind anonymous accounts and spew all kinds of wretched hate speech."

"I try not to pay attention. Too depressing. As for you... I thought you told me that before you retired, you never bothered with social media? You were better off."

"Emma—"

"Love—"

"There are sick individuals out there making threats against your life," Palmer's voice cracked. "What do I have to say or do to make you take it seriously?"

"I am taking it seriously. The FBI and the Secret Service investigate every credible threat. That's their job. You know this. We have to trust them to do their jobs."

"You're right, and I do trust them. I guess I'm just overtired."

"Palmer... Darling, look at me." Emma led them over to the couch. "I promise you I won't take any more chances than I have to. You know how important this trip is. It's my duty and responsibility as the titular head of the party to do everything in my power to get us the majority in the Senate. This is fundamentally important in order to clear the way for every good thing I swore to do when I came into office."

"I know," Palmer whispered.

"Imagine the things I can do in concert with a Democratic majority in both houses. Full, comprehensive immigration reform with a true path to citizenship." Emma snapped her fingers. "A real voting rights act." She snapped again. "Closing the wage and gender gap." Snap. "Universal health care with a private option." Snap.

"You've already achieved some of these things." Palmer's words sounded like a whine, and she knew it.

"Not in the ways we could with a solid majority. We could undo so much harm to environmental protections, climate change initiatives, consumer protections, education reform... The list goes on and on. We could enact proactive legislation and programs that would insulate and protect the most vulnerable and set the country up for success for decades to come. These are the reasons I became president. I've barely begun to scratch the surface of achieving the most vital parts of my agenda."

Emma stroked Palmer's hand. "You asked me if I always wanted to be president, and I told you the truth: that was never my ambition. But the fact is, I am the president. I will fight to my last breath to be the very best leader I can be—to do everything I can to leave this country in better shape than I found it."

"The country already is in better shape than you found it, Emma. You've restored the heartbeat of the presidency and the soul of democracy. You've replaced the politics of divisiveness with the policies of inclusivity. You've brought this country back from the brink of disaster and rekindled hope and faith where there was none. And you've done it all with kindness, compassion, heart, authenticity, transparency, and class. Whatever happens in these midterms, or two years from now on Election Day, I will never be prouder to be a citizen of the United States of America than I am right now."

Emma wiped a tear from the corner of her eye. "That might be the loveliest thing anyone has ever said to this president." She kissed Palmer softly on the mouth. "I promise you I'll be extra careful. I love you with all my heart, Palmer Estes."

"You're my heartbeat, Emma McMasters. Always remember how much I love and need you."

"Walk me out?" Emma asked.

"It would be my honor, Madam President."

✍︎❧

"Emma! Emma! Emma!" the crowd cheered.

"Hello, Miami!" she waved at the throngs of people stretched as far as the eye could see. "It's great to be here with you. It's especially wonderful to be standing side-by-side with your next U.S. senator, Representative Alyana Ortiz!" Emma grabbed Ortiz's hand and held it aloft.

"I am so grateful for the faith you all placed in me in 2020. Together, we turned Florida blue. Now I need your help to finish the job you sent me to Washington to do. With a solid majority in the Senate, we can ensure that every American has affordable health care, we can enhance worker protections..."

Emma rattled off the laundry list of accomplishments that a midterm election victory would make possible and then she invited Ortiz to address the crowd.

When the candidate had wrapped up her stump speech, Emma stepped up once more to exhort the audience to vote to restore humanity and compassion to our government.

"Thank you, Madam President. You really made a difference here today," Ortiz said.

"You're welcome. I can't wait to have you in the Senate. We need your voice and your passion."

"And so you shall have both."

Emma nodded and exited the stage. She spent several minutes on the rope line, shaking people's hands and taking selfies with them.

Several hours later, she repeated the same routine in Atlanta, where polls showed the upstart Democrat to be in a dead heat with the incumbent Republican.

By the time she reached her hotel suite in Atlanta, Emma was exhausted. She kicked off her shoes and headed for the shower.

When she was clean, dry, and comfortable, she retrieved her personal cell and texted Palmer. *I'm done for the day, love. All safe and sound and tucked in for the night. If you're available, I'd love to hear my favorite voice on the phone.*

Less than thirty seconds later, her phone rang. "What took you so long?"

"Very funny. How are you, darling?"

"Tired. Whiny because I miss my fiancée. Lonely. Did I mention I miss you?"

"You might've worked it into the conversation."

"What did you do for the rest of the day?"

"Graded midterm exams. Want to trade places?"

"Eh. How were they?"

"Mixed bag. I can see where some of the more motivated students really studied and mastered the material. On the other end of the spectrum are the ones who obviously thought they could BS their way through."

"Ah, Professor Estes, don't be too hard on the lads and lasses."

"That's your position? Because I'm sure when these kids get jobs in the intelligence sector, their superiors will go easy on them when they fudge their way through a briefing for the president."

"You make a good point. I retract my statement. Go on with your ruthless self."

"That's better."

Emma loved that Palmer was in a playful mood. It was a lovely counterpoint to the morning's stress.

"Emma?"

"Mm?"

"I miss you."

Emma smiled into the phone. "I miss you too. The rally in Louisville is an outdoor, lunchtime affair. I'll be home in time for dinner tomorrow night. Can I interest you in an evening at my place?"

"I'll check my calendar and ask my social secretary to pencil you in."

"Ha. Anything special you want me to ask the chef to prepare?"

"You know the only thing I care about is spending time with you. I wouldn't care if we had leftover spinach salad."

"Ugh. Is that what you're eating tonight?"

"What else?"

"We have got to expand your repertoire."

"It's worked for me for many, many years."

"Yeah, well, I'm not asking the White House chef to make my wife a wilted spinach salad, like ever."

"Once I'm married to you, that makes me First Lady. I can ask her to make it for me myself."

"I knew there would be a downside to all this marriage business."

"You should've thought of that first. Want to retract the proposal?"

"Never." Tears threatened.

Palmer must've sensed it, because her next words were, "Emma? Darling? I was kidding. I was just joking around."

"I know." A single salty drop streaked down Emma's face.

"What happened there?"

Emma huffed out a breath. "Long day, I guess."

"Are you all right? You want me to come down there?"

The offer made Emma smile. "Now? It's kind of late."

"I can catch a flight and be there within three to five hours."

"I'm glad you left yourself a window. You're incredibly sweet, but no. I'm fine. Really. Just overtired and emotional."

"For the record, you can't get rid of me that easily. I'm not going anywhere, Emma. Not without you. You're my heartbeat. I cannot wait to be married to you."

"I love you so much, Palmer. I didn't know my heart had the capacity to love another this way. You're everything to me. I hope you always know that. I hope I do enough to show you that."

"You do, darling. It's getting late. Are you going to be able to get some sleep?"

"I hope so. The sooner I get to sleep, the sooner I get to come home to you."

"I'll be waiting. Call me when you're done in Louisville?"

"The second I get in the limo."

"You're going to be great. Go get what's-his-name elected."

Emma laughed. "I hope the voters remember his name."

"I love you, Emma McMasters."

"I love you, Palmer Estes."

"Stay safe for me."

"Always. Goodnight, love."

"Good night, darling. Sweet dreams."

Emma disconnected the call and laid the phone on the bedside table. Tomorrow night she'd be lying in Palmer's arms again. She fell asleep with a smile on her face.

CHAPTER TWENTY-THREE

E mma squinted into the bright sunshine. At least the weather in Louisville was picture perfect. The temperature was a pleasant sixty-eight degrees, and she was glad she'd eschewed the light coat she'd brought along for the trip. The venue for the rally was the University of Louisville campus. She loved the energy of college campuses. They reminded her of her own student days, when she'd believed anything she wanted was achievable with enough hard work and dedication.

Although she no longer was that naïve young woman, she still believed that with hard work and dedication almost anything was achievable. That included coming away from the midterm elections with a solid majority in the Senate, a steady majority in the House, and a mandate to complete the agenda she'd laid out in her campaign two years ago.

"Madam President, I am so thrilled that you could make it today. I know you've got a lot on your plate. I can't tell you how much I appreciate you taking the time to give my campaign a push. This is going to give us exactly the kind of boost in visibility and fundraising that will get us over the finish line."

Emma shook hands with former state senator turned candidate, Thomas Engelbright. "You're welcome. I've heard great things about you and I'm looking forward to seeing your face in Washington come January."

"Yes, ma'am. I love your optimism."

"Madam President, they're ready."

Emma nodded at the aide. "Here we go."

She trotted up the three steps to the stage, with the candidate right behind her. She waved to the crowd as the now-familiar enthusiastic chant swelled to a crescendo: "Emma! Emma! Emma! United we stand!"

"Hello, Louisville!" She resisted the urge to shield her eyes from the glare of the sun off the Student Activities Center windows. "I'm excited to be here. Thank you all so much for coming out today. I know, weather like this makes it a hardship to be outside, right?"

The audience laughed. "I'm here today to support state Senator Thomas Engelbright. Senator Engelbright is exactly the kind of leader we need in Washington. Please help me give him a warm Louisville welcome!"

When the candidate finished speaking, Emma stepped back to the podium to deliver the call to action with her stock stump speech. Fifteen minutes later, she concluded by saying, "With your help, we can take the Senate and finish the job you all sent me to Washington to do. My friend, Thomas Engelbright, knows what's important to Kentuckians, and he's prepared to deliver for you."

Emma signaled Engelbright to join her. Together, they stepped out from behind the podium and held their joined hands aloft.

A searing pain pierced Emma's chest and she staggered backward. All around her she heard screams and the sounds of people running. Bodies were on top of her. She thought she recognized Scott.

"Madam President, can you hear me?"

"Yes." Her breath came in short spurts. The pressure was unbearable.

"You've been hit. We're going to get you out of here. You hear me? Stay with us."

Emma heard snatches of urgent barked orders. She felt herself being lifted and set back down on something softer.

"Pneumothorax. Get the chest tube inserted." It was the voice of her personal physician, Air Force Colonel Raymond Stark.

Another sharp pain caused her to cry out.

"Sorry, Madam President. That's the chest tube going in. Breathing should get easier now."

The pressure in her chest eased and she drew in a wheezing breath. She was hungry for air, so she pulled in another breath.

"Ready to roll?"

"Let's move!"

"The ambulance is here, ma'am. We're going to transport you now."

Emma blinked and tried to focus. "What's going on?"

"You've been shot, Madam President. Your lung collapsed. We've re-inflated it so you can breathe easier. We're taking you to the hospital now."

"Palmer..."

"Ma'am? Stay with us."

Emma heard the sirens screaming. She spotted Scott next to Doctor Stark. Scott's face was ashen, his hands covered in blood. She grabbed his lapel. "25th Amendment," she croaked. "In case... Follow protocol," she managed. Another searing pain, this one different from the last.

"We're losing her. Step on it..."

And then...nothing but a bright, white light.

✧✧

Palmer ran her fingers through her hair. Thank God this was the last of the exams she had to grade. Maybe she'd treat herself to a nice, light, late lunch after this. She didn't want to spoil her appetite for dinner later with Emma.

"Oh, dear God, no!"

Palmer heard the cry through the common wall with Professor Madeline Twilliger. She was half out of her seat when the professor in question rushed in. She carried her laptop in shaky fingers.

"Madeline?" Palmer stood the rest of the way and came around the desk.

"Have you seen this? Oh, my God." Madeline set the laptop down on the corner of Palmer's desk and put her hand over her mouth. "Oh, Palmer. I'm so sorry."

"What's going on...?"

Palmer's voice trailed off as a shaky video clip filled the laptop screen and a breathless anchor intoned, "Again, this is footage filmed moments ago by our sister station in Louisville, Kentucky. President Emma McMasters has been shot. Her condition is unknown. This is our first look at the video. You can see..."

Palmer stumbled against the side of the desk. It couldn't be… She glanced up in even more confusion as Nichelle and two Secret Service agents filled the doorway, virtually pushing Madeline out of the way.

"Nich?"

"Come with us, Palmer. Now." Nichelle's voice trembled and tears pooled in her eyes. "Hurry." Nichelle grabbed her by the sleeve and yanked. Palmer snatched up her phone and stuffed it in her back pocket as the Secret Service agents propelled her out the door.

They all ran double-time, an especially impressive feat for Nichelle, who wore heels.

"Nichelle?"

"Not here, Palmer. I'll tell you everything on the way."

They reached the motorcade, which to Palmer's surprise was parked in front of her building. Secret Service agents stood on high alert, covering all directions. The cars were idling and one of the agents guarded the open passenger door of the nearest limo.

The two agents that had come to her office hustled Palmer and Nichelle into the car, slammed the door, and the motorcade sped off.

Palmer wanted to scream. She needed answers, and she needed them now. They careened around a corner. "Nichelle. Talk to me. What is going on?"

Finally, Nichelle faced her on the seat. "I-It's Emma, Palmer. She's been shot."

Palmer slumped against the seat. Somehow, she'd hoped she'd either misheard the news anchor, or the anchor had gotten it wrong.

"She's a tough girl, Palmer," Nichelle said, as if that made a difference to a bullet.

Palmer slipped on the persona that years of combat had ingrained in her DNA and would allow her to function. First, she should prioritize what she needed to know and formulate questions. "How bad is it?"

"Bad. I'm not going to sugarcoat it."

"Tell me." Palmer could barely force the words out.

"I can only tell you what we know so far."

"We're here, ma'am," one of the Secret Service agents interrupted Nichelle.

"Where's here?" Palmer asked.

"The South Lawn. We're taking one of the helicopters from the presidential fleet to Andrews and getting on a plane. Come on."

Palmer followed Nichelle onto the chopper and buckled in for the short hop. She wanted to shake the story out of Nichelle, but she recognized that she would learn nothing more until they could have some privacy.

Nichelle took her hand and squeezed. Tears were close to the surface, and Nichelle blinked to keep them at bay. Palmer squeezed her hand back.

They remained like that until the helicopter put down. The skids barely touched the landing pad before the Secret Service had them on the move again, this time onto one of the 747s that made up the presidential fleet.

Palmer noticed that there were other members of Emma's close staff boarding the plane as well. Nichelle took her hand again and led her to a small office near the front of the plane. She closed the door behind them and indicated Palmer should buckle in.

She'd hardly settled into the seat before the plane accelerated down the runway.

"Nichelle, please." Her voice cracked.

The light had gone out of Nichelle's eyes. Palmer recognized the signs. She was in shock. "She'd finished her remarks and she and the Senate candidate were getting ready to exit the stage. Everything happened so fast." Nichelle stared off into space.

Palmer pressed forward. "And?"

"It was a sniper with a high-powered rifle, probably hiding on the second floor of the Student Activities Center. The bullet hit her in the chest and punctured a lung. They inserted a chest tube on the spot to help her breathe. She was conscious and still talking when they got her in the ambulance."

Palmer closed her eyes as her body started to shake. She wrapped her arms around herself.

Nichelle looked at Palmer, but it didn't seem as if she really saw her. "You know our Emma, she's a by-the-book kind of president. She's lying there, shot in the chest, and the first thing she does, right after asking for you, is to give the instruction to invoke the 25th Amendment, turning power over to Vice President Elder."

"Nichelle... What's the situation now?" Palmer tried to get her to focus.

Nichelle's voice lacked affect, and her demeanor was matter-of-fact. "Apparently, in the ambulance, she died."

"She..." Palmer's head spun. Blood rushed to her temples. She put out her hand to keep from falling out of the seat, even as the seatbelt kept her in place.

Finally, tears flowed down Nichelle's cheeks. "They were able to do CPR and bring her back after only a few seconds, though, and she regained consciousness. After that, it only took them a few minutes to get to the hospital. They got her inside and they were talking to her and evaluating her. Then, Doctor Stark and the trauma surgeon said she died again, right before their eyes."

Palmer's heart jolted painfully and she covered it reflexively with her hand. Nichelle didn't seem to notice; she was in her own world.

"They did two chest compressions, and again, she came right back. Doctor Stark spoke to Vice President Elder and me on his way into the operating room. He said it was the craziest thing. They determined that something really unusual must be happening, so they've rushed her directly into surgery. That's where she is right now. That's where we're going."

Palmer tried to process the information and get to the bottom line, wishing more than anything that Nichelle had led with the headline. "So, Emma is alive?"

"As far as we know."

Palmer rocked back and forth. *She's alive and in surgery. She's strong and a fighter. She'll fight to stay.* A sob pierced the cabin, and Palmer belatedly realized it came from her.

The sound seemed to jolt Nichelle back to the present space. She unbuckled her seatbelt and knelt next to Palmer's seat to give her a hug. "This is your Emma. She's young and in great shape. If anyone can make it through, it will be her."

"The news had footage..."

"The deputy press secretary was the one with the president on this trip. He's got his hands full." Nichelle returned to her seat and buckled in again. "Olivia is on board here somewhere. She's also interfacing with the press, trying to hold them at bay and keep them from disseminating uncorroborated or false information. Doctor

Stark will hold a press briefing once Emma's out of surgery, right after he talks to you."

Palmer's mind fixed on a question. "Did they get the bastard?"

"I don't know that. Scott was with Emma. He covered her with his own body. He was in the ambulance. He can tell us more when we land, which should be soon. I was told the flight would only take us about an hour and fifteen or so. There's a helicopter waiting to take us from the airport to the hospital."

"All the Secret Service agents had their guns drawn when you came to get me. Why?"

"We don't know if Emma was the only target or if you're in danger too. So, for now, you get protection."

Palmer nodded. Until they knew the motive and were confident that they'd found the shooter and determined whether he or she was a lone wolf, the Secret Service wouldn't take any chances.

A steward knocked on the door. "We're getting ready to land, ma'ams."

"Thank you."

Palmer sucked in a ragged breath. *I'm coming, darling. Hang on for me.*

Palmer needed some space. Like a good soldier in the middle of a battle, she'd held it together until this moment. But now, as she waited for Emma to come out of surgery and Emma's personal doctor to come out and give his report, she craved the privacy to grieve and process.

"I need a minute," she said to Jemelle, who had been assigned to protect Palmer once she arrived at the hospital. She liked Jemelle. So did Emma.

Emma. Reflexively, Palmer put her hand over her heart and rubbed the sore spot. For so long she'd been alone. Now? Now, she couldn't imagine a life without Emma in it.

"I hear you. I have to come with you, but you can grab a cup of coffee from the cafeteria down the hall." Jemelle murmured into her comms, "Panther is on the move."

Palmer bought coffee for herself and a cup for Jemelle, who was doing her best to be simultaneously protective but not intrusive.

Palmer sat down at a booth in the corner and pulled out her phone. She held it in her hands for a long time before opening the CNN news app and clicking on the top story, which declared, "President's life hangs in the balance."

Palmer kept the volume loud enough for only her to hear as she viewed the video coverage. The anchor repeated what was known. The president was shot from long range while speaking at a rally in Louisville, Kentucky, for U.S. Senate candidate, Thomas Engelbright, shortly after noon.

The anchor intoned, "I'll warn you that this footage is very graphic, and you might want to look away."

Palmer hesitated only a moment. She needed to see what had happened—needed to understand it and to make sense of the senseless.

The video showed a relaxed and beaming Emma standing side by side with the candidate. She took his hand, stepped away from the podium, held their arms aloft, and...

Palmer flinched as she watched the smile on Emma's face morph into shock and pain. She staggered a step and fell backward as she clutched at her chest. A second later, Scott entered the frame. He dove on top of Emma along with several other agents.

The video lost focus and the camera veered to the side. The videographer obviously had been jostled. Next, the camera panned the frantic crowd as panicked people scattered in all directions. A second later, the lens focused back on the stage, where Scott and other agents guarded the fallen president as paramedics worked on her at the scene.

The video ended and the screen cut back to the anchor. "At this hour, millions of people around the globe are keeping a vigil for President McMasters, praying for her survival."

Palmer's head jerked up when Jemelle touched her on the arm. She pressed a handkerchief into Palmer's hand. That was when Palmer realized she was crying.

"Thanks."

"You're welcome."

Palmer had one question on the top of her mind: *Did you guys get the bastard?* But she wasn't sure what the rules were with regard to this sort of thing, and she didn't want to put Jemelle in an uncomfortable position, so she left the topic alone. She wiped her eyes and drained the rest of the cup.

"This is my fault." Palmer muttered.

"What did you say?" Jemelle asked.

"I said it's my fault."

"How's that?"

"My gut was screaming at me before Emma left for the trip. As a soldier, I always survived by trusting my gut. If I shared more forcefully how I felt, maybe she wouldn't have gone and…"

"Hey." Jemelle waited for Palmer to make eye contact. "This isn't on you. Some unstable person with a gun took a shot. Every one of us charged with protecting the president feels like you do right now, only one-hundredfold, because it's our job to keep her safe. That's on us. This isn't just professional—it's personal. You and the president, you should never have to worry about her safety. It's our job to make it so you don't have to do anything but go about your business. You and the president, you trust us to keep y'all safe. We let you down."

"No, Jemelle. All of you did your best. I know that. Emma knows that too."

Jemelle held up a hand and she whispered into her comms, "Roger that. We're on the way." She addressed Palmer. "She's out of surgery."

Palmer took off at a run with Jemelle on her heels. She skidded to a stop just as Doctor Stark rounded the corner. "How is she, Doctor?"

"There you are, General. The president said to tell you you're stuck with her."

Palmer let that information sink in. "She told you that?"

"She did, although to be fair, she was on a lot of pain medication at the time."

"Is she all right?"

"She is now."

Palmer released the breath she'd been holding.

"I've never seen a scenario like this, and I've been practicing a long time. Come here, I'll show you."

Doctor Stark walked Palmer over to an x-ray viewer and held up an x-ray. "The bullet entered the right front chest just below the right breast, breaking this rib, here. This should've made the president very lucky, indeed, since the rib deflected the bullet, which was aimed for her heart. The bullet exited the body, here." He indicated the spot on a second x-ray.

"Had the bullet not hit the rib, it most certainly would've killed the president. As it was, the placement of the chest tube to re-inflate the lung gave her immediate relief. This is why it was baffling when not once, but twice, she died, even though the lung was inflated and the bullet missed all the other vital organs."

Palmer flinched at the words.

"The surgery revealed the crux of the problem. A piece of the broken rib splintered off and pierced the heart, causing blood to fill the pericardium—the sac around the heart. Normally, a patient would bleed to death in minutes from a hole in the heart. The president, as it turns out, only had a small hole in the right atrium of the heart from the tip of that broken rib. This hole caused blood to slowly fill the pericardium. In ninety-nine percent of cases, the blood flooding the pericardium literally crushes the heart, causing death."

Palmer's legs gave way, and she fought to keep her feet under her. *Oh, Emma.* Palmer steadied herself with a hand on the wall. *Emma's alive. She's in recovery. She's the one percent. Hold onto that.*

Doctor Stark continued his graphic explanation. If he noticed the effect his description was having on Palmer, he ignored it.

"When CPR was performed in the ambulance, the small tear in the pericardium caused by the rib, reopened. That let all the blood out, allowing the heart to beat again and reviving the patient. The lack of pressure on the pericardium then allowed that small hole to seal itself temporarily, preventing her from bleeding to death. At that point, the cycle started all over again, until she was in the trauma bay and died again."

Palmer thought her own heart would give out, but she forced herself to hear what the doctor had to say.

"After we opened her chest and performed the emergency thoracotomy, she died a third time. At that point, while we were inside the chest cavity, we were able to get a clear view and pinpoint the exact sequence as it happened in real time."

Now, Palmer's heart stuttered. Emma died a *third* time? Palmer slumped against the wall.

"During surgery, we were able to remove the rib fragments and repair the hole in the heart. We installed a clean chest tube to allow any excess fluid or air from the chest cavity to drain. We also performed a pericardial window procedure, where we cut a square hole in the pericardium so fluid would never tamponade—"

"Would never, what?"

"Sorry. Medical term. So that the fluid wouldn't crush her heart again."

The idea of Emma's heart being crushed robbed Palmer of breath. She nearly missed what the doctor said next.

"We left a heart drain behind temporarily, until the area begins to heal. This drain will likely be removed at the same time we take out the chest tube, probably in a week's time." Doctor Stark finally focused his full attention on Palmer. "Are you okay, ma'am? Your pallor…"

"I'm fine," she lied.

"Do you have any questions for me?"

She could absorb the medical technicalities over time. Right now, Palmer needed to know only one thing. "Is she going to be all right?"

"Yes, as long as we can keep her free from complications, she's going to be just fine. She's a very lucky woman. This is a one-in-a-million outcome."

"When can I see her?"

"She's in recovery now. She should be out in another couple of hours."

"Thank you, Doctor."

"You're very welcome, General. I've got to go give a press conference."

"Right. Thank you for taking the time to explain it all to me in detail. It helps."

"The president is as tough as they come. She'll be all right."

"She has to be," Palmer whispered, after the doctor walked away.

CHAPTER TWENTY-FOUR

E mma swallowed and wished she hadn't. Her throat felt like she'd ingested broken glass. She heard beeps and whirring. The smell of disinfectant permeated the air. Her chest and side felt like she'd been filleted like a fish. The one familiar thing was the feel of Palmer's hand in hers.

Palmer. Carefully, Emma cracked open one eye, and then the other. She blinked several times, until her surroundings came into focus. A hospital room? She closed her eyes again as everything came flooding back. She'd been finishing up her appearance in Louisville. Flashes of memories flitted like kaleidoscopic images in her head.

Standing in the sunshine on a stage... An explosion in her chest... Gasping for air... Screaming and chaos... Clouds in the pristine blue sky... Scott's face... Her personal physician, Doctor Stark... Sirens... A bright white light... Peace... Shouting... A doctor in scrubs telling her to stay with him...

Realization dawned and fear raced through her veins. She'd been shot. Someone had tried to kill her. Had they succeeded? "P-Palmer?" Emma struggled to open her eyes again.

"Emma? Darling? I'm right here."

Palmer's face swam into view. Was she crying? "Don't..." Talking hurt. Everything hurt. Emma closed her eyes again. She was so tired.

Palmer. Emma had to see her beautiful face again. She felt fingers lovingly stroke her hair. She willed herself up from the depths of wherever she was and swallowed again, determined to push words out. "Don't..." She cleared her throat. "Don't cry, love."

"Okay." Palmer's breath tickled her ear. "I love you, darling."

Palmer kissed her forehead. At least that didn't hurt. "I love you too. Hospital?"

"Yes."

"Shot?"

"Y-yes."

Emma absorbed that information. "Hurts."

"I know. But the doctor says you're going to be good as new."

"Mm. So tired."

"Rest. I'm not going anywhere, darling."

The next time Emma opened her eyes, Palmer still held her hand. The room was dark save for a low light over the bed.

"Hi, beautiful." Palmer's face came into view above her.

"Hi. Hurts."

"I know, darling. Do you want me to get the nurse or the doctor?"

"Not yet." She squeezed Palmer's hand. "Tell me."

Palmer nodded. She looked haggard. Her eyelids were swollen and her face was pale.

Emma ran her thumb over the back of Palmer's hand. "I'm sorry."

"You're sor... What for?"

"Scaring you."

"Darling, you didn't do that. I just need you to stay with me. Keep fighting, okay?"

"I promise." Emma swallowed. Her throat was so sore.

"You want some water?"

She nodded. Palmer placed a straw between her lips. "Thanks." She winced as her chest and side turned to fire. "Ouch."

"I know."

"Tell me," Emma repeated.

"Are you sure?"

"I need to know."

"Okay."

Palmer broke down several times in the telling. Emma encouraged her to finish. They both needed to get through this. How else could they process the trauma and get past it? When Palmer finished, Emma patted the bed in invitation. Gently, carefully, Palmer sat on the very edge.

"I remember parts of it," Emma said. "Just bits and pieces. Snatches of conversation, sensations, impressions, really." She hesitated. Should she share her revelation? *Palmer should know.*

"I can tell you this," Emma began. She considered how to convey something she never expected to know. "Dying isn't painful or hard, my love." She felt Palmer tense next to her. "It's nothing to be frightened of. All I felt was… I was so at peace. I felt love. That's the best way to explain it. I felt an indescribable love fill me."

"The idea that you died…" Palmer's voice trailed off as her body shook.

"Shh, love. I'm right here. I'm not going anywhere. I remember thinking that I needed to live for you, for us. Your love brought me back."

"CPR brought you back. Doctor Stark brought you back. Surgery saved you."

"Ever practical Palmer."

"Let me get the doctor or the nurse to give you something for the pain."

Emma closed her eyes. "If I take opioids, I can't fulfill my Constitutional duties. I can't take pain meds and be president."

"About that… Do you remember insisting on invoking the 25th Amendment? Apparently, in the ambulance, you instructed your people to make sure protocol was followed."

Emma narrowed her eyes and tried to remember. She'd seen Scott, she'd asked for Palmer… "Yes. So, did they execute the order?"

"They did. Vice President Elder is holding down the fort."

"Harrison is a good man."

"He is. Take the morphine if you need it, darling. You have to stay ahead of the pain."

As painful as her side, chest, and throat were… "Why does my throat hurt?"

"They had to intubate you and put you on a ventilator for the surgery."

"Oh."

"I bet your chest and side hurt like a son-of-a-gun too."

"You have no idea. Why is that?"

"The surgeon had to make a large incision to spread your ribcage so that he could remove all the rib fragments and sew up your heart."

"Oh." A frisson of fear spread through her. "Will I have permanent heart damage?"

"The doctor says no. Let me get him for you. He can tell you himself and answer any of your questions."

"Not yet."

"But you're in so much pain."

"I just need to be alone with you. Please?"

"Of course," Palmer answered. Palmer smoothed the hair back from Emma's face.

"I love you, Palmer." She was getting sleepy again.

"I love you, Emma Jean. Thank God you have a strong heart."

"Mm. You're my heart." She felt herself drifting.

"Sleep, darling."

"Mm…"

❧❧

"Ow." Sharp pain shot through Palmer's neck. Gingerly, she raised her head and turned it to the side to get the kink out. She'd fallen asleep in the chair with her head resting on the bed against Emma's hip.

Emma. She still was asleep, as she had been for the past several hours. The nurse from Emma's dedicated medical staff had checked on them several times. Emma's vital signs were good. The two drains sewn into the skin of her right side above the incision appeared to be working properly.

Palmer had taken a peek at the dressing that wrapped loosely around Emma's torso. The nurse told her Emma's incision ran all the way from her sternum to a little more than a quarter of the way around her back on the right side.

I almost lost you. Correction, I did lose you. Three times. Palmer's heart jerked. If she stayed in that head space, thinking about what happened, and how close Emma had come… *No.* There would be time for her to unpack her feelings later. Right now, all that mattered was that Emma was here, breathing and alive.

"Hi." Doctor Stark stepped into the room. "How's she doing?"

Palmer stood and stretched. "She's been uncomfortable and in significant pain when she's been awake, which hasn't been often."

"The nurse tells me she's refused any pain medication except for Tylenol."

"Much to my dismay," Palmer said. "What do you think, Doctor? Shouldn't she take the morphine? Wouldn't she be more comfortable?"

The doctor walked around the bed and checked the dressing. "She would, but I understand why she's resisting."

"I understand why she's resisting too, but surely she can't run the country in this condition."

"Actually, at the moment, her mental faculties are sharp enough and it is within her power to transmit the papers indicating that no disability exists. Assuming the relevant parties agree, she could resume the presidency right now."

"You get an A in Constitutional law, Doctor Stark," Emma said as she opened her eyes. Her voice remained rough. Palmer returned to her seat and took Emma's hand.

"Ah. Good to see you, Madam President. How are you feeling?"

"I've always wondered why doctors ask patients that question when they know full well that the patient feels like she's been hit by a train."

"It's the first question we're taught to ask in medical school. So, what questions do you have for me?"

"I hardly know where to start. First, I want to say a huge thank you to you and whoever else saved my life and sewed me back together."

"You're welcome, Madam President. That's why we're here."

"And here I thought you took the job because you wanted to see the world for free from Air Force One."

"I'm glad you haven't lost your sense of humor."

"Not yet." Emma shifted uncomfortably. "Ouch."

"Unfortunately, you're going to be saying that quite a bit for the next little while," Doctor Stark said.

"What's the next step?"

"Well, your security detail and I would really prefer to get you back to our home turf as soon as possible."

"And how soon is that?"

"You're twelve hours post-surgery—"

"I am?"

"You are."

"Wow. Time flies."

"Anyway, as you know, we have a full medical and surgical suite on board Air Force One. I've got a full team here. We could move you now."

"Is that wise?" Palmer asked. Belatedly, she realized the doctor might have construed her question as a challenge to his judgment. "I'm sorry. Obviously, this isn't my area of expertise. What I mean is, is it really okay to move a patient who's been through such a major trauma so soon?"

"It's a fair question. Normally, we'd want more time before taking such a step..."

"But there's nothing normal about dealing with a president who's been shot and is in a less-than-ideally secured and protected environment," Palmer finished for him.

"Exactly. For obvious security reasons, the Secret Service would like to leave this place in the rearview mirror and relocate the president to Walter Reed. I have no objection to that, especially since we've got full, familiar facilities at our disposal there."

"Understood."

"I'm ready," Emma said.

"Very well. Madam President, I would strongly suggest to you that you allow us to give you prophylactic treatment for pain for the purposes of this transfer. I promise you, you'll thank me later. Every time we transfer you from a bed to a gurney and back to a bed, and there will be multiple transfers, will be jarring and truly painful. You think about it. I'll be just outside getting the process moving. General Estes can give me your answer."

Palmer felt the tension in Emma's grip. "Emma, please?"

"Let me talk to Nichelle first. Is she here?"

"Of course." Palmer stepped out of the room for the first time since they'd wheeled Emma out of recovery. Secret Service agents on high alert covered every inch of the isolated area in the ICU wing where Emma was the only patient. She spotted Nichelle in a makeshift conference room, huddled with National Security Advisor Edwards, his deputy, the deputy chief of staff, Olivia, and the deputy press secretary.

Olivia noticed Palmer first and sprung up from her chair. "How is she?"

Palmer blinked. She'd been so focused on Emma that she'd managed, until this moment, to shut out the rest of the world. Of course, her staff would have been informed of her condition and the trauma team would've held one or more press conferences detailing the president's condition, but until the staff could see her for themselves... "She's..." To her mortification, tears filled Palmer's eyes as the enormity of it all came crashing down on her. She turned away. *You're scaring them.*

With great effort, Palmer reined in her emotions and faced the group. "She's a fighter. She's in significant pain, but she's doing just fine."

"Oh, thank God." Nichelle came around from the other side of the table and pulled Palmer into a tight hug. "That's our girl," she whispered in Palmer's ear. "She's got this."

"She's asking to see you."

Nichelle followed Palmer into Emma's room. "Madam President," Nichelle said. Her voice shook.

"Hi, Nich."

"It's good to see you."

"It's good to be here to be seen, let me tell you."

"I bet."

"How's it going? Is everything all right?"

"Vice President Elder is doing a fine job. He wanted me to be sure to convey to you his and Beverly's best wishes."

"I'll call him as soon as I can."

"Yes, ma'am. The crisis plan is working well. The vice president and cabinet members met in the Situation Room for an extended amount of time. I attended remotely. They worked well together. All appropriate world leaders and Congressional officials were informed, and everything is stable."

"Nobody's trying to take advantage of the situation?" Emma asked.

"No. The Russians, the North Koreans, the Chinese, and the Iranians all are on their best behavior."

"And the Senate majority?"

"Rallying around the president in this unfortunate and tragic time."

"And the public?"

"Fully informed and praying for you, Madam President."

"Good." Emma rested her head back against the pillow.

Palmer could see her energy waning. She motioned to Nichelle to wrap it up.

"Madam President, you should rest."

"Doctor Stark tells me he and the detail would like to get me aboard Air Force One right now and get me out of this joint."

"Yes, ma'am."

"The good doctor wants to dope me up on morphine for the trip. That means I can't be restored—"

"With all due respect, Madam President, Vice President Elder is calm and doing an excellent job holding the ship steady. I think you should accede to the doctor's judgment." Nichelle looked to Palmer for help.

"Emma, as soon as we touch down at Andrews you can refuse any more medication. The doctor says your system will be clear within two hours of the last dose you take, and you can resume your duties. At least let them get you home with minimal discomfort."

Emma seemed as though she might fight them.

"Don't be stubborn, darling. The more comfortable you are, the faster you can heal. It's a short-term/long-term thing. Please?"

"How can I refuse you anything?" Emma smiled at her. "Okay. But only for the duration of the trip. Once I'm settled at Walter Reed, I take nothing but Tylenol. Are we clear?"

"Clear," Palmer and Nichelle said simultaneously.

"And I want a secure connection and conversation with the vice president before I get too loopy to think."

"Done," Nichelle said.

⪻⪼

Emma's eyes felt like they were glued shut. "Ugh. Ouch."

"There you are." Palmer fussed with her sheets. "How are feeling, darling?"

"Did you get the license plate of the truck that ran me over?"

"Working on it," Palmer answered.

Emma made another effort to open her eyes. She blinked several times and the room came into focus. This wasn't Air Force One. "Where...?"

"Walter Reed."

"Already?"

Palmer laughed. "Yeah. Time is relative. You've been out for a while."

"Damn morphine."

"Don't knock it. Even with that, you were in tough shape on the trip."

"Don't remember."

"Just as well."

"Everything okay?"

"By all accounts, the trip was successful from a medical standpoint. Your condition is the same as it was. While you were out, they did an echocardiogram to check on the heart valves and the chamber. Doctor Stark says everything is holding steady."

"Good." She felt herself fading again. "Palmer?"

"Yes, darling?"

"I love you. No more morphine."

"Understood. I love you too, darling." Palmer kissed her closed eyelids. "Rest."

"Mm-hmm."

Emma pushed the considerable pain away. She'd been at Walter Reed for a little less than three hours. Over Palmer and Doctor Stark's objections, she'd insisted on getting dressed and putting on makeup for the solemn occasion of resuming the presidency. They'd compromised in the end on a presidential sweatshirt and a pair of sweatpants. Only the sweatshirt would be visible above the covers.

Now, at 5:13 a.m., a little more than seventeen hours after she'd relinquished the presidency, Emma was set to take it back.

She regarded the assembled gathering in her hospital room. Olivia, Nichelle, and an official photographer, had remained at the hospital after the flight from Louisville. She intended to make sure that after this piece of business was concluded, they would go home and catch up on some much-needed rest. The other members of the group consisted of Vice President Elder, the President Pro Tempore of the Senate, the Speaker of the House of Representatives, and the staff secretary who held in his hands the letter of transmittal certifying that no disability existed that would prevent Emma from resuming her office. Each of them had interrupted their sleep to be here.

"Madam President, it's so good to see you."

"It's good to see all of you as well. I want to thank you all for your flawless execution of your Constitutional duties during this crisis in our government. I know our country was in the best possible hands."

Vice President Elder said, "Maybe so, Madam President, but we are so glad to be able to witness this moment. It's clear to all of us that you are fully capable of discharging your duties as president, and we will so certify as soon as you sign that letter."

The staff secretary handed Emma the letter, and she affixed her signature to the bottom line.

"Welcome back, Madam President."

"It's good to be back."

"We'll leave you to rest now."

"Harrison? Will you stay a minute, please?"

"Of course."

When the rest of the group had gone, Vice President Elder pulled up a chair. "How are you really?"

"I'm not going to lie. I don't recommend taking a bullet to the chest."

"Madam President, I…" Tears filled the big man's eyes. "I'm really, really glad to see you. Beverly and I were so worried."

"I want you to know how much I appreciate your steadiness and integrity, Harrison. I am so fortunate to have a vice president that cares about this country and our promises to the American people as much as I do." She reached for his hand; the motion sent shards of agony through her body.

"Hey. Are you okay? Should I get the nurse?"

"No. I'm fine. Just a reminder of my limitations."

He took her hand. "You rest and get well. I'll carry as much of the load as you need me to. Tell me what I can do."

"I'll need you to be my surrogate on the campaign trail for a while. We have got to take back the Senate."

"We will."

"Also, I'm not above using this moment to push through some of those pieces of gun legislation that have been stuck in committee or on the majority leader's desk. If this doesn't prove our point, I don't know what will."

"I understand. Trust me, I'll be breathing down their necks on this issue. Anything else?"

Exhaustion and pain warred within, and Emma needed to rest. She'd extended herself farther than she should have, and she knew it. "I'm sure I'll think of something."

"When you do, I'll be ready." He squeezed her hand affectionately one more time. "I'm really, really glad you're here."

"Thanks, my friend. Me too."

CHAPTER TWENTY-FIVE

Emma winced. When Doctor Stark had told her she'd be saying "ouch" often, he hadn't been kidding. The pain below her right breast from the bullet wound warred with the agony in her ribcage where the surgeons had pried her ribs apart to get to her heart. At least the scratchiness in her throat was gone. And the physical therapy and nursing staffs had managed to get her up a short while ago for a brief walk up and down the hall. She'd take the small victories.

She glanced over to the rollaway bed where Palmer finally had fallen into an exhausted sleep. When she categorically refused to leave Emma's side, the staff had gotten creative. Emma wanted to kiss each and every one of them.

"Madam President?" Scott stood awkwardly in the doorway.

"Come in, Scott. I'm relieved to see you. Are you all right?"

"Me?" His face registered shock as he came to stand next to her bed. "I'm fine, ma'am."

He failed to meet Emma's gaze. "Scott, I need you to look at me." She waited for him to comply. "This isn't your fault. You have to know that."

"It's our job—my job—to protect and keep you safe. That should never have happened, ma'am. When this is over, I'll tender my resignation—"

"You will do no such thing. I won't hear of it."

"Ma'am—"

"Scott, listen to me. I don't care how good you are at what you do—and I can't imagine anyone doing your job better—if there's someone out there determined enough to get a shot off, there's nothing anyone can do to stop it."

"You should wait until I give you my report."

Emma's heart fluttered. "Do you have something?"

Palmer roused from sleep and came to stand opposite Scott on the other side of Emma's bed. "What's going on?"

Scott's gaze shifted from Emma to Palmer and back again.

"Whatever you've got to say, you can share freely in front of General Estes, Scott."

He nodded. "Of course, ma'am." He took a deep breath. "I can report that we've made an arrest. We got him."

Emma's mouth formed an *O*. She gripped Palmer's hand.

"Yes!" Palmer said.

Emma swallowed hard as she steeled herself to hear the details. "You said, 'him.'"

"Yes, ma'am. His name is John Henry Eustice, twenty-eight-years old, Caucasian, from just outside of Buffalo, New York. We caught up with him at a truck stop outside Columbus, Ohio."

"You're certain it's him?"

"Yes. Positive. We've got him dead to rights."

"He acted alone?"

"Yes, ma'am."

"How…?" Emma's head spun. "How can you be sure?"

Scott cleared his throat. Emma thought he looked profoundly uncomfortable.

"Ma'am, you know that we investigate every credible threat to you. We follow hundreds of message boards and social media sites, we vet correspondence sent to the White House, etcetera. On the occasion of your inauguration, you posted a tweet."

Emma briefly closed her eyes. She remembered the tweet.

"In response to that tweet, you received many congratulations and well-wishes. You also received some pretty nasty comments, including one from an anonymous account that referenced the car accident in which your wife was killed."

Scott handed her a piece of paper. On it was printed the suspect's response to her tweet. Emma recalled the comment. Seeing it again on paper, the venom in the words robbed her of breath.

Ur so-called wife's death is on ur hands. You should've died w/her. It should've been u 2. You both should've died for ur sins.

Now u have 2 live w/letting her die alone 4 the rest of ur life. How does that feel, bitch? Don't worry. U'll burn in hell w/her when ur time comes.

That comment had followed another one that showed an image of her in the crosshairs of a gun sight.

"I remember this," she said softly. Palmer's hand tensed in hers, and Emma gave her a wan smile. "It's okay."

"At the time, we flagged that and several other comments, but the accounts went dark so quickly. We decided to wait to see if they popped up again. They didn't. So, we put them on a back burner."

"Until this happened," Emma said.

"Yes, ma'am. Immediately, we began combing through every social media post for clues. We ran down every threatening comment or tweet. I remembered that particular comment because the language matched that used by some white supremacist groups that have been active in the past few years.

"I had my people and the FBI do some forensic work. With the proper warrant in place, they combed back through and found an IP address to go with that closed account. We traced the IP address to Eustice."

John Henry Eustice. Why did that name sound familiar? Emma's eyes opened wide. "Wait. I know that name. The big rig that smashed into Heather's car that day was driven by a long-haul trucker..." Her blood went cold.

"Yes, ma'am. That truck was driven by the same John Henry Eustice."

"But that was an accident. State police investigated..." Emma's mind couldn't process this.

"No, ma'am. We now know, based on the suspect's own admissions, that it wasn't an accident at all."

Emma opened and closed her mouth several times, incapable of believing these seemingly disparate incidents were connected.

Scott continued, "In terms of the attempt on your life, we determined that Eustice transported a cargo load from Buffalo to Louisville the day before yesterday—the day before your appearance. His dispatcher confirmed this for us, and further informed us that Eustice had called in on Saturday night and specifically requested the route to Louisville for the next morning, even though he'd been scheduled on a different route. The dispatcher groused about accommodating him on such short notice. She also indicated that Eustice was running late for his return route to Buffalo. She was able to pinpoint his location in Columbus, which is how we found him so quickly.

"We were able to confirm his identity and waited for him to exit the truck, which he did. At that point, we surrounded him and took him into custody without a struggle. We transported him to Louisville for his initial appearance before the U.S. Magistrate. We also set up surveillance around the rig and obtained the appropriate search warrant. We discovered the rifle inside that rig. Ballistics matched it to the fully jacketed round that passed through you and that we were able to recover at the scene yesterday."

"Oh, my God." Emma began to shiver. Palmer grabbed an extra blanket and covered her, holding her tenderly, obviously mindful of her injuries.

"He can't hurt you any more, darling. I've got you."

Scott cleared his throat. "Ma'am, if this is too much…"

"No." Emma struggled to keep her teeth from chattering. "I need to know all of it. We both do." She covered Palmer's hand with hers.

"Once we had him in custody, he was very talkative. He admitted to all three incidents. He was anxious for us to know that he believed you were in the car with your wife the day of the accident. At first, he was very disappointed that you were not, but eventually he came to believe that it was even better. In his words, 'that bitch would live the rest of her life suffering alone.'"

Emma gasped.

"When you won the presidency, he became agitated. He used a dark account to send that tweet on Inauguration Night. He vowed that he would bide his time. If an opportunity presented itself, he would do something about it."

Scott indicated Emma and Palmer. "When the photographs of you two at the restaurant hit social media Saturday night, he lost it entirely.

"As he told us, 'There's no way that c-blank-blank-t,'" Scott substituted for the full word, "'gets a happy ending.' That's when he hatched the plan to drive to Louisville.

"He says he holed up in the Student Activities Center overnight, hid in a supply closet until it was time, and took the shot from a second-floor window he'd scouted out earlier. He slipped out of the building in the subsequent panic. We will do a full review of how he was able to get into that building with a sight line. We will review every procedure, every action, every—"

"I know you will, Scott. Good work getting him so quickly."

"We have a press conference scheduled within the hour to make the announcement. The press already has an idea that something big has happened.

"Eustice will make an initial appearance tomorrow morning in a Louisville courtroom with airtight security and be transferred at an undisclosed time to avoid any chance of..."

"Lee Harvey Oswald and Jack Ruby," Palmer finished for him.

"Yes, ma'am. We are still building our case. We're tracing all of his movements over the past decade. We know that he attended white supremacist rallies and had loose ties to some domestic terrorist organizations. We are gathering evidence from his residence, interviewing known contacts, scrubbing his computer, his phone, and his tablet. We're examining phone records, emails, texts, tracing the weapon..."

Emma couldn't hear any more. She needed time to process—time to find a place to put all this so that it didn't drown her. "I'm sure you're being very thorough. Thank you, Scott. I'll have Olivia interface with you so that my statement on the matter dovetails with your press conference."

"Yes, ma'am."

"Keep me posted."

"Yes, ma'am." He turned on his heel and left Emma and Palmer alone.

"Are you okay, darling?" Palmer sat on the edge of the bed.

Emma shook her head. She didn't trust her voice just yet.

"What can I do?"

"Hold me."

Palmer kissed Emma's forehead. "I can't wait to do that properly. For now, this will have to do." Palmer took Emma's hands and put them to her lips. "I love you, Emma. We'll get through all of this together."

"I know," Emma answered. "I love you too. It's just... It's a lot to take in, you know?"

"I do. You don't have to figure it all out today. Get some rest. You'll feel better for it."

Emma nodded. "Palmer?"

"Yes?"

"Stay with me."

"Always."

⋖⋗

Palmer stuck her head around the corner and peered into Emma's bedroom in the White House residence. Emma was semi-reclined in the hospital bed that had been brought in so that she could finish her convalescence and work from "home." A thick briefing book was propped on her lap. Her eyes were closed.

Palmer crept into the room the rest of the way and pulled up a chair. In repose, Emma's face lost the stress and strain of the past two weeks. Had it really been only fourteen days since that awful day? In some ways, it felt like years ago, even though the reminders were ever-present.

"You're staring," Emma said. She cracked open an eyelid.

"You're beautiful. It's hard not to stare." Palmer kissed her on the lips.

"Sweet talker."

"I brought these for you." Palmer produced a dozen red roses in a cut crystal vase from beside her chair.

"They're gorgeous. Thank you."

Palmer placed them on the windowsill where Emma would be able to see them from her bed.

"How was your day?"

"Lecture, office hours, reporters waiting for me outside the classroom…the usual." Palmer decided to hold back the other piece of news; now wasn't the time. "How was your day? Did they take the stitches out?"

"They did. They said everything was healing up nicely." Emma's voice caught, a detail Palmer didn't miss.

Palmer scooted onto the edge of the hospital bed and faced Emma. "Darling, it's okay to grieve over the scars. Trust me, I've been there."

"Oh, Palmer." Emma burst into tears, and Palmer gently held her. "It's hideous. I'm hideous."

"You are nothing of the sort. You're beautiful, inside and out." Palmer kissed the top of her head and helped Emma get settled in a more comfortable position.

"Damaged goods."

"Emma Jean McMasters, look at me." Palmer tilted Emma's chin up. "Is that how you view me?"

"Of course not!"

"Right. No double standards here."

"But—"

"But, nothing. When I see those scars, I think about how precious life is—how precious you are—and how very lucky I am that you're still here. It's a miracle. It's a reminder to live every day as if it's the only one we'll have."

Palmer grabbed the box of tissues off the bedside table and handed them to Emma. "Darling, I know nothing about any of this has been easy. I understand better than most."

"I know you do."

Palmer hesitated. From the moment Scott had laid out the details of the assassination attempt and the back story behind it, Emma had withdrawn into herself. If the topic came up while they were together, Emma changed the subject. They'd needed to talk for days now, but Palmer kept putting it off, waiting for the right time. Perhaps there was no such thing. If she waited much longer, Emma could be lost to her for good.

"I'm struggling a little bit, and I really think talking it out would help. Would it be okay if I shared how I feel with you?"

Emma blinked away the last of her tears. "You can always share anything with me."

Palmer nodded and took a deep breath. "This is hard for me." Emma tensed and Palmer gave her what she hoped was a reassuring smile. "You've got a lot going on. I'm not talking about the job you're doing as president. My God, it's like you never missed a step."

Palmer fidgeted with her engagement ring. "But in private moments, when it's just you and me, it's like something essential in you has shut down. You're so quiet. It's not the sadness—that's to be expected. It's as though you're living in your own internal world, and I'm not any part of that."

Emma opened her mouth to say something, and Palmer held up a hand to stop her. "Please, let me finish. Then you can say anything you want, okay?"

"Okay." Emma's voice was so small. Palmer wondered if she was doing the right thing.

Unless everything is out in the open, this will never work. Palmer took another deep breath and plowed ahead. "In case this is part of what's going on for you, and I can't imagine how it could be otherwise, I want to make something really clear."

"Okay." Emma drew out the *O*.

Palmer hated that wariness crept into Emma's eyes. She would say what she needed to say, and figure out the rest later.

"Emma, I know how much you loved Heather. She was your world for more than thirty years. What happened to her was tragic. To know that it wasn't an accident... Well, I can only imagine all the emotions you must be feeling around that."

Emma shivered and Palmer pulled Emma's hand into her lap. "Darling, you didn't stop loving Heather just because she died. Anyone who expects that you did or that you should, doesn't know the first thing about love."

"I'm in love with you, Palmer. Please, tell me you know that." Tears brimmed in Emma's eyes again and threatened to spill over.

"I do. What I'm trying to say is, it's okay that you're still holding space in your heart for Heather. I've got rather a soft spot for her myself. After all, she had the excellent taste to love you and she made you happy for many, many years."

Now Emma's tears did fall. They flowed down her cheeks like a river bursting its dam. Palmer took Emma in her arms, cradled Emma's head against her chest, and let her cry herself out.

"Shh. It's okay, darling. Everything's going to be okay. That's right. Let it all out. You can't keep holding all that inside you; what's more, you don't have to. I don't want you to.

"It's okay to miss her. It's okay to mourn her. It's okay to share all that with me. I'm not a replacement for Heather. I don't see myself that way or view what you feel for her as a threat to what you feel for me. What you and I have... It's different than what you and Heather shared. It's not more, or less. It's just…different. It's uniquely ours."

Emma gulped in air as her sobs subsided. "Ouch." She put a hand against the center of her chest.

"Here. Lie back." Palmer helped her get more comfortable in the bed. She stroked her hair and wiped away a half-dried tear.

"I-I'm so afraid to hurt you, Palmer. So afraid that you'll misunderstand how I feel. You're right. Heather always will be part of me, part of my life. But that life is over. I have great memories and sad memories and every once in a while, something will remind me of her or something we did together and I'll feel a pang of sorrow. But that doesn't mean I don't cherish you or the new memories we're making or wish it could be different."

"I know."

"I love you with all my heart, Palmer Estes. Always remember that."

"I always will. And you must always remember that Heather and your memories and moments are welcome in our lives. I'll listen and hold your hand when you're sad, or angry about the injustice of what happened to her, or I'll laugh with you at a funny recollection. I just need you to be open and honest and share. Open, honest communication is the only way we can heal and move forward. Together, Emma."

"Always together, Palmer." Emma shifted to the side and patted the vacated space next to her. "Apropos of that… I've been thinking, I don't want to wait. One thing I've learned in all this is how precious and short life is. I want us to get married, and soon."

Palmer smiled. "Funny, I've been thinking the same thing."

"Did you have a date in mind?"

"Did you?"

Emma nodded. "The day after Christmas."

Palmer absorbed that. "Does the date hold particular significance to you?"

"Doctor Stark says I'll be fully healed and recovered in six weeks. I asked him, because I want to be whole and healthy when I walk down the aisle. Six weeks would put us in the middle of December. I've thrown in a couple extra weeks for good measure."

"Makes sense."

"Also, Christmas week is as slow a week as we'll get in terms of work flow for both of us. We could get married here in the White House and hole up until after New Year's at Camp David."

"Very practical, Madam President."

Emma snuggled into Palmer's side. "And nothing says romance like a Christmas-time wedding."

"Sold."

"Really?"

"Really," Palmer said, as she claimed Emma's lips. "We should start practicing the part where I get to kiss the bride."

"Mm-hmm. I think it's going to take a lot of practice."

"Good."

CHAPTER TWENTY-SIX

E mma stood in the Oval Office, staring out into the darkness. Every last nerve was on high alert. The polls would close in most states where the U.S. Senate was in play within the next few minutes. "Now is the moment of truth," she muttered.

So far, exit polling had been in the Democrats' favor. In addition, the Democratic National Committee's internal polls over the past few weeks indicated that the assassination attempt on Emma and her handling of the matter had caused her approval rating to skyrocket. Correspondingly, all of the Democratic senatorial candidates had experienced a nice boost in the polls as well.

Emma knew, though, that polls were no substitute for actual vote tallies. She checked her watch and made her way gingerly to the private residence. She'd invited Nichelle and Max over to watch the returns with her and Palmer. It was her first week back, on a limited basis, in the West Wing. She'd promised Palmer she wouldn't overdo it and already she was pushing it.

When she arrived, Palmer, Nichelle, and Max were snacking on crudités, cheese and crackers, and chips and salsa.

"How can you eat at a time like this?" Emma asked.

"How can you not?" Nichelle asked around a slice of brie.

"You look tired," Palmer said. She led Emma over to the special lift recliner they'd brought in for her comfort. Palmer helped her ease into the chair. If Emma was going to tell the truth, it was a relief to get off her feet and into a semi-reclining position.

"How's the wedding planning coming along?" Max asked.

"Ours or yours?" Palmer countered.

"First, I have to get Nichelle here to say yes."

"Get off it, Max."

"I didn't start this conversation." He held his hands up in innocence.

"In answer to your question," Palmer said, "invitations are scheduled to go out in the mail this week. Thank God for Vicki, the White House social director. All we have to do is say yes or no to whatever suggestions she makes."

"Lucky you," Max said.

"No kidding."

Emma watched the comfortable interplay between Palmer and Max, grateful for their easy friendship. She was glad that Palmer had suggested that they find a way for Max and Nichelle to participate. They were the closest thing Palmer and Emma had to family.

"Are you okay?" Palmer whispered in her ear. "You really do look beat."

"I'm fine. I'll be relieved when tonight is over."

"I bet. You're going to get your majority; I know it."

"I do love your optimism."

"Here we go." Nichelle cranked up the sound. They'd decided to watch MSNBC because Emma preferred their political director's maps and graphics.

"Here's what's at stake in tonight's election," the anchor intoned. "There are thirty-four seats in the U.S. Senate that are up for grabs out of one hundred total seats. Of those thirty-four, twelve seats are currently occupied by Democrats. The remaining twenty-two seats are currently filled by Republicans. At present, the Republicans hold a razor-thin one-vote majority in the Senate."

"Not for long," Nichelle said.

"The polls are just closing in the battleground states of Georgia, Florida, North Carolina, Ohio, Pennsylvania, and Kentucky. The polls will close one hour from now in Wisconsin.

"You will remember that it was at a campaign rally for Democratic candidate Thomas Engelbright…"

Nichelle dove for the remote and shut off the television. Emma cut her a grateful look.

"I didn't know you could move that fast," Max said.

"I can when it's a national emergency."

"Good to know."

Palmer got up from the couch and perched on the arm of Emma's chair. She kissed her on the top of the head. "Can't wait until they stop feeling it necessary to show that footage."

Emma squeezed her hand. "You are not alone."

The phone rang and Emma picked it up. "This is President McMasters."

"Congratulations, Madam President," the chairman of the Democratic National Committee began. "You have yourself a bouncing baby majority."

Emma had to struggle to hear him over all the background noise. "Did you say—"

"I certainly did. We held all our Democratic seats and captured Georgia, Florida, North Carolina, Ohio, and Kentucky. Exit polls indicate we're going to take Wisconsin too."

Emma wanted to weep with joy. "That's terrific. You did a fabulous job, Mr. Chairman. I congratulate you and your staff and thank you for all your hard work."

"You're most welcome, Madam President. With you at the top of the ticket, our job was easy. I'll talk to you tomorrow."

"Enjoy your well-earned celebration. Goodnight." Emma motioned Nichelle to turn on the television once again. She needed to see the numbers for herself.

"We did it," Nichelle said, as the projections rolled across the screen.

"We did it," Emma agreed. "We got our ironclad majority."

"I'll get Olivia working on a statement for your approval," Nichelle said.

"Good. I want to talk to each of the winning candidates personally to congratulate them and let them know I'm looking forward to working with them come January."

"Emma…" Palmer's voice was an admonition.

"This is my job, love. I have to do this."

"You have to rest."

"I promise I will, just as soon as I take care of business." Palmer was right, of course. Emma was beyond exhaustion and she'd pay a heavy price for overdoing it.

Still, her party had just achieved a goal thought beyond their reach just a few short months ago. It was incumbent upon her to set the tone for the remainder of her first term and to lay the groundwork for her reelection campaign. That work began tonight.

❧❦

Palmer tapped her fountain pen against the legal pad and observed the patterns in the water droplets that pelted the window outside the Treaty Room. The bleakness of the mid-November day matched her mood. She set the pen and paper aside.

"That was a heavy sigh." Emma came around the back of the chair and leaned in for a kiss.

"I didn't hear you coming."

"So I gathered." Emma lowered herself slowly onto the couch and patted the space next to her. "Sit with me?"

Palmer obliged. "What are you doing here at this hour? Not that I mind."

"Plenty of normal people knock off for the day at five o'clock in the afternoon."

"True. Since when are you 'normal people?' Are you tired? Hurting? Are you okay?" Alarm bells rang in Palmer's head.

"I'm fine. Each day I feel stronger and my endurance is better." Emma intertwined her fingers with Palmer's and stroked the back of Palmer's hand with her thumb. "I thought I'd spend some quality time with my fiancée."

Palmer smiled. "I think that's a great idea. So, why do I feel like there's an ulterior motive hiding in there somewhere?"

"Possibly because you know me well."

"Should I be afraid?"

"Why would you ask that?"

"Because you've got your 'serious' face on."

"Do I?" Emma asked. "I wasn't aware that I had a serious face, but since apparently I do… You shouldn't be afraid. The better question is, should I be?"

Palmer's eyes opened wide. "Have I given you any reason to believe you should be? If I have, I'm sorry. There's nothing—"

"Palmer Estes, you've been distracted and distant since the midterms. Weren't you the one who told me that the way forward was through open and honest communication? I can't help feeling as though there's something you're not telling me. Are you having second thoughts about the wedding?" Emma's voice cracked.

Palmer's heart stuttered. "What? No! Are you kidding me? I can't wait to be married to you." Palmer traced the outline of Emma's face with her free hand. "I am so in love with you, Madam President. I'm counting the days."

"Then, what is it? And don't tell me it's nothing, because I know that's not true."

Palmer hung her head. She should've told Emma about it the same day. Now she'd caused her needless worry. "You're right."

Emma stiffened beside her and Palmer felt even more miserable.

"It isn't you, darling. Really, it doesn't have anything to do with you or us... At least not directly."

"What does that mean?"

Palmer walked over to the desk and rummaged in her briefcase. She returned with an envelope held loosely in her fingers, sat down, and faced Emma. "This came to my office a couple of weeks ago." She held it out to Emma, who took it with trepidation.

Emma read the return address and blinked several times. "Is that...?"

"My mother?" Palmer closed her eyes and willed herself to stay detached. "Yes."

"She wrote you a letter?"

"Yes. Assuming it's really her."

"Did you vet it?"

"I did. I believe it's authentic."

"I'll have the Secret Service verify it," Emma said.

Palmer shrugged. "I'm not sure it matters."

"What do you mean?"

"I haven't decided if I'm going to do anything with it."

"Palmer..."

"Read it."

Emma teased the pages out of the neatly slit open envelope. She glanced over the top of the letter at Palmer.

"It's okay. I don't have any secrets from you, darling. I just... I guess I haven't yet figured out how I feel about it."

"Understood. Still, I wish you'd told me about it before now."

"You had so many things on your plate already—"

"Nothing is more important than you, my love."

"Just read it."

"Okay."

Palmer watched silently as myriad emotions crossed Emma's face as she read the contents of the two-page letter. When Emma had finished, she set it aside and pulled Palmer to her.

"I'm sorry I didn't know about this sooner. No wonder you've been so distracted. That's quite a jolt after forty years of silence. Are you all right?" Emma ran her fingers through Palmer's hair and held her close.

"Honestly, I don't know what I am. When it arrived, I let it sit on my office desk unopened for several days. I couldn't decide whether or not I wanted to know what she had to say."

"Assuming it's really her," Emma said.

"I'm confident it is, darling. I remember her handwriting, and there are things in it that no one else would've known—my favorite childhood foods, the games I used to make up to play by myself. The details are all accurate."

"Are you certain no one could've gleaned any of that information some other way?"

"I can't see how they could've. But if it makes you feel better to have the Secret Service investigate, that's fine with me."

"I will. For our purposes right now, though, I think we should assume it's really her."

"It's her. She included some pictures of us as a family when I was little. I remembered them."

"Where are they now?"

"I threw them in a box in the closet at my apartment with other old keepsakes."

They sat in silence for several minutes. "Palmer?"

"Mm?"

"You know I will support whatever decision you make."

"It's sounds like there's a *but* in there."

"She's reaching out. She wants to make a connection. I know this must be such a shock to you after all this time—"

"Doesn't it strike you as a little bit convenient that I'm the president's fiancée and now she's interested?" Palmer inhaled deeply and made a concerted effort to tamp down the anger and bitterness building inside. "I am a four-star general and a Silver Star recipient. You acknowledged me at the State of the Union. Unless she was living under a rock, she already knew enough to find me. Why now? And why doesn't she mention my father? Not even once?"

"You'll never know unless you ask her," Emma said quietly. "I think the bigger question is whether you want to continue to live your life carrying that anger and resentment inside you or whether you want to face it head-on, get the answers that sixteen-year-old girl deserved but never got, forgive, and achieve closure."

Palmer gazed once more out the window at the rain. "This is the reason I hadn't told you about the letter yet. I don't know how I feel or what I want. I-I'm so conflicted and confused."

"It's no wonder, love. This is quite a curveball." Emma moved closer and trailed her fingers along the contour of Palmer's jaw line. "Whatever you choose, I'll love you just the same."

"The teenager in me wants to punish her—to spurn her the way my parents spurned me."

"Perfectly understandable."

"The adult me, of course, recognizes that the healthy choice is to meet with her as she asks, listen to what she has to say for herself, and be done with it."

"Also a good option."

Palmer turned bruised eyes to Emma. "What do you think I should do?"

"This has to be your decision, love."

"What would you do in my place?"

Emma pursed her lips. She was silent for so long, Palmer wondered if she would answer.

"First, I'd be every bit as torn as you are." Emma grew quiet again. "I guess I'd fall back on something I believe deeply, which is that forgiveness heals. Forgiveness is as much—maybe more— for me as it is for the person at fault."

Palmer turned Emma's words over in her mind. She asked the next question carefully. "That's why you don't harbor anger toward John Henry Eustice, even though he tried to kill you and succeeded in killing Heather? Even after that hate-filled diatribe he spewed at his initial hearing and again at his arraignment?"

Emma closed her eyes and nodded. "I'm not going to tell you I don't have my moments, because that would be a lie. I'm human. But, every time I get angry, I catch myself and forgive him again.

Forgiveness is for me, not for him. He has to live with what he did. Because of his guilty plea at arraignment, he'll spend the rest of his life in prison. He made his choices. I can't change what happened to Heather or to me, but I can choose whether I let him and his actions have power over me going forward.

"I choose love. I love myself and you enough that I want to focus on our love and the love I carry in my heart. Of course, forgiveness is an ongoing process, it's not a one-time event."

Palmer nodded. What Emma was doing required strength and fortitude. Did she have that kind of courage when it came to her parents?

"Have I told you lately how truly remarkable you are?" Palmer kissed Emma on the forehead, then the nose, and finally claimed her lips. The kiss was tender and reverential. "I'm so glad you're you. You make me want to be a better person."

"You don't need me to be the best you can be, Palmer. You've been doing that all your life."

Palmer took another deep breath. If Emma could forgive a man with so much hate in his heart, the very least Palmer could do was hear her mother out. "Will you meet her with me?"

"If you want me to be there, I'd love to stand by your side."

"I always want you with me, Emma."

"Good. Because you're stuck with me."

"That's what Doctor Stark said you told him to tell me after surgery."

"Ah. I'm glad he passed along my message."

"That was the moment I knew you were going to be all right."

"I knew I was going to be all right in this world the moment you told me you loved me."

"Sweet talker."

Palmer leaned forward and kissed Emma again. Emma continued to heal, and Palmer knew she wasn't ready yet to make love. That was understandable. Palmer would wait as long as it took until she was ready. She just needed Emma to know how much she loved her, so she infused the kiss with everything that she felt, everything she hoped for, and everything she knew they would share together.

Together. Palmer liked the sound of that.

CHAPTER TWENTY-SEVEN

Emma stood back and observed as Palmer changed into the fourth outfit she'd brought with her to the White House for this occasion. "This is a new side of you, Palmer Estes. Interesting."

"You are not going to make fun of me right now."

"I'm not making fun." Emma hid a smirk behind her hand.

"How about this? Does this look okay?" Palmer wore a pair of sharply creased black trousers, a sky-blue silk blouse that made her eyes pop, and a sleek black jacket.

"You look gorgeous." Emma walked over and encircled Palmer in her arms. "Then again, you looked sensational in the first three outfits too."

"Don't mess with me right now, McMasters."

"I wouldn't dare." Emma leaned up for a kiss. "You're a knockout. If your mother isn't impressed, I am."

Palmer broke the embrace and stepped back to take one more look in the full-length mirror. "You're easily impressed."

Emma's eyebrows raised into her hair line. "Is that so? Tell that to the Senate majority leader."

"Who cares what he thinks? He's a lame duck."

"Very true."

Palmer finally stopped fidgeting. "This is as good as it's going to get."

"Did you want to critique my outfit too?"

"You always look impeccable."

"Thanks, I think." Emma threaded her arm through Palmer's. "Lunch is set up in the Old Family Dining Room. Nothing fussy or ostentatious."

"I'm sure it will be perfect."

Emma pulled them to a stop before they reached the door to the Center Hall and turned Palmer to face her. "It's okay to be nervous. I'm willing to bet your mother is anxious too. Imagine, having to explain yourself in front of a very protective president of the United States."

"Are you planning to go all badass on my mother, Madam President?"

"Only if she hurts the most important person in the world to me."

"Fair enough. I love you, Emma. Thank you for doing this with me."

"I love you, Palmer. Always together. Remember? And whatever happens today, she can't touch what we have. She can't hurt you."

"Right," Palmer agreed.

Emma reached up and touched her lips to Palmer's. "Shall we?"

As they arrived at the dining room, Emma signaled to an aide that he could show Mrs. Estes in. Emma had to admit, she was curious. What would Palmer's mother be like?

She didn't have to wonder for long. The aide opened the door to admit a woman who was the spitting image of Palmer or, more accurately, Palmer was the spitting image of her, minus twenty-five years. She had the same flaming red hair, although hers was tinged with gray. Despite her years, she walked with ease and good posture. Her eyes were that same shade of vibrant blue as her daughter's. In person, Emma had no doubt that this woman really was Palmer's mother.

"Come in, Mrs. Estes. Welcome to the White House," Emma said.

"Thank you, Madam President. Please, call me Helene." She stepped forward and shook Emma's hand, but her eyes never left Palmer's face. "H-hello, Palmer. You're looking well."

"Hello." Emma noticed that Palmer stood rooted to the spot. She made no effort to shake hands or hug her mother, nor did she address her by any of the normal terms one might use for one's mother.

"Thank you for seeing me. I know it must've come as quite a shock to you to hear from me after all this time."

"It was."

"Why don't we sit down?" Emma suggested. "Lunch will be served any second." Emma had asked the staff to set the three places at one end of the dining room table. She sat at the end, putting Palmer and her mother opposite each other.

Mrs. Estes continued to stare at Palmer. "I'm sorry. I know, it's rude to stare. You remind me of myself at your age, back when I didn't have any gray hair."

Emma felt Palmer's body vibrating. Palmer believed small talk was a waste of time, but it was a necessary staple in every politician's toolbox. *Time to step in and help out.* "Mrs. Estes, Palmer tells me you were a librarian. She certainly inherited your love of reading and classics."

"Helene, please. Yes, even as a young girl, Palmer read far above her grade level. While other kids wanted to hear Dr. Seuss at bedtime, my daughter begged for *Oliver Twist.* If she wasn't running somewhere, she was reading somewhere."

Emma smiled. Helene's affection for that young girl was evident in her voice.

"You're still a bookworm, then?" Helene asked Palmer.

"I collect first editions of the classics."

"Oh, that's perfect!"

The staff served the first course, Irish potato soup.

"Palmer tells me your maiden name was Fitzgerald and that your parents hailed from the old country. I thought you might enjoy a little taste of your heritage."

"How thoughtful. Thank you." Helene scooped up a spoonful. "Oh, this is delicious. My compliments to the chef."

"I'll be sure to pass that along." Emma watched Palmer out of the corner of her eye. She could tell that Palmer would combust if they didn't get past the niceties soon.

Palmer sat ramrod straight. "You said in your letter that you wanted to share some things with me—that there were things I should know," she said. "I'm listening."

Helene nodded warily. "All right." She put down her soup spoon. "I don't know how much you remember of your father."

"Too much," Palmer answered too quickly. Emma squeezed her leg under the table.

"I can imagine how you must feel, Palmer. Your father wasn't an easy man."

"That's putting it mildly. Wasn't? Past tense?" Palmer asked.

"Yes. He passed away a few weeks ago from a massive heart attack. I wrote you that letter the day after the funeral."

Palmer blinked, but said nothing.

Helene wet her lips. "You probably don't know this, since he died before you were born, but my father—your grandfather—was an enforcer with the Irish mob. He also was a heavy drinker and a gambler. The more he drank, the quicker he lost his money. And his temper? Let's just say you didn't want to be around if he came home having lost at cards."

"What does this…" Again, Emma squeezed Palmer's leg. "Go on."

Helene nodded. "My mother, God rest her soul, did her best to get me out of that environment. She managed to hide some of the cash my father brought home before he could gamble it away. Little by little, she stashed away enough money to send me off to a good boarding school here in the U.S. That's how I ended up getting a proper education."

The main course, Irish stew, arrived. "I'm sorry," Emma apologized. "It seems as though I may have misjudged the best meal to serve."

"No. That was very thoughtful of you. This actually brings back good memories." Helene tasted the stew. "Just like my mum used to make."

They ate in silence for several moments, and then Helene continued. "By the time I'd finished school, my mother had passed away. I couldn't go home to live with my father. I just…couldn't."

"I met George—your father—by accident. He was being tutored in English composition by a friend of mine. Well, my friend got sick one day and asked me to fill in." Helene smiled at the memory. "He was dashing, and handsome in that British way—a charming rogue, I thought, and my ticket out.

"So, I convinced myself that I was in love with him. We got married pretty quickly. It wasn't until a few years later that I realized how very much like my father George was. By then, I had you, Palmer." She gazed lovingly at her daughter. "I didn't make enough on a librarian's salary to raise a child on my own. I couldn't see a way out. Instead, I tried to find a way out for you."

Emma stole a glance at Palmer. Her face was impassive.

"When you showed such talent and potential as a runner, I cheered. I thought, 'Here's your ticket out.' And when the opportunity came up to send you to that camp... Well, it seemed like the perfect solution."

"Until you and Daddy showed up unannounced."

"Yes, until then. Showing up that way was your father's idea." Helene bowed her head. "When your father went after you... I-I saw the expression on your face, Palmer. I knew how hurt you were that I didn't stand up for you. I can't tell you how hard that was. It broke my heart—"

"*Your* heart?" Palmer exploded. "You left me to fend for myself. I was sixteen years old. Sixteen, Mother. How could you live with yourself?"

Helene recoiled from Palmer's words. "It wasn't easy, I can tell you that. But I could see what would happen if you came home, Palmer. I think he would've killed you. I truly believed the most magnanimous, selfless thing I could do was to let you go—to give you a chance in life.

"There was a part of me that was glad you liked girls. I thought you'd be spared the kind of bad choices my mother and I had made."

Palmer's eyes opened wide. "You didn't care that I was one of those 'perverts?'"

Helene shrugged. "Remember, I was a lot worldlier than your father. I went to an all-girls boarding school. I knew what was what. It never bothered me. For your father, it was as though it was a threat to his manhood." She said the last with disgust.

"I convinced myself that you would be safer—better off—by yourself. You were so smart and resourceful. I was certain you'd make a success of yourself."

Palmer crossed her arms. "You left me with nothing."

"That wasn't true," Helene said quietly. "When your father went to get the car, I found your coach. I slipped him all the cash in my purse and begged him to take care of you. I think he would've done so regardless, but my giving him an extra push in that direction couldn't hurt." She glanced up at Palmer. "He was a good man, your coach."

"Yes, he was. He and his wife treated me like their own."

Helene nodded, obviously pleased to know that.

"I told him you were a smart, well-behaved girl, and that you would do well in school. I told him I would send him money whenever I could for your upkeep, but that he was never to let you know."

"You..." Palmer's jaw went slack.

"Oh, yes, Palmer. You were my pride and joy. You were my great hope—the one good thing I did in my life." Helene smiled wanly. "It was all very James Bond. I had your coach send me progress reports at school so that your father wouldn't know I was keeping track of you. I saw every report card. When you got into the University of Oregon, I could barely contain myself."

Emma's heart soared watching the metamorphosis in Palmer as a truth she never suspected sank in.

"As you grew into an adult, I lost track of you. Once you graduated high school and moved out of your coach's basement..."

Palmer gasped.

"Yes, I knew where and how you were living, Palmer. I told you, I kept very close tabs on you. But once you'd graduated, your coach stopped sending me updates and once I retired from school, I didn't have the privacy or easy resources at my fingertips to conduct my own search. If your father had found out I was tracking you..."

"He might've killed you."

"Yes," Helene answered softly. "I believe he might have."

"Why did you stay?" Palmer asked. "After I was gone, you could've left and supported yourself."

"Maybe so, but I wouldn't have had enough money to keep sending to your coach for you."

"And after I graduated?"

Helene shrugged. "I'd made my bed."

"That's crazy. You weren't much older than I am now."

"I wasn't as strong as you, Palmer. But, I promised myself that as soon as George was gone, I would make it my life's mission to find you again. Imagine my surprise when your engagement to the president and accompanying picture were splashed all over the covers of every newspaper in the world."

Something niggled at Emma. "You didn't see my first State of the Union address where I singled out Palmer as one of my honored guests, Helene?" she interjected.

Helene laughed. "I'm sorry to say so, Madam President, and I don't mean to hurt your feelings, but George would rather have impaled himself on a bed of nails than watch a speech by a Democratic president, and especially a lesbian. To him, you were the anti-Christ."

That surprised a laugh out of Emma. "Oh, my. Well, perhaps my marrying his daughter is the perfect outcome."

"Oh, trust me, I've done a jig about that more than once," Helene said. She turned serious again. "Palmer, I recognize that all this is a lot to digest. You may never forgive me for being absent for all these years. If you don't, I want you to know I understand. I really came to tell you this: never, in forty years, have I stopped loving you. You were the best part of me. I'm so proud of you. I want you to know you were always loved and wanted. I am a woman of many flaws; I know that. I've made massive mistakes in my life. But the one thing I did right was to set you free to soar. I love you." Helene bent her head and began to cry.

Palmer jumped up from her seat and came around the table. She lifted her mother into a hug and held her tight. "Thank you for coming. Thank you for telling me. You're right. I'm going to need a lot of time to process. But, when I'm done and ready, I'm glad I'll know where to find you."

"Me too."

Emma rose and folded her napkin, mostly so she would have time to compose herself. This was the kind, compassionate Palmer she'd fallen in love with.

"Mrs. Estes…Helene… I can promise you this: you will never, ever have to worry about your daughter again. I love her with all my heart. She's the most amazing person I've ever met, and I assure you I plan to take care of her for the rest of my life."

Helene smiled through watery eyes. "I can see the love between you two. It's the kind of fairy tale I used to dream of for myself as a young girl. Nothing could make me happier." She shifted from foot to foot. "I'm sure you both have a lot to do. I don't want to take up any more of your time. You've been so kind and generous to invite me here."

Emma took Palmer's hand and they walked Helene to the door. "Thank you for coming, Helene. That was a courageous first step."

"I only wish I'd had the moxie to do it a long time ago." She gazed up at Palmer, as if memorizing her face. "You're every bit as beautiful as I knew you would be, Palmer. I'm proud of you." She waved on the way out.

As the door closed behind Helene, Emma opened her arms to Palmer. Palmer leaned against her and began to sob.

"It's okay, love. It's okay to be sad, to be overwhelmed... It's okay to be. We'll work through it all, together. I promise." *The road to healing begins with forgiveness.*

CHAPTER TWENTY-EIGHT

The lights on the White House Christmas tree twinkled, making patterns on the otherwise darkened walls of the Blue Room. Emma leaned into Palmer, more content and at peace than she'd been since before the assassination attempt.

Tomorrow, they would be married in a grand ceremony in the East Room, in front of friends, members of both houses of Congress, Supreme Court justices, Cabinet members, foreign dignitaries, military brass, celebrities, and Palmer's mother. Tomorrow at one o'clock sharp, she would be only the second president in U.S. history to be married in the White House—the first was Grover Cleveland, who married twenty-one-year old Frances Folsom in this very room in on June 2, 1886.

"What are you thinking about, darling?" Palmer's voice was soft in Emma's ear.

"Us. History. How happy I am. You pick."

"Wow. That's a lot."

"I'm a complicated woman."

Palmer laughed. "No kidding."

Emma turned and encircled Palmer in her arms. "You still have time to back out. The wedding's not for another..." She consulted her watch. "...fifteen hours."

"No way." Palmer swept an errant strand of hair off Emma's face. "I cannot wait to be married to you."

"I cannot wait for you not to sneak out in the middle of the night anymore. You're going to stop doing that, right?"

"The lease to my apartment expires on January 1st, so unless I'm going to be living on the street, you're stuck with me."

"Whew!"

"But for tonight, I'm still going back to my place to sleep."

"Palmer…"

"It's bad luck to see the bride before the wedding. I'll stay until you fall asleep, like I always do, but I am not waking up with you in your bed in the White House until I'm your wife."

"How ridiculously quaint, old-fashioned, and stubborn of you."

"All traits I assume you love or you wouldn't be marrying me. And I prefer tenacious to stubborn. It sounds so much better that way."

Emma pulled Palmer down for a long kiss. "I love everything about you, Palmer Estes. Every quirk, every trait, every… everything."

"Thank you." Palmer's voice broke.

"For what?"

"For loving me. I never thought… I never believed there would be someone like you for me. I convinced myself that I was unlovable. So, I gave up."

Emma nodded. She understood. "I thought after I lost Heather that I was done—that I would live the rest of my life with memories of what it felt like to be loved and to love, but never experience it again in this lifetime. You showed me how wrong I was, Palmer. You fill my heart with so much love. Most people are lucky to find one love in a lifetime. I've been twice blessed. I don't know what I've done to deserve that—to deserve you—but I'm grateful for it every day."

Palmer kissed the backs of Emma's hands. "Thank you for fighting to stay alive. If you had died that day, I don't think I would've survived it. I would've died with you, of a broken heart. I couldn't believe that the universe would be so cruel as to show me what life could be—what unconditional love could be—and then rip it away."

Emma swallowed the lump in her throat. "I remember thinking you'd had so much taken from you, I couldn't leave you that way. I had a choice, Palmer. In those timeless seconds when my heart stopped, I was given a choice. I chose love. I chose you. And I will continue to choose you for the rest of my life."

"And I you, darling. Is it tomorrow yet?"

"Almost." Emma threaded her arm through Palmer's. "Walk me home?"

"Of course."

"Stay the night?"

"Until you fall asleep."

"Darn tenacity."

"Yep." Palmer touched one of the branches of the Christmas tree. "It's beautiful. But not nearly as beautiful as you."

"Sweet talker."

"Merry Christmas, darling."

"Merry Christmas, my love."

A light dusting of snow covered the running path along the Potomac River. Palmer pulled the cap lower over her ears. Her breath came out in frosty puffs.

"Are you nervous?" Max asked. He ran easily alongside her as Secret Service agents flanked them on all sides.

"What kind of question is that to ask a bride?"

"Well, are you?"

Palmer punched him playfully in the arm. "Yes, and no."

"That was perfectly clear. Not."

"I'm nervous about the crowd and about being scrutinized by so many people, and that doesn't even count the press corps, not to mention the live televised coverage of the ceremony."

"It's pretty historic. The first president in more than a century to marry in the White House, and the first lesbian wedding ever held there."

"Thanks. This is a great pep talk, Max."

"I'm here for you."

"What I'm not nervous about is marrying Emma."

"That's good, because she's perfect for you in every way."

"Yeah, she really is." Palmer knew she sported a goofy grin. She didn't care.

"For the longest time, I worried that you'd never open yourself up enough to let someone in," Max said. "You were so wounded inside. Then, I watched you open bit by bit for Emma, until your heart finally cracked wide open. I can't tell you how happy it makes me to see you happy, my friend."

Palmer smiled at him. "When did you become such a hopeless romantic?"

"I think you know when. I saw Nichelle across that room at the Commander in Chief's Ball, and I knew I was in love. I know that sounds crazy, but it's true."

"I know. I looked over and saw you chatting her up and I thought, he's a goner. I'll be a son-of-a-gun."

"You know, I take pride in the fact that I introduced you to your bride."

Palmer glanced at him questioningly.

"It's true. It was that same night. President McMasters said she wanted to meet some of the members of the military, rather than dance and dash. I humbly asked if I could introduce her to you."

Palmer's eyes opened wide in recognition. "That's right. Huh. I guess you should get a finder's fee, after all."

"I'll settle for a periodic double date."

"You're on."

They reached a bend in the trail, and Palmer turned them around for the return run home. "Can't be late for my own wedding."

"You've never been late for anything in your life."

"Right. And this won't be the first time either." She picked up the pace.

"By the way," Max tossed off casually, "she finally said yes."

"What?" Palmer nearly lost her footing before regaining her stride. "You're pulling my leg, right?"

"Nope."

"When? How? Why am I only finding out about this now?"

"Slow down, General." Max laughed. "I popped the question again yesterday morning over Christmas presents. I had the ring sitting on the end of one of the branches of her tree. I got down on one knee and told her what was in my heart."

"She said yes," Palmer said excitedly. "Oh, my God. I'm so happy for you. Why do you think she said yes this time?"

"I'm pretty sure it was your and the president's happiness rubbing off on her. I think she saw how good love could be, and I think she realized she really wanted that for herself."

"When's the date?"

"I didn't want to push my luck, so I didn't press her for one, but we agreed that it would be within the year. With the president gearing up for her reelection campaign, we have to time it to fit in the cycle."

"Now that's romantic. Pfft," Palmer said. "I'll see if I can convince Emma to help you."

"I'd really appreciate that."

They turned onto Palmer's street. "Okay. Well, here we go. See you in an hour?"

"See you soon. Be on time."

"Make sure you and the team polish those ceremonial sabers."

"Yes, ma'am." Max peeled off toward the base.

Palmer headed for the shower. She took extra care with her makeup and mess dress uniform and still was ready with time to spare. She stepped over several packing boxes, looking for one in particular. She found it in the corner of her home office, labeled *Keepsakes*. Carefully, she undid the packing tape, opened the box, and reached inside.

She pulled out a sealed plastic bag with the pictures her mother had sent her. For several moments, she stared at the face of the little girl with the toothless grin, proudly holding up a first-place medal, standing next to her beaming mother. She remembered the track meet—it was the first one she'd ever run—the one that hooked her on the sport. She also remembered that it was the first time her father had ever told her he was proud of her. She was glad her mother would be here today and glad she'd followed Emma's advice and heard her mother out.

Palmer had come a long way since she'd been that young, lost girl. Her phone buzzed, nearly scaring her out of her skin. She snapped it up and read the text message.

What are you doing right now?

Palmer smiled and shook her head. *Counting the minutes until I'm married to you.*

Me too. See you soon, my love. I miss you.

See you soon, darling. I promise to stay the whole night tonight.

Palmer replaced the picture in the bag and the bag in the box. She re-sealed it and set it aside. The past would always be part of her, that was true, but today? Today was the start of the rest of her life. Palmer couldn't wait.

࢘ৎ

Emma regarded herself in the mirror. The custom Vera Wang gown was gorgeous and managed to hide all of her scars while showing off her shoulders and a hint of décolletage. Her hair and makeup, done especially for the occasion, were impeccable. Experimentally, she turned first to the left and then the right. The pain wasn't too bad. Her goal had been to walk down the aisle whole and healed, and she would achieve that.

Emma walked over to a drawer, opened it, and pulled out her jewelry box. She lifted the lid and withdrew her old wedding ring—the one Heather had given her.

"I know you and Palmer would've loved each other, Heather. I also know that you're up there cheering me on, ecstatic for my happiness. She fills me with more joy than I ever thought I could feel again. You and I did it, Heather—we won the presidency. I never could've gotten here without you. Now it's time for a new chapter, a new beginning. I know in my heart that's what you would want for me. Thank you for being my guardian angel. I hope you'll always watch over us. We're going to need the help."

"Madam President, are you ready?"

Emma shoved the ring back into the box, returned the box to the drawer, and closed it.

"I'm ready."

Nichelle came the rest of the way into the room and whistled. "You look amazing."

"I'm paying you to say that."

"No, you're paying me to tell you the truth, remember?"

Emma nodded. "Is it really okay?"

"It's so much more than okay. It's perfect. Palmer's a lucky woman."

"I'm the lucky one."

"You're both lucky. And speaking of lucky..." Nichelle waved her left ring finger in front of Emma's face.

"Oh, my God! You said yes."

"I said yes."

"Oh, Nich." Emma hugged her. "I'm so happy for you."

"Thanks. You know, I didn't think I'd want to be married. After all, I'm married to the job. But, watching you and Palmer, I realized that was an excuse. I could find balance if I wanted to. I was being a coward. Deep down, I thought if I didn't get married, I couldn't fail at it. The truth is, if I don't take the chance to trust love, I can't succeed at it either."

"That's profound." Emma said. "And for the record, I'm incredibly proud of you. Max is a great guy."

"Yeah, he really is."

"Did you set the date?"

"I told him I'd have to consult the election cycle calendar and figure out the optimal window—"

"You're kidding me, right?"

"No." Nichelle looked genuinely baffled.

"Nich. Our approval ratings are at a record high. Polls across all demographics indicate a renewed faith in government, a restoration of harmony, empathy, respect, and hope. We have an unbreakable majority in both houses of Congress. We've mended our relationships with our allies, re-entered key treaties, restarted the economy. We are about to achieve every legislative goal…"

Emma started counting them off on her fingers: "Climate change solutions, universal health care, fixing our broken education system, tackling racial inequalities, immigration reform, voting rights, restoring integrity in government…"

Nichelle rolled her eyes. "It's your wedding day. You're not supposed to be thinking about politics."

Emma smiled broadly. "Thank you for making my point. You walked right into that one, my friend. You set the date, our reelection campaign will work around it."

"That was tricky."

"That's why I'm president and you're not."

"Is that why?"

"One among many reasons."

"Let's go get you married while your head still fits through the door."

"Capital idea. Thanks for helping me get ready, Nich."

"Trust me when I tell you, it was an honor and a privilege."

They headed toward the Red Room, which would serve as Emma's staging area. Nichelle gave her a kiss on the cheek and left to find her seat in the front row.

∽⌒∾

Palmer stood in the Green Room at the threshold to the East Room. She could hear the murmurs of the crowd as they settled in their seats.

"You look great, General. Are you ready?" Max asked.

"You look pretty smart yourself, General." In fact, Max cut a nice figure in his mess dress uniform.

He gave her a kiss on the cheek. "I'm so happy for you."

"Thanks for the run this morning, and thanks in advance for putting together the Saber Arch."

"Thanks for including me in your special day. That means a lot to me." Max gave Palmer one more kiss on the cheek and left to take his seat next to Nichelle.

The string quartet struck up the wedding march music, Pachelbel's "Canon in D." Palmer took a deep breath to settle her nerves. *You have nothing to be nervous about. Emma will be by your side the entire time.*

As if right on cue, the door from the Blue Room opened. There stood Emma, beaming and resplendent in white. Palmer swallowed hard. *You take my breath away.* Palmer's heart beat out of her chest. This woman was about to be her wife.

When Emma arrived next to her, Palmer leaned close. "You are the most beautiful vision I've ever seen."

"Sweet talker." Emma winked.

They proceeded out of the Green Room and paused at the doors leading from the Cross Hall into the East Room.

"Are you ready?" Emma asked.

Emma's smile was radiant and Palmer momentarily lost herself in her eyes. "Can we elope now?"

"Very funny."

"With you by my side, darling, I'm ready for anything."

Emma threaded her arm through Palmer's. She nodded at an aide, who spoke into her comms. Within seconds, Patrick Monahan, the lead singer for the band, Train, began playing the signature first guitar chords of their hit song, "Marry Me."

Palmer leaned over and whispered to Emma, "Perk of marrying the president. Top-notch live entertainment."

"I was just trying to impress the girl. Is it working?"

"It worked a long time ago, darling, and it didn't require any theatrics at all. Just you being you."

The doors to the East Room opened, and Emma and Palmer began their walk down the aisle together. The room was packed, with everyone standing, and all eyes were on them.

Palmer recognized so many faces: Britney standing next to a handsome man she presumed was her husband; Doctor Seth Radin, the man whose platoon she'd saved in Desert Storm; her co-pilot, former Warrant Officer Stephen Oakes; all of the members of the Joint Chiefs of Staff, including former Chairman Dutton; the four senators Emma had saved with the raid in Syria; all of the living past presidents, save one, and their spouses; Palmer's mother; members of Emma's staff—Trent, Miranda, Olivia, David, their deputies, CIA Director Fishel; the NSA and his deputy and the rest of Emma's Cabinet; Emma's personal secretary, Jeannie Tribden; Vice President Elder, his wife, Beverly, and their two children, and many more whose faces were familiar to Palmer, but whose names she did not know.

They reached the front of the room and the small stage where newly minted Supreme Court Justice Carolyn Burr would perform the wedding ceremony.

All the butterflies Palmer had been experiencing floated away on the moment. Palmer had eyes only for Emma. She forgot about the guests, the television cameras, the media, and everything else and focused on the one thing that mattered most to her in the world, Emma.

Justice Burr led them through the vows they had written for each other.

Palmer took Emma's hands. "Emma, I've never known anyone like you. Your heart, your compassion, your caring and concern for others, your integrity… These are all qualities that anyone who knows you has witnessed in abundance. But it's your remarkable ability to love with your whole heart that's the most extraordinary part of you."

Palmer took Emma's ring from Justice Burr. "Emma Jean McMasters, with the placement of this ring on your finger, I do solemnly swear that I will love, honor, and cherish you all the days of my life. You are the best part of me and you own my heart. I will love you to the end of days and beyond." Palmer slipped the ring on Emma's finger.

Emma smiled up at her. "Palmer, you have more courage and heart than anyone I've ever met. If ever I want to know if I'm doing the right thing, I just ask myself, 'What would Palmer do?' and there's my answer. Your steadiness, steadfastness, honor, and endless capacity for love light my days and warm my nights."

Emma took Palmer's ring from Justice Burr. "Palmer Estes, with the placement of this ring on your finger, I do solemnly swear that I will love, honor, and cherish you all the days of my life. You are the best part of me and you own my heart. I will love you to the end of days and beyond."

Justice Burr announced, "As you have pledged yourselves to each other in love, I now pronounce you eternal partners in love and marriage. You may kiss the bride."

"I love you, darling Emma."

"I adore you, sweet Palmer."

Emma wrapped her arms around Palmer's neck and kissed her sweetly on the mouth, and cheers reverberated throughout the room.

Max stood and announced, "We ask that you all remain seated please, for the brides' recessional." He nodded at the five other uniformed, saber-carrying Army officers who would make up the Saber Arch. On Max's command, they formed lines on either side of the aisle, with Max as the last person on the left side of the arch. "Halt… Center face," he commanded. In perfect precision, the six turned and faced the center.

Palmer threaded her arm through Emma's and urged her forward until the two of them reached the first set of sabers. Max announced in a crisp, clear voice, "Ladies and gentlemen, honored guests, it gives me great pleasure to present to you for the first time as a married couple, President Emma McMasters, and General Palmer Estes. Present…sabers."

The six officers brought their sabers to their chins. "Arch…sabers." They created an arch over the center of the aisle.

Palmer and Emma strolled through the arch until they reached the last pair of saber-bearers. Max and his counterpart lowered their swords to cross at waist level, effectively blocking Palmer and Emma's passage. "Ma'ams, it is traditional for us to require a kiss to secure passage."

Emma smiled broadly and kissed Palmer to the cheers of the crowd. Max and his counterpart lifted their sabers for the couple to proceed. As Emma passed, Max tapped her lightly on the backside with his saber. "Welcome to the Army family, Madam President."

"Hooah," Emma replied.

Beyoncé, who stood off to the side, broke into the Etta James classic, "At Last," and Emma and Palmer exited the East Room to the beat, much to the delight of the guests.

Emma pulled Palmer into the Green Room before the crowd overtook them. "I wanted a minute alone with you to tell you how beautiful you look, and how proud I am to be your wife." Emma claimed her lips in a searing kiss that went straight to her center.

"You expect me to want to go to the reception when you kiss me like that?"

"I propose that we make short work of the reception. Marine One is ready to take us to Camp David as soon as I say the word."

"Word," Palmer said.

"Very funny. Let's stay for a respectable hour—long enough to mingle and make everyone feel important—and then sneak away."

"Fair enough."

Forty-five minutes later, they'd made the rounds. "Have we greeted everyone we needed to greet? Please say yes?" Palmer cooed in Emma's ear.

"Almost. Looks like someone's trying to get your attention," Emma said.

Palmer followed Emma's gaze. "Ah. This is someone you should meet."

"I'm intrigued," Emma said.

Palmer took the woman's hand.

"Congratulations, Palmer. I'm so happy for you."

"Emma McMasters, I'd like you to meet my friend, Britney Reynolds, and her husband?" Palmer raised an eyebrow in question.

"Yes, this is my husband, Jason."

Jason stepped forward. "It's a pleasure to meet you, Palmer. I've heard a lot about you. Madam President, congratulations."

"Thank you." Emma said. "Britney, Palmer tells me I have you to thank for nudging her to take a chance on me."

"I did that?" Britney regarded Palmer quizzically.

"You did," Palmer agreed, "with an assist from Mary Oliver. 'What do you plan to do with your one wild and precious life?'"

"Aha. And here I didn't think you were listening."

"Good thing for me, she was," Emma said. "I'm truly glad to meet you both. I really hope you'll be able to come visit us sometime."

"I'd like that," Britney said.

Palmer added, "Good to see you, Brit. Nice to meet you, Jason."

Emma tugged Palmer by the hand. "Quick, now's our chance." She signaled to Nichelle, who commandeered Max to run interference for them. "Have fun you two. I'm told your bags already are on board. All you have to do is change your clothes."

"Thanks, Nich." Emma kissed her on the cheek, then kissed Max on the cheek also for good measure.

"We love you guys. Get out of here."

Palmer and Emma exited out a side door and headed for the residence to change for the trip to Camp David and their honeymoon.

❧❦

If Emma and Palmer thought they were going to slip away quietly, they were sadly mistaken. As Emma led Palmer outside and onto the South Lawn, they were greeted with a shower of rice, courtesy of their wedding guests.

Emma narrowed her eyes at Nichelle and Max, whom she spotted encouraging the activity.

Palmer wrapped her arm around Emma's waist. Together, they stopped and waved to the gathering. As they continued on their way to Marine One, Palmer nuzzled Emma's ear. "I have a question for you, Madam President."

Emma felt the vibration of Palmer's voice right down to the tips of her toes. "Let me guess, you want to know if we'll be consummating our wedding vows tonight? The answer to that is an emphatic yes."

Palmer grinned. "That wasn't the question, but I'm glad to know that's on the wedding night agenda."

"What was your question, love?"

"Now that I'm First Lady, do you think they would let me fly this bird?" Palmer pointed to the waiting helicopter and waggled her eyebrows.

Emma laughed heartily. "Not a chance, stud."

"Can't blame me for asking."

"Since we're in the spirit of asking things," Emma countered, "I've got a question for you too."

"What is it? Whatever it is, the answer is yes."

Emma raised an eyebrow. "Hmm. I might have to reconsider what I was going to ask."

"I say go with your first question. If that goes well, we can entertain the next one."

"Sounds good to me," Emma agreed.

"What was your original question?"

"Are you planning to stay the night?"

Palmer's smile lit up Emma's world. "Oh, I think you can count on me planning to spend every night, darling." She pulled Emma up just short of the steps, took Emma's face in her hands, and kissed her lovingly on the mouth. "Always together."

THE END

About the Author

Lynn Ames is the best-selling author of sixteen books. She also is the writer/director/producer of the history-making documentary, "Extra Innings: The Real Story Behind the Bright Lights of Summer." This historically important documentary chronicles, for the first time ever in her own words, the real-life story of Hall-of-Famer Dot Wilkinson and the heyday of women's softball.

Lynn's fiction has garnered her a multitude of awards and honors, including six Goldie awards, the coveted Ann Bannon Popular Fiction Award (for *All That Lies Within*), the Alice B. Medal for Lifetime Achievement, and the Arizona Book Award for Best Gay/Lesbian book. Lynn is a two-time Lambda Literary Award (Lammy) finalist, a Foreword INDIES Book of the Year Award finalist, a Writer's Digest Self-Published Book Awards Honorable Mention winner, and winner of several Rainbow Reader Awards. *All That Lies Within* was additionally honored as one of the top ten lesbian books overall of 2013.

Ms. Ames is the founder of Phoenix Rising Press. She is also a former press secretary to the New York state senate minority leader and spokesperson for the nation's third-largest prison system. For more than half a decade, she was an award-winning broadcast journalist. She has been editor of a critically acclaimed national magazine and a nationally recognized speaker and public relations professional with a particular expertise in image, crisis communications planning, and crisis management.

For additional information please visit her website at www.lynnames.com, or e-mail her at lynnames@lynnames.com. You can also friend Lynn on Facebook and follow her on Twitter, YouTube, and Instagram.

Published by
Phoenix Rising Press
Asheville, NC

Lynn Ames books are available in multiple formats through
www.lynnames.com, from your favorite local bookstore, or
through other online venues.

CPSIA information can be obtained
at www.ICGtesting.com
Printed in the USA
BVHW040359240221
600911BV00009B/331

9 781936 429202